Gail Anderson-Dargatz grew up in rural British Columbia, Canada. She has published a collection of short stories, and is author of *A Recipe For Bees* and *The Cure for Death by Lightning*, which became instant best-sellers in Britain and Canada, and won many prizes including a Betty Trask award and was shortlisted for the Canadian Giller Prize in 1997. Gail Anderson-Dargatz now lives on Vancouver Island with her husband and their young son.

ALSO BY GAIL ANDERSON-DARGATZ

The Cure for Death by Lightning

A Recipe for Bees

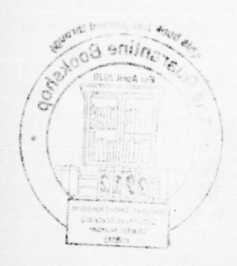

A Rhinestone Button

GAIL ANDERSON-DARGATZ

Virago

A *Virago* Book

Published by Virago Press 2003
First published in Canada by Alfred A. Knopf 2002

Copyright © Gail Anderson-Dargatz 2002

The moral right of the author has been asserted

A CIP catalogue record for this book
is available from the British Library

ISBN 1 86049 841 8

Typeset in Berkeley Book by M Rules
Printed and bound in Great Britain by Clays Ltd, St Ives plc

Virago Press
An imprint of
Time Warner Books UK
Brettenham House
Lancaster Place
London WC2E 7EN

www.virago.co.uk

For Floyd

Once upon a time, in the land of Uz, there was a man named Job. He was a man of perfect integrity, who feared God and avoided evil.

BOOK OF JOB

ONE

Job Sunstrum *felt* sound, and *saw* it. He held the hum of a vacuum cleaner in his hands: it was an invisible egg with the smooth, cool feel of glass. A sensation so real he followed its curve with his finger. He left the vacuum sitting in the kitchen, running, occasionally for hours at a time. Listened to the vacuum's whirr with his eyes closed and smoothed the glass egg in his hands. He rose from these sessions calmed, refreshed, clear-headed. Untroubled, for a time, by the fear and guilt that dogged him.

Others might have called this pastime meditation, but not Job, as contemplation of nearly any kind other than prayer was discouraged in the circles he travelled. 'It's not good to leave the mind empty,' said Pastor Ludwig Henschell from his pulpit at Godsfinger Baptist. 'An unoccupied mind is the playing field of the devil.'

The voices of the congregation as they sang a hymn produced, for Job, concentric rings of colour, like the rippling circles falling rain created on the surface of a slough. His friend

Will's voice was the deep blue-green of a spruce tree. Stinky Steinke's was the blue-black of a crow's wing. The sopranos' circles were small and brilliant, in dazzling whites, yellows, peaches, pinks. Penny Blust's was the colour of pink lemonade. The altos tended to the purples, like Barbara Stubblefield's, the blue-violet of flowering borage. Circles of colour that rippled outward, blended with one another. A vision Job experienced *out there*, projected a half foot in front of him, as if onto a transparent screen through which he saw the world around him.

Job sometimes stopped singing, lost his boundaries of self to the pool of colours, in the same way that he expanded, then dissipated, into the expanse of prairie and arching sky as he drove the paved roads. He startled awake to his shrunken self when the hymn came to an end, just as he did while driving when he met an oversized stop sign or rumble strips, a series of bumps on the asphalt that warned mesmerized drivers of an upcoming intersection. But when he was submerged in the congregation's singing he also felt a certainty, a thrill of recognition as if he had unexpectedly seen a beloved on a strange street in an unfamiliar city. The passion of *aha!* Of *eureka!* Though what it was he knew, what it was he had discovered, he couldn't say. It was a feeling that lasted for just a moment after the song was over. A *knowing*. At these times he knew God was real with the same instinctive confidence with which he knew how to breathe.

It was a phenomenon he kept to himself. He had tried telling his best friend, Will Stubblefield, when they were still children. Job and Will waited for the school bus together at the Sunstrum mailbox. Sang with each other in the junior church choir. Competed against one another with their 4-H calves at

2

Whoop 'er Up Days. Visited each other's homes after school, slept in each other's bedrooms, and once when they were twelve they spent the night out in the field together, though Job's mother had made Jacob, Job's older brother, join them to make sure they didn't get into trouble. Plagued by mosquitoes and smelling of insect spray, they snuggled in their sleeping bags and, with Jacob snoring beside them, waited for a show of northern lights.

Just before midnight the adventure took a turn. 'I'm cold,' whispered Job. 'Mosquitoes driving me crazy.' He wondered at his brother's blissful sleep, how the mosquitoes' whine and bites didn't wake him. At fourteen, Jacob had grown stinky and large with burgeoning manhood. Job watched his step with his brother, anticipating his moods as he did his father's. Just as his father would inflict the strap, Jacob would trip him up or wrestle him to the ground, twisting his arm behind his back.

'Let's zip our sleeping bags together,' said Will.

Job listened a moment to hear that his brother was still asleep. 'I don't know.'

'It'll be warmer.'

Job, who was used to doing as he was told, or merely asked, zipped his sleeping bag to Will's as quietly as he could for fear of waking Jacob, who, he sensed, would put an end to this sleeping-bag business. Jacob rolled over, snorted. The boys eased their way into their bed and Job pulled the edge of the sleeping bag over his face, to warm his nose, to ward off the insistent mosquitoes.

'You ever kissed a girl?' said Will.

Job weighed his answer briefly, and decided to answer truthfully. 'No.'

'Me neither. Let's practise. With our pillows.'

Job felt a queasy warning in his stomach that he felt each time he was about to step into unknown territory. The whole of Job's sexual education, as provided by his father, had been delivered in two sentences: 'Keep that thing in your pants,' and, after Abe had shot a feral tomcat dead just as it was mounting a barn cat, 'That's what you'll get if I ever catch you screwing around.' He knew his father suspected that he had begun to abuse himself. One cold night, Job had taken his mother's blow-dryer from the bathroom cabinet and used it to warm himself under the blankets. The warmth was a relief, but it was the hum of the blow-dryer he enjoyed most. It generated a smooth cylinder in his hand, one he could run his hand up and down. It had the feel of glass, as if he were holding his mother's clear glass rolling pin, one of the few wedding presents that had survived the years. He closed his eyes and stroked the cylinder, visible only to him, enjoying its smoothness, thrilling at the *knowing* that came along with it. He didn't hear his father's knock and Abe walked in on him, blow-drying his thighs under the covers, stroking his invisible cylinder, his knees making a tent of the blankets.

'Stop that!' said Abe.

Job pulled the blow-dryer out from under the covers, turned it off. 'What?'

Abe waved a great paw at him. 'Whatever it is you're doing.'

'I was just warming up.'

'That's your *mother's* blow-dryer, for God's sake. It's just *sick*.' Abe slammed the door shut behind him.

As Will rolled on his belly and nuzzled his pillow, Job watched in the half light, listening to his brother's breathing, hoping

4

Jacob was still asleep. He felt Will's hand on his thigh. 'It's okay,' said Will. 'If we're just pretending.'

'Pretending?'

'Like you were a girl.'

'I'm not a girl.'

'No, I mean like if you were a girl, and I was a boy. Or if I were a girl. See?'

Job didn't see. A familiar fuzzy confusion descended on him. Here was another thing he couldn't fathom. It was as though everyone else, at school, at church, in town, was operating under a different knowledge than he was. For reasons he was unsure of, but were certainly his fault, he had been left out. He stared up at the sky, the muscles of his legs and arms held stiff as Will touched his private place. It didn't occur to him to object, say no, and after the first wave of fear, Will's touch felt good. He relaxed a little, lifted his nose from the flannel of the sleeping bag for fresh air.

'Look at that,' said Will, as if his hand weren't someplace private, as if he were scratching his leg. 'Beautiful.'

Above them the sky breathed ghostly northern lights. At first the greenish-white lights hung like draperies between him and the night sky. But soon the corona moved directly overhead. Job was no longer facing the curtain of light; he was under it, as if he were lying beneath the draperies, gazing at the swirl of fabric from below.

'They're all right,' Job said, to deflect from what was going on in the sleeping bag. 'But I like the colours of the dishes better.'

'Huh?' said Will.

'The dishes? When you wash them? That squeaky sound? The colours are better, like in an oyster shell.' Job loved doing dishes, the wash of transparent colours very much like those his mother's voice produced. If he'd had things his way, Job would have spent all his time in the kitchen. As it was, his mother, Emma, snatched Job in from outside chores on the pretence of helping him with his homework and they baked together, then ate whole pans of cinnamon buns by themselves, on the sly, before washing the dishes to hide the evidence. Job found reasons to help Emma out in the kitchen to listen to her voice, the sheen of colours sliding across his view like the shifting gloss of northern lights but in the pastel colours of blue, pink and yellow found in soap bubbles or in Emma's opal ring. A vision almost exactly like the one Job enjoyed when running a wet finger around the rim of a glass.

Will stopped his fumbling under the covers, moved his hand away. 'What are you talking about? What colours?'

'You know, when you run a finger over a dish when you're washing it? Or around the rim of a wet glass, and it rings? I like those colours better.'

'Colours?'

It was at that moment that Job realized others didn't see the world as he did, didn't feel and see sound. Once, when his mother asked why he liked washing dishes so much, when she couldn't even bribe Jacob to do them, he fumbled for words to describe the wonder of the colours he heard, the feeling of *aha!*

His mother ignored him, as she did when she thought he was talking nonsense, and went on chopping carrots.

He tried explaining to his father how he knew the cows were in heat, often before the bulls knew, by listening to their bawls. 'Their bellow goes really dark when they're in heat,' Job told his father, 'like chokecherry.' He meant the colour of chokecherries when they were ripe, near black and shining.

'Chokecherry?' Abe asked, his voice prickling on Job's arm.

Job nodded. 'Its shape changes too. It's more like a flag. Don't you think?' This making perfect sense to Job, that a cow would want to advertise when it was time.

Abe shook his head, wandered off chuckling.

His parents' reactions were strange, but it hadn't occurred to him until this moment, lying in the sleeping bag with Will, that they didn't see the world as he did, that they didn't hear colours. The best his parents and Will could hope for was this night sky, stars flickering through the greens and reds of the northern lights.

The aurora twisted, pulsed. At times seemed close enough to touch. He found himself relaxed, lulled, drifting, asleep.

After that night Job never invited Will for another sleep-over, and their friendship began its slow decline. In past summers he and Will had run down the coulee hill on the Sunstrum farm to the lake below, thrown off their clothes and swum naked in the muddy water. One Halloween they stuck a pair of rubber boots into one side of a round bale in the Sunstrums' field by the side of Correction Line Road, a stuffed shirt and John Deere cap out the other, a reminder of the nightmare farmers faced of being pulled into the baler and rolled into a bale themselves. Together they had filled a mayonnaise jar with moths, then smuggled the jar into the Leduc movie theatre and let the insects loose to flutter up to the projection booth, their huge, flickering shadows cast upon the screen.

When Job's prettiness earned him the nicknames Pansy and Fairy, Will wouldn't have anything more to do with him; he avoided Job at church and ignored Job's stilted stabs at friendly chatter as they waited for the school bus in the winter dark. He stood several yards away and kicked snow so those riding on the bus could plainly see he and Job were not friends.

Job's mother, Emma, was killed when Job was thirteen, as she and Abe tried to pull-start a tractor. Emma was on the 730 Case, pulling the 930 Case that Abe was riding. When the tractor was rolling at sufficient speed to get it going, Abe took his foot off the clutch, and the tractor skidded for that moment it took to turn the engine over. The chain between the two tractors went suddenly taut and snapped. It whipped back and hit Emma in the head. She was dead before the ambulance arrived.

Godsfinger women brought casseroles, cookies, squares and sausages; they filled the fridge, then the freezer. Godsfinger men took turns harvesting Abe's second hay crop, then his grain, and stood kicking dirt beside him. They didn't expect talk. Abe felt blessed by friendship the first week, sick in the gut the second, took to bed the third week and shot Barbara Stubblefield's dog the fourth. Everyone, even Barbara, understood. The dog had been killing Abe's bantam chickens that ran loose around the yard. You can't break a dog of that once it starts.

Abe cried at night, and his boys heard him through the thin walls of the house, but he didn't tolerate their tears. When Job, smelling the cinnamon buns the church ladies brought, began sniffling in the kitchen, Abe slapped the table and demanded, 'Quit that or I'll give you something to cry about.'

Job learned to hold the tears in, raising his eyes to the ceiling and biting an indent into his lip that took months to heal. But the tears still came, at odd times, as he worked his numbers in math class. Or struggled to concentrate on what Mrs.

Walsh was telling him in English. Not thinking of his mother. Kids sniggered. Teachers led him by the arm into the hall and patted him on the shoulder, then left him alone with his perplexing tears. It felt like punishment. The shame of being singled out and left in the hallway, the embarrassment of having to return.

He was plagued by a series of illnesses: stomach aches and sore throats; rashes and a spotted tongue. A speeding heart that woke him sharply from sleep, or brought him up short as he strode to the house. Heart palpitations that left him feeling faint and weak, afraid for his life. He cooked and baked to calm himself. The pans of almond squares and cinnamon buns he had made with his mother when she was still alive. His mother was still here, in the kitchen. Her presence in the tidy, childish handwriting on her recipe cards, the Band-Aid she'd stuck over the word *devil* in the devil's food cake recipe in her *Joy of Cooking*. Her smell in the apple pies he made, loaded with cinnamon. Her voice in the squeak of the dishes he washed, the sheen of pastels through which he saw the kitchen.

Job, like Emma, was slender and possessed a white-blond head of curly hair that cascaded past his ears in ringlets. His delicate, heart-shaped face gave him an angelic prettiness. Farmers in the area called him Pretty Boy or Princess.

Abe avoided looking Job in the eye because he saw his wife there, in Job's sweet face, in the curls that framed it. He forced crewcuts on him. Job stared at the sign above the barber's mirror that proclaimed *You won't find a better barber until you reach the next world*, and ground his teeth, but said nothing.

In high school, he had endured nipple twists from boys who danced circles around him with limp wrists or called down the hall, 'Hey, Princess, where's your purse?' In the locker room, after scoring a goal on his own net, Job even took ribbing from the guy named Chuck with the harelip. 'Look at this guy. There's hardly a hair on his body. What do you do? Shave your legs?'

Job felt a kinship with his biblical namesake. Perhaps God, in a fit of pride, had been tempted into another wager with Satan over the faithfulness of a good servant and was testing him. But instead of the boils He'd inflicted on the biblical Job, which could, in these modern times, be cleared up with lancing and antibiotics, God had imposed on Job Sunstrum this prettiness. Anywhere else Job's good looks might have won him friends and his choice of wife. But Job lived in big-farm country, where many men lost a finger to a sickle on a mower or to a spinning auger by the age of thirty-five. They wore baseball caps, given to them by farm-implement or bull-semen salesmen, with promotional slogans like *Western Breeders* or *Snap-On Tools*, or simply *Case*. Men were not pretty in Godsfinger, Alberta.

Job felt like the gimpy calf in his father's herd. Some congenital failure of the ligaments had made the calf walk awkwardly upon its knuckles, to fall to its knees when standing still for any length of time. It hobbled behind the herd, never keeping up, and called plaintively to its mother when left behind. It couldn't compete at the grain trough or at the round-bale feeder and was bunted out of the way by the other calves. It learned to eat alone. To live apart.

Jacob left home to attend a Saskatoon Bible college, set on becoming a preacher, and Job spent his late teens and early twenties nearly cloistered on the farm. He didn't drive much because he found the effort fatiguing. The steady rumble of gravel hitting the undercarriage of his father's Ford created a tumble of shimmering blue spheres, rolling and bouncing like lottery balls. He knew the balls weren't really there but found himself batting them away as he fought to concentrate on the road.

Trips to Edmonton or Wetaskiwin or Leduc were painful, overwhelming. The roar of passing vehicles filled his hands with rough shapes, one barely registering before another took its place. Car honks exploded in blinding white light, like the flashbulbs of cameras aimed at him. The shrill whine of an ambulance siren drove needle points into his cheeks. Music thumping from car stereos or blasted from cafés threw rings of colour at him. All of it blending, expanding, like balls of cookie dough flattening in the oven, obscuring his view, grabbing his attention. He came home from these few trips exhausted, swore to shop in Godsfinger, if at all.

In winter, Job loaded up the silage wagon from the pit where the silage was stored and dispensed it into the feeders. On very cold days the tractor often wouldn't start and he'd spend hours fiddling with the machinery. It was sometimes a day or two before he could feed the cattle.

If he could bring the cows to the feeder, rather than the feed to the cows, it would save a lot of work. So that's what he did. He converted the rectangular silage pit into a feeder by placing steel feeding panels at one end. The silage in the pit was ten feet deep and usually fell towards the feeding grate as the cattle ate away at it, replenishing the supply.

The feeder worked, though Abe argued it shouldn't. Daily. When he came to Job once again complaining that the stack of silage was about to topple over and crush the cows eating with their heads through the feeding panels, Job said, 'I'll get right on it.' But didn't. He went into the house to put on morning coffee.

He was standing on the stoop to call his father in for a cup and a warm cinnamon roll when he heard the *woomph* of silage falling and the screech of twisting metal that shot out fingers of lightning in all directions. He ran to the feeder and found the tractor still running. Abe had been about to knock the wall of silage down and was chasing a cow from the feeder when the silage overhead collapsed, crushing him under the feeding panel. Job pulled Abe out from under it and ran to the house to call for an ambulance. He returned with a blanket that he lay over his father.

Abe's voice was a whisper, but still prickly. It brought up goosebumps on Job's arms. 'It hurts to breathe,' he said.

'You'll be all right. The ambulance is on the way.'

'If you'd built that thing right, it wouldn't have collapsed on me. Didn't I tell you it was gonna collapse?'

At the hospital, all the chairs in the waiting room were taken. Job leaned against the wall and found some comfort in smoothing the invisible sphere that the electric hum of fluorescent lights overhead produced in his hand. He sat in the first chair to come free, then gave it to an elderly woman. Leaned against the wall again until he grew tired. Sat in a kiddy's chair at a table of toys and watched a boy of three drive a car over the stomach of a teddy bear.

His father was on the operating table with an aortic aneurysm. The young doctor had explained how the blow to Abe's chest had caused the blood vessel to balloon out like a blister on an old tire, ready to burst.

Job felt so heavy he thought he'd never be able to stand again. He stayed sitting, even as he felt the touch on his arm and looked into the face of the doctor, her hair hidden under a green surgical cap. 'Mr. Sunstrum? I'm sorry. Your father didn't make it.'

He hugged his knees and watched the child playing with the toys on the table, and started to cry, though he felt no emotion, nothing at all. The boy, noticing his tears, offered him the teddy. 'Bear?' he said.

Job, alone on the farm. He turned down offers of help from Godsfinger men, supper invitations from their wives. He blamed himself for his father's death. Thought everyone else did too.

He felt nothing in his hands when listening to the vacuum. Its hum no longer produced the feel of a glass egg, and Job became less inclined to use the machine. Weeks of grit accumulated on the kitchen floor. The congregation's singing was muddied and yellow, like the colours of a photograph left too long in the sun, and Job stopped going to church. No one phoned or stopped by to check on him. He walked through his days with the feeling that at any moment he might become lost, and no one would know to search for him, or care.

It was Barbara Stubblefield who contrived to steer Job back into the fold. A big woman, at least five foot ten. Heavy set. Square face. Bifocals. A taste for sweater sets. She was quick to criticize an unkempt lawn, a messy house. On the other hand, she'd nailed her collection of promotional caps that farm-supply salesmen had given her to the tops of fence posts bordering Correction Line Road. Over the years, kids had painted faces on the fence posts under the hats, so now there was an army of clowns standing at attention along her property line.

The consensus after Emma's death had been that Barbara would end up with Abe. It wasn't often a widow and a widower ended up living side by side like that, both with teenaged sons ready to work the farm. But Abe had never asked Barbara out to a pancake supper, and had in fact avoided her at church.

She believed she'd been healed of her borderline diabetes by a television evangelist who read her prayer request for healing during his broadcast. Members of the church, however, attributed the cure to the fact that Barbara had given up coconut-coated marshmallows in compliance with her doctor's orders to lose weight.

Barbara was a poultry farmer, so she began, as always, with a chicken. Once a week, on Friday mornings, she stopped in on Job before heading to the ladies' auxiliary meeting. She dropped a frozen fowl on the table and announced, 'There's your dead bird,' and talked of little other than church as Job stared at her red, cracked hands. She wouldn't take money for the chicken, so he had to listen. There was no getting around it.

One Friday morning Barbara brought her son Will over, and dropped him off as she went to the auxiliary meeting. Will had moved back from B.C. to take over his mother's poultry farm. Barbara, now sixty, was moving into a post-war bungalow in the middle of Main Street, and she'd taken on the job of mayor, as no one else wanted it.

Will came sporting a beard and smoking an Old Port cigar and talked animatedly about his travels around British

Columbia, working in logging camps and mills. He carried the conversation, a trait Job was always thankful for. They took a stroll to look over Job's herd. The cows ran away when they saw Will coming, a near stampede to the end of the pasture.

'You've got old man's cows, eh?' said Will. 'Never see anybody else. Only used to you and your ways.'

'I guess,' said Job, thinking of the days, years before, when he farmed with his mother and father. The cows wouldn't run then, even when a semen salesman wandered down to find Job and Abe in the fields, offering caps and brochures. His cows had betrayed him. Will knew he was without friends.

From then on Will came over on Friday mornings instead of Barbara, bringing a frozen chicken. He drank coffee and offered Job compliments on his baking, and talked farming for the most part, markets and prices, his hopes for the poultry, but he managed to slip in a word or two about the goings-on at church. Whose son had married. Whose father had died. Then, two months after his return, he finally got around to it. 'Why not ride to church with me Sunday morning,' he said. 'Pick you up at nine-thirty?'

Job agreed, recognizing the net that had caught him. But he was surprised at the effect of the service. Friendly, familiar faces greeted him. The smell of the church, of old wood and years of coffee, canned milk, comfort. The singing produced, for Job, that pool of sound, splashed with the individual voices of the congregation. Radiating circles, Will's voice spruce blue-green, Barbara's blue-violet. Rings of colours spreading, blending with all the others. Filling his visual field, projected, out there. Real. With the colours came the excitement, the certainty. God.

TWO

Job accepted the Lord Jesus Christ as his personal saviour. Again. Coffee and hand-shaking afterwards. Mumbles of 'Glad to have you back, Job,' and 'Good to see you.' Slaps to the shoulder. Community.

At home he found the glass egg back in his hands when he turned on the vacuum cleaner. Saw the pastel sheen when he ran a finger around the rim of a glass or squeaked a clean dish. A remembrance of his mother's voice. He found a new enthusiasm for keeping house.

He thought for certain that Will would drop him as a friend now that he was back at church. Another fish caught. He was right. Will stopped coming over on Fridays and sat with others at church. Never offered him another frozen chicken. But Job was hungry for a friend. He invited Will for supper, with the excuse that he owed Will a cheque for the barley he'd trucked over the week before. Job started cleaning the house at noon. Cooked a dinner of fried chicken, a bowl of potatoes whipped with butter, peas grown in his own garden that he served with fresh baked buns on his mother's best china and glassware. Candles out, table shining like a candelabra.

He gave up on Will arriving at all by eight. At nine, Will turned up four hours late with an excuse about running into one of his old buddies in Edmonton. The chicken had gone cold and greasy in the fridge, peas to mush. Job apologized, offered to microwave him a plate. When Will declined, said he'd eaten in the city, Job apologized again, made tea and put out a plate of frozen shortbread, then sat staring at it, unable to come up with anything to say. He wished he were adept at conversation, quick with a joke.

'I like your jars,' said Will, pointing at the gallon jars lined up along the tops of the cupboards, in which Job stored beans, dried peas, pastas, flour, cornmeal and rolled oats.

'Pickle jars,' said Job. 'I get them from Crystal, at the Out-to-Lunch Café.'

'Ah,' said Will.

They sat in silence for some minutes.

'Well,' said Will. 'It's getting late. Sorry about supper.'

'No, no,' said Job. 'I'm sorry it's cold.'

'All right then. I'll see you later.'

Will had left the driveway before Job realized he hadn't given him the cheque for the barley. Will would think him stupid, or he'd think Job was trying to get out of paying him. That Job was holding a grudge because Will had turned up late. Job rolled it over in his mind and didn't sleep that night; he tossed and turned on guilt and hurt. He got up at five, emptied the macaroni out of one of his pickle jars, the beans from another, and took them and the cheque over to the poultry farm when he knew Will's hired hand, an acreage kid with pock-marked cheeks, would be doing chores. He handed him the cheque and the jars to give to Will when he woke.

Later in the day Will came over, said Job needn't have gone to all that trouble. He knew he'd get the money sooner or later. Did he really want to give up the jars? Job felt foolish and apologized again. Said sorry when Will insisted there was no need to apologize. Felt stupid for it.

'Look,' said Will. 'I'm sorry I missed supper. Why don't I make up for it? Come by the house tonight. I'll cook.'

It was the first of many dinners. Will made Job sit at the kitchen table as he served beef stroganoff, hamburgers, Beef Rouladen, having completely lost the taste for chicken himself.

At times, when Will hugged Job goodnight, or laid a hand on his shoulder, asking if he wanted more coffee, another slice of lemon loaf, Job was moved to tears and had to look away. Thankful for his small kindnesses, thinking himself undeserving. He wondered that the friendship endured.

Job tried to grow a beard like Will's and failed, took up cigars instead. He didn't smoke them but chewed on the tip as if he were just getting around to it. He kept a package in the freezer and took them out when Will stopped by for coffee. He believed they made him seem worldly, well-travelled, as Will appeared. But he gave them up, as did Will, when Stinky Steinke, heading the church board, pointed out that the constitution forbade smoking.

Then, one Sunday, a year after Will's return, despairing that her son would never find a wife and give her grandchildren, Barbara Stubblefield invited Penny Blust, the daughter of a friend from Leduc Pentecostal, to come to Godsfinger Baptist. She was a petite girl of nineteen, with blonde hair cut just above the shoulder and held back with barrettes. Clear pink skin and pale blue eyes. A tight, permanent smile already etched into her face. She seasoned her conversation with phrases that few at Godsfinger Baptist would use. 'The Lord is leading me into the ministry,' she said when Will asked her what she was going to do now that she was out of school. 'Not as a pastor, of course, but maybe the youth ministry, or working with children. Or maybe I'll go overseas, into missions. I tried doing home care, you know, helping out cripples, old people in their houses. But I relied on myself, didn't take it to the Lord, couldn't handle cleaning pee off the floor around toilets. So I figured I'd take a year or two off, before going to Bible college. Work at Dad's Dairy Queen until I'm a little more spiritually mature.'

Barbara had Penny sit between her and Will and kept Job safely on her left. She invited Penny and Will over for supper. Within a week she had Will take Penny to a movie in Edmonton, and in a month got him bringing the girl flowers.

Job once again spent his Saturday nights alone, listening to the vacuum cleaner, smoothing the glass egg in his hand. He felt dispensable, a friend of convenience.

One Saturday evening Will was at the door, dressed in a town shirt, tugging at his beard, asking Job to chaperone Penny and himself at the movie that night, and for nights to come. 'We want to save ourselves for marriage,' he said. 'We're afraid – I'm afraid – if we spend too much time alone we'll succumb to temptation.'

Job nodded. Given half a chance he would succumb himself.

So it was that Job found himself accompanying Will and Penny on most of their dates. Penny seemed flattered by the attention of two men. She hugged them both when Will dropped her off before driving Job home, and kissed Job on the cheek. In the dark of the movie theatre she often took Job's hand as well as Will's. The fact of her hand in his seemed a near impossibility, a hummingbird miraculously caught in flight.

Job built his herd, bid on new blood at the Ponoka auction. Went into pure breeds for a couple of years, for the status; left because of the expense. Finally fell back on the cow-calf operation. He made a fair living and saved a bit. Joined a Tuesday-night Bible study, held in Will's kitchen, and brought baked goods to church and community dinners, even though, as a bachelor, he wasn't expected to. He canned crabapples and made saskatoon jam and gave the jars away at Christmas, tied in bows, just like the women of the church did.

He kept to the women, baked alongside them in the church kitchen, made squares, pies and muffins to sell with theirs to raise money for the church. He was told by the women that he'd make a wonderful husband, and if they were younger they would snap him up for themselves. He was told by the men he'd make someone a fine wife. That bothered him. But still, he felt a part of something. Though he did not have a wife and family, at least he had friends.

THREE

 Then came a year when his tightly coiled life popped its twine and unravelled like a round hay bale dropped to asphalt from a speeding truck.

First, Jacob. He phoned from the Edmonton airport on a March morning, just as Job came in the house from checking for new calves in the calving pen. 'I need a ride home,' he said. His voice prickling across Job's arms as Abe's had.

Job tugged at the twisted cord of the telephone, said, 'Sure.'

'I'm waiting at luggage claim. See you in half an hour.'

As he drove up to the airport, Job figured his brother was making the trip home by himself, taking time to finally settle the estate. Jacob hadn't been home since Abe's funeral three years before, when he brought his wife, Lilith, and their eight-year-old son and stayed a week. Jacob had met Lilith, the daughter of a missionary family posted at Frog Lake, at Bible school. He had brought her to Godsfinger just once before bringing her home to marry. Lilith gave birth to Ben six months later. Jacob claimed he was a preemie.

The week of the funeral, Jacob and Lilith slept in Abe's room and Job gave up his bed to Ben. He slept out in the old hired hand's cabin on a folding cot. Ben was family, sure enough: pretty face so much like Job's, on a meat loaf of a body. Oversized hands and feet. His nails were chewed to the quick and he had the nervous habit of plucking the hairs from his arms. When he told a story, waving his hands in the air, Jacob told him, 'Look at you, talking with your hands like a Frenchman.' A thing Abe had said.

Lilith spent two hours in the bathroom each morning, came out painted up, eyebrows sketched on, hair glistening with spray. She wore dentures, not because her teeth had rotted, but because she had thought her own teeth ugly and had them all yanked.

Lilith, Jacob, Job and Ben sat around the kitchen table for most of those days, eating sliced meats and cheeses, home-made buns and squares, leftovers from the church-basement reception that had followed the funeral. Around them the kitchen was pretty much the same as it had been when Emma was alive. A metal-legged table sat in front of the window overlooking the vegetable garden. Beside it there was a cabinet with sliding glass doors that housed Emma's good china and glasses. The only new addition was the microwave sitting on a shelf over the portable dishwasher.

The cupboards, installed the year Job's grandfather died and Abe took over the farm, were painted white with square metal pulls. On the walls, framed pictures of grain elevators made from wheat, a calendar, a photograph of the farm taken from the air.

Jacob talked and talked, of the church where he was pastor and his small accomplishments, but not of Abe. Though he'd thought of Abe's safety deposit box straight away and asked Job for the key. Abe had made Jacob executor to his will and had left no special instructions on leaving the farm to Job. He'd made it clear he wanted things split evenly between the two boys, though he had talked as though Job would be the one to take over.

Jacob told Job he didn't want the farm. 'I've got my church, and like Dad kept telling me, I'm not farmer material.'

Job remembered his father had put it more bluntly. 'He's useless,' Abe had once said, right in front of Jacob, who stood behind him at the kitchen door, wilting in his rubber boots. Jacob's crime, that time around, was to break the handle of a spade clean in two. He was handicapped by clumsiness, his limbs growing faster than his capacity to control them. But instead of awkwardness, Abe had seen in Jacob the chief reason for the farm's failure to prosper. 'You're trying to ruin me, aren't you?' he'd asked Jacob. 'Trying to make me go broke!'

Before Emma's death, Jacob might have been his mother's kitchen help, while Job did chores outside with his father, but Jacob had lacked skill there as well: he'd knocked freshly canned jars of saskatoons to the floor, splattering purple berries across yellow linoleum. Dishes slipped from his thick fingers and cracked on the Arborite counter. Emma had thought him purposeful, trying to get out of helping her, and chased him from the kitchen.

Jacob was a copy of his father in build if not in talent. A belly that strained the buttons of his shirt. Hands and feet of a giant on a six-foot frame, giving him the bearing of a troll. A head too big even for that inflated body. He'd been called Moose at school. Meat loaf. Later, after he accepted Jesus Christ as his Lord and personal saviour at Godsfinger Baptist Camp, he was called Friar Tuck, less for his piousness than the frequency with which he bought candy at the tuck shop. Job had seen strangers on the street stop and gape at his brother.

'You'll have to go to a lawyer and settle things,' said Job. 'I won't be able to take out a loan until you do.'

'You've got cows to sell. You'll be all right.'

'What if a tractor breaks down, or I have to buy equipment?'

'I'll get right on it,' said Jacob, but didn't. He took on a church in Ontario, then another in Saskatchewan. Always had a reason why he couldn't come home.

As he drove to the Edmonton airport, Job figured he'd finally get things settled. But Lilith and Ben were waiting at the luggage carousel alongside Jacob. Lilith's dress rumpled, cheeks splotched from crying. Ben silent, his pretty face a mask. Beside them a pickup load of luggage: suitcases and boxes of clothes; downhill skis; a birdcage; boxes of Jacob's pastoral files and books; Lilith's sewing machine; the disassembled crib that had been Ben's; photo albums wrapped in plastic grocery bags; garbage bags full of quilts Lilith had made from old dresses; the brown stoneware dishes Abe had given them as a wedding present, packed in their original box. All of their lives folded, bundled and stacked.

'We'll be staying awhile,' Jacob said.

Job picked up one of the boxes, loaded it onto a trolley. 'How long?' he asked.

'Not sure. Just 'til we can get back on our feet.' He gave Job a half hug, one arm around the shoulder. Job was surprised to see tears in his brother's eyes. 'Sorry it was such short notice. I didn't know what else to do.'

Job didn't ask what had happened, and his brother didn't volunteer. He bought Jacob and Lilith an old station wagon from Jerry Kuss, moved a few of his things into the old hired hand's cabin, where he shifted thirty years of accumulated junk into one corner to make way for the cot, a table, a couple of chairs. He let Jacob, Lilith and Ben take over the house. They seemed to expect that he would and it seemed the thing to do. There was no plumbing in the cabin, and Abe had plowed over the outhouse that had once served it. Job had to run to the house to use the facilities, and once there, he had his sister-in-law to contend with. It was simpler to stand behind the cabin to relieve himself.

Job was taking his first whiz of the morning behind the cabin when Ben came looking for him. The squeak of dry snow underfoot, like the sound of Saran Wrap being balled up, shooting off a cloud of transparent blue. Job hurriedly arranged himself and was zipping up his jeans when Ben turned the corner on him. 'Dad needs help. He's got a calf that won't come out.'

Since his arrival, Jacob had been some help over the calving season, checking on the cows in the morning so Job could sleep in until seven-thirty or so. But he needed help with every small problem that arose. Job took the midnight and three o'clock watch, checking for signs that the cows were close to calving, assisting them in labour, and warming newborn calves under a heat lamp if necessary.

Job walked with Ben towards the calving pens. Around them a flat landscape covered in barley-stubbled snow. The farm was miles from the buzz of a highway, in a blanket of quiet so thick Job could hear the pit-a-pat the chickadees made as they hopped along the branches of the cottonwood and willow his grandfather had planted around the farm as a windbreak. The *flit flit* of their wings as they flew from branch to branch left blushes of tawny rose in the air.

'Got any matches?' Ben asked him.

'No.'

'Why don't you get a haircut? You look like a girl.' Something Jacob had told Job at nearly every visit.

'What do you want matches for?'

'No reason.'

A crow flew up from a fence post as they passed. The first crow Job had seen that year. His mother had always said that you should look to the first crow of the season to tell you what your year would be like. If you saw a crow resting, then you could look forward to a relaxing year. A crow flying in the air made for a busy time. A crow coming in for a landing meant things would slow down after a fast start. Job couldn't remember what a crow taking off meant.

'Is it true you didn't talk 'til you were just about five?' asked Ben.

'That's what they tell me.'

'How come?'

'I don't remember.'

'Dad says he talked for you. You'd point things out and he'd tell your mom what you wanted.'

It was a story Jacob had brought up at every family gathering, gatherings that were few and far between after he left for Bible college. Job had once asked him why he didn't come home more often. 'It's the old prodigal son thing,' Jacob had said. 'I get a better reception if I'm not around too much. If I'm always home, Dad won't give me the time of day.'

'When Dad went to school you talked all at once, right?' Ben asked. 'Like you'd known how to talk all along.'

'That's the story.' As Jacob told it, Job's first words had been, 'Can I have a glass of milk?' When his mother asked him why he hadn't talked before he said, 'I didn't have to.' Jacob had always been the talker in the family. While other boys played football at noon hour, Jacob holed up in the library to read the encyclopedia, and after school lectured Job on whatever he had learned that day. He was Job's only playmate until Job went to school.

While Jacob wouldn't play football with the other boys, he would toss a ball around with Job after school, or rough-house on the lawn before chores. Job often gave up on these games; he was so much smaller, and would always lose, but Jacob would bribe him with gum or offer to take over some chore if Job would only keep playing. They would trip each other up, jump on each other's back, shove and push and throw each other down in the shadow of the looming silos.

The Sunstrum farm was split in two by Correction Line Road, running east to west. The occasional driver heading into Godsfinger had to drive right through the Sunstrum farmyard. A few months following Emma's death, Abe had taken advantage of that bit of luck by painting *Jesus is Lord!* on one of his two silos, and *Hallelujah!* on the other. As an after-thought, on the roof of his barn he painted *This is cattle country. Eat beef.*

Job kept meaning to paint over the lettering on the silos, or better yet to take the silos down. He agreed with the sentiment all right, but the enthusiasm of the four-foot lettering embarrassed him. In any case, the silos weren't of use any more. They had long ago been replaced with the cement silage pit that Job had converted into a feeder. The silos were becoming dangerous; the soil beneath them was giving way to their weight and each year both silos leaned farther south. The summer before, Job had been forced to climb them in order to wrap cables around them both, to tether them to steel rods forced into the ground to secure the silos from collapsing.

'My dad won't let me have any,' said Ben.

'What?'

'Matches.'

'You a firebug?'

'No.'

'I was a firebug,' said Job. 'Got me in a lot of trouble with my old man.'

'*You* were a firebug?'

Job had started setting fires following his mother's death, after his father had been baptized in the Holy Spirit. He lit brush piles and the garbage in the burn can at first, made it his job to fire up the tank heater in the stock tank. Fires his father couldn't fault him for. But he later carried boxes of Redbird matches in his pocket so that when the compulsion hit, he could simply light a match and drop it in the dry grass around the farm.

It was the sound of fire that drew him first. The pops and crackles of a flame filled his vision with tiny explosions, a private display of fireworks, silvery white and tinged with green, like the back of a poplar leaf blowing in the wind. With the fireworks came brief, intense bursts of excitement, oddly mixed with a peaceful feeling. It was the *eureka!* he'd found nowhere else for a time following his mother's death.

'I nearly set the cabin on fire once,' he said. 'Got it out though.' A grass fire Job had lit had licked up the wall of the hired hand's cabin, sending panicked mice scurrying from under the building, darting between Job's feet as he beat the fire with a wet burlap bag. He managed to get the fire out by himself, but the west wall of the cabin was scorched black. He was strapped for that fire as he was strapped for almost every fire he set.

'I lit this fire in the garbage can,' said Ben. 'Sparks from it set our lawn on fire and burned the lawn furniture and Mom's plants. Dad beat the crap out of me because he said I'd nearly burned the house down and it wasn't even our house. It was the church's, and how was he going to explain it to the church board? He lied. He told them he'd been cooking on the Hibachi when a fire started. He said he didn't want them to think he didn't have his son under control.'

'Look, you like fire, you can have the job of keeping the fire going in the stock tank heater. But don't light any other fires. Okay?'

'Cool!' Ben picked up a fist of snow, patted it into a ball. 'Dad didn't want to come back to the farm, you know.'

'Oh?'

'He said he didn't have any choice. We didn't have any money, no place else to go. Mom wants to stay. She doesn't want Dad to go back into preaching 'cause she's tired of moving from church to church. She says she's tired period. She says she's tired of Dad.'

'I'm sure she didn't mean that.'

'She said it was Dad's fault she duct-taped that kid's head to a desk.'

'She duct-taped a kid's head to a desk?'

'He was hyperactive. Always running all over junior church. So she got real mad and duct-taped him to his desk. She had to cut the duct tape out of his hair and his parents asked how come his hair was cut funny and they found out and they yelled at Mom, and Dad got fired because he couldn't control his wife and we had to come here.'

'She thought that was your Dad's fault?'

'Because he's a preacher and she's his wife and she has to be nice all the time because everybody's always watching everything she does. She says sometimes she wants to explode. She says sometimes she feels like killing somebody.' Ben hurled the snowball at the silo that read *Jesus is Lord!* Missed. 'Dad kind of gave in. Said he'd stay on the farm and give it a try.'

Jacob was kneeling on the straw of a calf pen, working behind a cow that was lying on its side. He stood when he saw Job, let him take over. The calf's legs were just sticking out the cow's back end. Chains above the calf's hooves with pull handles hooked to the chains. The cow still tied by its halter to the corner post. Sloppy. Job untied the halter, let the cow's head drop. She wasn't going anywhere. He repositioned the chains above the calf's ankles, ran a second loop above the hooves to distribute the load; the feet were already swollen from too much pulling. 'Hand me that rope,' he said. Jacob passed it to him, and Job slung it over his shoulder. 'Hear you might be staying awhile.'

Ben glanced at Job and kicked a frozen cow patty, but said nothing, his face flushing red. A look on Jacob's face that Job had seen on his father's, before he got the strap. Job regretted he'd said anything. He knew Ben would be in for it now.

Job rolled up his sleeves, wet his arms with water from the pail Jacob had brought with him, then with birth fluid from the cow's vagina for lubrication. The smell of cabbage and liver. 'So you're staying.'

Jacob held the top of his right arm, as if nursing an injury. His hands the size of dinner plates, the colour of ham. 'I don't know what else to do. We're broke. I doubt I can find another position after what happened. I'm sure Ben told you about that as well.'

Job said nothing. He reached into the cow's vagina to check for the position of the calf's head. When he didn't find it laying on the legs, he pushed back against the base of the calf's neck.

'What're you doing?' asked Ben.

Job grunted from the strain. 'Head isn't coming. Got to push the calf back, to reposition it.' Not an easy thing, pushing against the cow's contractions. But it had to be done, and quickly, or the calf might die. The cow too, by the look of her. She'd pushed for ages and was bawling high and long in pain, a noise that created a shower of brown sparks in front of Job, like a spray of dirty water from a garden hose. 'You've just been pulling on the two legs here,' he said.

'Yeah, so?' said Jacob.

Job didn't bother trying to explain. He'd only end up making Jacob look foolish in front of his son. The calf's head was bent back. Jacob could have pulled for hours and got nowhere. It seemed he'd forgotten the basics, that he needed three things to pull a calf: two feet and a head, or two feet and a tail. He should have reached in to make sure both feet were from the same calf, and that it wasn't twins, that he wasn't pulling one leg from each.

Job grabbed hold of the calf's nose, and held its jaw so its bottom teeth wouldn't cut into the uterus. He swung the head around, so it rested on the front legs. Worked the rope in around the calf's head, behind the ears.

'Okay, tug gently on the chains.'

Jacob took both handles, pulled.

'Gently!'

With his left arm still up the cow, Job held the calf's head with his left hand, and tugged on the rope with his right, as the calf was pulled from the cow, slid to the ground. A gush of amniotic fluid. The sweetish smell of newborn calf.

The calf's tongue was sticking out, swollen and blue. Job hauled the calf up by the back legs, held it as high as he could.

'He's got to make sure the fluid drains from the lungs,' Jacob explained to Ben. Hoping to save face, Job thought, to appear like he knew a thing or two about this business.

Job lay the calf back on the ground, pushed the tongue back in and covered the calf's mouth, then blew into a nostril to clear the way and get the calf breathing. It snorted, drew breath. Thrashed. He grabbed the old cow's head and pulled her off her side so she was lying normally and had an easier time breathing. Then he washed in the bucket of water and took a handkerchief from his pocket to wipe his hands. He felt the confidence of being in his element. He knew cattle. A skill Jacob didn't possess. 'The calf was in a normal position except its head was dropped to the side. When that happens, it doesn't matter how much you pull. Calf won't budge. It's a common mistake, if you haven't calved much.'

'Well,' said Jacob. 'Learn something new every day.' But he didn't look happy about it.

'So what would you do here?' said Job. 'Build a herd? You never took much interest in farming.'

'More to the point, I was never much good at it, right?' said Jacob. 'Yeah, well. Remember that story Grandma Sunstrum always told? About how her dad sent her into the field to pick rocks with her brothers, and she came home saying she couldn't find any rocks? Sometimes I didn't know what I was doing, but sometimes I just wanted to get out of the work. I wanted to read my books. I hated working with Dad. All he did was yell at me.'

'You know you're welcome to stay awhile,' said Job. 'I can sell a few cows and hire you for the summer if you want. I could use a hand with field work.'

'I'd appreciate that. Anyway, I don't know that I'd end up farming. It may come down to selling this place.'

'But Dad was born into this house,' said Job. 'Granddad built it. We can't hand it over to strangers.' Or more to the point, what would he do without the land? Who was he without this farm? He'd imagined he'd live his life here, as his father had. It was an assumption Abe had planted in him, one that he'd never questioned.

'I'm not saying we will sell. I'm just saying it may come down to selling. In the future. We'll have to settle my part of the inheritance sooner or later. You could always buy me out.'

'The bank isn't going to loan me the money to buy you out. My income isn't enough.'

'You could sell a quarter.'

'We've only got the two quarters. I need it all to keep the operation going. An investor may buy it and rent it back to me, but that's a long shot. In any case, the house is on one quarter, the outbuildings on the other. If I sell either one I'll have to go to the expense of building.'

'You see how it is,' said Jacob. 'If you aren't going to buy me out, then we're going to have to find a way to share the land.'

Job took a step back into a steaming cow patty. Felt his heart tattoo a rapid beat. He saw the months, maybe years, before him, living in that shack, eating canned tuna sandwiches, without mayonnaise, because he didn't want to deal with Lilith, who'd taken over his own kitchen. He wouldn't be able to bring a woman home to entertain, or promise her anything. He felt as he did when he drove the tractor too close to a slough and was pulled in, one back tire spinning uselessly, the other still on firm ground but arching its way inevitably into mud.

FOUR

Then Ed. The summer following Jacob's return, Job dropped in on Will early one morning, unannounced, and found Ed sitting at the kitchen table in nothing but his Stanfield's. Morning bristle on a wrestler's chin, dark ruffle of chest hair, arms as thick as thighs. He made no attempt to cover himself. Will had answered the door in a terry bathrobe. 'This is, ah, Ed. He'll be staying with me. Working with me.'

Ed didn't act like a hired hand, didn't live in the trailer on the other side of the yard but moved right into the house with Will, ate every meal with him. Made supper alongside Will when Job was over. It was clear Ed wasn't a guest; he was family in a way Job wasn't. Although Ed didn't impose himself when Job went out with Penny and Will, he was there, in the kitchen, during the Tuesday-night Bible study when Job found himself complaining, again, about the lack of eligible young women in the area.

'You just need to get out more,' said Ed.

Job supposed this was true. Other single men his age drove up to Edmonton discotheques looking for a date. Or went to the Godsfinger Bar and Grill for a beer and bum darts, a game in which contestants put quarters in the fabric of their butt cracks, walked a space, then released the quarters into a cup; or chicken bingo, for which bets were placed as to where on a numbered grid the bird in question would take a shit. Or, as a last resort, single guys went to the karaoke nights at the Godsfinger community hall, where residents sang from lyrics typed onto recipe cards. On the Saturday nights that Job didn't go out with Will and Penny, he stayed in his farm kitchen with his cat in his lap, listening to his vacuum cleaner.

'Even if I found somebody, how would I entertain?' said Job. 'I can't bring a woman into that cabin.'

'A girl would understand,' said Will. 'It's just a temporary situation.'

All of them were crowded at the kitchen table. Job in jeans and a Sunday shirt. Wade in his NAPA Auto Parts cap and Jerry Kuss in his white cowboy hat, neither thinking to take them off inside the house. Penny in a sweatshirt with a picture of a cat on the front. Ruth Swanson, sitting head and shoulders above them all, with the hands of a basketball player. Ed in jeans and undershirt, though there were ladies present. Will in his Mackinaw, itching his beard. A duck, wearing a diaper, sat on his foot.

Job took a sip from his coffee. 'Jacob's talking about staying, running the farm.'

'He's no farmer,' said Will. 'Never was.'

'I know it. He knows it. But they've had some problems. Lilith wants to stay put for a while.'

'You happy about that?' said Will. 'Farming with him?'

Job shrugged. 'What choice do I have? Dad left half the farm to him.'

'Even if he does stay, that's no reason why you can't go out, have a little fun,' said Ed.

'Yeah, but who with?'

Godsfinger wasn't brimming with single women. Job had found his one and only date at Jacob's wedding reception, held at the Godsfinger community hall. Amanda Krumm was a second cousin from Saskatchewan; when Job watched her from across the community hall, she gave him the eye in return. As they petted in his father's pickup behind the hall, it never occurred to him that she might try to take his shirt off. He didn't notice she'd undone several buttons until she spoke.

'Your chest is so smooth. And your arms. What do you do? Shave your arms?'

'No.'

She ran a finger down his cheek. 'And the skin on your face, it's so soft, like a woman's. You don't have to shave, do you?'

There was wonderment in her voice, as if she had just seen a rare eastern bluebird, flitting cerulean in the lilac. It was true, at nineteen he shaved only occasionally and even then he shaved just for himself, to say he could. His beard was a scattering of downy white hairs.

'You *are* a man, right?' She giggled. It rose like hiccups and wouldn't stop. Job asked politely if Amanda would please leave the truck and then he drove himself home, abandoning his father at the reception, though there'd be hell to pay. He knew his embarrassment would be all over that hall within the hour.

'Why not put an ad in the personals?' Ed asked.

Job took a sip from his coffee, didn't bother answering.

'I'm serious,' said Ed. 'That's how I hooked up with Will.'

Around them the kitchen was more or less as Barbara had left it, though nowhere near as tidy. Three days' worth of dishes in the sink. Stacks of newspapers in the corner. A bag of Pampers Newborns on the counter. Two weeks of grit underfoot. But the walls, the tops of cupboards, and the fridge, were covered with Barbara's fridge magnets and framed inspirational sayings, knick-knacks. Chickens, mostly. A ceramic-chicken cookie jar on top of the fridge. A chicken mobile dangling above the window. Thirty or more sets of chicken salt-and-pepper shakers scattered here and there. Gifts from friends who felt it necessary to give her chickens for her birthdays and at Christmas. Barbara had once told Job that she had never liked these chicken trinkets but felt duty bound to display them all, in case one of the friends who'd given them should drop by. She'd left it all when she moved into town, bought everything new. But didn't want Will to throw anything out.

'It's one thing to find a job through a newspaper ad,' said Penny. 'It's another to find a wife that way. It's sort of desperate.'

'Who said anything about a wife?' said Jerry. 'Why not just someone to have a few laughs with. A little hootchy-kootchy.'

Jerry had little trouble finding women, though he couldn't seem to hang on to them. He had the cowboy look that the local women went for. Brilliant blue eyes in a sunbaked face. He'd opened a country mechanics shop in his father's old machine shed. Scraped a meagre living until he went back to church and joined the local Christian businessmen's association, and changed his business name from Kuss Repairs to Good Samaritan Towing and Repairs. Business went up thirty per cent.

'Exactly,' said Ed. 'I'm just talking about someone to get out with, so you're not always hanging your sorry ass around here.'

'How about Liv?' said Ruth. 'You seem to get along with her.'

Liv worked at the co-op, waitressing in the café, manning the tills in the grocery, and had a habit of sitting at Job's table when things were slow, sharing a coffee and a bit of gossip with him. She sliced him larger pieces of pie than the other waitresses did. Spooned on bigger dollops of whipped cream, ice cream. She'd moved to town with her husband, Darren Liebich, several years before, just after Darren's mother had died and left him the family home in the centre of Godsfinger, a grand turn-of-the-century two-storey house with elaborate fretwork on the veranda and upper balcony. Darren was a trucker and wasn't home much. He and Liv had a son about eleven or twelve, Ben's age, named Jason. Liv had an easy way about her, a ready laugh that produced, for Job, a fall of tiny silver balls. He liked her. She was one of the few women his age, other than Penny and Ruth, who he felt comfortable talking to.

'She's married,' said Job.

Will picked up the duck, put it on his lap, stroked its head. 'She and Darren split. Mom said his truck was parked over at Rhonda Cooper's several nights in a row.'

'She doesn't mow her lawn,' said Penny. 'There were complaints. Barbara said she gave Liv a warning. If she doesn't tidy up her yard, Barbara's going to fine her.'

Will put the duck on Ed's lap, stood to get the coffee pot. 'That's my mom.' Barbara not only judged and awarded ribbons on the vegetable and flower arrangement entries at the fall fair, but placed sticky notes on the winners and losers alike with what she felt were helpful criticisms: *These carrots should have been cleaned better and had the hairy root ends cut off*, or, on Liv's blue-ribbon flower arrangement, in which she had used a pretty yellow button flower, *Tansy is a noxious weed. Why you used it is beyond me.*

'She *is* pretty,' said Job.

'She's fat,' said Penny. 'You're not really thinking of asking her out?'

'I'd ask her out,' said Wade. 'If I were you.'

They all turned to Wade and waited for him to say more. But he put a whole almond square in his mouth and chewed. Wade and Jerry were best friends, though what kept the friendship going was anyone's guess. Wade worked in the Leduc auto-parts store that Jerry frequented, and Job supposed that was how the friendship between the two had been struck. But while Jerry grated, Job liked Wade. He didn't expect talk, rarely spoke. There was something in his manner that demanded respect. Maybe it was his silence. Like Proverbs said, 'Even a fool is thought wise if he keeps silent, and discerning if he holds his tongue.'

Job reached for Ed's lap to stroke the duck's head but yanked his hand back when the bird lunged for him. 'I don't think she's fat,' he said.

'She's got thick ankles,' said Penny. 'And she dresses weird.' Liv wore ankle-length skirts with sandals in summer, army boots in winter, when the other women wore jeans and sweatshirts adorned with pictures of cats and horses or dressed for Sunday in frocks from Kmart. She'd let her hair grow to her bum, dyed it red with henna, kept it in a thick braid for work and wore dangling earrings so heavy they stretched the holes in her earlobes. Stinky Steinke called her a hippie.

Penny crossed her arms. 'She's always got scruffy kids hanging around her place.'

'They're visiting her son, Jason,' said Ed. 'And she volunteers for that crisis line, helps kids out. I like her. I'd say go for it, Job.'

Job glanced at Penny. 'Nah, she's damaged goods,' he said, and realized at once this was something his father had said of a woman with a history, something he disliked his father for.

Jerry snorted, shook his head. 'I guess going to the bar is out.'

Job didn't bother answering. The few women who set foot in the Godsfinger Bar and Grill: sixty-year-old, chain-smoking Beulah, who filed her nails to a point and took trips to Vegas and cruises to Alaska. Pamela Wragg and the Reddick sisters, who participated in the bar's sporting nights, in games of bum darts and chicken bingo.

'There's always Crystal,' said Will. He grinned. The co-op's Out-to-Lunch Café was run by the cook, Crystal Briskie. Her real name was Janice, but following her divorce, when she'd reverted to her maiden name, she'd felt a change in her first name was also in order. She was a short, chunky woman in her mid-fifties whose fashion was inspired by Dolly Parton. Blonde hair piled on her head. Cleavage showing even as she deep-fried the hand-cut potatoes. She wore spiked heels while she worked, and never failed to complain that her feet were sore. She didn't go to church and Job gathered she didn't have much use for religion. She once told Job, 'You need to find yourself a good woman who'll take care of you. Give you some loving. It'll change everything. Make all that church business look like the nonsense it is.'

Job often took his coffee into the kitchen to talk with her while she cooked and sometimes helped her out, ladling up soup or flipping burgers. The sound of sizzling patties on the grill, bursts of orange and red that blended into each other like the food colouring his mother had dropped into vinegar to colour Easter eggs. 'Why don't you come work for me?' she said. 'Better yet, take over running this place. I've had it with the complaints.' He liked that she enjoyed his company. He liked that she found him useful in the kitchen. But she was fifty. And smoked. And never went to church, and had two sons nearly his age.

Will refilled Job's cup.

'So why not ask Ruth out?' said Jerry.

It was a cruel thing. Ruth looked out the window. Job studied his coffee. He'd given some thought to asking Ruth out. With her obvious physical strength and her no-nonsense spirit of mind, she would have made an excellent farmer's wife. But just standing next to her made him feel inept. He didn't like the thought of asking *her* to get the Kellogg's box down from the top shelf.

'Ah, I'm just joshing,' said Jerry. 'You'd look like a couple from a mock wedding.'

Ruth, and then Job, laughed from relief, for there it was, the truth of the matter.

'If I wasn't seeing Will, I'd go out with you,' said Penny. 'What I mean is, it's just a matter of you meeting some girls. You're gorgeous.'

Will put the coffee pot back on its hot plate. 'Penny's right, you're a good catch,' he said. 'Just nobody knows it. I think putting an ad in the personals isn't such a bad idea.'

Job played with the handle of his cup, stared down at his wavering reflection in the coffee. He didn't share the same ruggedness of the local men, like Reuben Brostom, who had once killed nine gophers with one shot. Or Rusty Gronlund, who, after his arm was chopped off at the elbow when he tried to yank wet hay out of a clogged baler, had driven himself, and his severed arm on ice in his beer cooler, the half-hour drive to the hospital. But Job had his own charms.

Will sat back down and Ed handed him the duck. Job reached for the duck again, trying to make friends, but pulled a throbbing finger from its beak. It was a mallard. He'd given Will the clutch of eggs it had hatched from. A nest he'd run over with the mower the summer before, killing the mother duck, who, in her broodiness, wouldn't fly off the nest to save herself. Job was too late to rescue the mother but gathered three unbroken eggs. Took them over to Will, who'd tucked them under a broody hen. Will was there to watch them hatch and he peeled the last of the egg away from this duck. Made a pet of him. First around the yard, later in the house so he wouldn't fly off in the fall. Barbara demanded that Will diaper the bird, for it was she who cleaned the house, twice a month. Insisted on it.

Will held the duck's beak closed together a moment, as punishment, and put it to the floor.

'How about that radio show,' said Ed. '"Loveline." You ever listen to it?'

Job shook his head.

'The first part of the show they interview people who call in, one at a time. Others call in and try to convince the host why they should go out with one of the people interviewed. They're all trying to sell themselves. The only thing is they stopped taking farmers because most of them lived too far away. But we could work that out somehow. It's on tonight. We could phone.'

'No, no.'

'I'll phone for you. Set it up.'

'No. Please don't.'

'Leave it alone,' said Will. 'Why not let us get on with our Bible study?'

'Fine,' said Ed. He grabbed a couple of Job's almond squares, strode from the kitchen, clicked on the television in the living room.

Job, Will, Wade, Jerry, Ruth and Penny got down to the business at hand: determining the will of God. They had gone through the Bible-study course 'Figuring Out the Will of God' twice in the last year, and Job was still confused. He knew how to ask in prayer. But how to be sure of God's answer? Why could he never get a clear sign from God, when others who shouldn't be certain claimed with confidence that God had spoken to them? Edith Spitzer waylaid people on the street, announced that God had told her to pass on a message, then lectured them on the dangers of mowing over outdoor electrical cords or making toast next to the kitchen sink, or on the importance of wearing safety goggles.

Edith, or Dithy as she was called – among other things – had lost her husband, Herb, and all her children when their car was hit by a train at the Millet crossing. With the loss of her family, Dithy Spitzer became obsessed with the safety and health of others. She fancied herself a traffic cop, strode out into the street to stop a car if she saw a pedestrian waiting to cross, or if she thought the car was going too fast. After years of ushering her off the street, the RCMP had given in to her fantasies and presented her with a fluorescent vest so at least she would be seen. On to it she'd fashioned a holster, in which she carried a water pistol that she fired at drivers who didn't yield to her frenzied demands to stop.

44

Just last week she'd grabbed Job's arm as she met him in front of the co-op, whispered, 'God told me to tell you that you've got to get out more.' When he yanked his arm away, walked on, she pulled out her water pistol and shot him in the back of the head.

Job's was a problem that had long vexed the faithful. Gideon himself had felt it necessary to ask God for a sign, and then test the sign he got. He laid a fleece on the ground overnight, asked God to put dew on the fleece and not on the ground if God backed his plan to save Israel. And God did. But that could have just been condensation. So Gideon laid out the fleece a second night, and asked God to put dew on the ground this time and not on the fleece. A sure sign. In the parlance of Job's community, testing God's will in this manner was called putting out a fleece.

Job knew he shouldn't bring simple decisions before God: like, what socks should he wear? What should he cook himself for dinner? But he knew he had to ask God for help in making any major decision, like, should he buy a new truck? Job's truck was a moody red Ford that had belonged to his father and only started when God moved it to. He kept meaning to take the truck over to Jerry's to get the starter fixed, but found it useful for ascertaining God's will. If the truck turned over he went into town. If it didn't, he didn't.

An hour into the study, Ed called from the living room. 'Hey, Job. Phone.'

'I didn't hear the phone ring,' said Will.

'Who is it?' Job asked. The duck followed him into the living room, its diapered tail swinging back and forth.

'How should I know?' said Ed.

Job took the phone, said 'Hello?' Listened to music for a few moments. 'Hello?'

'Hello, Job from Godsfinger. I'm Roly Redman and you're live on "Loveline." So, Job, tell us about yourself. I understand you're in real estate.'

'No. I'm a beef farmer. Cow-calf operation. Who is this?'

'Uh-oh. Sounds like you pulled a fast one on us, Job. We don't take farmers. Most of you live too far away for our callers to hook up with.'

'Take farmers for what?'

'This is "Loveline." Edmonton's dating show. And you're on the air.'

He watched Ed pick up the duck. 'I'm sorry. Somebody's played a joke on me.'

'We've got you on the air now, Job. Why not tell us about yourself? What do you like to do, besides farming? What do you do to entertain yourself when you don't have a date on a Saturday night?'

Job thought of himself in the kitchen, listening to the vacuum cleaner, stroking the invisible glass egg in his hands. His cat sucking her tail at his feet. 'Not much,' he said.

'Come on, there must be something you like doing.'

'I cook.'

'Great! Gals love a man who cooks. Don't you girls?' Canned giggles, a womanly *whoopee*. 'So what kind of cooking? Taiwanese? Tex-Mex?'

'Just cooking. Home cooking. I like to bake.'

'Great! Cookies, cakes, that sort of thing?'

'Almond squares. Matrimonial cake.'

'Matrimonial cake. The way to a woman's heart. So what are you looking for in the way of a girl, Job?'

'I don't know. A Christian.'

'Okay, a Christian. What else?'

46

'That's about it.'

'All right, girls. We've got a guy who bakes squares and ain't picky. If you think he's the one for you, give us a call later in the show. Now we're on to our next caller, Rick from Castle Downs. Hello, Rick. You're live on "Loveline."'

Job hung up the phone. Turned to find Ed and Will, Jerry and Wade, Ruth and Penny all watching from the living-room doorway.

'So?' said Ed.

'You didn't give them my home number?'

'No. I gave them this number. You should hear back within the hour. Come on, let's listen to the show. Hear who calls in for you.'

There was Cindy, who water-skied in the Shuswap during her vacations and thought she'd be perfect for Rick from Castle Downs, who was into dirt biking. Sandy from Beverly, who was hoping for someone to talk to and liked the voice of Andy from McKernan. Shelly from Londonderry, who wanted the number of Phil because she was looking for a man with a steady job. Call after call, but none for Job from Godsfinger, who cooked and baked and would take any Christian girl who might accept him.

Then a call from Debbie. 'I feel God is leading me to have coffee with Job from Godsfinger.'

'Can you tell us why?'

'Well, as I said, God is leading me.'

'No particular reason, eh?'

'I think God telling me to is reason enough.'

'You got a point there, Debbie. All right, Job, if you're listening, you're going to get a call from Debbie from Millwoods. Let's move on to the next caller.'

Ten minutes later, the phone rang. Job picked it up. 'Hello. Job Sunstrum speaking.' He was caught by the formality of his voice. Like a bank manager.

'This is Debbie Biggs. I heard you on "Loveline."' Her voice nasal, a cluster of little balls, like frog's eggs, the colour of a John Deere tractor. 'I wouldn't normally phone into a show like that,' she said. 'But God led me to.'

'Well.' He cleared his throat, glanced back at Ruth, Wade, Penny, Will and Jerry standing at the living-room entranceway, watching. The duck waddled across the floor towards him.

'Besides, I liked the sound of your voice. The way you described yourself, with such *vulnerability*. You did say you were Christian, didn't you?'

'I was looking for a Christian, yes.'

'So what do you look like? No, don't tell me. I want to walk into the restaurant where we meet and pick you out *intuitively*.'

'*Intuitively?*' The duck pulled at the laces of his boots. He brushed it away with his foot.

'I feel that we should *know* our soulmates immediately, when we first meet them. We just *feel* something click inside. Something inside us says, "That's the one for me." You know what I'm saying? I *always* know when someone's my soulmate. Oh, listen to me, babbling on. I'll let you talk now. Go ahead.'

'I, um—'

'I've put you on the spot. We can talk when we get together.'

'Yes, we could meet.'

'How about next week? I'm busy this weekend. Say, Friday? That's my day off. You can get away from the farm on a weekday, right?'

'Sure, Friday.'

'How about noon at Maxwell Taylor's. You know, the restaurant on Calgary Trail?'

'I was wondering if you could come here, to Godsfinger. I'm not much for the city, and I wanted you to see me in my element.' So she'd know what she was getting into right away. So he wouldn't be hurt later.

'All right, I guess. Okay. Sure.'

'At the Godsfinger co-op. The Out-to-Lunch Café. You can't miss it. It's the only restaurant in town.'

'The *only* restaurant?'

'Well, they serve coffee at the gas station. And there's a bar, but—'

'The co-op will be fine.'

Will tapped him on the shoulder, mouthed, 'Photo, get a photo.'

'I was wondering if you'd send me a photo. It's Job, Job Sunstrum at general delivery, Godsfinger.'

'Sure. I could do that. Sunstrum. General delivery. Godsfinger. All right. See you next Friday. Ciao!'

Job put the receiver in its rest, stared at it. This was the girl God had in mind for him?

'So you got a date!' said Will.

'I guess.'

'What do you mean, "I guess"?' said Ed.

'I was thinking, what if she isn't who God has in mind for me?' What if he went out with this woman just because she was the only one who phoned, and they got married even though she wasn't the one destined for him by God, and then she ran off with the local MLA who came knocking from farm to farm during election time as Mrs. Ireland had, or took up living in sin with the rendering man as Jean Milner had, after he came around to pick up a cow who'd died from bloat. That would prove to everyone that Job hadn't been listening to God whispering in his ear when he made his choice of wife but that he had been listening instead to the devil.

Ed threw up his hands. 'I don't *believe* you people.'

'So you put out a fleece,' said Will. 'Ask for a sign.'

'What do you expect?' asked Ed. 'A bloody burning bush?'

FIVE

After he'd done chores, before he had breakfast, Job began his day with a Bible reading. He read through his Bible twice a year, starting with Genesis, finishing with Revelations. He was in Acts now, Saul on the road to Damascus. Saul before his name change, still persecuting Christians. A flash of light and God was speaking to him. As straightforward as that. No room for doubts.

Job tucked his bookmark into his Bible. Penny had given him the bookmark on his birthday. A purple laminated card with gold lettering that read, 'A day hemmed in prayer seldom unravels.'

He closed his Bible, looked around at the hired hand's cabin. The bare plywood walls, the pile of junk in the corner: socket sets, drill bits and Vise-Grips; stomach tubes and pill pushers. A box of equipment for inseminating the cows: French guns, sheaths, gloves and lubricants. Dehorning wire and handles; castrating rings and tools; hoof trimmers and hoof knives; halters and calf pullers. He couldn't bring Debbie Biggs home to this.

He reached across the table for Debbie's letter. The day before, he'd walked out across the road to the mailbox that had been knocked crooked from a game of drive-by mailbox base-ball. He'd found her letter inside, along with a pile of flyers and an electricity bill, and opened it there at the mailbox. Her photograph had slid out and fallen to the gravel below.

Job looked down at the snapshot now. She was pretty, pretty enough to intimidate Job. She appeared to be in her early twenties, and somewhat heavily made up. Job worried that a woman concerned about her appearance might not like getting her hands dirty around the farm. But there was no telling from a photo.

He put the photo back in the envelope, tucked the letter in his breast pocket and opened the cabin door to step outside. Maybe Will was right. He should put the matter in God's hands, put out a fleece.

Job looked over the farmyard, the silos that read: *Jesus is Lord! Hallelujah!* His cows in the pasture and the far bank of the coulee beyond. He prayed silently for a sign from God, that something might fly overhead if God expressed approval. Maybe a duck? He stopped praying, and waited for a reply.

All around him the farm was sketched in the simple lines of a child's drawing, painted in the primary colours of a kinder-garten paint set. The house, a child's rendition of a house: a white box topped by a red peaked roof. A power line stretched out to thin, elderly power poles that trailed away in descend-ing order into the horizon in both directions. Beyond, rolling fields of brilliant primary yellow, canola in flower. One line defined the prairie horizon. Perfect white and fluffy clouds receded one after the other into blue.

At first Job heard nothing except the northeastern wind

that whistled through the windrow of blue spruce behind the house, a sound that rolled tiny bluish balls, the shape of woollen pompoms or tumbleweed, across Job's field of vision. Then the whine of a yellow Ag Cat, a biplane, popping purple-pink fireworks in the air in front of Job, like the burst of a chive flower. The plane flew so low he could see the jubilant, ecstatic expression on the pilot's face. Arnie Carlson. His wife, Annie, washed dishes alongside Job at church functions, but after nearly twenty years of marriage, she had given up trying to talk her husband into going to church. Arnie had stopped farming his father's land years before, rented out the fields surrounding the yard and got himself a pilot's licence. For a moment Job locked gazes with him. Was this the answer to his prayer? *Please God*, Job prayed, *if you want me to go out with Debbie, make Carlson circle around the house.*

The plane banked, circled the house. Job's heart leapt, fell. Carlson would have circled anyway, to say hi, as he always did when he flew over. This was no sign from God. Just Carlson showing off.

Job walked across the road to watch the plane as the door to the house slapped shut. Jacob stepped out onto the stoop and hung onto the top stair rail with both hands. He looked down at Job as if he'd never left the pulpit. Even now, resting at home, he wore a town shirt and striped tie. Perspiration circles ringed each underarm. A tense smile etched into his huge face. He could have been the old man himself.

'You get Carlson in to do crop-dusting?' he asked Job.

'No.' He watched the plane fly over the silos. 'I got a letter from the girl I told you about. From the radio show.'

Jacob watched the plane fly over the north quarter as if he hadn't heard. 'So what's he doing?'

53

'Just giving us a show, I guess.'

'He's flying like he sees something. Keeps going over that same spot. Could be a cow down. Or a grass fire.'

'No smoke.'

Job's tortoiseshell cat, Grace, was at the screen door, meowing to be let out. Job had removed the screen at Lilith's request, as she didn't like the ratty look of it, but he hadn't got around to putting the new screen in. The cat could have hopped through the hole to go outside but from habit sat there waiting for someone to open the door.

'You going to find out what Carlson's after, or what?' said Jacob.

'Yeah. Sure.'

Job followed the cow trail towards the field Carlson seemed to be interested in. He passed a patch of scorched grass, fire-blackened fence posts. A discarded box of Redbird matches. Ben's handiwork. He looked back to see Ben and Jacob, following at a distance. Carlson's plane buzzed low overhead.

Job trotted up a small rise, found himself staring down at a swirling depression in the barley field, as if God had pressed the barley flat with his finger, leaving his seal of approval for Job's date with Debbie Biggs.

Ben caught up to Job just as he stepped into the centre of God's fingerprint. 'Cool! A crop circle!' Job's shoulders fell. *Of course.*

The plane landed with a bump and a hop in the hayfield just as Jacob walked up to meet Job and Ben. He had a limp and the rocking gate of the obese, his joints giving out after years of holding up his weight. 'Why's this barley lodged?' he asked. 'You tramp it down?'

'No.' But Job at once felt guilty, as if he *had* made the circle himself.

'You put too much fertilizer here?'

Carlson climbed the fence and walked through the grain towards them in cowboy boots, sunglasses, a short-sleeved western shirt and jeans with grass-stained knees. A bad case of helmet head. 'You got a crop circle!' He squatted down, placed the palm of his hand over flattened barley. Nicotine stains on his fingers, dirt under the nails. A couple of skinned knuckles. 'It's hot. Can you feel the heat?'

'It's sunny,' said Jacob. 'The plants are absorbing the heat.'

'Probably radiation,' said Carlson. 'Shouldn't let the kid too close.' Although Arnie wasn't known for his concern over safety. Annie Carlson complained that each spring, when her husband came home from a day of crop-dusting, stinking of weed spray, she had to get him to undress outside the house or all her houseplants would wilt.

Ben hunched down beside him, put a hand to the barley. 'It *is* hot!'

'It's hot 'cause it's sunny,' said Job.

Ben shook his head. 'Aliens.'

'The kid's right,' said Carlson. 'They leave this tell-tale mark when they land. Their ships flatten the grain. Or sometimes they're trying to communicate with us, by drawing pictures in the fields. They've been landing for years, see, but only started communicating with us about five years ago, when they started drawing pictures in fields in England. Now they're talking to us! I hope you don't mind. I radioed this in. Pete said he'd call ITV news.'

'There's no such thing as aliens,' said Jacob.

'Sure there are,' said Carlson.

'They're not aliens,' said Jacob, his voice easing into pastoral authority. 'They're demons trying to make everyone *think* they're aliens.'

'Why the hell would a demon want to go and do that?' said Carlson.

Jacob limped forward, into the crop circle. 'It feeds into the whole evolution conspiracy, doesn't it? Demons want us to believe in evolution because it undermines the Bible, undermines man's place at the pinnacle of creation. If everyone comes to believe there are other worlds, other intelligent creatures, that makes us just another creature. Jesus dying on the cross to save us doesn't make a whole lot of sense then, does it?'

Carlson ran a hand over his scalp to flatten his hair. 'I don't mean any disrespect, Pastor Sunstrum. That whole God's-son-dying-to-save-us thing never made much sense to me. Evolution makes a hell of a lot more sense.'

'Sure evolution makes sense,' said Jacob. 'God came up with the idea. He planted the evidence of evolution. He made the world have the appearance of great age, and he put the fossils in place so it would look like there was evolution.'

There was no denying there were fossils. With each pass of the fields Job churned up more fossilized wood. The farm was strewn with it. He took it home and used it as book ends.

'God is outside time,' said Jacob. 'He knew there were going to be evolutionists, so he put the fossils under the earth at the time of creation to see who would be faithful to his word. Do we listen to the humanists? Do we trust what we see with our own foolish eyes, what we hear with our own puny ears? Or do we have faith and believe what God told us happened, in the Bible? That's the test.'

Carlson scratched his neck. 'But if God knew there would be evolutionists, then he'd also know who would be faithful and who wouldn't, wouldn't he? So why go to all the trouble of planting the fossils in the first place? It seems kind of, I don't know, deceitful.' When Jacob opened his mouth to reply, Carlson held his hand up. 'No offense, but I just want to take a look at this crop circle; I didn't come for a sermon.'

Jacob's face the colour of pickled beets. But he smiled. 'None taken. We've all got a right to our beliefs, no matter how misguided. I'm heading back to the house.' He took a few steps, turned. 'Come on, Ben.'

'I want to watch the plane take off.'

'Now!'

'All right.' But Ben didn't move.

'I said now!'

'I could use Ben's help moving the bull to the other herd,' said Job. Though he'd already done it.

Jacob let his shoulders drop. 'All right. But don't take long. Lilith will have coffee ready. You know how she gets when we're late.'

Ben nodded his thanks to his uncle as Jacob limped away.

The faint, sweet smell of insecticide clung to Carlson. Over this the smell of petroleum, the lines of his hands sketched in oil. 'I seen lots of things in fields that look like crop circles, you know,' he said. 'Fairy rings, crops that grow quick and collapse over old manure piles or fertilizer spills. But never an authentic crop circle.'

'It could be somebody playing a joke,' said Job.

Carlson shook his head. 'Too well done. Though I pulled one over Stinky Steinke years ago. You know how I drop those automatic flagmen after each pass, to see where I've sprayed?'

Job nodded. The flagmen: six-foot lengths of folded, filmy paper, like toilet paper, fastened to six-inch squares of cardboard.

'I ran out of them while I was dusting Steinke's canola. So instead of going back to base for some more, I flew real low, dropped my wheels into the canola, lifted off again, to mark the line where I'd sprayed. When I stopped in on Stinky he said, 'Somebody's been driving in my field but I can't figure out how he got in there.' There were no tire tracks coming or going, see? Just the touchdown in the field. I never did tell him. Still hear him worrying over it now and again.' He took off his sunglasses, wiped them. 'I should be going too,' he said, walking off. 'Crop circle. Wild.'

Job and Ben watched Carlson circle over their heads and tip his wings before flying off. They walked the cow trail back home, both of them with their hands shoved in their jeans' front pockets. Job saw his own curls in the back of the boy's head. Cut short though.

'If there *were* aliens,' said Ben, 'and they weren't like Dad said, devils, then God would have made them too, right?'

'I suppose. If there were aliens. God even made Satan.'

'But we look like God. The Bible says we were made in God's image. Right?'

'Right.'

'So, what does the aliens' god look like?'

'It's like your dad says. There are no aliens. There's only one God.'

'But if there *were* aliens, would God look like *them*, with a big grey head and stuff?'

'Your dad wouldn't like you talking about this.'

'Dad doesn't like me talking about anything.'

A tree had fallen over the path, but the cows simply stepped over it rather than deviate from the route. Ben and Job stepped over it too. Here and there the cows' hooves had gouged deep, muddy holes in the trail. When a track grew too deep to traverse, the cows just walked a few steps over, matching the curves and undulations of the first. Creatures of habit.

Job followed his nephew up the stairs and into the house, took off his boots and sat at the same seat he occupied as a child, with his back to the window. Jacob at the head in Abe's old seat, Ben in Jacob's.

Lilith, hair flying like a banshee's, shrieked into the kitchen brandishing a broom, chasing Job's cat. Grace skidded across the linoleum, scrambled to safety under Job's chair, behind his feet, and sat on the register. 'What she do now?' asked Job.

'Just found it sleeping on my bed. I'm allergic, you know.'

Job leaned down to give the cat a scratch, but she jumped from his hand, jittery from the chase. Grace was the only cat on the farm Job had allowed in the house. She lived there still, as she had claimed it and refused to sleep in the cabin. When he had slept in the house, Job often woke in the night to find her lying on his chest, staring down at him, her eyes shining. A comfort, that something in this world found him fascinating. But frightening too, eyes glittering in dark. He had petted her, sparks showering from her coat in the dry night air, until she fell asleep purring, sucking her tail.

Lilith set cups and spoons, a bag of Dad's Oatmeal Cookies on the table and fell into her seat opposite Job. Two years before, she'd been overcome by a bout of palsy and hadn't regained full function of the right side of her face. It gave her a sour look, as if she had just smelled something foul. The expression never left her face, even when she smiled, giving whatever she said a cynical edge. 'So, we've got a crop circle out there, do we?' she said.

'You should've heard Carlson go on about it,' said Jacob. 'He thinks we've got UFOs landing in the field. Or aliens trying to communicate. I tried to tell him it was Satan's work, but he wouldn't listen.'

'But God made the aliens too, didn't he?' said Ben. 'I mean, if there were aliens? Job said they'd be God's creation too.'

Jacob slapped the table, making Lilith and Grace jump. 'What have I told you about talking like that?'

He finished off his cup and set it down. Lilith jumped up to grab the pot and poured him another. 'Ben, you got anything to tell me?' said Jacob.

It was what Abe had always asked before he gave his boys the strap. A fly landed on Job's plate and tasted the cookie crumbs with its feet. Job overturned his empty water glass on it and watched it buzz in panic.

'About what?' said Ben.

'Anything at all.'

Ben reached for another almond square. Job admired the boy's ability to look nonchalant. 'No,' he said.

'Are you sure?'

'Yes.'

'All right. Go to your room and get ready for a strapping.'

'What for?'

'You know what for. If you'd told me about that fire you set in the field, I wouldn't have to strap you.'

'Yeah, right.' He didn't try to deny he'd set the fire, or give his father any more lip. He slid from the table and went to his room, slammed the door behind him.

Grace sat on Job's feet, hoping for a handout. 'I got a letter from that girl who phoned into the radio show,' said Job. 'Debbie? She sent her photo.' Job slid the photograph across the table to Jacob.

'That's no way to meet a girl,' said Lilith. 'It's embarrassing. What are you going to tell people when they ask how you met? "I was so desperate I bought an ad to find a wife"?'

'It wasn't an ad.'

'Why don't you go to Bible school?' said Lilith. 'Find yourself a girl there.'

'*Bridal* school,' said Job. 'I don't see how that's any better than meeting a girl through "Loveline." The only reason girls go is to find a husband.'

'Worked for me,' said Jacob. He winked at Lilith, but she turned and stood to clear away the cups and plates.

'Anyway, I'm too old for Bible school,' said Job.

'Now what's the matter with that cat?' said Lilith, pointing at Job's feet. 'She been into some catnip?'

Job looked down at Grace rubbing her chops over his feet. He had in fact sprinkled a little dry catnip into his socks earlier in the day, afraid of losing the cat's affections to Ben or his brother or, worse yet, to Lilith. He scratched Grace's neck. 'She just misses me,' he said, and blushed at the lie. How small and sad his life was. Living in a shack, arranging dates over the radio, buying the affections of his cat. He felt at once overwhelmingly sorry for himself.

Jacob picked up the photo of Debbie Biggs. 'Huh.' He slid the photo back across the table to Job. 'I got a call this afternoon from Pastor Jack Divine. He's agreed to come down for the revival Saturday.'

'*The* Pastor Divine?' Jack Divine hosted an hour-long Sunday program on a local Edmonton radio station. 'How'd you pull that off?' he asked Jacob.

'You know we were at Bible college together,' said Jacob. 'I gave him a call, to let him know I was back in the area. We had lunch and I asked him to swing by our revival, as a personal favour. You should have seen Stinky Steinke. He was thrilled.' Jacob rubbed his fingers together in the sign for money. Then he slapped his knees. 'Well, I better get to it.' He limped to Ben's bedroom, pulling off his belt.

Job listened for the first slap of leather on skin, and Ben's cry. A brief burst of radiating red lines, followed by a flash of white light. He stared up at the plaque that his mother had hung above the stove many years before, words from Proverbs surrounded by wild rose blossoms: *A gentle answer turns away wrath.* Job stood to rifle through the kitchen cupboards, anything to keep his hands busy. He was sorry Jacob was strapping the boy. But there it was, a father's prerogative. Abe had given Job the strap for each and every one of the fires he set, using a piece of leather horse harness hung by the fridge. Abe had waited a few minutes after telling Job he was giving him the strap, so he wouldn't strap while angry. 'Hitting in anger's a beating,' he told Job. 'I don't give beatings. I'm not a violent man. My dad was a violent man.'

Job's grandfather had been a little man, though he refused to believe it. He had married a woman nearly a foot taller than him, and wore clothes meant for a much larger man. As Abe told the story, his father went into the general store to order shirts, instructing the clerk to bring in size forty-two. The clerk sized him up and without saying anything, ordered the size Grandpa Sunstrum really needed – thirty-six. The shirts arrived, and Grandpa Sunstrum tried them on in the store, triumphantly declaring them the best fitting shirts he'd ever had. Then, on changing back into the clothes he'd arrived in, he noticed his new shirt was not in fact a forty-two. He made the clerk send back the shirts that fit and eventually got his size forty-twos in. Whether the story was true or not, Job remembered his grandfather in shirts that hung loose as a child's play clothes.

Each time Abe warned Job that he was about to give him the strap, Job sat in his room, waiting for his sentence to be carried out with the same mix of fear and numbness, he imagined at the time, as a man on death row. Some time later Abe would walk into Job's room, carrying the strap in both hands like an offering. He asked Job to take down his pants and lay from the waist over the bed, and he hit Job's bare behind with the strap, just once. The sound of leather hitting skin made a good solid smack, very much like the crack a wet towel would make when Jacob flicked it at Job's behind after the baths they shared. The strapping stung, and Job's behind felt hot for an hour or two afterwards, but the real punishment came from the shame of exposing his behind, from the embarrassment of being caught yet again, the confusion he felt over his compulsion to set fires.

Abe administered the strap until Job was sixteen and had become 'too big to handle,' as Job heard his father tell Pastor Heinrich over coffee in the Sunstrum kitchen. Pastor Heinrich himself had recommended from the pulpit that parents stop strapping their boys when they turned fourteen, and that, for girls, strapping should certainly be stopped before the onset of menstruation, well before age eleven, 'to avoid any suggestion of impropriety.'

Lilith rolled the portable dishwasher over to the sink and glanced at Job as she loaded the supper dishes. 'What are you looking for?' she asked.

'My jujubes.'

'I threw them out.'

'You threw out my food?'

'I hardly call that food. I didn't want Ben eating any sweets. We think he might be hyperactive or something.'

'Those jujubes were mine.'

'Well, I am sorry. I'll buy you more jujubes. You can keep them in the cabin.'

'You rearranged the cupboards.'

'Just so they make sense.'

'They made sense.' Now alert for changes, he scanned the kitchen and living room. His books were gone, the shelves bare, except for a copy of *Nervous Christians*, which said anxiety and nervous tension were caused by Christians relying on themselves, rather than the Holy Spirit. He'd filled three shelves with books, collected over several trips to the Salvation Army thrift shop in Wetaskiwin, because if he happened to meet a woman in town and invited her back to the farm for a home-cooked meal, he wanted to appear well read. But he'd only read a handful. Over several lonely nights the previous winter, he'd read *The Story of Margarine*, *Manures for the War-Time Garden* and *Extraordinary Popular Delusions and the Madness of Crowds*, the latter of which he'd only got halfway through; it dealt with the many and varied ways in which humans were fooled by their own desires into believing the ridiculous, and for reasons he could not define, he found these stories unsettling.

After Pastor Henschell's sermon on avoiding the polluting effects of media, he'd intended to throw all the books out and restock from the *Christian Book and Record Store* in Edmonton, worried that if he met a woman at church and invited her home, she'd see all those unsavory books on the shelves and would think him a backslider. Nevertheless, he picked up *Nervous Christians*, waved it in front of Lilith and demanded, 'What did you do with my books?'

'They're in a box in the car. I thought I'd take them to the thrift shop. Jacob needed the room for his books.'

'But they were *my* books.'

Lilith hooked the dishwasher nozzle to the faucet and started up the machine. The sloshing water and the whirr of the motor put invisible spiny cones in Job's hands that pricked his palms. He flicked his hands as if to drop them, but the sensation persisted. 'Can't the dishes wait?' he said. 'The machine's not even half full.'

'If I don't, I'll run out of cups and cutlery.'

Jacob strode out of his son's bedroom, red-faced. 'Can't you two shut up?' he said. 'Squabbling like children. I could hear you through the door.'

The phone rang and Jacob answered it. Lilith switched off the dishwasher. She and Job listened to Ben's sobs, to Jacob's side of the conversation. 'Uh-huh, uh-huh. Well, I don't know.' Finally he said, 'All right then,' and hung up the phone. He sat at the kitchen table. 'There's a camera crew on the way here. They want to interview you.'

'A what?' said Job.

'That was a guy from ITV. They're coming out this way for

another story and want to talk to you for a spot for the evening news, to end off the show. About that crop circle. They'll be here in about twenty minutes.'

Job jumped up, ran for the door. 'There's no time. I don't have any clean shirts.' He scrambled to the cabin, got himself dressed in a clean pair of jeans and a T-shirt. Ran back to the house to see if he could borrow a clean shirt from Jacob.

Job slid off his runners and walked into the kitchen, just as a cat screech set off an explosion of green jagged lightning. Grace, wet through, shot out of the dishwasher as Lilith opened the machine. The cat slid across the floor into the kitchen hallway and scrambled out the hole in the screen door.

'What the *hell*?'

'Your cat shit in my shoes!'

Job looked behind him into the hallway, directed by Lilith's bony finger, and saw a two-sectioned turd in Lilith's yellow Sunday pumps. 'So you put her in the dishwasher?'

'Just for a minute. It's not like I was going to let her drown.'

Job saw in Lilith's eyes the wild look he'd seen in gadding cattle, cows crazed by the larvae of warble flies burrowing into their skin, and decided against pressing the matter further.

'I need a clean shirt,' he said.

'Jacob's shirts would be way too big.'

'Does Ben have anything that would fit? Some oversized shirt?'

'Not big enough for you.'

'How about you?'

'You want to borrow one of my blouses?'

'I've got to find a shirt. I can't go on TV like this. What would people think?'

'Borrow one from Will, then.'

Job slipped on his runners, ran to his truck, praying that it would start. When it didn't, he headed down the road for Will's house at full run. As he reached the poultry barn, Will was just getting out of his truck in the yard. Ed came out of the barn to meet him. Job was about to raise a hand to catch their attention when Will kissed Ed on the lips. It was brief and tender, the kiss a husband gives a wife on returning home. He brushed something off Ed's cheek and grinned before heading towards the house.

Job turned the corner, hid behind the barn, felt the sun-hot wall against his palms as he listened to Will's footfalls on the steps to the house, the duck's quack greeting him as he opened the door, the screen door snapping shut.

Job headed back home, slowly now, his feet in concrete, his skull a pot of churning porridge. The heads of timothy grass in the hayfields were a stunning green, lit from within. A thing he'd never seen before, or noticed. Then a startled squawk, a flurry above him, a *thwack* to the back of his head, the bounce and quick flicker of feathers, and his hands were in front of him, instinctively reaching out for the thing falling into his arms. A duck.

A beautiful thing. A bufflehead. A large white patch on the back of its head; shimmering forest-green and eggplant plumage on the front. Black and white body. He felt for a pulse and found it was dead. Checked for a bullet hole and blood, but there was none. He remembered a thing his father had said, that ducks sometimes die of heart attack in the air. The exertion of achieving flight.

Job's head began to throb. He nestled the duck like a baby, in the crook of one arm. Checked his scalp. Found a tender spot at the cap of his skull but no wound. He saw a blaze of dust stretching up the road, turning into his driveway, and couldn't think who it would be. He quickened his step before realizing with a start that the dust was the television crew. But he didn't run. He felt a strange mix of drowsiness and clarity, and the landscape was different somehow. The colours of sounds were muted, faded. The crow's caw was a transparent tongue of sky blue, not the usual wedge of navy. When he followed the fenceline towards the house, the shush of his legs passing through grass was hardly visible, though usually it offered up a pleasant sunflower-yellow haze. Now there was nothing but a shimmer.

Job carried the bufflehead to the steps of the house, where Ben waited, his eyes still puffy from crying. 'They're at the crop circle. Dad told me to wait and tell you. He went into town for some meeting. What's that?'

'A duck.' Job carried the bufflehead out to the crop circle, prodded by his nephew's questions. Had he shot it? Found it dead? Job didn't answer. Words were too unwieldy, too heavy to bring up from inside himself. Even walking seemed difficult. All he was certain of were the silky feathers of the dead duck.

'They've got a couple of other men with them who they're going to interview,' said Ben. 'Crop-circle experts. They're in a hurry. We should run.' He took Job's arm and tried to get him to pick up his pace. At other times Job would have run to the crew so they wouldn't have to wait, apologized for the inconvenience he had caused, blushed in the effort to make peace. But at that moment he couldn't fashion in his mind the thing that was being asked of him.

A cameraman had set up just outside the crop circle. He wore a military-green vest with many pockets and didn't bother to greet Job. Inside the circle, there was an interviewer Job recognized from an Edmonton news show, casually dressed, holding a mike. With him were two middle-aged men, both dressed in suits.

The interviewer held out a hand. 'Mr. Sunstrum. Thought we were going to miss you. I'm Dave Nash of ITV. I'll be interviewing you and Mr. Mayer and Dr. Fisher here. All right?' When Job didn't answer or even nod, he asked, 'You okay?'

'Yes.'

'What you got there?'

'Duck. A bufflehead.'

'A pet?'

'It's dead.'

'All right then. Tell us what you thought when you first saw the crop circle, Mr. Sunstrum. What did you think caused it?'

'I thought it was God.' He realized this was a mistake. But felt committed now, caught in the truth.

'God?'

'A sign, from God.'

'A sign?'

'I was trying to make a decision. So I prayed. Asked God for a sign. Something in the air. I thought maybe a duck. Then Carlson was in the plane flying overhead and . . .'

'The crop circle.'

Job saw he was sinking, paddled harder. 'But then Carlson was talking about aliens writing messages in the barley, or that maybe the circle was where a UFO landed. And my brother explained how all that talk about aliens is a demon conspiracy. So now I don't know what to think.'

'A demon conspiracy?'

69

'The devil trying to get us to believe we're not the only people in the universe, so that salvation doesn't mean much. My brother's a pastor.'

'I see. A unique theory, Mr. Sunstrum. Well, there you have it, folks. God – or maybe the devil – reaches out and touches folks in Godsfinger.' He turned to one of the other men. 'Dr. Fisher, what do you think caused the crop circle?'

'There's been all kinds of explanations for crop circles, anything from dust devils to plasma vortexes or ball lightning to landing marks left by alien craft. But most likely it's pranksters.'

'Some argue that the crop circles are too complex to be built by pranksters,' said the interviewer.

'I've made them myself. I fixed up this piece of two-by-four with wire stuck through a hole on each end. I held onto the wire and pushed the board down into the grain with my boot. Nothing to it. Leaves that swirling pattern everyone gets so worked up about.'

'But that hardly explains the molecular change the wheat undergoes in these crop circles,' said Mr. Mayer.

'There is no molecular change.'

Job stepped back, out of view of the camera, and looked down at the duck. He couldn't think for a moment why he was holding it. He listened to the other men talk and talk, couldn't catch onto what they were saying. Aware of the ache at the back of his head.

Dave Nash lowered his mike, coiled its cord. 'All right, Dr. Fisher, Mr. Mayer, Mr. Sunstrum, thank you very much. I think that's all we need. Karl, make sure you get a shot of the silos and that barn roof. We can splice it into the interview with Sunstrum. *Jesus is Lord! Hallelujah! This is cattle country. Eat beef.* Christ. And the dead duck. This is too good.'

70

Job followed several yards behind the crop-circle experts, the cameraman and Dave Nash as they hauled their equipment back to the van. He watched Ben leap around them like a magpie on an ant hill, pecking bits of attention from them. Mr. Mayer and Dr. Fisher continued to wrangle. Mr. Mayer, red-faced and angry; the doctor, quiet and assured, pulling out a notepad as he got into the van next to Mayer, calmly sketching out his defence as they drove off.

Job watched the van drive away, pulling a cloud of dust behind it. Held up a hand as Ben waved to him from the stoop of the house before going inside. He wondered again why he was carrying a duck, realized with a sting of embarrassment that he'd held it throughout the interview, though now he couldn't recall what he'd said. The television crew and the interview – they seemed unlikely. As unlikely as a crop circle forming in his field in answer to a prayer. As unlikely as a dead duck dropping from the sky onto his head. As unlikely as seeing Will kiss another man on the lips.

Job winced as the throbbing of the lump on the back of his head came sharply into focus. He picked up a shovel that was leaning against the barn wall, carried it with one hand up to the house and laid the duck on the bottom step before scooping out a hole in the flower bed. He laid the duck to rest, and quickly shovelled dirt to cover its one open eye.

SIX

For the first thirty years of the town's life, Godsfinger was called Hay Lake, after the lake that disappeared in dry years, giving surrounding farmers a fertile field of hay to cut. But then the sky set about renaming the place. A tornado touched down one summer, blasting a swath through town, lifting the church whole into the sky like the body of the chosen on the day of resurrection, before slamming it down again. Everything was destroyed, except for the cement cold room, in which the ladies' auxiliary kept fruit and preserves for church suppers and pie-making events. Not a single jar of preserves was lost.

Members of the congregation built a new church on the old foundation that same summer and conducted services until the second tornado hit, exactly a year to the day after the first, lifting the roof of the new church like a great winged bird, casting it a half mile to the corner of Steinke's farm. Without the roof, the walls fell; what was left looked like a flattened cardboard box. Upon seeing that second tornado approach, the church secretary fled downstairs to the concrete cellar to hide among the preserves and rose from rubble into daylight carrying a jar of strawberry jam.

The following Sunday the pastor then, Fritz Hofmann, preached a fiery sermon in a crowded tent beside the church foundation. He claimed God had roared through town to give them a taste of the end of the world, so believers would know their deliverance was close at hand, so sinners would have no excuse on the day of reckoning. From the manse, he had watched the tornado touch down in the field, he said, 'like God's finger writing the commandments in front of Moses!' And went on to suggest the town should be renamed Godsfinger, to commemorate the two catastrophes, to remind everyone of God's everlasting power over them. In the end, the town council agreed, as public sympathy had been swayed by the disaster.

Disaster is said to come in threes, and even though the congregation rebuilt a second time on the old foundation, everyone stayed away from the church on the anniversary of the tornado and breathed a sigh of relief when the day came and went without catastrophe.

Godsfinger might have become a bedroom community to Edmonton, as nearby St. Albert had. But the stench of Hanke Bullick's feedlot on one side of town, Stinky Steinke's dairy on the other and Stubblefield's poultry farther out kept potential buyers from the city from settling there. No one in Godsfinger liked the stink, but almost everyone understood, as they carried their own farm odours: the sweet smell of horse or cattle, the foul scent of pig, or the worst of odours in Job's mind, poultry. Stubblefield's poultry barns were situated a half mile west of Godsfinger on Correction Line Road, so when the wind blew east, it brought the foul stench of chicken manure into town with it. As it stood, the whole town was composed of one dead-end street with a strip of shabby buildings running down each side, crowned at the end by Godsfinger Baptist Church.

There was little to keep the town going. The old brick bank still stood, but its windows were boarded over. Residents had to go to Leduc or Millwoods to do their banking. The Godsfinger Bar and Grill kept chugging along, though the upper floor hadn't been operated as a hotel for years. Hanke Bullick, who owned the bar as well as a feedlot, occasionally rented rooms by the month to young people just stepping out or to ancient bachelors down on their luck, but they never stayed long. The rooms were sun-baked in summer, freezing in winter.

Sheeler's Auto Repair had been running for nearly twenty-five years, though rumour had it Sheeler was thinking of retiring, closing things down. The beauty salon closed and reopened every couple of years. It was currently owned and operated by Annie Carlson, who cut both men and women's hair. A doctor from Leduc visited a worn office next to the salon two mornings a week. The three grain elevators had been taken down and Hosegood's sausage factory had gone bankrupt almost a decade before, though the building still stood, empty and boarded up, at the opposite end of town from the church. Beside the factory, an Esso gas station did brisk business.

Children in grades one through twelve were bussed to Godsfinger from surrounding farms, and it was this school that kept the town alive. That and the Out-to-Lunch Café tucked in the front corner of the co-op. Fifteen years before,

Crystal had covered the café walls in fake wood panelling, decorated them with laminated jigsaw puzzles of cats, horses, an empty farmhouse on the prairie, and hadn't changed a thing since. Plastic plants dangled from macramé hangers over the windows. On the ceiling, a brown swell of water damage. Stinky Steinke, Gerhard Schultz and Walter Solverson sat like elements of the decor at their table by the counter, in a daily, informal meeting of the church board.

Job came into the café wearing his Sunday best, dress corduroys and a white town shirt, wishing he'd gone into Edmonton to meet Debbie. Hadn't thought of these prying eyes. He waved at Crystal, who blew him a kiss from the kitchen, nodded at Steinke, Schultz.

Solverson with a double chin, the sideburns he'd worn since the fifties, dyed with Grecian Formula, though he was otherwise bald. 'Saw you on the news,' he said. 'You believe all that stuff you said about that crop circle?'

Job pulled back a chair at his usual table by the window, said nothing. He didn't remember much of what he'd said and was afraid Stinky Steinke would tell him all about it.

'What was with the duck?' said Steinke. He had a long, thin face, a neck that had lengthened and shoulders that had sagged with age, giving him the general appearance of a ketchup bottle. A sign placed on the side of the Steinkes' barn by the salesman who sold him the equipment had proclaimed his barn to be a Barn-o-matic, a self-cleaning model. Cows, locked into stanchions, shit into gutters. A chain propelled by an electric motor dragged the manure down the gutters and up a chute that dumped the manure outside into a shit-spreader. Steinke made a practice of spreading his manure right behind the hall during community events. It was his way of saying,

'I'm working and you're not,' and it was this routine that had earned him his nickname.

'You got yourself a new pet or something?' Steinke cradled the air in his arms. 'There he is holding a duck. Rocking it like a baby.' He laughed with Solverson and Schultz.

Liv refilled their cups and brought the pot and a cup to Job's table. The smell of oranges about her. Her voice had been the purple of flowering heliotrope, but it was faded now, transparent. Job watched her voice, a sprinkle of lavender falling across the skin of her face as she spoke. 'Why *were* you carrying a duck?' she asked.

Job grinned, talked into one shoulder. 'It hit me on the back of the head. Guess it died in flight. I caught it before it hit the ground. Then I couldn't think what to do with it.'

Liv's laugh was still a rain of silver balls. 'What are the odds? Too bad the cameras didn't catch that. So, what can I get you?'

'Just coffee for now. I'm meeting someone.'

'Will?'

'No.'

Liv raised an eyebrow but didn't push for more information. She carried the pot back to the counter.

Noon came and went. Job drank, stared out the window at Liv's house up the street. An overgrown lawn filled with bird feeders and sunflowers had sprung from the seeds birds had scratched to the ground. The cheerful heads of the flowers were pointed Job's way, following the sun.

Jerry tied his dog to the garbage can outside the door. A Samoyed and German Shepherd cross, white with a tail that curled over its back. It tried to nose its way through the door as Jerry came in. 'What happened? Date stand you up?'

Job felt the room turning his way and huddled over his empty coffee cup.

Jerry took off his cowboy hat, laid it on his table, turned his chair to face Job and settled in. He called to Liv, 'Hey sweetie, can a guy get some coffee around here?'

Liv poured Jerry his coffee and took the pot around. As she refilled Job's cup she asked, 'I hear right? You got a date?'

Job watched the coffee pour into his cup. 'Sort of.'

'Hang on a sec.' She set the pot down behind the counter, picked up a plate and an orange and sat at Job's table to peel it. 'Don't worry,' she said. 'I'll leave when your date turns up. I'll just keep you company 'til then.' She nodded at Steinke. 'Keep the boys from making a scene.' She separated each section of the orange, arranged them into a flower on her plate, cut each section into three and sucked the juice from each bit before chewing. She had a cupid's bow mouth. Job had once over-heard Darren say, 'Hey, Kissy Lips,' on greeting her, before slapping her butt. 'So, how'd you meet this girl?' Liv asked.

Job etched a line in the checkered tablecloth with his thumb. 'I haven't met her yet.'

Crystal came over to the table. Her stiletto heels pock-marked the linoleum. She leaned over the table, so close Job could smell the cigarette on her breath. A jangle of bracelets. Pointy nails painted coral. 'What's this I hear about a date?' she whispered.

'A blind date,' said Liv.

'Somebody fix you up?'

He looked up at the wasp trap hanging over the door. 'Not really.'

'What did you do?' said Crystal. 'Put an ad in the personals?' She laughed, then stopped. Job felt the blush sweep across his face.

'She heard me on "Loveline." That radio show. Ed phoned in and lied. Said I was a real-estate agent. Then handed me the phone.'

Liv laughed. 'That shit.'

'Oh, crap,' said Crystal. 'I got to get back to the grill. Fill me in later?'

Job watched her tap back to the kitchen.

Liv ate a chunk of orange. 'So I guess you don't know what this woman looks like.'

'She sent a photo.' He pulled it from his breast pocket and watched Liv suck the juice from her fingers before taking it.

'Huh,' said Liv. 'Pretty.' She ate another piece of orange. 'You hear Darren and I split?'

Job hoped he looked surprised, as if he hadn't heard. He tried to think of something to say, but found himself dumbfounded, feeling the same mild panic he felt when he tried to come up with something to write on sympathy cards.

Liv leaned over the table in the way he liked, giving him her attention in a very physical way, with her whole body turned to his. 'So, did you believe that stuff you said on TV? Or were you putting those guys on?'

He turned his attention outside, to Jerry's dog tied to the garbage can. 'Oh, I don't know.'

Jason pushed through the café door wearing jeans and a jean jacket and a striped blue T-shirt. His dirty-blond hair stood straight up from his head. He had Liv's milky complexion, round face and wide smile, though he was lanky like his father. All arms and legs. He tripped over his own foot as he ran over to their table. 'Job! Saw you on TV!'

'No running in here,' said Liv.

Jason sat. 'Can I come over and see the crop circle?'

'Sure,' said Job. 'Your mom tells me you're getting pretty good on the sax.'

Jason scuffed his runner against linoleum. 'Not really.'

Liv rubbed a hand down her son's arm. 'He plays and plays, throws his music across the room when he doesn't get it quite right. Then he gathers up the pages, starts again. He's a perfectionist. Doesn't get it from me.'

'So did you see any aliens or anything?' Jason asked.

Job caught Steinke watching, laughing. 'No,' he said. 'No aliens.'

Liv popped the last of the orange in her mouth, pushed her chair back and stood. 'Looks like I better get back to work.' She waved a hand at the window. Outside Debbie Biggs stepped from a red Mustang. Job sat up straight. Felt his heart thud against his chest and his hands go moist.

'All right, Jason. Let's leave Job alone. He's meeting someone.'

'Can I come over to see the crop circle today?' he asked Job.

'We'll see,' said Liv. 'Job might be busy.' She winked at Job, then walked Jason up to the counter and brought him a slice of blueberry pie.

Debbie Biggs stepped through the café door and looked around the room. She had breasts big enough to garner stares, though she'd apparently done her best to conceal them by wearing a loose sweater and jacket with oversized shoulder pads. Job put his hand up to get her attention, but she'd already locked gazes with Jerry. He nodded at her and she sat at his table and stayed there. Job waited for Jerry to clear up the mistake, but Debbie went on sitting with him. She laughed too loud and curled her hair with her finger. Jerry leaned into the table and stared deeply into her monumental breasts. He caught Job's eye and winked.

Liv came back to Job's table and whispered, 'That's your date, isn't it?'

Job nodded.

'What's she doing with Jerry? You want me to go get her?'

'No! No.'

'I imagine Jerry will tell her.' When Job said nothing, she said, 'Want some pie?'

Job stabbed his blueberry pie and watched Liv carry the pot over to Jerry and Debbie. He looked down, blushing, at his half-finished pie when Liv pointed his way. Then Debbie Biggs was there, standing beside him. 'Job?'

'Yes, hello,' he said, standing.

'I'm Debbie.'

He shook her hand, stepped forward to pull out her chair just as she stepped back, plunging a heel into his toe. He gasped, apologized.

'I'm the one who stepped on your toe.'

'Yes, of course. I'm sorry.'

He sat and tried to think what to say. Out the window Jerry's dog struggled back and forth past the café window, with its tongue out and tail wagging, dragging the now-upturned garbage can to which it was tied, trying to get a scratch from Dithy Spitzer. A trail of garbage littered the sidewalk behind the can.

Debbie cleared her throat. 'So, you're a farmer?'

'Yes.' He watched Liv sashay over to Steinke's table, carrying three plates, the soup-and-sandwich special. Tuna sandwiches. Tomato soup. He wondered why talking with Liv was nearly effortless, like talking with Ruth. Or Crystal.

'Cow-calf operation,' he said finally. 'Though I should tell you that since my brother came home, I'm living in the hired hand's cabin. I've got no place to entertain. And there's some confusion over the farm. After my father's death the estate was never settled. Now my brother's back home. I don't think he really wants to farm. He's a pastor. I could never be a pastor, standing in front of all those people and everything. Although when I was a kid I sometimes played the accordion at the community hall, for weddings and showers, that sort of thing. The accordion was my father's idea. I wanted to play bass guitar. But then my dad didn't allow any rock in the house.' He stopped short, having completely lost his train of thought.

'You were telling me your brother moved back home.'

'I just wanted to let you know. In case it made a difference. I'm not sure what you have in mind. I mean what your expectations are. About what I can offer.'

'I'd like a cup of coffee.'

'Oh, yes, sure. Sorry. I don't usually talk this much. I guess I'm just – Liv? Can I get another coffee, please?'

He went up to the counter to get it, came back and sat, and found himself staring at Debbie's breasts as she squirted creamers into her coffee.

'Implants,' said Debbie.

'What?'

'They're not real.'

'I'm sorry. I didn't mean to—'

'It's okay. When I had them done, I wanted men to stare. Then I found Jesus.'

Job, pawing his mind for something to say, watched as Dithy, dressed in her fluorescent vest and brandishing her water pistol, strode into the street in front of Will's truck. Ed was in the passenger side. Will stopped so he wouldn't run Dithy over, but drove on when she started to give him one of her lectures. She aimed her gun and sprayed his back window before he parked at Sheeler's Auto Repair, in front of the sign that read *Cadillacs Only* in pink lettering.

Job patted his back pocket for a hanky. When he didn't find one, he used a paper napkin to give his nose a discreet blow. Then he noticed the whistle that rattled from his nose, a sound just like the one that issued from the red toy whistle on the cowboy hat his father had given him one Christmas. He'd blown that red whistle all Christmas Day, conjuring a blue bowl that was suspended in mid-air in front of him, as if he'd come across the half shell of a robin's egg caught in a spider's web. Until Abe yanked the ball from the whistle so it would never trill again. Now here was that same sound, coming from his nose, bringing with it an image more vibrant than any sound had produced since he'd seen Will kiss Ed, since the duck hit him on the back of the head.

He rubbed a hand over his mouth and whistled from his nose, watching through the blue eggshell as Dithy confronted Will. Her hands up, water pistol waving in the air, pointing back at the street. Ed, with his massive arms folded over his chest, watching from the other side of the truck, grinning.

Job pushed a fork into his pie, left it there. Tried not to stare at Debbie's breasts but couldn't look her in the eye. He settled on her right earring, a large square of metal with a round of pearl-coloured plastic glued to it. He groped for words, came up empty. Whistled through his nose because the robin's eggshell brought on a feeling of calm.

Debbie squinted at him. 'Maybe I should go.'

'No! I was going to ask if you wanted to go to our revival here, tomorrow night. Pastor Divine's leading a healing service.'

'Pastor Jack Divine? Of Divine Ministries?'

'He's a friend of my brother's.' A half lie.

Debbie placed a moist hand on Job's arm, stroked as she might comfort a poodle. Shook her head. 'This just isn't going to work. I sensed immediately we weren't soulmates. And this man over here?' She pointed a red fingernail at Jerry. 'I knew, as soon as I walked in the door, he was the one God led me here to meet. I mean, you're beautiful and all, but God has led me to want more. God wants me to have things. He wants me to have a large house and a new car. Can you give me the things God wants for me?'

Job shook his head. But then neither could Jerry.

Liv brought the coffee pot to the table, poured.

'You see how it is,' said Debbie. 'But I want to thank you. If you hadn't phoned into "Loveline," I wouldn't have come here, and I wouldn't have met Jerry.' She gave Jerry a little wave. He waved back.

'God sure moves in mysterious ways, don't he?' said Liv. 'You want pie or anything?'

'No, I've got to go,' said Debbie. 'Jerry's taking me out to his cabin at Pigeon Lake.' She stood.

Jerry made his way over to the table. 'Hey, aren't you that crop-circle guy?' he said, grinning. 'Saw you on the news last night, Job.'

'You were on the news?' said Debbie, sitting again.

'Yeah, he's got this crop circle in his field.' He laid a hand on Debbie's arm, helped her up. 'I'll tell you about it later.'

Liv with her hand on one hip. 'That's a buck for the coffee.'

'Oh, I thought Job—'

'I mean for you and Jerry here.'

'Oh, yes.'

'I'll take care of that,' said Jerry. He followed Liv to the checkout.

Debbie smiled, looked at the toes of her pumps. 'Yes. So. Thanks again.'

Job kept his eyes on the plastic plant in the macramé hanger. He wouldn't look at Stinky or the other boys on the church board. 'It was nothing.'

'I guess we're going. Ciao!'

Job slumped into his chair and watched them leave. He tried to conjure the blue robin's egg, but his nose whistle was gone. A snuff box made a circle in the back pocket of Jerry's jeans as he untied his dog from the garbage can. He led Debbie and the dog off to his truck, leaving the garbage strewn across the sidewalk.

Liv sat across from Job. 'She was quite the, ah, woman. And Jerry was quite an ass, eh? Stealing your date like that?'

'I guess.'

'Why'd you let him get away with that?' When Job said nothing, she said, 'Turn the other cheek and all that?'

Job drank his coffee and watched Jason pick up the last of his pie and carry it over to their table. The boy sat and ate with blueberry-tinted lips. Job wondered at the colour of his own. Had he talked to Debbie with bits of blueberry stuck between his teeth? He pushed his cup away and fished in his pocket for change.

'It's on the house,' said Liv. 'Anyone who can endure that little scene deserves it.'

Job felt his eyes water up and his lip tremble in an effort to hold back tears. He looked away, at Dithy striding down the street.

'Actually, I wouldn't mind seeing that crop circle of yours either,' said Liv. 'You hear so much about them.'

'Yeah!' said Jason.

Job nodded, pinched his nose. 'You can stop by any time.'

'Could you give us a ride now? I don't drive.'

'You don't drive?'

'I let my licence slide. You heading home soon?'

'Now, I guess.'

'How about I put together a picnic lunch and we eat it in the field?'

She disappeared into the kitchen for a few minutes and came back carrying a co-op grocery bag.

'I've got something for you,' she said. 'A treat guaranteed to put a smile on your face.'

She pulled a folded paper towel from the bag, then offered him a plump dried fruit from within it.

'What's this?'

'Medjool date.'

'It's warm.'

'Nuked it. Brings out the flavour.'

Job took a tentative bite. The flavour was sharp, sticky-sweet, a revelation. He nibbled at the date, then popped it whole into his mouth, pressed it against the roof of his mouth. He watched as Liv ate hers, the fruit between her lips.

'Good, huh?'

'Wonderful.'

'Another?' When he nodded she tore a bit of flesh from a date and pressed it to his tongue. Her fingers lingered on his lips. Then she put her hand on Jason's head, and smoothed his hair until he yanked his head away.

SEVEN

Liv held the grocery bag in her lap as she sat next to Job in the truck. The warmth of Liv's thigh next to Job's as they bounced down the gravel road, past the row of clowns along the Stubblefield farm. When they pulled into the yard, Ben was spinning donuts on the trike, a three-wheeled all-terrain vehicle Job used to work on fences or to check the cows. Ben couldn't get enough of the trike. Job had put him to work on it chasing cows.

Ben drove the trike to the passenger side and nodded at Jason as he got out. 'Cool!' said Jason.

'We're going to take a look at the crop circle,' said Job.

'Want a ride?' Ben asked Jason. They were off in a flurry of dust, Jason on the back of the trike, hanging onto Ben's shoulders so he wouldn't fall off.

'That thing safe?' Liv asked.

Job shrugged. 'More or less.'

As Job and Liv followed the cow trail out to the crop circle, the grass along the fenceline of the adjacent pasture rustled as if an animal were passing through it. Job called, 'Kitty, kitty?' and listened.

'What?' said Liv.

'Thought it might be my cat. She hasn't come back home. Lilith put her in the dishwasher while the machine was running.'

Liv laughed. 'She did what?'

He realized his mistake. There'd be hell to pay from Jacob if word got out. 'Don't tell anyone. Please. I don't think Lilith could live it down. Or Jacob.'

'The cat survived?'

'Yeah, but I haven't seen her since.'

Liv laughed and laughed, a waterfall of tiny silver balls. Tears at the corners of her eyes. Job found himself laughing with her, and the incident seemed less tragic now, less crazy.

The boys, having checked out the crop circle, were making their way back to Job and Liv. Ben pulled the trike to a stop next to them. 'You already done with the crop circle?' Liv asked.

'Yeah, it's cool,' said Jason. 'Just not what I thought. I mean, it's just knocked-down wheat.'

'Barley,' said Job.

'Whatever.'

'Aren't you going to come with us, have something to eat?' said Liv.

'I'm not hungry.'

'Guess I shouldn't have given you that pie. All right. See you later. Have fun.' She waved as the boys took off through the field.

As Job and Liv reached the crop circle, a hay devil swept up around them, making mischief with Liv's skirt, lifting it clear up to cover her face, to expose her pink cotton panties, her sturdy legs. A shiny, inch-long scar on her shin. Liv pushed her skirt down, red flooding her face. So she could be embarrassed, thought Job.

She turned her back away from Job as she unloaded the grocery bag and poured coffee from a Thermos. Job sat with her, an arm propped up on one knee, watching as she set out a checkered tablecloth, napkins, cutlery. He looked down at her leg, the scar there. 'Where'd you get that?' he said, pointing.

She pulled her skirt to cover it. 'It's nothing,' she said. 'I was helping my dad load the pickup with firewood when I was six. I loaded up my arms too full, you know, trying to impress Daddy, so I couldn't see where I was going. I walked into the rough edge of the log, cut a gash to the bone.'

'Must of hurt.'

'Yeah. Dad said, "Why weren't you watching where you were going?" He was pissed he had to take me in to get stitches and couldn't finish picking up the wood. He said I'd made him waste a day. He couldn't see I was trying to impress him, you know?'

Job nodded. At the age of five, at Tom and Clara Dumkee's wedding reception, Job climbed the stairs to the stage of the Godsfinger community hall, danced by himself to Sem Gillespie's accordion rendition of 'Some Enchanted Evening.' Abe grabbed him from the stage, spanked him several times. Shouted, 'Show-off!' His voice bristled across Job's arms like the gristly lick of a cow's tongue.

Job plucked a couple of oranges out of the grocery bag and did his one-hand juggle. Trying to impress. He dropped the oranges.

'Here,' said Liv. She took the oranges, and a third from the bag, then she stood and juggled. 'The idea,' she said, 'is to keep your eye on one spot above you. Keep your back straight, move your feet for balance and throw like this.' She threw an orange up in an arch and caught it in her other hand. 'Let your hands throw to each other,' she said. 'They know where they are.' She did this without effort, sending the oranges into the air one by one until she appeared to have a tiny, vibrating, swirling sun in her hands. She tossed Job the oranges. He fumbled, catching one, letting the other two fall to the ground.

They ate and talked of who was ill, who had cancer. Who'd been hailed out, who'd been bankrupted and lost their farm. Who'd just died, or was about to. Who'd hung themselves from their barn rafters that month because they were about to lose their farm. The usual talk.

'Will you have to move?' asked Job.

'I don't know. I want to keep the house. It's not like Darren wants it. He thinks his dad's still prowling around the place. I kind of like living with a ghost.'

'You've seen it?'

'Yeah. I think so. I got up to use the washroom and was washing my hands when I looked into the mirror, into the room behind me. The bathroom door was partially closed, but in the dark space between the door and the door frame there was this old man watching me. Scared me. I swung around and there was no one there. I was so sure I'd seen the ghost. But then I kind of exaggerated when I told people about it, for effect, so after a few tellings my story kind of muddled the memory of it.' She shrugged. 'When I saw the thing, I was still half asleep. The ghost could have been a dream that fol-lowed me into the bathroom.'

Job had known Darren's father, of course. Albert Liebich wasn't a man who tolerated opposition to his opinions. He'd thrown the whole congregation into an uproar at an annual general meeting when he put forward a motion forbidding anyone at church to use the word *luck*. To say there was such a thing as luck, he said, was to suggest that God was not omnipotent. 'God,' he said, 'does not play dice.' It was a testament to the power he wielded that, in the end, the motion was passed. From then on, *luck* was no longer used by the pastor during a sermon, or by the board, or printed in the church bulletin. The ladies' auxiliary no longer held *potluck*, but *cooperative*, dinners.

'Darren says one day the ghost walked up to the house and stood off the deck, looking in through the window right at him. It was pouring rain, but the ghost's coat didn't get wet. Then he just disappeared.'

'That'd creep me out,' said Job. 'Having my dead dad watching me all the time.'

'It's not so different from how your God watches you all the time, is it?'

Job chewed on that thought for a moment. 'So you'd want to keep the house,' he said, 'even with the ghost living in it?'

'Sure. We'll have to wait and see how the settlement turns out, of course. I always thought the house would make a great bed and breakfast. And people like haunted places. It'd be great for tourists. Though why would anyone want to stay in Godsfinger?'

'How about a tea house? We could use a restaurant in town.'

'And pass up the lovely atmosphere of the Out-to-Lunch Café?' She laughed. 'Anyway, I like to cook, but not for big groups.'

'Nothing to it. Of course, for something like a tea house you'd need to take better care of your lawn. To attract people in.'

'Oh, I would, would I? That's the thing about this town. Everyone and their dog's got an opinion on how you should run your own affairs. I've got Barbara Stubblefield banging at my door, telling me I've got to Roundup my whole lawn, sunflowers and all. And to plant grass. Keep it mowed within an inch of its life. Like I've got the time for that.'

But neatness did count here. If a farmer didn't keep a neat yard, he was talked about. When a farmer bought a new piece of land, it was said of him that he planned on getting the land into shape. That meant the farmer would work on making the soil fertile, but it also meant he would quite literally change the shape of the land. Having the fields rectangular made tractor use easier and so a farmer would go to great lengths to accomplish this. He would remove sloughs, bush and even hills. It led to an exact way of thinking, Job supposed, that extended to landscaping around the house.

Liv waved a hand. 'I'm sorry. It's just everybody in this town is so caught up in how they think things should be. Barbara's so set on her idea of what a lawn should look like that she can't see what's there. When I told my mother about Barbara wanting me to Roundup the lawn, she said, "What kind of crazy person objects to sunflowers?"' She laughed, then started to cry.

'You okay?' said Job.

She picked up a paper napkin, wiped her nose. 'I'm sorry. I don't know what I'm crying about. It just seems to come and go. One minute I'm fine. The next I'm bawling.' She gathered the Styrofoam cups, paper plates and cutlery and put them in the grocery bag, keeping her eyes on these small tasks as her tears wound down. She was embarrassed by her crying. Job liked her for that. 'You know, I've never been to your place before,' she said.

'I could show you around.' But made a note to avoid the cabin, Lilith in the house.

The motion of their legs through the hay crop sent sulphur butterflies fluttering up from the flowering alfalfa. The familiar aching heaviness of hay fever filled Job's sinuses, made his eyes water. He pinched his nose, trying to stop a sneeze, and patted his back pocket for a hanky. When he found none, he blew his nose with the expertise of a farmer, by blocking one nostril with an index finger and blowing sharply towards the ground with just the right amount of force to avoid ending up with goo on his shirt.

Liv laughed, hollered, 'Gross.'

Job was aware of a shift between them. That she laughed at his nose blowing wouldn't have mattered before, when she was with Darren, but it embarrassed him now. He searched for some bright thing to please her with. Broke off a sprig of deep purple alfalfa flower with his clean hand, gave it to her, chewed on another himself.

'It's sweet!' said Liv.

'Wait.'

He watched the tastes sweep across her face.

'Now it's like chewing on grass . . . Now it's bitter, like old spinach.'

'And it's got an aftertaste, like when you eat fresh chives.'

'Yeah.'

'The yellow ones are sweeter.' He picked up the pace. 'I've got an idea. Something I used to do when I was a kid.' And just the month before, but he felt silly admitting to it.

He slid through the barbed-wire fence of the adjacent pasture, where his cows grazed, held the wires apart for Liv. Chose a clean patch of grass and lay down. Liv lay beside him.

'Now what?' she asked.

'Wait.'

They stared at the blue sky. 'What am I waiting for?'

'You'll see.'

One of the cows came towards them, and then they all came, bringing with them the flies that landed on Liv's and Job's faces, their arms. The soft thud of hooves hitting grassy earth, the click of their knuckles popping as they put their hooves down. Their snorts and sideways chewing, calves suckling, the rush of urine. The month before, the sounds had produced a flickering show of colour as if on a screen just in front of Job: lozenges of sage green, splotches the orange-red of mountain-ash berries, tongues of deep purple the colour of ripe saskatoons, streaks of steely blue, spirals the pebbled orange of a Christmas mandarin. Colours and shapes that overlapped, blended with each new sound. He had lain listening to it for hours when he was a boy. Better than TV. Now, nothing. He put a finger in each ear, wiggled them, pulled his fingers out. Still nothing.

A daddy-long-legs crawled up Liv's arm but she didn't brush it away. Earlier in the week Job had heard Lilith shriek when a spider scuttled across the kitchen floor. She'd fled the room and wouldn't come back in until Jacob assured her he'd caught the spider and taken it outside. A grasshopper leapt on Liv's belly and hopped away. The smell of cow shit, grass burps, urine and the incomparable smell of the cows themselves. Hot. Animal. 'They smell something like horses,' she whispered. 'I can smell their breath. It's grassy.'

'Fermenting grass.'

The cows moved forward, all at once, until Job and Liv were completely surrounded by a circle of cows. 'They'll step on us!' said Liv, but they didn't. From this angle, with their bodies against blue sky, the cows were giants, each of them Paul Bunyan's ox. They ran their muzzles along Job's and Liv's bodies, sniffing them. 'They have such big lashes,' she said. 'That one looks like she's crying.' A long stream of water ran from the cow's eye down her muzzle.

'You have to watch that. Sometimes it's an early sign of pink eye.'

'See the light coming through the fine hairs on their ears,' said Liv. 'And the water drops on their noses.'

One of the cows licked the bottom of Liv's sandals. Job sat up suddenly and waved his arms. The herd scattered.

'What did you do that for?' Liv said.

'Watch.'

One by one the cows came back again, sniffing, sizing them up, until the herd had again formed a circle around them.

'I can do that again and they'll come back. And a third time. After that they kind of lose interest. Most people think they're stupid. But if there's anything new in their pasture, they've got to check it out.'

Liv touched the skin at Job's collar and ran her fingers down his neck and along his lips. Leaned to kiss his cheek. Job turned to face her. Her hazel eyes. Her breath a mix of oranges and sweet coffee. Her lips on his, at first ticklish, then pressing. He felt her tongue on his lips, then in his mouth. Found his hands exploring on their own, the soft folds of Liv's blouse, the skin at her waistband, her back. He wondered if he knew how to unhook a bra with one hand and was surprised when he found that his hand did.

A car spitting gravel along the road came to a stop and started up again. Then the sound of the trike, buzzing in their direction. They sat, scattering the cows. Liv rearranged her shirt, her bra. Job shifted himself to a safe distance. They said nothing as the boys drove up on the trike. 'A bunch of kids are driving their car in the field,' said Jason. 'They were heading towards the crop circle, then turned around when they saw us coming.'

Job stood up, watched with Liv as a white Rambler hopped through the field, its back end kicking up like the hind end of a jackass, before coming to an abrupt stop in the mud of one of the many sloughs that dotted the field. Kids hoping for a field party in the crop circle. A Godsfinger tradition, though Job had never been to one when he was a kid; he'd never been part of the crowd.

'Stupid kids,' said Ben. 'Now they're stuck.'

'I should help them,' said Job.

'You still want to help them after the mess they made in your field?' said Liv.

Job shrugged. He jogged back to the yard to get the tractor and drove down Correction Line Road and around to the far gate. As he glanced back to see how close the rear tire was to the ditch, the chug of the tractor and the rumble of gravel hitting its undercarriage produced a tumble of blue balls much like the sound he heard as his truck drove the gravel roads, but faded now, much more transparent. The tire spun, threw up gravel. A stream of motion that suddenly came to a halt. Job's tumbling blue balls and each pebble the tractor wheel churned up hung suspended in mid-air. Each tread was clearly defined, as if the tire were motionless. A moment that stood still.

Then the honk of a truck. The blur of tire, spit of dirt. Job felt a jolt, a sudden awareness of self, as if he had been driving the prairie roads in a daze and was shaken awake by rumble strips. He rubbed the steering wheel, leaving sweaty thumbprints, as he was passed by a Chev pickup pulling another Chev with a chain. The kid driving the lead vehicle gave him the finger and yelled in protest as the Chevs sped past.

In the field, three boys were standing shin-deep in mud, trying to push the Rambler out of the slough. A fourth was in the car, stomping the gas pedal to the floor, going nowhere. Job didn't recognize any of them and guessed they were teens from Leduc or down from Edmonton who had seen the interview. He drove the tractor into position. Said nothing to them as he fashioned a chain to the undercarriage of the car, pulled it free. Once he removed the chain, the boys sped away without saying thanks or apologizing, embarrassment hot in their faces. Job drove the tractor back to the yard before walking out to the field. He met Liv following the cow path, heading towards the yard, carrying the grocery bag.

'Where are the boys?' he asked her.

'They went back to the house. Jason lit up when Ben said he had an amp for his guitar.' She waved a hand at the slough where the car full of boys had been stuck. 'It was nice, what you did. Pulling that car out. Most farmers around here would have left them in the mud. Or charged them a fee for pulling them out.'

Job laughed. 'I thought about it. But they're just kids.'

Liv took the elastic out of her hair, pulled her mane free of the braid and pushed it back over her shoulders; it rippled down her back. A killdeer cried out and flew in front of them, tripping along, dragging its wings as if injured, to gain their attention and lure them away from its nest.

Liv shifted the grocery bag to her left hand and reached for Job's. He gave hers a squeeze and let go. 'Did I move too fast?' asked Liv. 'Or is it because I'm still married?'

'No.' Though it was that. 'I'd like to spend some time with you again, really.'

Job plucked the heads of the timothy grass and chewed off the soft ends as he walked, trying to think of something to say. He thought of how, as children, he and Jacob had put the heads of that grass into their mouths, pretending to smoke cigarettes. 'You ever have time sort of stop on you?' he asked finally.

'All the time. Every afternoon at the café. You've seen it. It's deadly.'

'No. I mean, like, say you're watching something that's moving and it just sort of stops.'

'Like when you look at a fan?'

'A fan?'

'A ceiling fan. Like at the café? Sometimes I can see the individual wings of the fan, not just the blur of it going around. A trick of perception, I guess.'

'I guess.' But the moment on the tractor hadn't felt that way. He'd lost himself. Felt that time had actually stopped.

They walked on, saying nothing. Liv stopped as Job took a few paces. She said, 'I've really got to take a piss. You mind?'

Before he'd comprehended what she was asking, she stepped a few feet away, lifted her skirt and squatted in the grass. Job turned away. It was a thing a man did, pissed in the field or behind the barn to save going back to the house. Job saw men standing beside the open doors of their trucks along the highway, trying to look like they were just taking in the expanse of prairie, while their stance and the puddle forming at their feet gave them away. He'd heard old Harry Kuss tell Jerry he kept a toilet roll in his truck in case he 'got caught up short' and had to find a lonely field in which to deposit his night-soil. But this, thought Job, was not something a woman did. Yet here was Liv, peeing, when she'd been embarrassed that the wind had exposed her thighs.

She joined him again, patting down her skirt. 'You didn't mind me taking a pee, did you?'

'No. Not at all.' But he walked a little ahead of Liv until he felt stupid for it and slowed his pace. Tried to salvage things. 'So, you ever go to church?' he said, thinking he might ask her to the revival.

'Not since I was a kid.'

He carried the disappointment a few feet. 'I was going to ask if you wanted to come to our revival this weekend,' he said. 'Pastor Divine is leading the service tomorrow night.'

'Who?'

'Pastor Jack Divine? He's got a radio show. It's a healing service.'

'Like, miracle healings?' she said.

'I could stop by your house. We could walk over together. So you don't have to walk in alone.' A fear Job imagined in others, harboured in himself.

'Yeah, maybe. I've never been to one of those things.'

As they neared the yard, a mouse skittered out from under a round bale and ran in front of them. With the instinct of habit, Job took one stride to step on the mouse, killing it. The mouse was crushed under his boot without the crunch one might expect. It was the same feeling he experienced stepping on a fresh cow patty: revulsion, regret. Then he realized that if

Liv hadn't liked the way he blew his nose, she likely hadn't been impressed by this display of his mouse-killing skills.

'Can't you let the barn cats kill them?' she asked. She walked on ahead of Job to the yard, chucked the grocery bag in the burn can.

As they reached the house, Jason charged out onto the front stoop. Lilith pushed open the screen behind him. 'I won't have that kind of behaviour in my house!' she yelled. Ben in the doorway behind her.

Jason ignored her, strode across the yard towards Liv and Job. 'What did you do now?' said Liv.

'Nothing.'

'He threw a chair across the kitchen,' said Lilith. 'Nearly broke the glass in the cabinet.'

Jason pointed at Ben. 'He punched me.'

'I punched him in the arm,' said Ben. 'We were just horsing around.'

Liv scowled down at Jason. 'What the hell's the matter with you?'

Jason waved a hand at the house. 'He wouldn't let me play his guitar.'

'It's his guitar.'

'But he said I could. Then he wouldn't let me.'

'So you threw a chair?'

Jason said nothing. He looked as perplexed about his actions as Liv did.

'I won't have violence in my house,' said Lilith. 'I'll have to ask you not to bring your son around again.'

Liv put her hands to her hips, pressed her lips together and looked as if she might lash into Lilith, but said nothing. She took Jason's arm. 'Come on, let's go.'

Lilith slammed back into the house, pulling Ben inside with her.

'I'll give you a ride,' Job called after Liv.

Liv lifted a hand, but didn't look back. 'We'll just hoof it back to town. It's not much of a walk.'

'Really, I don't mind.'

'It's fine,' she said over her shoulder. 'We could both use the exercise. Jason needs to cool down.'

'So I'll pick you up for the healing service tomorrow? About quarter to seven?'

'Miracle healings?' said Jason. 'Like when they fall down and get cured?'

Job nodded.

Liv turned. 'Thanks for the offer, but I think I'll pass. It's not my bag.'

'Can't we go, Mom?'

'No.' She waved and was on Correction Line Road, walking Jason down the line of Barbara Stubblefield's fence posts with their caps and faces. The row of clowns.

'If you change your mind,' Job called after her.

She lifted a hand, but didn't turn.

Hands dangling, he watched her figure grow smaller down the road. He stood there long enough that a woodpecker flitted over, landed on his boot, pecked at the shining shoelace holes and shat on his toe.

EIGHT

Job turned into the gravel parking lot of the church and parked the truck. The church sat smack in the middle of God's acre, a cemetery the original church board had laid out in alphabetical order to avoid conflicts. Each of the five Steinke graves was covered in a blanket of cement, a row of neatly made beds. Before, this tidy plot had been a mess of whirligigs that Dithy Spitzer had mounted on the graves of her husband and children: angels her deceased husband, Herb, had made using the mermaid pattern he'd found in a book at the Wetaskiwin library, but instead of tails he'd given them skirts, and painted their bosoms white. They did the butterfly stroke each time the wind caught them, arms twirling like windmills.

The church itself was little more than a peaked roof on a white box resting on a basement foundation. It might have been mistaken for a community hall if it weren't for the sign on the lawn that read *Godsfinger First Baptist Church* and listed the times of worship, Bible classes, ladies' auxiliary meetings, prayer meetings and the exhortation *Plan Your Week With God*. There was a kitchen in the basement, just beside the cement cold room that members of the ladies' auxiliary filled with their canning and the sacks of potatoes and carrots they grew themselves. Foodstuffs they used to make a bit of money, catering the weddings and funeral receptions that were held in the church basement. Junior church rooms skirted the reception room, the kitchen. Each of these rooms was windowless and filled with tiny chairs and miniature tables. Their cement walls were covered with pictures of Jesus, Noah's Ark and lambs.

Job laid his tray of almond squares on the table set up in the foyer outside the sanctuary along with other offerings from the ladies of the church. He'd had to pull a frozen batch from the freezer, as Lilith was making it increasingly clear that she didn't want him in the kitchen. Missing his time at the stove, he'd offered to make dinners now and again, but Lilith had only responded, 'My cooking isn't good enough for you?'

In the church foyer, the smell of coffee, canned milk. A few of the women hovered over the table, arranging plates and adding more cookies and squares. Something in Job, his prettiness, his eagerness to please, made them offer him hand-knitted socks and recipes they hid from other women. Job was aware of his effect and soaked in their affections, the delicate sheen of their voices so like his mother's. He felt at home with them in a way he never felt with the men. Though tonight their voices held no sheen, showed no colour at all.

'I see Jacob's got us a holy roller tonight,' said Annie Carlson. She wore her hair long and held back with a white plastic band; her face was hardened and lined by the sun.

'Pastor Divine,' said Job.

'He's not going to make us speak in tongues, is he?' said Mrs. Schultz. 'I went to one of those services in Edmonton with my daughter last winter. Her idea, not mine. All that babbling and not one person there to interpret. Where's the sense in that?' She had a fringe of white hair, black button eyes set in folds of skin. Face like an apple doll's.

'And they get them falling into the arms of catchers,' said Annie. 'If it really was the Holy Spirit making them fall over, what would they need catchers for? The Holy Spirit would make them fall light as a feather.'

Job said nothing. They all knew Job's father had been given to charismatic outbursts in church: at times, moved by the Spirit, he stood up in the middle of the sermon, raised his hands and spouted gobbledegook. This in a prairie Baptist church that frowned on glossolalia as embarrassing theatrics, not God's attempt to communicate. The congregation had expected that sort of thing from the likes of Job's father, who was, after all, a reformed sheep man and Lutheran, not born to cattle farming, much less the life of a German Baptist. Or from Barbara Stubblefield, whose occasional convert stayed a month or two before disappearing, never to return. She'd married into the church, been raised a Pentecostal. Couldn't be expected to act properly. Even so, Abe's loud, emotional testimonials had been frowned on, just as evangelizing was not, in practice at least, encouraged; it seemed impolite, presumptuous, embarrassing at best. After several warnings, Abe had been asked to step down from the church board.

Ruth strolled over and wrapped an arm around Job, tucking him under her armpit. 'So, Job, how'd that date go?'

Job bit into one of Annie's sugar cookies.

'That good, eh?' said Ruth.

'What's this about a date?' asked Annie.

'It wasn't a date,' said Job. 'We had coffee, that's all.'

'Who with?' asked Mrs. Schultz. 'Liv? From the café? I heard she and Darren split.'

'No. I mean, I've had coffee with her. But we're just friends.'

Will wandered to the table along with Jerry and Wade. Will's beard was newly trimmed, showing the square of his jaw. Wade was without his NAPA cap, his greasy hair patted down but not combed. All three men carried coffee cups in their hands and looked uncomfortable in their Sunday shirts and clean jeans. They wore no ties. The younger men of the church only wore ties and suit jackets for weddings and funerals.

'It was a woman from Edmonton,' said Ruth. 'He met her through "Loveline." The radio show.'

'We're talking about Debbie?' said Will.

'"Loveline"?' said Annie. 'Really? Are you going to see her again?'

'No,' said Job.

'So, this girl wasn't your type?' asked Mrs. Schultz.

'More like I wasn't her type,' said Job. He glanced at Jerry.

Will wrapped an arm around his shoulder and squeezed. 'Ah, well,' he said.

Job jerked away as Penny joined them. Pretty in a lace-collared blouse, red pleated skirt. Hair pulled back with red barrettes. Annie and Mrs. Schultz withdrew as Penny took Job's arm, and went back to refilling plates, fussing with arrangements.

'What's wrong?' asked Will.

'Nothing,' said Job.

'He's pissed with me,' said Jerry. The hair on his scalp was flattened from his cowboy hat. He lifted his cup as if proposing a toast. 'Job, the, ah, Lord laid what happened with Debbie upon my heart.'

Job cast a sorrowful look to the floor, but was pleased. Jerry felt guilty.

'I never should have gone off with Debbie like that.'

Penny pulled Job close. 'You ran off with Job's date?' she said.

Job leaned into Penny. The warmth of her arm. The smell of baby powder. 'It *was* a pretty crappy thing to do,' he said.

Jerry lifted his chin, drank his coffee. 'She was cuter than her picture. Anyway, she said we were soulmates.'

'So you're going out with her?' said Will.

'She's staying out at my cabin.'

Job lowered his voice. 'You're *living* with her? You're *back-sliding*?'

'It's just a little holiday, that's all.'

Job felt a hand on his shoulder. Jacob. 'Got somebody for you to meet.'

Jacob led him over to a large man dressed in a dark blue, wide-shouldered suit and striped tie. A wave of grey-streaked hair swept from his right temple over the top of his head to his left, and was held in place with hairspray. Men in Godsfinger accepted their hair loss as a right of passage – 'Grass don't grow on a busy street,' his father had said of his own baldness – and if they felt it necessary to hide it, they wore the baseball caps the salesmen had left them.

Jacob put a hand on the man's arm. 'Jack, this is my brother, Job. Job, this is Pastor Divine.'

Pastor Divine shook Job's hand. His wedding band and the gold rings he wore on both pinkies were large and square. Nails buffed to a shine. 'Jack. Call me Jack.' A million-dollar smile like a crop-insurance salesman paying a visit to the farm. A practised voice, oily and smooth.

'Jack may have a solution to our problem at the farm,' said Jacob. He patted Job's arm. 'Excuse me, Jack. I'll let you and Job talk. I've got to get things set up at the podium.'

'Sure, sure.' He turned to Job. 'Jacob's done nothing but talk about you since I got here. What a skilled farmer you are, how well you'd fit into my ministry.'

'Me?'

'I've been running this ongoing campaign from my church. Workshops on how to evangelize with the Holy Spirit. The men and women I train go out and evangelize on the streets. The problem is, our campaign has been too successful. We've got all these new converts coming to my church, but they drift away after a few weeks because there's nothing for them. We had fourteen converts in the last campaign. Rod here is the only one still with the church.' He pointed at a young man in a Hawaiian shirt, eating from his paper plate hand over fist. 'I've got him sleeping on a cot in my basement. We need a place where we can isolate men like him from temptation.'

Rod turned and caught Job looking at him. He winked.

'Jacob says you've got something of a situation on your farm,' said Pastor Divine. 'That you might have to sell the family farm.'

'You want to buy my farm?'

'No, no. Jacob and I were thinking of a different kind of arrangement. I'm overloaded with work as it is. I can't take my campaign to the next level. I need someone like Jacob to do that. I've offered him a job. To head up the project.'

'What project?'

'To build a halfway house. A place for our converts to get to know the Lord, get back on their feet. A kind of church camp for adults. That is, if you're willing.'

'I don't understand.'

'We want to put the halfway house on your farm.'

Job took a step back. 'Oh, I don't know.' He had never given handouts to the homeless men and women he'd passed on Edmonton streets. He was afraid of being taken advantage of, or laughed at. They seemed world-wise in a way that he wasn't. Like the ragged man in his forties with a beard and a golden retriever carrying a backpack. The man muttered as Job passed, 'Wolf got my dog pregnant.'

'What?' said Job.

'Spare some change?'

Pastor Divine waved a hand. His rings flashing. 'We'd start small at first. Put up just one building that would serve as a bunkhouse, kitchen, meeting place. Later, as we put more buildings up, that first building could serve as a mess hall and meeting place. We can finance it with donations and use volunteer labour. Have work bees on the weekend. Make it fun. Get members of my church and maybe some of your locals involved. Make them feel a part of things. Once things are up and running, those converts who come to stay will be working on the farm, as part of their rehabilitation.'

'Jacob's agreed to all this?'

'He's taken the job as project manager. But of course everything, even his job, hinges on you agreeing to the plan. But don't feel you have to commit to anything right away. All I'm asking is that you give it some thought. But consider this: if you agree to participate in the project, you won't have to sell the family farm or buy out Jacob, and you'll be getting free labour. Free labour! It's a farmer's dream.' He reached into a pocket, slapped a promotional pamphlet for his workshops into Job's hand. 'Just think it over. In the meantime, I run a workshop every couple of months on how to evangelize with the Holy Spirit. Why not come to the next one?'

'I'm right in the middle of field work.'

'Well, at least come to one of my services. Check us out. See what we're about.'

Penny took Job's arm. 'Aren't you going to introduce me?'

'This is Penny Blust. Pastor Divine.'

'Penny, is it?' He pulled a pamphlet from his jacket. 'I'm running some workshops you might be interested in.'

Jacob wandered over to Job as Divine walked off with Penny. 'Well, what do you think?' said Jacob. 'Isn't he great? A real character.'

'Why'd you tell him we were interested in that halfway house idea? I don't want a bunch of strangers on my farm.'

'Our farm. Anyway it's just something to think about. I've got to find some way to make an income. Speaking of which, you got any cash on you?'

'Just a fifty.'

'Great.'

'It's all I've got on me.'

'You know I'll get it back to you.'

But he hadn't paid back Job for the station wagon, or the two hundred he'd borrowed nearly five years earlier.

'What's it for?'

'Tonight's offering.'

'You don't need that much, do you?'

'It's important that I appear to be behind Pastor Divine one hundred per cent.'

Job opened his wallet and handed over the fifty as he pointed a chin at the drummer, guitarist and keyboardist testing out their equipment onstage. 'Where'd the band come from?'

'When Jack heard this wasn't a charismatic church, he volunteered to bring a worship team down with him, to get things rolling. There's the band, and then them.' He pointed at several women and men scattered around the room in pairs. A few of the men wore dress scarves around their necks and carried leather briefcases. They wouldn't have stood out more if they had worn jesters' caps.

'Why aren't they sitting together?'

'So they just look like people interested in the revival. And it's easier to get the crowd to respond if the worship team is dispersed throughout the church. It creates an atmosphere conducive to healing.'

'Conducive to healing?'

Jacob nodded to the front of the church where Will sat with Penny and Barbara. 'Will's waving you over.'

'Yeah, I see him.'

'Aren't you going to sit with him?'

'Not tonight.'

'Guess I better get onstage. Showtime.'

Job took a seat in the last pew, where the late people sat, and kept his eyes focused on the pamphlet Pastor Divine had given him. He felt a rustle and bump as someone sat down beside him. Dithy Spitzer, the front of her fluorescent vest spotted with bits of almond square. Job stared straight ahead, at Jacob and Jack Divine sitting on the platform behind the pulpit. The two men guffawed at some joke between them, knowing they were watched by everyone in the room and making a show of it, confidence like a rash on their faces. Pastor Henschell sat in a chair beside them, hugging his King James, smiling as if he had heard the joke.

'Did I tell you I haven't drank a cup of coffee in fifteen years?' said Dithy. 'You drink coffee? Bad for the nerves. You're nervous, aren't you?' When he didn't reply, she said, 'God told me, "Talk to that young Job. Tell him he's got to get out more." When was the last time you went anywhere?'

Job had in fact left Alberta only once, for a cattle show in Denver, on invitation from Hanke Bullick, a barrel-chested, red-faced silverback who owned the feedlot that sat directly behind Main Street. He had thumped his chest in the Sunstrum kitchen with Job's father over the issue of gun control, and come fall he liked nothing better than to take a case of beer and his rifle out to neighbouring farms to pick off deer. He was heading down to Denver without the wife and saw in Job a gift for keeping his mouth shut. He took Job to a hockey game the second night in Denver and handed him a beer, then another, then a third.

Job accepted the beer as it seemed best not to refuse Hanke anything. To say no was to ask for confrontation. Besides, even Abe had encouraged Job to at least try a beer. Seeing an unhealthy tendency to extremism in his son, Abe had quoted Ecclesiastes to him. 'Do not be overrighteous, neither be overwise – why destroy yourself?'

With each drink the colours he heard just kept getting brighter and brighter. The slashing sticks, the hissing skates and the crowd's roar created a pool of sound showered with rings of golds and blues, reds and yellows that he sank into, rose from and sank into again, losing his sense of self to them. It felt good at first, much like standing with the

Sunday congregation, listening to a hymn. The alcohol took away the edge of anxiety that usually overwhelmed him in crowded places, in the city.

The Americans played a dull game and offered an intermission show of twenty naked women – wearing nothing but skin-coloured skates and feather headdresses – skating in line. Job was horrified, couldn't believe the spectacle, ran off to find an empty stall in the bathroom, where he kneeled and, leaning on the toilet, prayed for forgiveness at having seen this debauchery.

Spying the back of Job's shoes under the stall door, Bullick thought he was sick and drove him back to the hotel before intermission was over. 'Got to teach you to drink,' he said, then left him to scrub the sin from his body in the shower.

Job dreamed that night of naked women with feathers in their hair, dancing on the frozen waters of Hay Lake. They ran tiptoe on their skates across bright snow, giggled up the bank of the coulee as he chased them. He singled one out from the rest, as if culling a cow from the herd, and she became a horse, black flank shining in the sun as she ran up the snowy bank in front of him. Job scrambled through the snow and caragana of the coulee, struggling to keep up. He wanted her skin in his mouth. Once at the top, the mare stopped, offered her dark flanks to him. He jumped her, climbed her back, bit the base of her neck, pushed his penis into her and thrust and thrust.

He woke abruptly, with the first spasm of orgasm. Grabbed the head of his penis at the sensitive line of his circumcision, pressing it against his body to stop himself from coming further, wincing as pain travelled up and down his penis. He could not stop the dreams, the confusing spasms that haunted

111

his sleep, but he could stop the pleasure and inflict on himself this pain instead.

Penny turned in her place next to Will, scanned the room, smiled when she found Job. She waved for him to come sit with them and then her smile fell. Job saw Liv making her way down the pew, her bracelets jangling on her wrists. Her broomstick skirt was transparent. He could see the yellow shorts she wore underneath, her sturdy legs. On her feet a pair of East Indian leather sandals. He shifted for her, bumping a hip up to Dithy Spitzer. 'What are you doing here?' he asked.

'Oh, well. I thought I'd check things out, for a laugh.'

'Where's Jason? I thought he wanted to come.'

'Darren had a run to Vancouver, so I asked him to drop Jason off at his grandma's in the Shuswap. He'll be staying there a couple of days. I needed a little time to sort things out.'

She scrutinized the church, the white crossed windows, the unadorned wood panelling on the walls. 'Kind of drab in here, isn't it? Where're the stained-glass windows?'

Job looked around him, saw that Liv was right. Usually for him it was filled with the colours and shapes of voices, music, but other than the rough wooden cross made from two-by-fours that hung behind the pulpit, there was little in the room to demonstrate that this was a church. There was no altar to speak of; that would be too Catholic. The only spot of colour belonged to the orange of the pew seats. Stinky Steinke had weathered a shower of complaints from members over the hardness of the pews, but there wasn't any money in the treasury for upholstery. So he stapled to the benches remnants of the orange shag carpet he'd pulled from his living-room floor.

Liv took Job's hand, held it on her lap. 'I wanted to apologize about Jason's behaviour, and I'm sorry I got grossed out about the mouse. I just didn't grow up farming, that's all. I'm not into killing things. I had a good time out in the field.'

Job pulled his hand away, glanced at Penny. Will turned to see what Penny looked at and caught Job's eye.

Liv crossed her arms. 'What?'

'It's just, *not here*,' he whispered.

'Ah. I'm not acceptable?'

Job glanced across the aisle. Elsie Hosegood was watching. 'It's just that you're married.'

'You want me to leave? You did invite me.'

'No. Stay. Please stay. I just can't be . . . affectionate here.' He looked to see if Penny was still watching. She was. So was Jacob. He scowled at Job, shook his head. Dithy patted Job's knee, chewed and grinned, winked.

'I'll be good,' said Liv. She sat straight like a child in a junior-church chair.

'I had a good time too,' Job whispered. 'In the field.'

'You're not going to blow your nose like that again?'

'Not here.' He pulled a red cloth hanky from his pants pocket and tucked it back in.

Jacob rose, and without making an introduction, slipped a sheet into the overhead projector, and got them standing and singing a series of unfamiliar songs.

Liv sang along, keeping an alto harmony. Rings the purple of heliotrope. Though faded, transparent, like the voices of the others. Job cocked his head in case his ear still held water from his shower, dampening his hearing. At the end of the first song he whispered, 'I didn't know you could sing.'

Liv grinned. 'It comes back to you. Church choir.'

'Church?' said Job, surprised.

'United.'

'Ah,' said Job. This explained everything.

The worship team worked themselves up in the process of trying to work up the crowd. Hands in the air, trying to touch the Almighty. A few bobbing from the waist, as if greeting an important Japanese businessman, chattering a steady stream of gobbledygook punctuated intermittently with 'Yes Jesus, thank you Jesus.'

Liv leaned against Job, smelling of orange, her hot breath thrilling his neck as she whispered, 'You think deaf people ever speak in tongues?' Nearly an hour of singing later, she asked, 'Do you always sing this much?'

'No. I think Jacob's trying to create an atmosphere conducive to healing.'

'Conducive to healing? He'll have us hallucinating from exhaustion if this goes on much longer. Half the congregation has sat down.'

The more elderly members of the church had taken their seats, including the usually enthusiastic Harry Kuss, Jerry's dad. Born again when he was ten and cleansed in the blood of the living Christ for nearly sixty years, Harry still found it necessary to rededicate himself to Christ each time a preacher made an altar call. Job's father and others visiting in the Sunstrum kitchen had often speculated that Harry was carrying a monkey on his back, that he was hagridden by a sin that had haunted him ever since his wife had gone off the deep end and had to be institutionalized at Ponoka. He embarrassed

114

everyone by holding up a hand when he sang, and held one up now, even as he sat.

Job shifted his weight to his left foot to relieve a cramp. Dithy Spitzer, finally tiring, sat heavily in the pew beside him. Liv plopped herself down. Men and women visiting from Bountiful Harvest, Divine's church, came and went to get coffee from the foyer and returned with their cups but without embarrassment, while members of Godsfinger Church shifted in the pews in agony, praying for the service to come to an end so they could use the washroom.

But the singing went on. Job found himself swaying and fought the urge to hold a hand up in praise. He did hold a hand up, just above waist level, to better see the faded rings of colour, the singing, projected against the skin of his hand. Until he saw Annie Carlson watching him from across the aisle. She shook her head slightly, undoubtedly thinking Job was getting too caught up in the music, holding his hand up like a charismatic, about to embarrass himself. He put his hand down and held it there, and put up with faded colours projected against the grey suits of the men in the pews in front of him, their bald heads.

Jacob had one hand up, Pastor Divine had them both up. Pastor Henschell kept his arms close to his sides, though he sang on, one foot tapping out the rhythm. Penny and Barbara held both hands up over the crowd, but they were the only ones, other than Harry Kuss, from the home congregation. Will didn't join her. Several women from the worship team stepped into the aisle and danced, hands in the air. The old floorboards thumped out their praise. They sang the chorus over and again, a song Job had never heard before but could not pry from his head for days after.

The song wound down. The dancing women went back to their seats. The bobbing men quieted. Pastor Divine stepped to the microphone. He didn't bother to introduce himself. 'We'll sing some more praise songs later,' he said.

They all sat, Job taking his place between Liv and Dithy Spitzer. Dithy shook her head and muttered, 'Praise songs.'

'Tonight we're going to heal some bodies,' shouted Pastor Divine. 'We're going to heal some souls. Tonight you will see miracles in this church.' He thrust a finger at the audience. 'Miracles! The Holy Spirit is going to bring miracles on this church tonight! Do I hear Hallelujah?'

Members of the worship team called out 'Hallelujah!' A second later Harry Kuss echoed them.

'God *wants* you to be healthy. God *wants* you to be *wealthy*. Did you know that? God *wants* you to be healthy *and* wealthy. If you are ill, you're going to leave this place healed. If you were hurting financially, you are going to leave this place rich. I guarantee it. Tonight I'm going to tell you about how faith can heal. About the anointment of the Holy Spirit. I don't know I'm anointed by *feeling*. I don't wake up with my hands on fire! Faith isn't a feeling. How many of you are married?'

Hands went up, nearly the whole crowd.

'Do you wake up each morning thinking, Gosh I feel romantic? Men, do you hand your wife roses every day and serenade her all night long? Are you lovey-dovey every day?'

Laughter across the crowd, a warming.

'But you stay married, don't you? You know love isn't about those big rushes of emotion you might still get from time to time. Love isn't always a feeling, it's a commitment. Faith isn't a feeling, it's a commitment. It's saying, God, I'll believe in you when things are bad, and I'll believe in you when things are good. If faith *were* an emotion, most of us would feel like God asked us out on a date and then stood us up. Am I right?'

Job sat up. *Yes.*

'But God is never unfaithful. He'll never stand you up. And we can't afford to stand him up. Faith is a decision. If all of us made that commitment, we'd never want for anything. There'd be no need for doctors. Doctors are for people who haven't made that commitment, who don't have enough faith.'

Liv choked out a laugh. Mrs. Schultz turned to look at her.

Dithy muttered, 'Not enough faith,' and shifted in her seat.

The pastor pinched his nose and grinned. 'Let me tell you a joke. A chicken and a bull were talking about what to offer their master for breakfast. The chicken said, "Let's give him eggs and sausage." The bull says, "Well for you that's an offering. For me that's commitment."'

Laughter across the crowd.

'Which are you? A chicken or a bull? Are you ready to die to yourself? If you're not, you're a chicken. You're a disciple of convenience. There's lots of so-called Christians out there willing to make an offering, but you won't see them making a commitment. They'll give that egg but won't die to themselves. They follow God's laws when it suits them. But if you're ready to make a commitment to Jesus, then you're a bull. You'll give up your needs and desires to Jesus. You'll die to your own desires. You'll *die to yourself.*'

'*Die to yourself?*' whispered Liv.

'Um, give up yourself in service to the Lord,' said Job.

'What do you mean "give up yourself"?'

117

'You know, give up your wishes, desires, give up your self interests, *give up your self*, become an empty vessel, so God can work through you.'

'You mean like take possession of you?'

'Sort of. Yeah, like that.'

'This is a good thing?'

Pastor Divine spread his arms wide. The gold on his fingers caught the overhead lights. 'Being healthy, being wealthy is all about getting your faith, your money out there working for you. You seed, what? Two bushels to the acre when planting barley? And don't you get seventy, a hundred bushels back? That's God's prosperity. That's his abundance. It's the economics of nature. You put a little into the farm, you get back tenfold.'

'Always worked the other way around on my farm,' Steinke called out. 'I gave tenfold, got nothing back.'

Laughter, fluttering petals of pale yellow, rose over the heads of the crowd. On previous Sundays, the laughter had been a deep sunflower yellow. Job put his pinkie in his ear, worked it, and looked again at his pinkie to see if there was wax.

'You don't have to take my word for it,' Divine called over the laughter. 'You can try it out for yourself. Ask the Lord to tell you how much to put in that offering plate, then *name your seed*, an' ou'll get it. The Lord will provide.'

' r seed?' whispered Liv.

. It was new to him.

tell you all about it.' Divine stepped away ed up the young man in the Hawaiian

whispered, 'You know that guy?'

onton with Pastor Divine.'

'Hi. I'm Rod. I did like Pastor Divine said. I listened to what the Lord was telling me to put in the offering plate. And he told me to put more than I had in, more than I had in my bank account. But I wrote the cheque anyway, and put it in the offering envelope, and I named my seed. I wrote what I wanted on the back of the envelope. I was thinking my cheque would probably bounce, but because the Lord told me to do it, I figured I better have faith.'

'Does he really believe God spoke to him?' whispered Liv.

'Yes. No. It's more like an expression. It sort of means he got an idea. But from God.'

'How does he tell it's from God?'

'He just knows.'

'What if it's from the devil, pretending to be God? Or what if it's like you said, just an idea that popped into mind? Why credit God for an idea you had yourself? I mean, how would you know the difference?'

'If it's a good idea it comes from God. If it's a bad idea it comes from the devil.'

'So you don't have any ideas of your own?'

Mrs. Schultz turned, shushed them. Job lowered his voice further, leaned closer to Liv. The smell of oranges. 'If they're bad they may be your own ideas. Or if you have doubts. The devil could plant those. Or they could be your own doubts. Either way, they didn't come from God.'

'So you never have any good ideas of your own?'

'Oh, I don't know.'

Rod jammed both hands in his front pockets. 'Then this friend of mine turned up with the money he owed me, and it was the exact amount of the cheque I put in the offering plate. Then a few days later, another guy I knew was buying a new leather jacket and he asked me if I wanted his old one, because it was still in really good shape, and I couldn't believe it, because that was what I asked for on the offering envelope, a leather jacket. I named my seed and I got it.'

Pastor Divine stepped back to the microphone as Rod took his seat in the front pew next to Penny. Penny smiled at him as he sat down, and leaned over to whisper in his ear.

'Thank you, Rod,' said Divine. 'The Lord will provide. Name your seed and plant it. God will give back tenfold. Give what God tells you to give. Amen. At this point we usually hand buckets around, but tonight God is telling me to help you plant that first seed. He's telling me to get the heads of the household to bring their offerings to the front.' He picked up a Kentucky Fried Chicken bucket from beneath the podium and held it up. 'Men, as heads of the household, bring your offering, hold it high in the air so God can see it, bring it up front and put it right in this bucket I'm holding, so God and everyone in this room can see you are investing in God's financial system.'

'That's a good tactic,' whispered Liv. 'Forcing everyone to show what they're giving. He's sure to get more that way.'

'It won't work here,' said Job.

'Come on down,' said Pastor Divine. 'Don't be shy.'

Job looked around, along with everyone in the congregation, embarrassment rippling across the room. No one discussed money here and no one, except Dithy Spitzer and the children who made offerings of quarters and dimes, put his offering in the plate without having first wrapped it in the clean white church envelopes with *God loveth a cheerful giver* printed across the bottom. Years before, Abe had put a motion before the board to have the members' yearly contributions published along with their names in the last church bulletin of the year, to encourage more enthusiastic giving, but was firmly voted down six to one.

'Come now, people,' said Pastor Divine. 'What you give tonight will come back tenfold.'

Dithy snorted, muttered, 'Tenfold.' Clacked her dentures against the roof of her mouth.

Jacob stepped forward with a fifty dollar bill, held high for everyone to see and placed it in the bucket. But no one else came up. Not even members of the worship team. Perhaps they felt they were making enough of a contribution to the event.

Pastor Henschell whispered in Pastor Divine's ear.

'All right,' said Pastor Divine. 'Pastor Henschell has suggested we hand the buckets around. So, attendants?'

Steinke and Solverson passed the Kentucky Fried Chicken buckets row to row, starting at the front. The offering bucket made its way down the row. Liv handed it on to Job without contributing. He put in an envelope he'd prepared at home and handed the bucket to Mrs. Spitzer, who made change from a five.

'All right,' said Pastor Divine. 'Let's have a few more praise songs!'

The congregation stood, sang.

'I feel the Spirit in this place,' Pastor Divine boomed over the voices.

Many church members stopped singing, uncertain of what to do. But the worship team went on singing, and some spoke in tongues quietly.

Pastor Divine took the microphone off the stand, carried it out to the front pew and waved a hand in front of him. 'I feel the Holy Spirit here. It's very thick here, over this section of the crowd. Do you feel it? The Holy Spirit swells on our song, on our praise. It's very thick here tonight. Here it comes. I can feel it swelling!'

The music swelled, and the singing and the speaking in tongues swelled with it. Then just as it started, the din subsided into gentle singing, whispered glossolalia. 'Feel that?' said Pastor Divine. 'The Holy Spirit's like the wind, comes and goes. Here comes another gust!'

The cacophony rose again. A woman from the worship team shouted out as if in pain. The music quieted. 'That was just a breeze,' said Pastor Divine. He pointed at the ceiling. 'Somebody turn off these fans so we can feel the breeze of the Holy Spirit.' Steinke flicked off the switch, the fans slowed to a stop. 'Here comes another gust. Feel it!'

The noise rose yet again and Job could almost feel the breath of the Holy Spirit on his face. He felt Liv's, for certain. 'You believe this guy?' she said.

'Who feels the Holy Spirit on them?' Hands shot up, eager children with the right answer. 'Come forward.'

A line of fifteen formed down the aisle, all city folk. Some from the worship team, others as neatly dressed but without the air of professionalism. Likely they had come down from Bountiful Harvest as well. Volunteers to spread the fire. Or out for a night's entertainment. Job could see the fun in it, the excitement of meeting God head-on, touching the divine on a Saturday night.

'Catchers!' said Pastor Divine. 'I need catchers!' Men from the worship team stepped forward, braced themselves to take the weight.

Pastor Divine talked into the face of the first woman, waving a hand gently back and forth in front of her. 'I see the Holy Spirit over you, enveloping you. It's like a bubble. Nothing else

122

can come inside. No germs. No bacteria. When the Holy Spirit is over you, you are clean!' The woman swayed back and forth in response to his hand, as if she were a puppet. He made a sizzling sound, touched her forehead and yelled, 'Fire!' The woman fell back into the catcher's arms. He laid her gently on the floor and moved on. The woman convulsed on the floor as if suffering from an epileptic fit.

'He's doing a stage hypnotist's show,' whispered Liv.

When the pastor had finished knocking down the row of people, he climbed over them to get back to the front. 'I should mention that if you're too shy to come forward tonight, or if you have someone at home who is sick, bring a cloth handkerchief to me and I will anoint it for you. Cotton or linen handkerchiefs work best, but don't bring me man-made fibres like nylon or Saran Wrap or aluminum foil like some people have. It doesn't hold the anointment. Though in a pinch, toilet paper works quite well.'

Liv's laugh high and clear across the congregation, a tumble of silver balls. Job inched closer to Mrs. Spitzer.

Pastor Divine glanced at Liv before carrying on. 'All you have to do is be open to the healing that Jesus has already given you. I'm just the doorman. I open the door so God's healing can take place. All you have to do is be willing.' He held out a hand, picked his way between the bodies of those slain in the Spirit. 'The Holy Spirit is blowing through again. Feel it! It's thicker down here. You!' he said, pointing at Dithy. 'The Spirit's in you.' He pointed at Liv. 'But not in you! You are empty of the Holy Spirit!'

Liv laughed.

Pastor Divine stepped into the pew, put a hand on Job's shoulder. 'But the fire's on you! Stand up!'

Job stood.

'The Spirit of healing is thick on you. You'll feel it in your hands as heat. Are your hands hot?' He kept command of the microphone, didn't point it at Job.

Job felt the heat in his sweaty hands. Nodded.

'You can heal, did you know that? Anyone can heal if they've got the Holy Spirit in them, anyone.'

He took Job by the arm, led him to the aisle, shifted the foot of one slain in the Spirit to the side. 'Who needs a healing?'

One of the slain jumped up, took her spot at the front of the line, others from the city behind her. A big woman, in a shapeless green dress. Swollen ankles.

Pastor Divine asked, 'Where are you hurting?' and tipped the microphone to her.

'I've been clinically depressed for a year. I'm on medication.'

'You believe you can be healed?'

'Yes.'

'Then be healed!' He took Job's hot hand, placed its palm on the woman's forehead. The woman fell back, into the arms of a catcher.

The next woman in line said she had arthritis, and fell backwards before Job touched her. 'It's your proximity,' explained Pastor Divine. 'When you're filled with the Holy Spirit, you can just walk into the room and everyone in it will be drunk on the Holy Spirit. All right. You've got the hang of it. Touch their forehead and command them to be healed in Jesus' name.'

'Is that what I say? *Be healed in Jesus' name?*'

'Sure. Whatever the Holy Spirit lays on your heart. That's what you say.'

Job's hands shook. He cleared his throat, coughed. 'What's your ailment?'

The woman in front of him was in her late fifties, heavy-set. Her dark eyes followed Pastor Divine as he made his way over bodies, and she boomed into the microphone. 'Diabetes,' she said. 'Borderline. I'm on a restricted diet. Miss my chocolate.'

Job coughed into his hand, saw a momentary look of disgust flit across the woman's face. 'You got a cold,' she said.

'No. Just a tickle in my throat.'

'The last thing I need is a cold.'

He rubbed the cough onto his pant leg, reached for the woman's forehead. She ducked. He waved his hand in the air around her head, hoping it appeared authentic. 'In Jesus' name,' he commanded, 'be healed!' But lost his voice, trailed off into a squeak. Coughed.

The woman didn't fall backwards, and instead looked him in the eye. 'I didn't feel anything.'

'The Holy Ghost has moved on,' said the catcher behind her. The woman stomped back to her pew, and the others in line drifted off.

Job, let off the hook, fled through the sanctuary doors to the foyer and poured himself coffee. His hands shook. He felt like he'd run a marathon. His heart pumped; he smelled the stink of anxiety from his pits. He drank, staring through the window of the sanctuary door, resolved to stay in the foyer until the service was over. He didn't know how he'd face Liv.

Inside the sanctuary, everyone, save those lying in the aisle or dancing, was fanning themselves with the pamphlets for the evangelical workshops Pastor Divine and Rod had placed on the pews. With the fan off, the combined heat of their bodies was stifling. Almost everyone had the wilted look of week-old tulips. Harry Kuss slumped in his seat and let out a snore loud enough for Job to hear in the foyer. Laughter scattered across the room.

'There's another manifestation of the Holy Spirit,' Pastor Divine said. He carried the microphone down to the first row. They all listened to Harry snore. 'It's as if he's saying amen to what I've been saying.'

He carried the mike back to the pulpit and threw a hand in the air. 'Jesus is going to heal you of that demon you've got riding on you. You got the demon of cancer? He will cast that demon out! You got the demon of arthritis? He will cast that demon out!'

'Demon?' Dithy called out. The congregation turned to look at her.

'Yes!' Pastor Divine jabbed a finger at Dithy. 'Demons! Now I've got a word of caution for you. Not every illness is caused by a demon. Sometimes God's got a plan for you. Sometimes God has something to teach you. Yes, God teaches through misfortune. Let me say that again, God teaches through misfortune!'

Dithy stood. 'No!' she said. 'You're wrong!' She worked her way out of the pew. Liv clapped her hands and laughed. 'What did I learn from losing everybody I ever loved?' Dithy cried out. 'You tell me!'

Jacob and Pastor Henschell jumped up to intercept her. But before they could reach her, Dithy pulled the water pistol from her vest and aimed it at Pastor Divine. 'Oh my God!' he screamed. 'She's got a gun.'

Those slain in the Spirit scrambled on all fours into nearby pews and huddled at the feet of members of Godsfinger Baptist, clearing the way for Dithy. She aimed and fired. A stream of water hit Pastor Divine between the eyes. He stumbled back, touched his face to find there was no blood there, only water. Took a handkerchief from his breast pocket, mopped his face.

Jacob and Pastor Henschell pulled Dithy down the aisle. 'The bumper stickers are right!' she called out.

Job stepped aside as Jacob and Pastor Henschell pushed open the sanctuary doors. Dithy struggled there a moment, braced herself against the door frame, turned her head back to glare at Pastor Divine. 'Shit just happens!'

NINE

Job stepped out onto the church steps, rolling his shirt sleeves down, his fingertips puckered from washing the revival crowd's dishes. He'd slipped downstairs to the kitchen with a pan of cups and plates during Pastor Divine's wrap-up prayer, embarrassed to face Liv after the show he'd put on. Hoping, too, that she'd come downstairs to find him. But she was gone with the rest, and he was left to lock up the church. The sun had just set. Under red-tinged clouds, a ribbon of brilliant yellow, the colour of an egg yolk taken from a chicken allowed to run the yard.

Jacob was waiting for him in the truck, sitting in the passenger side with the windows rolled down. Mosquitoes buzzing around him. He slapped his arms. 'Mind giving me a ride home?' he said. 'Lilith took Ben home in the car.'

Job got in, pulled the door closed behind him. 'Why you got the windows open?' he said. 'Aren't the mosquitoes getting to you?'

Jacob slapped a mosquito on his neck. 'Just hot, I guess,' he said.

But Job smelled a fart. Jacob had opened the windows to air out the truck, so Job wouldn't notice he'd passed wind. It was a thing Job himself might have done. He held his farts in until church was over, or until dinner was done if he was eating with Jacob, Lilith and Ben in the kitchen. He took his gas outside. But Job had always imagined Jacob had the confidence to weather such trivial embarrassments, in a way that Job himself did not. A surprise to find he didn't.

The truck wouldn't start. Jacob got out and pushed, while Job leaned into the frame of the open door until they got the truck rolling. Job jumped in, put it in gear and popped the clutch. Waited for Jacob to catch up to the truck and get inside.

Job pulled out of the parking lot. 'You see Liv leave?' he asked.

'Saw her hanging out in the hall for a while as everybody filed out, like she was waiting for somebody. Didn't see her leave. You invite her?'

'She'd never been to a revival before.'

'I heard she came by the farm with that kid of hers.'

'She and Jason wanted to see the crop circle.'

'And he smashes up the kitchen?'

'He didn't!'

'Threw a chair.'

Job watched Liv's house come and go. Sunflowers like heated stove elements in the evening light. A shadow in motion across the window.

'I understand Liv spent some time with you out in the field.'

Job laughed a little. 'We're just friends.'

'She's got a husband. What does she need with friends?'

'She and Darren split.'

'I see.'

They passed Dithy Spitzer's yard, covered in whirligigs her husband, Herb, had made before his death, pounded into the tops of fence posts scattered about the lawn: chickens that pecked, Indians who paddled canoes, mermaids who swam, airplanes with moving propellers, pigs in rowboats, and ducks with feet that twirled. After this, the caps and clown faces on the fence posts that marked the Stubblefield property line. Will's house, the poultry barns. The smell of chicken shit.

Job gripped the steering wheel. Left wet thumbprints there. 'You ever have a friend who was doing something really wrong?' he said.

'I guess,' said Jacob. 'Not really.'

Now that he thought of it, Job had never heard Jacob talk as if he had friends. Acquaintances, yes. Jacob bragged of the few well-known people he'd met, like Pastor Divine. But even when Jacob and he were kids, Jacob's conversations had always been about things he'd read or seen on television, never about the people in his life. It occurred to Job that the only real friends Jacob had were his family.

'What if you did have a friend who was doing something?' Job said. 'Would you confront him? Or would you let him work it out himself?'

'This is a Christian we're talking about, I take it. And this thing he's doing is a sin?'

Job nodded.

'Confront him. Think of what happens if you don't, and he keeps doing whatever he's doing, and he never seeks God's forgiveness. Then he's heading for hell, isn't he? But take someone with you. Those scenes can get pretty ugly.' He glanced at Job. 'Something going on between you and Will?'

Job gave out a nervous laugh, like a billy goat's. 'No, why?'

'You wouldn't sit with him. What's he done?' When Job didn't answer right away, Jacob said, 'If you want, I'll be happy to go along with you when you talk to him. Ease the way a bit. That's a good part of what I do.'

'I don't think I could.'

'So what is it you think he's done?'

Job glanced out the driver's side window. Fireflies, hovering over the sloughs along the road, flickered on and off in the dusk.

'He's not a homosexual, is he?' said Jacob.

Job laughed. Coughed. 'What would make you say that?'

'You can't help but notice something's not right between Will and Penny. They act more like friends.'

'They've been saving themselves, for marriage.'

'But even then there's hand holding, hugging, sparks. I've seen sparks when Penny looks at you. Am I right?'

'I like her. If Will wasn't in the picture, I'd ask her out.'

'But he is in the picture.'

'Sort of.'

'Aren't they dating any more?'

'Yes.'

'Then what?'

'I just think his interests lie elsewhere.'

'He's got another girl?'

'No.'

'He is a homosexual, isn't he?'

'I don't know.'

'But you suspect he is.'

'Maybe. I don't know. That day the television crew came I saw Will kissing Ed. On the lips.'

'A brotherly kiss?'

Job had never seen a man kiss another for any reason. Men simply did not kiss each other in Godsfinger. They rarely hugged. 'It was a kiss on the mouth, like you'd kiss a woman.'

Job drove into the yard and parked near the house. They sat in the truck in silence for a time. A jet flew low overhead, lights blinking, heading for the Edmonton airport, prompting a nearby coyote to howl.

'We're just going to have to go talk to him,' said Jacob.

'Is that necessary?'

'We've got to save him, from himself. He's one of our brothers and he's sinning, and if he doesn't stop he'll be condemned to hell for all eternity. Don't you think he's important enough to save from that fate?'

'Yeah. I guess. Of course.'

'Keep in mind it's not just Will we're talking about here. Someone who isn't a homosexual can become one by having a sexual experience with someone of the same sex. Think of all the others who are at risk of becoming infected through contact with Will.'

Job felt a cold shock go through him, thinking of the night he and Will zippered their sleeping bags together.

'I think we should involve Pastor Divine,' said Jacob. 'He's had experience counselling homosexuals. And Pastor Henschell should be there, as Will's pastor. And I think we'd better have Barbara there. He'll need family support.'

'What about Penny?'

'No need to involve her yet. Not until we find out what's really going on. It could cause more harm than good to have her there. I'll do the phoning in the morning. We'll meet over at Will's place tomorrow night after he's finished chores, had a chance to have supper. Everything goes better on a full stomach.'

When Job and Jacob arrived, Barbara stood at the sink, washing Will and Ed's dishes. Pastor Henschell sat with Will and Ed at the kitchen table, nursing coffee, dunking cookies. Ed had changed out of his work clothes, but the stink of poultry was still on him. Will wore jeans, a white denim shirt. The duck slept on a cushion in the corner, bill tucked into its feathers. It jumped awake when Jacob closed the door behind him.

Jacob introduced Pastor Divine all around and took a seat. Barbara poured more coffee. 'All right,' she said. 'You got your coffee, you got your squares. Now tell me what this is about.'

'We've got some unsettling news, I'm afraid,' said Pastor Henschell. 'We have reason to believe your son may be a homosexual.'

Barbara turned her back to the table, sunk her hands into dishwater and rattled dishes. Water sloshed onto the counter.

Will laughed. 'I'm not gay.'

'Job saw you kissing Ed,' said Jacob. 'On the lips.'

'I may have been mistaken,' said Job. 'I was some distance away.'

The duck slid from the cushion, waddled over to Will and tugged at his pant leg.

'Did you kiss Ed?' asked Divine.

Will shook the duck off his pant leg and took a bowl down from the kitchen shelf. He opened the fridge and poured milk into the bowl. The duck followed him, diapered tail wagging.

'I kiss friends now and again.' He pulled a loaf of Wonder Bread from the top of the fridge and ripped a slice to shreds.

'Let's cut to the chase,' said Pastor Divine. 'Have you had sexual relations with Ed. Yes or no?'

Will laughed. A little. 'I'm not gay. It's a stage, that's all.' He dropped bits of bread into the bowl, pressed them into the milk with a fork and set the bowl on the floor. The duck fished in the milk for the bread, tipped its head back to gulp it down.

'So you're saying you *have* had sexual relations with Ed,' said Divine.

'No. We just horse around.'

'Define horsing around.'

Will leaned against the kitchen counter, then lifted a hand when he found a puddle from Barbara's dishwashing. 'I don't know.'

'Have you ever kissed Penny?' asked Pastor Divine. 'Passionately? Have you made out with her?'

Will glanced at his mother, her face of granite. 'Yes.'

Job crossed his arms and shifted in his chair. He had born witness to a few of their passionate kisses and had turned away with a stone in his stomach every time. The feeling not quite like finding a lover in the arms of betrayal. More like what he had felt as a child, coming home early from school and catching his parents at it. A scuffle and grunt from the closed door of their bedroom.

'Have you had sexual relations with her?' asked Divine.

'No. We decided to wait. Until we get married. It's important to us both. We want it to be special.'

Pastor Divine turned his cup clockwise. 'Have you kissed Ed in the way you kissed Penny?'

'I'm not gay.'

Barbara smiled at Will. 'Of course you're not gay.' She slammed a cup into the dish rack.

'This is serious business, Will,' said Pastor Divine. 'You've broken God's law. This is real sin we're talking about here.'

'What do you want me to say?'

'I want you to tell the truth. Before us. Before God.'

Will picked up the bowl from the floor and set it on the counter. Leaned into the kitchen counter with his arms crossed. When the duck pulled at the leg of his jeans, he picked it up, cradled it, kissed the duck on the head and smoothed its iridescent feathers.

Ed dropped the spoon on the table, a clank that filled the room. 'You want the truth, I'll tell you the truth. Though it's none of your goddamned business.'

Will took a step forward, brandishing a hand. The duck quacked.

'I love Will, and he loves me. If you want the bloody details I'll give them, if it's titillation you're after.'

Will settled back against the kitchen counter and hugged the duck. Pastor Henschell shifted in his chair and crossed his arms. Job contemplated Barbara's Smarties cookies; happy, childish mounds on the plate. He wished to God he had done his laundry so he'd have had a clean shirt that day the crop circle appeared in the field, so he would have had no reason to run over to Will's. He wondered why he had confided in his brother, if he had had a motive that he wasn't aware of.

They all listened to Barbara wash dishes. Job no longer heard the pastel sheen of dishes squeaking, but he saw shards of brilliant white light as she smashed a glass into the metal rinse sink. She wiped her hands dry, took up a broom and swept. 'How can he be gay? He goes to church. He's *Christian*.'

Pastor Divine leaned forward, chose an almond cherry drop from the plate and bit into it. 'From what Jacob's told me, the cause in Will's case is clear: his father died while he was still a boy, and you had to fill the role of both mother and father, running this farm, raising a son. No woman should have to do all that alone.'

'You saying this is my fault?'

Jack picked a sliver of maraschino cherry from between his front teeth. 'There's no blame here. It's just the way of things. A boy needs to identify with his father. Without that male influence and guidance, he's left with a big hole, a hole he tries to fill. With some boys that emotional need gets twisted, sexualized. He looks to sexual encounters with men to fill it. It's especially true when the mother has a strong personality, shall we say, a masculine personality. It just adds to the confusion of the boy.'

Barbara slumped in a chair and held the broom between her legs. Will adjusted the duck, held it in one arm like a football. 'It had nothing to do with you, Mom. Right from kindergarten I knew I was different. I was always more interested in hanging out with girls. I remember putting on nail polish, playing with dolls.'

'Don't tell them *that*,' said Ed.

'You see my point,' said Pastor Divine. 'Too much female influence. Here's an example of what I'm talking about. Look at this duck you got.'

'It's a pet,' said Will.

'In diapers.'

'I don't want it pooping all over the floor,' said Barbara.

'But the man's diapering a duck. If that doesn't tell you something's out of whack, I don't know what will.'

Will dropped the duck to the floor and crossed his arms. Barbara swept the duck into the living room. It waddled off, quacking its objections, head bobbing up and down.

'You can't blame Mom. It's not her fault. I remember having feelings for guys really early on. Long before Dad died.'

Job glanced at Will and away. He and Will zippered together in the sleeping bag. The northern lights above. The whine of mosquitoes that bit him. The smell of insect spray. Will's hand on his private place. Job was one of the guys Will had had feelings for. He felt faint; the room shifted away from him.

'I knew I was weird,' said Will, 'from what other people said, from what I heard on television. I mean, the worse thing you can be is a fag, right? It was like all the other boys knew something I didn't; they knew how to be boys. By the final year in high school I was really depressed. I thought of killing myself I don't know how many times. You remember in grade twelve when I didn't go to school for weeks?'

'You had pneumonia,' said Job.

'Wasn't pneumonia. I got to the point where I was so afraid I'd give myself away that I hardly said anything to anyone. I stopped going out with friends. Stopped leaving the farm. Then I stopped leaving my room.'

'You were just tired,' said Barbara. 'You worked too hard. You always work too hard.'

'I don't understand how you could keep it a secret from Penny,' said Job.

'She knew.'

'She *knew*?'

'I told her I had feelings for men. She said she loved me anyway, that she would help me through it, that we could talk about it. She felt God was leading her to help me change. That was her mission. You can't imagine what a relief it was to tell her. To tell somebody.'

'I can't believe she was that comfortable about it,' said Pastor Divine.

'Sometimes she got upset, scared that I would find some man and fall in love with him.'

'What did she say about Ed?'

'I said he was just a hired hand, that I wasn't attracted to him.'

Ed sat back, crossed his hairy arms. 'Thanks a pile, bud.'

'What did you expect me to say?'

'The truth, maybe.'

'I felt caught. I didn't know what I wanted. I wasn't sure you and I were going to stick together. I mean, it was all so new. Anyway, I don't know if she suspected anything or not. She seemed more, I don't know, clingy after Ed was on the scene. And once or twice she pushed to have sex.'

'And did you?' said Ed.

'I reminded her we wanted to wait, for the wedding.'

'And what did she say?'

'She wanted to push the wedding date up.'

'And what did you say?'

'I said why don't we think about it.'

'And did you? Did you have sex?'

'No!'

'You were using me,' said Ed. 'Hanging on to Penny and me at the same time. So you had a safety net either way.'

'Why are you getting jealous now? You knew I was still seeing Penny. You were living with me, for heaven's sake.'

'I thought it was just a cover, so the folks in Godsfinger wouldn't get suspicious. That was what I kept telling myself, anyway.'

'I told you straight up I wasn't ready to give up on my relationship with Penny. I told you that when you moved in.'

'Then you offered me a ring.'

'You gave this man a ring?' said Pastor Divine.

Ed held out his sun-darkened mitt and pointed at a thick gold band studded with a ruby. He twisted it to straighten it. 'It's beautiful,' he said. 'Meant the world to me. Now I don't know if it means anything.'

Job felt a hot shot, and wondered how he could be jealous. Did that mean he was gay? Will had never given him anything except those few frozen chickens, not even for his birthday.

Barbara rummaged in a drawer for a clean dishrag, lifted the ceramic-chicken cookie jar from on top of the fridge and dusted it.

'All right,' said Jack Divine. 'I think I've heard enough. Will, have you got any interest in getting rid of these homosexual feelings?'

'I've prayed to God every day to have them lifted. I've prayed that since I was a kid.'

'It's not just a matter of prayer. If you've got a hope in hell of beating this thing, you're going to have to put in some hard work of your own. None of this is going to come easy.'

'It's natural,' said Ed. He turned to Job. 'For God's sake, you've seen your own bulls go at it with other bulls.'

Job nodded grudgingly. If he was in the market for a bull, looking for a good breeder, he'd watch to see how often a bull rode others in the bull pen.

'But bulls don't think, they just act,' said Pastor Divine. 'They've got no control over their urges.' He tapped his chest. 'We do. God gave us minds. Choice. We can choose to sin. Or we can choose God's way. Besides, just because something happens in the natural world doesn't mean it's right, or that we should accept it. Two-headed calves are natural. Earthquakes are natural. Cancer is natural.'

'So you're calling what I am a disease.'

'In many ways it's like alcoholism, isn't it?' said Jacob. 'It might be there are some born with a tendency towards it. I don't think so, but it may be the case. But you'd hardly call alcoholism natural, and I don't think anyone would argue that we should just accept alcoholism as a lifestyle.'

The chicken head slid off the cookie jar, fell to the floor, smashed to pieces. 'Shit,' said Barbara. She put the headless chicken back on the fridge, retrieved the broom and dustpan, swept, dropped the pieces into the garbage can.

Divine tucked a finger under a tag on his Bible, flipped it open. 'Will, it's as simple as this: you continue in your homosexual behaviour and you will not be saved. It says right here, in 1 Corinthians 6: 9–10, "Do you not know that the wicked will not inherit the kingdom of God? Do not be deceived: Neither the sexually immoral nor idolaters nor adulterers nor male prostitutes nor homosexual offenders nor thieves nor the greedy nor drunkards nor slanderers nor swindlers will inherit the kingdom of God." You'll be in hell, with the thieves and alcoholics. Do you want that?'

'No.'

'Of course you don't.'

'But I've prayed. I've tried. I'd go months where I didn't head to Edmonton, not for that, in any case. I'd feel like I was back on my walk with the Lord and the shame was gone. Then the urge would sort of build up and I'd find myself back in the bars, or at the park, and there were these men—'

Pastor Divine closed the Bible, nodded. 'And the guilt and shame start all over again. And you make promises to God. I know. I've seen it all before.'

'But what can I do?'

'You're not going to listen to this nut?' said Ed.

'I think I'm going to have to ask you to leave,' said Divine. He stood, put a hand on Ed's shoulder.

'Will?' said Ed.

Will stared at the mobile of chickens flying over the table.

'You can't be serious,' said Ed.

Will glanced at him, and then at his hands.

'Fine.' Ed pulled the ruby ring from his finger, banged it on the table. 'I hope you're very happy with that little girl of yours.' He slammed the door behind him as he left the house.

As Ed's truck roared out of the yard, Barbara said, 'Why didn't you tell me? I could have gotten you counselling. We could have handled this privately.'

'You threatened to kill yourself if I turned out to be gay.'

'I did no such thing.'

'You came out of the post office carrying a *Good Housekeeping* magazine with a headline that said something like "What if your child is gay?" on the cover. You threw the magazine on the seat and said, "If my son was gay I'd shoot myself." I was fifteen and I knew I had feelings for men and could never say anything about it to anyone.'

Pastor Divine led Will to the table. 'You seem repentant, Will. That's an important first step. Now, are you ready to admit you need Christ? Are you ready to admit you can't make any changes without him, that you're powerless without him?'

'Yes.'

'Then you must confess your sin. It's just like the Bible says. James 5:16. "Therefore confess your sins to each other and pray for each other so that you may be healed."'

'I have confessed.'

'You need to confess to God, to Penny, to the church. There can be no more secrets or you don't have a hope in hell of healing. Do you understand?'

Will nodded, played with the lip of the cookie plate.

'I'll leave it to Pastor Henschell to arrange things so you have a chance to stand before the church and confess your sin of homosexuality publicly.'

'Is that really necessary?' said Pastor Henschell. 'It seems cruel, spilling this out in front of everyone.'

'Confession frees the sinner. There's nothing Satan loves better than a secret. Once it's all out on the table, Will's got nothing to fear. He won't be worrying about who knows and who doesn't and can get down to the business of healing. Besides, with the whole church knowing, there'll be more people watching that Will doesn't fall. He's going to need watchdogs.'

Pastor Divine gripped Will's wrist. 'You *can* make a change, with God's help. You're going to have to submit to the author-ity of a spiritual adviser. In this case I suggest Jacob. As he's got the time.'

Jacob, pleased, smiled and reached for a ginger snap.

'You'll abide by his decisions on what television to watch, what to read, who to spend time with, where you can go and when. You'll need a time of isolation, of focusing on the Lord. Barbara will have to help with that task, watching you every minute. Do you understand why that's necessary?'

'I guess.' He watched the duck bob and sway back into the kitchen. 'Not really.'

'You're going to be tempted. Even if the Holy Spirit lifts temptation from you – and he's fully capable of doing just that – if you slip from your daily practice of prayer and monitoring your unclean thoughts, then you can stray. Satan will be looking for a foothold, and before you know it you'll be back cruising the parks. That temptation isn't just going to go away. Jacob's right. It's just like the struggle of the alcoholic or the smoker or the glutton.'

Jacob slowed his chewing, eyed his cookie, but went on eating.

'You can't keep anything from Jacob. He'll call you on it. Barbara, you'll have to hold Will accountable, keep track of where he's going. Who he spends time with. What television he watches. Books he reads. You'll have to be on guard so that he doesn't spend time with old friends who might lead him astray.'

Barbara glanced down at Job and sniffed. Found a chicken salt shaker to wipe.

'It's important that no matter how embarrassed you feel, you must keep attending church,' said Jack. 'You'll need that fellowship, now more than ever.'

'A lot of folks aren't going to know what to make of this,' said Pastor Henschell.

'It'll be your job to teach them,' said Divine. 'Will's going to need compassion from the congregation. If he doesn't get that, he'll end up leaving the church and slipping into his old ways. I've seen it happen over and over.'

The duck tugged at Will's pant leg. Divine waved a hand at it. 'And for heaven's sake, get rid of that duck.'

Barbara swooped up the mallard, ripped off the diaper, opened the screen door and flung the duck out into the night. Job watched through the window as the duck fluttered through the yellow spill of the yard light, falling and labouring like a fledgling, a white sticky tab from the diaper stuck to its behind.

TEN

Two coyotes ate crabapples among the yellow leaves that littered the grass under the tree outside Job's cabin. Job watched them for a moment before tapping on the window. The coyotes looked up at him before trotting off.

Above them, crows darkened the sky. The crows were normally independent birds, sitting on fence posts or on roads in ones or twos. Job would see three or four gathered if there was a feast to be found: someone's carelessly tossed container of McDonald's fries, or the remains of a gopher hit by a truck and lying sadly by the side of the road. But this day the crows were flocking. They flew over the drying hay in the field to land in the cottonwoods surrounding the house, cawing to one another, disappearing into the leaves. When Job went outside to watch them, to listen to their coarse song, the metallic scrape of the screen door sent them into the air in the hundreds.

Job headed towards the house for breakfast. But stopped when he saw the barn roof. Kids, he supposed, had been up to a little mischief in the night, painting with a can of white latex and four-foot brooms. *This is cattle country. Eat beef.* now read *This is fag country. Eat me.* The kids hadn't bothered to scale the silos but wrote *Pretty Boy* along the base of one.

He was Pretty Boy. The message on the barn was aimed at him. A pause and thud in his pulse. Another. Then a rambling beat. He walked a little to assure himself he wouldn't drop, fall to a stilled heart.

Jacob and Lilith were at the kitchen table drinking coffee when he went in. Job guessed they'd been fighting. Neither looked him in the eye. Lilith served him up a couple of pancakes, eggs and sausages from the grill on the stove, where they sat warming.

'You see the barn? The silo?' said Jacob as Job sat down at the table.

Job nodded and dunked sausage into egg yolk and wrapped it in a pancake. He chewed. 'Where's Ben?'

'We asked him to take a little walk,' said Jacob.

'A walk?'

'We needed some time to talk. To you.'

'What about?' Thinking that Jacob was about to put on the pressure over the halfway house.

'Lilith wanted to talk to you right away,' said Jacob. 'But I wanted to give it a while, to think it over.'

'Think what over?'

Jacob took a sip of his coffee. 'Pastor Divine said a few things that made us think, about homosexuals, about womanly influence.'

'We don't want you spending time with Ben any more,' said Lilith. 'Not alone, in any case. As parents, we just can't afford to trust you, after all that time you spent with Will.'

146

'What does she mean?'

'We can't be sure you weren't infected,' said Lilith. 'By Will's ways. Will dated Penny for two years. But you – all those years without even one girlfriend. And how you went ape when I changed things around in the kitchen. No man cares that much about a kitchen.'

'But it was *my* kitchen.'

'You see?' said Lilith.

'Jacob. Tell her I'm not gay.'

'I don't think you're gay,' said Jacob. 'It's just that one thing that worries me. I remember that incident, when you and Will were boys, that night we all slept out in the field.'

Job's heart skipped a beat. 'What do you mean?'

'You know. When you zippered your sleeping bags together, and you thought I was asleep. Do I have to spell it out?'

'We were just kids.'

'I'm sorry, but we just can't take the chance,' said Lilith. 'I've got to protect my son. I can't tell you how frightening it was to wake up to that graffiti on the barn.'

Job felt the muscles in his thigh and neck twitch. His left index finger tapped of its own accord. He felt as if his body was lying on the vibrating bed he'd slept on that trip to Denver. His heart skipped, rolled like a snare drum, and then, just when Job thought he might be having a heart attack, caught its rhythm. But he couldn't catch his breath. Something was terribly wrong. He thought he may have con-tracted an awful flu, or that an internal organ had burst. He stood.

'What's wrong?' said Jacob. 'Where you going?'

'Town.'

'We're not finished here,' said Lilith.

Job staggered from the house, Lilith calling after him, and got in his truck and sped off. He wondered what day of the week it was. Dr. Mary Taylor was only in her Godsfinger office on Tuesdays and Thursdays, and only in the mornings. She was back in her Leduc office the rest of the week.

Job parked his truck in front of the doctor's office. As he got out of the truck he felt faint and had to hold on to the box to steady himself. Steinke walked by and, not looking him in the eye as he passed, muttered, 'Zipper.' For a brief, horrifying moment, Job thought Steinke knew, everyone knew, about the time he and Will zippered their sleeping bags together. But then he saw that the zipper of his jeans was undone. When he zipped, he found his hands were shaking and there was a gloss of sweat on the palms. He felt his heart jerk against his throat and thought he might vomit as he faltered into the doctor's office.

'I need to see Dr. Taylor.' The receptionist was a plump woman in a crisp, pink medics tunic, the kind he saw in the Sears catalogue. He didn't know her. Dr. Taylor brought her receptionists from Leduc. They seemed to change from visit to visit. 'Do you have an appointment?' she asked.

'I'm sick.' He started for the doctor's office door.

'You can't just barge in.'

'Is she with someone?'

'No. But that's not how it's done.'

Job pushed on anyway, afraid that if he stopped he would collapse on the floor or vomit at any moment. Dr. Taylor stood when Job opened the door and waved off her receptionist, who closed the door behind her. The doctor was in her late fifties, petite, sun-lined and freckled.

Job explained his symptoms through gasping breaths but

could not seem to get her to understand the severity of his plight. The smile on her face. 'I feel like I'm going to die,' Job said.

'Sounds like anxiety to me.' She leaned on her desk, across from Job. 'Classic symptoms. I know it feels scary. But it'll pass. You been under some tension recently? Worrying about anything?'

Job waved his hand in the air; he couldn't think where to start. But felt the breathlessness, the racing heart calming, now that he had an explanation.

'You know how many times you've been to see me over the last year?'

'No.'

'Eleven times. Headaches, backaches, stomach aches. Do you know what that says to me?'

'I'm a hypochondriac?'

'It says you need some fun, some relaxation. Take a vacation. Any place other than Godsfinger. You need to get out more. Or maybe, more to the point, you've got to find yourself a woman you really like. Get close, you know. A little intimacy goes a long way. A woman would do you a lot of good.'

'I've never been, you know, intimate.'

'Never?'

'A little petting. Once.' Thinking of Liv in the long grass, the cows around them, her hand up his back. Then he remembered Amanda Krumm in his father's truck. 'Twice.'

The doctor patted the air. 'Don't worry about it. Once you get close to a woman, start smooching, biology takes over. Your body knows what to do. It's hard-wired into you. Then after a while you'll learn the subtleties. Like a baby learning to walk. We were meant to walk upright. It's hard-wired into us. It just takes a little time to get the hang of it. Maybe you'll trip up. But in the meantime you'll still have a little fun. Try it. Go find yourself a girl.'

Penny was just leaving the co-op, heading for her parents' Ford Taurus as Job left the doctor's office. Job hadn't seen her since the night of the revival. He didn't know what to say to her, thought it best to start with an apology.

'It would have come out sooner or later,' she said.

'But if I had kept my mouth shut—'

'Then Will would have been doing *that*, and I wouldn't have known. Thinking about it makes me sick.' She threw her purse in the front seat. 'All that wasted time. I feel so stupid.' Her voice took on a little girl's squeak when she was angry, something Job had never heard before. Pink streaks, like a poorly washed window. He found himself wanting to keep her talking, to watch her voice. A vibrancy of colour here, in her anger, that he'd otherwise lost, even in the singing at church.

'Will says it's just a stage,' he said. 'He says he wants to marry you.'

'How could I marry him? He hardly ever wanted to touch me. And I thought that made him a gentleman.'

'He said you knew about his tendencies.'

'He told me he sometimes had fantasies about men. I had no idea he acted them out. I mean, he said he loved me.'

'I think he did. Does.'

'Then why didn't he want me? If I was attractive enough he'd want me. Barbara says those urges can be changed. She says I should wait and he'll come around.' Penny waved at the

150

window of the Out-to-Lunch Café. 'She just spent an hour trying to convince me. But it's over. I don't want anything more to do with him.'

'I'm sorry,' said Job.

Penny nodded down the street. Job turned to see Liv sitting in Darren's truck in front of the co-op. She waved and smiled.

'You two were pretty cozy at the revival,' said Penny. 'I heard she was over at your place.'

'To see the crop circle. Jason wanted to see it.'

'I heard she and Darren are back together, trying to work things out.'

Job watched his boot kicking gravel, the woodpecker shit still on the toe. 'Well, I should get back home,' he said. 'Field work. See you at church?'

'I can't go back there,' said Penny. 'The only reason I went at all was Will. And you. I think I'll head up to Pastor Divine's church this Sunday. Give him a try.' She took his hand. 'Why don't you come up with me? We could go out for lunch after. Make a date of it.' She kissed Job on the cheek, smiled at him as she got in her parents' car. 'Think it over. Give me a call.'

A brief thrill ran through Job. He watched Penny's car drive off, then turned, smiling, to find Barbara leaving the co-op. She looked up from the handbag she was rummaging through, caught sight of Job and walked the other way.

Liv called him over. 'How you doing?' she said.

'Okay, I guess.' Job glanced at the side of the truck, at the letters proclaiming *Liebich's Trucking*, then at his boot scuffing dirt.

'He's just driving me to Wetaskiwin,' said Liv. 'We've got a few things to settle. Listen, I heard some of the talk at the café. About Will. And some about you. Don't let it get to you, okay? It's just talk. It'll quiet down when something more interesting turns up.'

He wanted to ask, What are they saying? But he couldn't bear to. He already knew. Or guessed.

'How's Penny?' she asked.

'As good as can be expected. I guess she won't be spending much time around here any more. She's talking about getting involved with Divine's church.'

'I think she'd be very happy there.' Liv pasted on a fake smile, blinked twice.

'I take it you don't like Penny.' Or could she be jealous? The thought pleased him.

'I don't have much feeling for her either way. It just seems like her only goal as a good little Christian is to be cheerful all the time. You can do that with weed, if you want, and get a better result.' She turned her eyes on the storefront. 'So, where were you after the revival? I waited, but you'd disappeared.'

'I had to pack away the tables, clean dishes.'

'Couldn't they have waited?'

Job watched the Bullick kid make another pass on his bike, said nothing.

'Thought I'd see you at the café at least.'

'Things have been kind of strange.'

'I gather.'

Dithy Spitzer marched across the road, headed towards them. Job looked back down at his boots. 'So, what things are you settling?'

'What's that?'

'With Darren.'

Liv pulled at a thread on the hem of her shorts but stopped

when the hem started to unravel. 'We're taking Jason to see a counsellor.'

Darren banged out the co-op door. Cowboy hat tilted back to expose his forehead. Reddish skiff of stubble across his chin. Eyes like slough water before a storm. He carried two Pepsis and handed Liv one through the window. 'Hey, Job,' he said. 'Any more aliens land on your place?' He laughed as he walked around to the driver's side and got in the truck.

'Give me a ring,' said Liv, 'all right?'

'Yeah, sure.' But he knew he wouldn't, because at the moment he stepped back from the truck and waved, the only clear thing in his head was the image of Darren's hand on the skin of Liv's thigh.

ELEVEN

As Job watched Liv and Darren drive off, a cold spray of water hit him in the back of the head. And there was Dithy, water pistol aimed menacingly at him. 'You got to get out more,' she said. 'Go!' She sprayed him again, this time in the face. 'Go!'

He waved his hands to avoid another spray to the face, then stumbled back up the sidewalk and headed to his truck. He reached it just as a trike skidded to a halt beside him, raising a cloud of dust. Ben.

'What are you doing driving that thing into town?' said Job. 'Your dad will have your hide.'

'The bull, he's in the lake!'

'All right. Get in the truck. We'll come back for the trike later.'

Job dragged dust to the farm, picturing the worst: the bow of the bull's back like a whale's breaking water, its head submerged, drowned.

'Mom doesn't want me spending any time with you,' said Ben. 'Not alone.'

'Yeah. She told me.'

'You're not gay, are you?'

'No.'

'I had the trike down in the coulee. I left the gate open. It's my fault the bull got out.'

'You know you're not supposed to drive the trike down the hill. You could kill yourself.'

'You going to tell Dad?'

'I imagine he's not home, if you took the trike out.'

'He said something about meeting Pastor Divine.'

But when they reached the farm, Jacob was in the yard, just getting out of the car. He talked to Ben as if Job weren't there. 'What are you doing with Job? Didn't you hear a word your mother said?'

'Ben ran into town to tell me the bull's in the lake,' said Job.

'How'd you know?' Jacob asked Ben.

'He saw from the top of the coulee.' Job felt the corner of his eye twitch. A thing that always happened when he told a lie. 'I'd asked him to watch the cows. Pasture's running low. Thought they might try breaking through to the upper hay-field.'

'Well, let's go get the bull out of the lake,' said Jacob, sighing. As if he were in charge and this was one more thing he had to take care of. 'You,' he said pointing at Ben, 'stay here.'

Job drove the Case with the front-end loader down to the lake. Jacob followed on foot behind. Twenty-five feet out into water, past cattails and slough grass, out where a child could sink to his death in mud, the bull was wallowing. Job picked up stones, then, stepping up to the water, flung them at the bull, aiming to splash just in front of the animal's head.

155

'What're you doing?' said Jacob, catching up to him.

'Trying to get the bull out.'

'Why not just pull him out?'

'Might not have to,' said Job. 'Rather not get into the water next to him.'

The bull jerked his head back from the splash of each stone flung into the water, but stayed firmly lodged in muck. Job took a few quick steps into the lake, thinking he could scare the bull into pulling itself free, but only succeeded in getting stuck himself. He took a step forward but found his boot left behind. Job stepped back into the boot. He swung around, yanked his boot free, dragged himself forward to the bull.

An American bittern hidden in the reed canary grass sounded for all the world like a slough pump: *glump*, *glump*, *glump*. The lake smelled of mud and the slough mint growing around its edges. Coarse grass sliced into Job's fingers as he moved through it, leaving nicks like paper cuts. A sudden, eerie shiver ran up Job's spine, the same shiver he remembered from childhood when, stepping into slough water when he knew he wasn't supposed to, he found himself stuck knee-high in gumbo and in black water up to his waist. He feared his father's licking but was more scared of what dark, unnamed thing skimmed below the water's surface.

The old bull was tiring. Job smoothed his hand over its face and neck like he might a horse, murmuring to it, trying to calm the animal. The bull looked back with one wild eye. Job found himself caught in its stare. Startling, to be this close to such an alien consciousness. But then animals had no consciousness, did they? At least that was what Abe had taught his sons, that animals had no souls. It made butchering time easier, bearable. Yet there was a soul here – Job felt certain of it – a terrified soul.

He bent a little closer, scratched behind the bull's ear, looked into that one eye. 'There, there,' he whispered. The bull leaned its head into Job's hand as a dog might, enjoying the scratch. Job was rarely this close to his bulls, except for the times he pinned them in the chute for injections, or clipped their hooves, or treated a wound. It was never wise to make a pet of a bull, the way he made pets of some of his cows. A bull was unpredictable, calm one moment, pawing the ground the next. A creature ruled by raging hormones and drives. The bull's breath was loud, wedges the colour of raspberry sherbet, but transparent now. Job put a cheek to the creature's massive head to listen closer to its breath, but the colour did not intensify.

'You want a hand?' yelled Jacob.

Frightened by Jacob's shout, the bull flailed, flinging Job backwards. For a long, panicked moment Job found himself underwater as he tried to right himself. He gulped mud. Spat and thrashed. One foot made contact with the soft belly of the bull. Then, seeking earth, his feet sank into mud. He found himself groping the wiry hair of the bull's back. The bull snorted and twisted from his grasp and he fell backwards again. He felt another thrashing beside him, he thought for a moment that the bull had torn itself loose. But there was a hand at his neck, yanking his shirt collar, dragging him from mud.

Job caught air, struggled out of Jacob's grip. 'Leave me alone!'

'I was only trying to help.'

'If you hadn't yelled, the bull wouldn't have thrown me,' said Job.

Jacob dragged himself from the water, perched on a log and sulked.

Job slogged through slough grass after his brother, wet jeans heavy around his legs, then drove the tractor down to the water's edge and rejoined the bull in the mud, fashioning the chain loosely around the animal's neck. He attached the chain to the draw bar and drove the tractor forward, slowly, to gently lift the bull out of the muck neck-first. Freed from the mud, the bull fought its way back to shore, then, exhausted by the struggle, stood passively at the lake edge, snorting. Job unhooked the chain from the bull's neck and replaced it with a halter. It would be an easy matter, now, to lead the exhausted animal back home.

Job slumped down at the edge of the lower field where alfalfa and brome met wild rose brambles. 'I'm sorry for getting mad,' he said. 'Thanks for pulling me out.'

Jacob waved a hand. 'It's all right.' After a time he laughed. 'Remember when you got stuck in the mud out here and I tried to rescue you?'

'And got stuck yourself,' said Job.

'We called out for — what? — two hours before Dad came down to find us. Then he beats the crap out of me and doesn't lay a hand on you. He says, "You should have known better." Like I'd instigated it. He wouldn't believe me when I said I was trying to get you out.' He looked away, at the lake. 'You given any thought to the halfway-house project?' he said.

'It's not something I want.'

'Well, it's not really a matter of what you want, is it?' said Jacob. His voice slid into a pastor's lilt. 'It's about what God wants. You think I'm staying on this farm or thinking about

158

running this halfway-house project because I want to? If I did what I felt like, I'd sell this place right now, set up my own ministry someplace. But this was Granddad's land, and Dad's land, and you're set on keeping the farm in the family. And Lilith doesn't want to move any more. When Jack proposed this halfway-house project, I figured that's what God wanted for me. That's why everything happened to bring us here. So I'm staying.' He looked past Job's shoulder, and Job watched his brother's face sag in fatigue as the thought settled into him. Then the tense smile was back on Jacob's face. He gave Job's thigh a pat. 'Anyway, take it to the Lord. Ask God if he wants you to involve yourself in this halfway-house project or not. Let God make the decision. That's what he's there for.' Jacob stood up. 'I better get back to the house. You want me to take the bull up?'

'No. I'll do it.'

Job watched Jacob start his slow climb up the bank of the coulee. Maybe it was as simple as Jacob said. He'd pray for confirmation, ask God if the halfway house was what he wanted for Job and the farm. Or not. But the trick was to figure out God's answer. He gave it a try and said a prayer with his eyes open, in case God threw him a sign and he missed it.

A duck heaved itself onto the bank and waddled straight over to Job as if it were a city bird, hoping for a handout. A mallard, with a white shred of diaper stuck to its butt. Will's bird. It gripped Job's pant leg in its beak and tugged, then tugged again. Clamped hold of a bit of skin and yanked.

'All right,' Job yelled, kicking it off. 'I'll do it, I'll do it.'

'What was that?' Jacob called down from the hill.

'I said I'll do it.'

159

'What?'

'I'll check out Pastor Divine's church. If I like what I see, we'll go ahead with the halfway house.'

The duck wheezed out a quack, like the laugh of a child's pull-along toy, before waddling back to the water and disappearing into the bulrushes.

TWELVE

Job sat in a metal folding chair near the front of the church, watching as Pastor Divine worked his way down the line of those who came forward to be slain in the Spirit. Penny took Job's hand, her moist palm a thrill in his. She wore a pink blouse with a ruffle at the neck, and her hair was piled on her head in an elaborate do she might have worn to the prom. 'Isn't this exciting?' she said.

Ben slouched in his seat beside Job, kicking the underside of the empty chair in front of him. He was dressed much as Job was, in a Sunday shirt and clean jeans. Next to him Lilith chewed the side of her ring finger, her eyes on Jacob as he walked down the line with Pastor Divine, as one of the catchers for the slain.

Bountiful Harvest Church was an old Safeway building, with an S-shaped roof, and all the windows covered over in a light grey stucco. At the entrance to its parking lot there was a sign with an arrow that read *Miracles This Way*.

Inside, high above the crowd, fans churned the air. On the stage hung two childishly constructed fabric hangings, depicted flames of fire, of renewal, of the Holy Spirit. Between these flames hung an unpainted wooden cross.

Pastor Jack Divine had had the crowd stand and sing for nearly two hours before finally announcing it was time for the anointing. The air was stifling, filled with the stench of men's aftershave and sweat. A number of the women held their hands cupped in front of their chests in supplication, as if holding a bowl and waiting their turn for the bowl to be filled. Some held their hands higher, in the way small children ask, 'Up?' One man wore an ambulance driver's outfit. A woman in her forties danced in the aisles, twirling a bright pink flag tied to a stick.

Penny looked so happy, so certain, the excitement of meeting God rosy in her cheeks. It took Job's breath away. To feel that excitement, that certainty. To *know*. He felt instead as though he couldn't swim, the rescue rope was slipping from his grasp, and the boat was pulling anchor, leaving him adrift in this strange ocean. Pastor Divine had said there was no faking this; if God wanted you slain in the Spirit, he'd take you. If he didn't think you were ready, if there was something standing in the way, some secret sin, some flaw in your Christian character, then he wouldn't let the Holy Spirit flow. 'You can fake a conversion experience,' Pastor Divine had said, 'but you can't fake a baptism in the Holy Spirit.'

As Divine came nearer, Penny took her place in the aisle. Divine touched her lightly on the forehead. She fell into Jacob's arms, and he laid her gently on the floor.

'Why aren't you standing?' said Pastor Divine, stepping up

162

to Job's seat. 'Don't you feel the call to be baptized in the Holy Spirit?'

Job stood and shook his head, though now that he was standing before the pastor he did feel something. A gnarled burl of anxiety in the pit of his stomach that Pastor Henschell called 'conviction by the Holy Spirit,' and what others may have simply called guilt. Guilt over what he couldn't say, though on reflection any given day produced an abundance of things to feel guilty about. 'Yes,' he said.

'Well, which is it?'

'I want to be anointed.'

'It's not what *you* want,' said Pastor Divine. 'What *you* want means diddly-squat. What does God want? Do you feel God's call?'

Job glanced at Jacob. His brother's face was splotchy from the exertion of catching those slain in the Spirit. A bead of sweat ran down his cheek. He nodded at Job, as if to encourage him. 'I feel it,' said Job. He thought he felt it.

'All right then.' Pastor Jack pressed a hand to Job's forehead, and when Job took a step back but didn't fall, Jacob took him by the arm to steady him. 'Don't you feel the Spirit?' said Pastor Divine.

'No.'

'*Try* to feel the Spirit. Sometimes you've got to give it a little help. Open the door.'

'I'll try.'

'Why not try speaking in tongues?'

'I don't know how. I mean, God would have to do that through me, wouldn't he?'

'Loosen your tongue in faith.'

'How's that?'

'Say some nonsense words; try out some syllables. You know, like *nanana papa*, that sort of thing. You'll get over your inhibitions, and then God will help you out.'

'I'll try.'

Pastor Divine moved down the row, and Job mumbled as he'd been instructed, *nanananana*, *papapa*, watching as the anointed fell one after the other, their inhibitions shaken loose and dropped like a pocket full of coins. Lilith fell to the floor sobbing. A woman lay next to her, laughing. A boy in the seat in front of Job held his hands up, murmuring to the Lord as if to a lover. Others, rocking back and forth, clicked their tongues against the roof of their mouths.

Ben stayed slouched in his seat with his arms crossed. He'd refused to stand when Divine came on him and wouldn't look at his father. Job knew exactly what he was feeling, as Job himself, cringing in the pew beside his father, had gone through the same agonies of embarrassment each Sunday, and had endured cruel taunts about his father and brother at school. Jacob had joined in with Abe, standing in church when his father stood, waving a hand in the air, calling out, 'Thank you, Jesus!' or tottering back and forth in what Job supposed was a trance, gibbering in choppy, meaningless sentences that sounded vaguely Italian.

Abe had once derided that kind of public demonstration of faith as the rest of the Godsfinger Baptist congregation had. But then five months after Emma died, Abe had gone into town on a Saturday and hadn't come home for supper. He came back after eleven with a shine to his face, a vascular glow. Job thought he'd been drinking, and said so, out of surprise. He thought he'd get the strap for it.

'I am drunk!' said Abe, swinging an arm up and nearly

losing his balance, as if to demonstrate. 'I'm drunk on the Holy Spirit. The Holy *Spirit*.' He laughed, the first laugh since Emma's death, and fell into his easy chair, shaking his head at some thought.

Jacob said, 'You all right?'

'Better than all right. Haven't felt this good since—' He twirled a finger in the air to finish his sentence. 'I saw the Pentecostals were having a revival in Leduc this week. They promised healing, emotional healing. I thought, What the hell? Can't feel any worse than I do now. So I took myself out for supper and sat in the back pew. I thought there'd be all that chatter and wailing, the devil getting the better of them. But it wasn't like that at all. They got us singing and singing and singing. And it was fun! And then the Holy Spirit came down on the crowd.' He stood, threw his hands into the air. 'And I was healed!'

'What do you mean, healed?' said Jacob.

'I was baptized in the Holy Spirit and I was healed.' His eyes shone. 'Don't you see? I know I'm forgiven.'

Jacob offered his father a hug and said, 'That's great, Dad.'

Job backed into the kitchen counter and kept his distance, as if his father really were drunk. 'You mean, like, you spoke in tongues?' he asked.

'Yes! It was wonderful! I haven't felt this way since your mother and I were dating and we did that mock-wedding skit at Steinke's twenty-fifth anniversary. She was so beautiful in my suit and I looked so silly in her nightgown. Balloons here, you know.' He patted his chest. 'I couldn't stop laughing and I loved her so much.' Abe jumped, shouted 'Woo-hoo!' and landed, sending a shudder through the old floorboards of the house.

Job had been embarrassed by his father and brother, but jealous too. Jacob claimed that when he spoke in tongues, he felt a great warming of the blood, a sweep of emotion cresting over him as the Holy Spirit flowed in. He said he felt God's presence, and that he knew he'd been forgiven, something Job was never certain of.

Job tried again to loosen his tongue in faith. *Mamamama, papapapa, boobooboooo.* Nothing. He went on mumbling gibberish as he looked up to see Pastor Divine anoint the last in the row. A petite girl of eighteen threw herself back into Jacob's arms. There was no hesitation in her fall, no suspicion that he might not catch her. Jacob lay the girl to the ground and looked up, catching Job's eye. Job turned back to the stage and prayed for release, for the loss of self he saw all around him.

Jacob limped up to him, wiping the sweat from his forehead with his sleeve. He touched Job's arm. 'Still nothing?'

'No.'

'It's okay. Let's pray.' Jacob put a hand on Job's back and held it there as he prayed that Job might feel God's presence and his Holy Spirit might descend upon him. And so on. When he finished his prayer he said, 'Even if nothing happens here today, know that you've been *loved on*. Know that God loves you.'

A thrill that this might be true. The suspicion that it was not.

Jacob put on his pastorly smile. 'The Holy Ghost is going to work miracles on you, Job. I'm sure of it. Loosen your tongue. Have faith. Keep at it. It'll come. Just say whatever comes to mind. Don't worry if it doesn't make sense to you.' He patted Job's arm, then took Ben by the elbow and hauled him up so he was sitting straight. As soon as Jacob moved on, Ben slouched back down in his seat and crossed his arms. He glanced at his mother sobbing on the floor before kicking the underside of the seat in front of him.

Job looked down at Penny on the floor at his feet. Her eyes were closed. A smile flitted across her face from time to time and her arms jerked a little, much like a sleeping baby's. What was she going to think of him if God didn't allow the Holy Spirit to flow through him? He took a breath and began to mumble again, the nonsense syllables. The gibberish fell off his tongue easier this time, smoothed by Jacob's reassurances.

A memory flickered to mind. He was sitting as a boy in the pews, feeling trapped, desperate to move but compelled by his father's threats not to. He felt the desire to run or kick the pew in front of him. Anything that would let the anxiety dissipate. But then he felt a sudden shift of thought. Though his body was trapped in the pew, his mind was not.

It occurred to Job that he could let his mind soar again. He could think of the vacuum cleaner, the egg that the whirr had manufactured in his hands, the steady vibrations of the machine that ran through his body, soothing him. As his body relaxed into remembered sound, he realized he was no longer making up the gibberish that he spoke. The words poured out of him, still unintelligible, but with a rhythm, a flow, a sing-song cadence of their own. Was this what the others were feeling? It was as if he were submerged in a hot bath and had lost the sensation of boundaries between skin and water. For moments he rose to the surface, heard himself speaking and became aware of the room full of people, before sinking again, into a state of forgetfulness, losing himself.

Then he felt a shift, as if someone had turned up the volume of the noise surrounding him. He opened his eyes and saw swirls of velvet brown, splotches the deep maroon of a dried fig and streaks the colour of blood orange. Rich, deep hues that surpassed anything he'd seen at the Godsfinger church. He felt a nebulous shape in his hands that seemed to be generated by the hum of voices. Not a defined shape. Not the glass egg of the vacuum cleaner, but a shape nevertheless, a presence in his hands, a weight. Along with the shape and colours, he felt an absolute certainty sliding back into his bones. A knowing. It must be the Holy Spirit coming into his soul, he thought, and along with it a feeling that everything was all right, that he was okay, accepted.

He felt as he did after he ran down the coulee and back up the steep slope, when his heart stopped banging in his chest and he was resting at the top of the bank; it was a feeling of relief and release. He remained in this bliss for some time and then rose from it, as Penny and the others, one by one, pulled themselves from the floor and stumbled from their altered states like drunks from a bar. And like a drunk, Job hugged everyone close by, and mumbled that he loved them. Love felt like a tangible thing in his hands, a glass egg he could give to others. He felt deeply grateful to them all, though he was hard-pressed to think what for.

He understood now why his father had risen in Godsfinger Baptist, despite the disapproving and embarrassed stares, to wail and clack his tongue, and why Jacob had stood to do the same, not just to receive his father's blessing. It was for this feeling, like the shaky peace that followed a good run or a good cry. But more than relief, he also felt forgiven. For all the failures his father had pointed out. And for his father's death. For his clumsiness with words and his inability to say what he meant, or to act when wrapped in fear. For his anxiety with women who interested him. At that moment he felt there was nothing he couldn't forgive. He pulled Jacob into a bear hug, pressing his chest into his. He told Penny he loved her, and held her hands. He forgave Will for his strange tendencies. Understood it all now.

THIRTEEN

Job ran down the coulee bank, chasing a doe, in a light, warm rain that wetted the skin on his back, his forehead. He wondered at the speed he was capable of, his ability to keep up to the deer and almost, but not quite, overtake her, even as the deer left the valley floor for the far wall of the coulee, running up the steep slope through poplar, caragana and lanky saskatoon bushes heavy in deep purple berries. Branches whipped Job's face, pulled at his skin, but he kept running, his breath hot from his mouth.

A lion slid into the chase in front of Job, racing up the slope, gaining on the deer. *It will catch her*, Job thought. *The lion will kill the deer.* Just as abruptly as the lion had appeared, Job became the lion. He scrambled to grab both sides of the deer's rump with his claws and the doe came to an abrupt halt in front of him. He leapt onto her back and bit into the base of her neck with his powerful jaws. But instead of killing her, he mounted her and thrust his penis into her with quick, urgent lunges.

Then a clanking in the chimney. Job's consciousness leapt up startled from his dream. He reached down to stop himself from coming, then lay on the cot for a time, listening to his own rapid breath. Not three weeks after he spoke in tongues, forgiveness and love spewing from his trap like holy water, and he was back in league with the devil, as pulled by confusing lusts as he ever was.

He slid on a pair of shorts over his underwear and pulled on a T-shirt, and opened the stove door. He found a duck there, a lesser scaup, soot-blackened and flapping its wings, working up a cloud of ash. Job closed the door, rummaged through the laundry basket for a towel and opened the stove again. The scaup blinked at him, and lunged at his hand. Job draped the towel over the bird and pulled it out. He tucked it under one arm to open the door and found Ben there, ready to knock. The skin around his right eye was bruised and turning yellow.

'What's that?' said Ben.

'Duck.' Job didn't try to explain. He opened the towel, held the duck aloft. Watched as it flew over the windrow of spruce and off towards the closest slough.

'Dad wants you to come in for breakfast, so you can talk about the work that's getting done today.' That morning Rod was driving volunteers down from Bountiful Harvest for a work bee, to prepare for and pour the floating slab – the foundation and floor for the halfway-house building. The site had already been excavated by Jerry's brother, Alan Kuss. Job and Jacob had serviced it themselves, rolling out the plastic tubing for water, and running a power line from the farm's transformer to the building site, into the trenches that Alan had dug with his backhoe.

Job sank his feet into a pair of runners but didn't bother with a jacket or jeans. Fall was his favourite time of year. The days were sunny and warm, but the first overnight frosts of September had killed off the clouds of mosquitoes that pestered him all summer long. 'Where'd you get the shiner?' he asked Ben as they walked to the house.

'Nowhere.'

From the lake, the bang of a shotgun, followed by the whoosh of pellets exploding into the sky, like the pop and rush of fireworks blasting off. Then the quack and flurry of whistling feathers as a flock of mallards flew low overhead. Duck-hunting season had opened on Labour Day but was just getting underway at the lake; having grown fat in northern feeding grounds, the ducks were now returning to Godsfinger to feast on the grain swathed in the fields.

'So, how you like school?' Job asked Ben. He'd had little chance to talk to his nephew alone these past few weeks. He'd done as Jacob had suggested and made himself scarce around the house, taking most of his meals in the cabin. But he was growing tired of peanut-butter sandwiches, and he missed his kitchen, the smell of roasted chicken or cinnamon buns from the oven.

'It's okay,' said Ben.

'Make any new friends?'

Ben shrugged. 'A few.'

'You see much of Jason?'

'He's in my class.'

Job hadn't seen Liv since the day in town when she drove off with Darren. He'd avoided going into Godsfinger, and instead shopped in Leduc or Wetaskiwin. Afraid of the talk.

Lilith was at the stove flipping pancakes as they came in.

Jacob sat at the kitchen table, drinking coffee. He was dressed in some of Abe's old work clothes, a plaid shirt and jeans that Job had stored in the attic. 'You think we've got enough rebar?' he asked Job as he took a seat at the table.

'If we don't I can make a run up to Edmonton. How many people do you think will come out and help?'

'I don't know. Ten at least. Maybe fifteen. I asked the secretary at Bountiful Harvest to put a notice in the bulletin.'

'Pastor Divine coming?'

'He said he figured he'd better be here when the foundation was laid. To show his support.'

Lilith put a plate of pancakes on the table and pointed her spatula out the window. 'Who's that?' she said.

Job turned in his seat to see the figure walking down Correction Line Road. 'It's Liv,' he said, and watched as she turned into their driveway.

'You didn't ask her to come over, did you?' Lilith asked Jacob.

'Why would you ask her over?' said Job.

'Ben and Jason had an incident at school,' said Jacob.

'Jason beat up Ben,' said Lilith.

'No he didn't,' said Ben. 'He just hit me. Once.' He touched the side of his eye. 'I was sitting on the bleachers behind Jason at a basketball game and I had to take a piss.'

'Language,' said Lilith.

'So I patted Jason on the shoulder, so he'd move over, so I could climb down. He wouldn't get out of my way so I slapped him on the back of the head. Jason just kind of swung around and punched me.'

'It was an unprovoked attack,' said Lilith.

'He said he was sorry,' said Ben.

'We had to take it to the principal,' said Lilith. 'It was for the boy's own good. You can't let that kind of behaviour go unpunished. Mr. Pinchbeck was only going to give Jason a couple of detentions. But we pointed out that he has a record of acting out. So he gave him a three-day suspension.'

'If he was my kid, I'd give him a good walloping,' said Jacob.

'You know Liv's not going to do a thing about it,' said Lilith. 'And God knows when Darren's going to be home from one of his hauls again to deal with it. It's just not a stable home.' Lilith reached out a hand to Jacob. Job thought she might put her hand on her husband's, but she laid it palm down on the table next to his. 'Maybe we should invite her up to Bountiful Harvest, or see if Barbara can't get her going to Godsfinger Baptist. She did go to the revival.'

'She only went because Job was there.'

'So, Job, you invite her.'

Jacob shook his head. 'It wouldn't be appropriate. Liv is still married. Besides, the Lord's got to break her more before she'd be interested in going to church.'

The light tap of Liv's sandals on the concrete steps as she approached the screen door. 'Mind if I come in?'

'I suppose not,' said Lilith. 'Leave your shoes at the door. I just washed the floor.'

'Of course.'

'You want coffee?'

'Sure.' Her face was shiny from the walk. She took off her jacket and hung it on the back of a chair, then folded her skirt beneath her as she sat. 'Hello, Job,' she said.

He nodded and helped himself to a couple of pancakes, then forked a sausage from the plate Lilith set on the table. Trying to look nonchalant. Trying to look like the room wasn't veering away from him in all directions. He thought of Liv on the grass, and the cows all around.

'I'm sorry to interrupt your breakfast,' said Liv. 'I thought I better get out here early, before you get to the fields.'

'We have a work bee today,' said Lilith. 'We're putting up a building.'

'Yeah, I heard about that. Some kind of halfway house, isn't it? For street people?'

'New Christians,' said Lilith. 'Jacob is heading up Pastor Divine's program to get people off the streets.'

'Good thing to do, I suppose. What about you?' she said to Job. 'What do you think about all this? It doesn't strike me as the kind of thing you'd want to get involved with.'

Job glanced up at Jacob and thought it better not to voice his opinion on the plan. For a couple of weeks after his baptism in the Holy Ghost, he'd been wrapped in a sort of glow, a feeling that he loved everyone, could forgive everyone, of anything. He'd smiled at the clerks and customers alike in the grocery store in Leduc. He'd even waved at Will when he saw him working out in the fields, though, previously, he'd turned the truck around rather than pass Will's when he'd seen him coming down Correction Line Road. During those two weeks, he'd agreed to go ahead with the halfway-house project, but now the whole idea made him panic. What did he know of ministering to alcoholics and drug addicts?

'Well, anyway,' said Liv. 'I came to talk about this situation with Jason and Ben.'

Jacob shook his head. 'There isn't anything to discuss. Besides, we don't really have the time. I've got a work crew turning up here any minute and we have a bunch of last-minute details to hammer out.'

'I think we do have some things to discuss. It will only take a few minutes.'

'I really don't have the time for this today. Ben, go to your room and get changed for the work bee. Lilith, get me some more coffee, will you? And a couple of the cookies you got on the counter would go down nice.'

Liv laughed. 'Why don't you get them yourself,' she said. 'You got some kind of handicap?'

Jacob's face burned red, but he said nothing. He glanced at Lilith and she jumped up to refill his cup and bring him cookies. Job nursed his cold coffee. He didn't dare ask for a fresh cup, though Lilith would look hurt if he got it himself, thinking he was judging her a poor hostess.

'I talked to Barry Pinchbeck,' said Liv. 'Explained our situation at home and that Jason is going through counselling to deal with his anger. He agreed to drop the suspension.'

'He did what?' said Jacob.

'He suggested Jason write a letter of apology, and I agreed. That's why I'm here.' She held an envelope out to Jacob. When Jacob didn't take it, she put it on the table in front of him.

Jacob flicked the letter away. 'This means nothing. Your boy is out of control. He needs to learn a lesson.'

'He didn't think about it, he just reacted. The anger flashed out of him. He already apologized to Ben. And he's written this letter to you, explaining and apologizing for his actions.'

'As I said, I don't have time for this today.' Jacob pushed himself up from the table and carried his coffee cup into the bedroom. He closed the door behind him.

Job stared at his plate and felt the urge to run away, as Jacob had. He hated these scenes.

'Well,' Liv said to Lilith. 'I guess it's just you and me.'

176

'As my husband said, there's nothing more to talk about.'

'You don't have to let him order you around like that, you know,' said Liv.

'He's my husband and it's my obligation and privilege to be obedient to him. You would do well to do the same to your husband. It's very freeing.'

'Like hell it is,' said Liv. She pushed her chair back and grabbed her coat. 'Thanks for the coffee.' And she was gone, out the door.

Job jogged down the stairs after her. When he reached her, she turned. 'How can she defend him like that?' she said.

They listened to gunshots from the lake, then the *woosh woosh* of wings as panicked ducks flew so low overhead Job felt he could reach up and grab them.

'I haven't seen you at the café for a while,' said Liv.

'I didn't feel much like going into town, with all the talk.'

'There hasn't been that much talk, Job. Everybody's already moved on to the next round of gossip.' From the lake, a shout from the hunters. The bark of one of their dogs. 'I thought you were going to phone.'

Job shrugged. 'It looked like Darren was back on the scene.' He looked up. 'Is he?'

'I don't know. We're going to see the counsellor we take Jason to. She asked a pile of questions to see why Jason was acting out, about what was going on at home. At the end of the session she told Darren he was abusive.'

'He hit you?'

'No. He's way too smart for that. But Jason saw lots of scenes growing up. Me on the couch crying, Darren standing over me yelling and yelling. That sort of thing. I guess Jason kept it bundled inside, then, when puberty hit, it started bubbling out. At the end of the counselling session the counsellor said I could stay in the marriage if Darren was willing to go through counselling with me. Or I could leave and she could help me straighten myself and Jason out. But she couldn't do a thing if I stayed in the marriage and Darren didn't make an effort. It kind of shook Darren up, to see the effect he was having on Jason. To hear someone other than me saying it. He said he'd give it a try.' She shrugged. 'We'll see.'

As Job tried to think of something to say, he looked across the road, at the excavation site in his hayfield, the square of earth scraped down to the tan clay beneath the sod. The string and stakes that marked out the building site. The mounds of dirt covering the trenches in which he and Jacob had laid the power- and waterlines. Down the road a vehicle dragged dust towards them. Likely Rod driving the church van, bringing the volunteers. 'I'm sorry about all this with Jason and Ben,' Job said.

'It's not really such a big deal, not like Jacob and Lilith are making it out to be. The boys have settled things. They're friends, you know. Ben's been coming over to my place quite a lot during the days since school started.'

'You let him skip school?'

'It's not a matter of me letting him. He'd skip whether I turned him away or not. There's no place for a kid to go in this town. So he stops in at the café. Sometimes I give him coffee and lunch. He does dishes or cuts carrots, whatever Crystal's got for him to do, to pay for it. If I'm not at work he'll stop by the house, see if I'm home. He offers to do some work, so I got him mowing the lawn a few times, so Barbara won't fine me again. I just give him a safe place to go. If he didn't have it, I'm afraid of what he'd get into. He's a smart kid, but he's pretty messed up.'

178

'Does Jacob know?'

'I'm sure the school's informed him Ben's been missing so much school. There's got to be something going on with him at home. Sounds like Jacob gives him the strap a lot.'

'A father's got a right to discipline his son the way he wants.' Something Abe had always said.

Liv laughed. 'What about Ben's rights?' she said.

The church van pulled into the Sunstrum yard and parked. 'Well, I see Penny and your other church friends are here,' said Liv. 'I guess I better get going.'

'You're welcome to stay and visit,' said Job. 'Lilith is bringing out coffee before we get started.'

Liv laughed. 'No, thank you.' She lifted a hand as she walked off. Nodded at Penny as she got out of the van but didn't stop to talk.

Penny, in pink shorts, a pink T-shirt and flip-flops, slapped her way over to Job. 'What was Liv doing here so early?' she said. She glanced at his cabin and lowered her voice. 'She didn't stay overnight, did she?'

'No! Of course not. There was this incident at school, between Jason and Ben. She came to discuss it with Jacob and Lilith.'

'Huh.' But she didn't look convinced.

Rod came up behind them, dressed in a brand-new plaid work shirt and jeans that hadn't yet been washed. The creases from the store packaging still etched on his sleeves. 'Job, did you ever meet Rod?' asked Penny.

'No.' He shook Rod's hand. A tattoo of a cross on the back of Rod's knuckles. 'I saw you at the revival.'

Rod took a quick step behind Job. 'You're right!' he said. 'He does have a great butt!'

'Told ya!' said Penny, giggling.

Job swung around. Felt his face flush.

'Ah, we didn't mean nothing,' said Rod. 'Just having a laugh.'

Penny was changed in Rod's company. A flirtation went on between them of the kind that went on between co-workers, or a brother and a sister-in-law. A freedom provided by a line that couldn't be crossed. Something. Job couldn't quite put his finger on it. He didn't like it.

A woman leaned against the van. Black hair pulled back with a yellow scarf. Prominent cheekbones under tanned skin. A wide, full mouth painted in red lipstick. She smiled at Job, toyed with her hair and held him in a long look. Job felt a churning in his stomach and a sudden awareness of his groin.

'This is Jocelyn Pryer,' said Rod. 'Jocelyn's a nurse.'

'Glad to meet you,' she said. She took just his fingers and gave them a squeeze. Her hands were warm and a little slippery. There was a slick of suntan oil at her neck and on her face. The smell of coconuts about her.

Penny took Job's arm and pulled him close, as if she had made a claim on him. 'Jocelyn's just new to the church,' she said, and gave Job a knowing look.

Jacob tapped down the house steps as Pastor Divine pulled into the yard in his truck. 'Is this it for volunteers?' Jacob asked Rod.

Divine closed the truck door behind him. 'You wrote in the church bulletin you only needed a handful,' he said.

'But a few more than this would have been nice.'

'People are busy, with school back in. Speaking of which, I've got to run.'

'You aren't staying?'

'Looks to me like you've got things well in hand. Just came down to give the project a blessing.'

'We could use your help.'

Divine patted Jacob on the shoulder. 'You'll do just fine without me.' He clapped his hands together. 'All right. Let's gather over at the building site and have a prayer.' They stood in the excavation, and Divine said a prayer for their safety as they worked and that the work might be productive, that God might bless the project. Then Jacob walked Pastor Divine back to his truck. They stopped at the old wooden wagon wheels Job had bought at the Olson auction years before. A ribbon of steel around the wheels' circumference. Job had planned on nailing them on the gate in front of the house but never got around to it. Jack Divine pulled one up from where it lay in the grass beside the barn and inspected it.

Rod picked up a shovel and leaned, chin on hands, on its handle. 'So Job,' he said. 'What's your story? Penny's told me a few things. How'd you come to find the Lord?'

Job scratched his chin. 'I don't know. He was always just sort of there. I grew up in a Baptist church.' When Penny shifted away from him he added, 'My father was a reformed Lutheran.'

'Huh,' said Rod. 'I guess when you've grown up with this stuff the evangelical fire burns low, doesn't it? But for me, this is first-generation stuff. This is rare. This is meaningful. You understand what I'm saying? This is all new to me. I never set foot in a church until the day I was saved.'

'Rod lived on the street,' Penny whispered in Job's ear. 'He was a prostitute.'

'Ah.' Job didn't ask, from politeness, but wondered how this worked. Did women drive down the street in cars, looking to buy a night's pleasure? Had Rod stood on the street, dressed in – what? What did women find sexy? Very short shorts?

'Jesus came to me one night when I was stoned,' said Rod. 'I was in a doorway, you know, just having a snooze, and he was suddenly there, all shining and everything. And he was really built. He had, like, these really big muscles. Nothing like the paintings you see of him, all skinny and everything. I mean, he was *built*. He said, "I'll take care of you." And he did. The next day Pastor Jack stopped me on the street and invited me to his revival and I was saved that night. He cleaned me up, got me straightened out and gave me a place to stay.' Rod nodded at Jocelyn. 'How about you? What's your story?'

'Nothing very original,' said Jocelyn. She pulled the yellow scarf from her head and used it to tie her hair into a ponytail. 'About a year ago I found out my husband was screwing around and I fell apart. You know, crying all the time. My neighbour, Linda Bergen, you know her? Anyway, she brought over cookies and sat with me and listened to me gripe and cry. She invited me to go to Pastor Divine's church with her. She'd been so nice, so I went along. Then in church I had a crying fit. Linda said it was a sign Jesus was working on me. After the service, she and one of the deacons sat on either side of me. They got me to say a prayer, to accept Jesus as my saviour. Then all these other people came up and hugged me. And I felt better, like somebody cared about me.'

'Have you been baptized in the Holy Spirit?' said Penny. The look on her face that said, Probably not.

'Yeah,' said Jocelyn. 'I spoke in tongues.'

'You feel anything when the Holy Spirit comes on you?' Job asked. 'I mean, did things change for you?'

'Yeah, sure,' said Jocelyn. 'Kind of. Didn't things change for you?'

'At first I felt different. But now I don't feel like I thought I would.' After the vibrancy of that first service where he spoke in tongues, his colours had faded again. He had tried to get the Holy Spirit back during Pastor Divine's services over the weeks that followed, confessing his sins over and over silently, in prayer, but he couldn't catch the euphoria, or speak in tongues again, though he'd tried to loosen his tongue in faith as Pastor Divine had suggested. He spoke gibberish, feeling nothing, as he watched others fall into fits on the floor or light up in flames of giggles or go stiff and bob from the waist. The Spirit fell on them easily but left Job cold. He felt as though God was punishing him, withholding from him. He didn't know what other reason there could be for his emptiness.

'Once you're baptized in the Holy Spirit you've got to be on guard,' said Rod. 'Because Satan will really be on the attack now, seeding your mind with doubts.'

Job thought of that past Sunday, when, as Penny lay on the floor pushing out forced laughter, they locked gazes for a moment. 'You don't always feel something either, do you?' said Job, then wished he hadn't. An unwitting confession. But into it now.

'Feel what?' said Penny.

'The Holy Spirit, when you're speaking in tongues, or laughing.'

She laughed and glanced at Rod. 'I'm not faking it.'

'I sometimes give it a little help,' said Rod. 'As Pastor Divine suggested. You know, loosening your tongue in faith.'

'That's different from faking it,' said Penny. 'You've got to make yourself receptive to the Holy Spirit. I mean, it's not like you always feel something right away.'

Job mulled over this, that if Penny didn't always feel the euphoria and had to try to work up the feeling, then others might be doing the same. Maybe most of them.

Lilith walked down the steps in her sock feet, with two plates of cookies covered in tinfoil, and stepped into her rubber boots at the bottom of the steps. She shrieked, tossed the plates into the air and kicked a boot several yards away from her. A mouse scuttled from the boot, and Lilith ran back up the stairs, slamming the screen door behind her.

Penny jogged over to pick up after Lilith, and Rod followed to help her. Together they took the cookies and plates into the house.

Jocelyn sat on the side of the excavation site, and Job sat with her. 'So is Penny your girlfriend?' she asked him.

'No.' He wasn't sure what was going on between them. He hoped for something, watched for signs of Penny's intent, but didn't want to step in too soon after her breakup with Will.

'It felt like there was something going on between you two.'

'She was my friend's girlfriend.'

'Did this friend die or something?'

'No.' He didn't try to explain. It was all so embarrassing.

'How about that other woman who was here? In the long skirt.'

'Liv? She's married.'

'So, you're not seeing anyone?'

'No.'

'Well, maybe we could get together for a coffee or something sometime. Or maybe supper.' When Job didn't answer right away, as he weighed his options, Jocelyn threw up her hands and said, 'There I go again. My ex always told me I was too pushy.'

'No. Not at all.' From Will's field, the loud quacks of female ducks and the whispering calls of the drakes, as birds foraging in the swathed grain called to the flock circling overhead.

'Well then, I'm thinking of going to Pastor Divine's next workshop,' said Jocelyn. 'On evangelizing with the Holy Spirit. Maybe I'll see you there.'

Jacob crunched over the newly gravelled road to the construction site as Pastor Divine drove away down Correction Line Road. 'Jack took a real shine to those old wagon wheels,' he said.

Job glanced over to where they had lain. They were gone. 'He took them?'

'I offered them to him. He's going to use them in his garden.'

'But they were mine. I bought them at the Olson auction.'

'I didn't think you'd mind.'

'I was going to put them on the front gate to the farm. I just hadn't got around to it.' It made him angry, not just because Jacob had given away the wagon wheels without asking him, but because he had given them to Pastor Divine to garner social favour, as if he had to buy the pastor's respect. It was something Job himself might have done. *Had* done. He'd emptied his pickle jars to give to Will, just because Will had made an off-handed comment that he liked them. Two years before, after Solverson complained that he was late in getting his harvesting done and had no sons to help, Job volunteered to give him a hand. He drove his own equipment over to Solverson's, baled and brought in the straw just before the first snow of the season, neglecting his own crop as a consequence. Solverson was right there alongside Steinke at the Out-to-Lunch Café, giving Job the gears for neglecting to get his straw bales in before the snow. Too late, Job had realized Solverson was only complaining as he always did; he would have brought his crop in with or without Job's help. He didn't care one way or the other that Job helped him. More than that, he'd thought Job a fool for letting his own field work suffer, though he'd accepted the help readily enough. But Job said nothing more to Jacob about the wagon wheels, just as he'd said nothing to Solverson. What was there to say? The wheels were gone now. There was no getting them back.

'Where's Rod and Penny?' said Jacob. 'We better get this show on the road. The cement truck will be here at two.'

Job slapped dirt off his jeans. 'They went into the house. I'll get them.' Job didn't bother going inside; he didn't want to take his boots off. Instead he pulled open the screen door and called, 'Penny. Rod. We're ready to get started.'

Lilith stepped into the hall, wiping her hands on a dishrag. 'They went back outside.'

Job turned, scanned the farm, the construction site. 'I don't see them.'

'Penny said something about showing Rod that old cabinet of your grandmother's that's stored in the barn.'

The barn door was partly open. Job slid inside and stood a moment to let his eyes adjust to the darkness, and then to let his mind adjust as well. Rod pressed Penny against the back wall of a box stall. Her shirt was pulled up, and his hand was on her exposed breast. Penny's eyes fluttered open. She saw Job, made a startled squeak like that of a mouse underfoot and pulled herself from the kiss. Rod turned, wiping his mouth, and Penny said, 'Job,' and held out her hand. Then she laughed, nervously, as Job turned and fled, with the barn door swinging out after him.

186

FOURTEEN

Jacob, Lilith, Job and Ben drove up to Edmonton in the station wagon on a sunny October Saturday. All of them wore shorts and T-shirts, to take advantage of the last days of warm, mosquito-free weather. Earlier that week, over breakfast, Job had explained to Jacob that if he were serious about getting the halfway house to lockup before the weather turned, they should have used these fair days for a work bee, to put up the walls and roof. But here they were driving up to Pastor Divine's workshop on how to evangelize with the Holy Spirit. 'You can't expect people to turn up for a work bee without any warning,' Jacob had said. 'Besides, Pastor Divine's had this workshop planned for months. And he won't have another one now until after Christmas.'

The difference between those living in the city and those on the farm, Job supposed. In the city, people planned for things, committed to social engagements a week or two or even months in advance. But on the farm, where almost everything depended on the weather, people were less inclined to make plans or commit to a dinner out. A rainy day was a town day. A sunny day this time of year meant a farmer would take to the field because, any day, winter might arrive. Job knew that's where he should have been this day, on the combine, harvesting his barley. If he didn't get to it quickly, he might end up one of those poor sods he sometimes saw out combining in snow, guiltily. Farmers in the area would eye his field as they drove by and later, over coffee in their kitchens or in the Out-to-Lunch Café, speculate that perhaps Job had had some equipment breakdown. Or they'd say the things that Job himself had said of others, that he should get the lead out of his pants, that he was sloppy in his field work or just plain lazy. 'If we're not going to work on the building this weekend, then I should be out in the field,' he'd said to Jacob that morning.

'Pastor Jack will notice if you don't turn up,' Jacob replied. 'This is a workshop we're going to. There's only likely to be twenty or thirty people there.'

'But I've got to get that barley harvested.' And he knew Penny would likely be at the workshop. His first impulse was to find whatever excuse he could to avoid going himself, so he wouldn't have to face her. Yet he wanted to see her, to know if she was serious about Rod, or if what he had seen was merely a fling, a cure for heartbreak. Rod was a former prostitute after all, and perhaps he had seduced her. Did she regret it now? Had she taken it to the Lord for forgiveness? Job wondered if he was still in the running, if he had ever been.

'You've got to at least appear to make an effort,' said Jacob. 'Pastor Jack heard you didn't help out with the last work bee. That you took off after he left.' After Job had seen Penny in Rod's embrace, he'd headed straight for his truck, praying that it would start. When it did, he drove to the Out-to-Lunch

Café, flying to safety like a chicken to its roost. A familiar place. He had hoped to see Liv, to hear her silvery laugh, but she wasn't there. He was served by Arnie Carlson's daughter, Betty, a shy, ash-blonde girl of sixteen. Crystal was busy in the kitchen prepping for lunch. So he ate his pie by himself, then drove the back roads all afternoon, hunting, unsuccessfully, for the blue lottery balls driving over gravel had once produced. He couldn't face Penny that day, couldn't stand the embarrassment of listening to her explanation, if she'd had one. Later, over supper, Jacob had demanded an explanation from Job as to why he'd run off. Job had sat as numbly and silently as he had as a boy, when his father demanded to know why he kept setting fires. He didn't know. He had just acted.

'Don't think Pastor Divine didn't notice that you disappeared after he got you healing at the revival in August,' Jacob had said to Job that morning at breakfast. 'He told me he wondered just how committed to the Lord's work you were. If you had what it took to deal with new converts when we get things started up. I assured him that you did. For heaven's sake, Job, don't you understand what's at stake here? I need this halfway-house project to work. I need the salary. Otherwise we're looking at selling this farm.'

So here he was, riding in the back of the station wagon on his way to Pastor Divine's workshop. On the radio, a tinny country song he didn't know. The air conditioning in the car didn't work and all the windows were open partway. Job's thighs stuck to the vinyl of the car seat, and he squinted into the wind like a dog, the dream that woke him still sliding around in his mind. He'd been at the church camp where he and Jacob had spent two weeks of their childhood summers.

The camp bunkhouse smelled of dust and Pine-Sol. The bunks that lined the walls were two high, and on each bed lay a body. They were all dead, every one of them. Job walked down the length of the bunkhouse, touching each corpse on the forehead. He knew what to do. He had the power to wake the dead. All it took was an act of silliness, something to make them laugh, something to trick their consciousness into resurrection. He winked knowingly at them first, as if conspiring with them, but when this got no response he jumped around, flapped his arms and danced like a chicken. A few laughed and rose. He tickled the remaining dead under the chin, and on the soles of their feet, until they, too, rose. Suddenly he was dead, lying in a bunk. There was no one there to make him laugh. He struggled to waken but could not, and felt the panic of sleep heavy on him. Then he woke, dry mouthed, heart beating in his chest, a trapped sparrow thrumming its wings against a window.

Passing through Millwoods, Ben said, 'Can we stop at a gas station? I've got to use the washroom.'

'Why didn't you go before we left?' asked Jacob.

'I didn't have to go then.'

'You can wait.'

'No, I can't.'

'I could use a pit stop myself,' said Job.

'I'm driving,' said Jacob. 'I'll decide when we stop and when we don't.'

Job thought of himself at sixteen, asking his father if he could borrow the truck to go to a basketball game in Leduc. His father said, 'No, you can't.'

Job asked him, 'Why not?'

Abe had said, 'So you know I can still say *no*.'

190

But Job didn't press Jacob further. He tapped his foot on the station-wagon floor in the effort of holding it in.

Jacob caught his eye in the mirror. 'I meant to tell you we're all having dinner with Jack and his wife tonight.'

Job felt trapped; he knew he'd be in for some kind of lecture from Pastor Divine. Jacob had avoided telling him about the dinner earlier, so he wouldn't back out of coming with them. 'I've got chores,' said Job.

'I don't know how you're getting home then,' said Jacob. 'We won't be heading back until after supper.'

'Penny will be at the workshop,' said Lilith. 'You could get a ride home with her.'

Jacob glanced at her and then at Job through the rearview mirror. 'Your choice,' he said.

They came to the sign that read *Miracles This Way*, and pulled into the parking lot in front of the old Safeway building. Once parked, Ben jumped from the station wagon and ran into the church to find the men's washroom. Job followed, and found an empty urinal. Released a stream that made everything in the world right for a moment.

Job and Ben followed an elderly couple into one of the junior-church rooms off to the side of the sanctuary. Ben joined Jacob and Lilith, who had chosen seats in a middle row. Close to twenty other people sat on folding metal chairs around them. At the front, Pastor Divine organized his notes on a music stand. In the first row, Penny sat by herself. No sign of Rod. Job's heart leapt when she turned and saw him, and gave him a tentative smile. She was dressed in a sleeveless pink dress and matching flip-flops. She waved him over, and when he sat, she took his hand, as if nothing had come between them. She asked him how he'd been doing, but offered no explanation about why she had been with Rod in the barn, and he didn't ask for any, as Pastor Divine was already clearing his throat to speak.

Then Rod came into the room and handed Pastor Divine his Bible, before taking the empty chair on the other side of Penny. He was dressed up, in a salmon-coloured shirt and striped tie under a deep-blue suit jacket so big that it was obvious it didn't belong to him. His hair was parted conservatively to the side, and he had the clean, darkly handsome appearance of the young Mormons who occasionally came down from Edmonton to proselytize door to door through Godsfinger, despite the cross tattoo on the back of his right hand. Penny leaned into his shoulder and whispered something in his ear. He grinned at her. Job pulled his hand from Penny's grip.

Pastor Divine held his arms out and smiled. 'You are part of God's family!' he said. 'Everyone, stand and give each other hugs!'

Job looked around, aware of his arms dangling at his sides, as Penny hugged Rod. Then Penny turned to him and gave him a quick squeeze. The smell of her: Ivory soap and baby powder. When he held on, she gave him a pat on the back and pulled herself away. Job shook hands with Rod, but couldn't bring himself to hug him, or look him in the eye.

Pastor Jack stepped back up to the music stand. 'All right folks. Quiet down. Today I'm going to teach you to evangelize with the Holy Spirit. We'll spend part of the morning here, learning the basics, then, later this morning and all this afternoon, you'll put what you've learned into practice. You'll pair up, and each pair will go to a different part of town to witness.'

Jocelyn opened the door to the side of Pastor Divine. She smiled her apologies for being late as Divine went on talking, then tiptoed in front of him and took the seat next to Job. She smiled at Job, nodded. She wore a khaki T-shirt and shorts and black leather sandals. The smell of coconuts around her. A shine over the tanned skin of her chest.

'So you got the Holy Spirit working through you,' he said. 'And I'm sure everyone in this room does. How do you go about using that Spirit to bring people to the Lord?' He tapped his eyebrow. 'You start with the eyes. The eyes are the mirror of the heart. What we're talking about here is *discernment*. The Holy Spirit will lead you to read pain, fear, arrogance and failures in the eyes of others. And you're going to read sin in the eyes, guilt. I've gotten so good at this, I can just walk down the street and look into people's eyes and tell what's going on in their lives. I can tell when someone has murdered.'

Several people in the group said, 'Oh!' Job caught Jocelyn's eye. She smiled and raised her eyebrows.

'You see arrogance there,' said Pastor Divine, 'walk away. You see satisfaction there, don't waste your time. Revival happens when people come to a place of humility, inner need or depression, when everything is taken away. It's the Lord's way of making us ready to receive him. You're not going to bring a guy to the Lord if he doesn't think he's thirsty for God. You've got to make him see that he's thirsty. It's just like teaching a calf how to drink from a bucket. And how do you do that, Job?'

Fear like cold water shot through Job. Penny took his hand in both of hers and patted it. Job looked around, saw Jacob nodding, urging him on. All other faces blurred. He felt his stomach cramp.

'A prospective convert is just like a Holstein calf,' said Divine. 'A Holstein calf won't want to drink from a bucket. Its nature tells it to hold its head up, bunt its mother, suckle. So what do you do to get a calf to drink from a bucket?' He waited for Job to answer. A second chance.

'I raise Herefords,' said Job. 'You don't have to teach them to drink from a bucket.' Penny let go of his hand, crossed her arms and shifted her weight so she was leaning towards Rod. Jacob, too, crossed his arms and wouldn't look at him. Job realized too late that he'd just undergone a test, of sorts, and had failed.

Divine spoke directly to Job, instructing him as he might a child. 'You put your fingers in the calf's mouth and as it's sucking you bring your fingers into the milk, drawing its muzzle into the bucket. Then, once it's slurping, you take your fingers out.' Divine turned to the rest of the group. 'That's what you've got to do with a prospective convert. You've got to lead his head down into the bucket. You've got to teach him to bring his head down before the Lord, to be humble, to submit. All right. Let's get an expert up here to show you how to do it. Jacob?'

Jacob made his way to the front of the room and Divine wrapped an arm around his shoulder. 'Everyone, this is Jacob Sunstrum. In case any of you haven't heard, Jacob's heading up our halfway-house project, setting up a place so the people you bring to the Lord today will soon have a place to live and learn about the Lord.'

Divine pulled up a chair and sat. 'All right. So I'm sitting here, reading my newspaper.'

'Hello,' said Jacob.

'Hello.'

'I wonder, sir, where would you go today if you were hit by a bus and died?'

Pastor Jack sat forward, addressed the group. 'There, see, a direct approach. Don't beat around the bush.' He sat back, resumed acting. 'I suppose I'd be dead.'

'Yes sir, but where would you go? Heaven or hell?'

'Well, I don't know.'

'Have you been born again?'

'Born again?'

'Have you accepted Jesus Christ as your Lord and personal saviour?'

'Well, no. I guess I haven't.'

'Then you'll be going to hell.'

'Hell? I don't want to go to hell.'

'No rational man would. It's a terrible fate. Wouldn't you prefer to go to heaven if you had the choice?'

'I suppose, I would. Yes.'

'I can see in your eyes that you're feeling badly about something. There's something haunting you that you wish you hadn't done.'

'Excellent,' said Pastor Divine. 'See what Jacob did there? He brought my head down to the bucket, made me realize I was thirsty. How'd he do that? Guilt! I can't stress this enough: make use of guilt. It's the best tool in the evangelical toolbox. Everybody feels guilty about something. Make them feel the guilt in their bellies; fire it up! Make them thirsty for God's love. Make them frightened that they'll starve without it! Because they will! They're going to experience eternal death without God's love. Promise them salvation, the final solution for guilt. Then you've got them.' He turned to Jacob. 'How you going to do that for me?'

'It doesn't matter what you've done, how serious the thing is. God will forgive you. He already knows all about it.'

'He does?'

'Yes, and he loves you anyway. He accepts you anyway, just as you are.'

Pastor Jack turned to his audience. 'See what Jacob did there? He made the sinner feel that he could be forgiven, loved, accepted. That's what every sinner wants. When you let the person know God loves him and accepts him, then they can't help but be blasted by the Holy Spirit. It's now that you want to lead the sinner to God. Go for it, Jacob.'

'God wants you to come to him. He wants you with him in heaven. If you're serious about wanting to go to heaven, then I would lead you in a prayer right now. It would take less than five minutes.'

Pastor Divine sat forward and addressed the group again. 'See there, he made it clear it wouldn't take long. People don't have a lot of time these days.' He sat back and looked at Jacob. 'What kind of prayer?'

'You'd repeat after me, asking the Lord Jesus into your life, to forgive your sins and give you a clean heart. Then you'd have the same salvation that I have. I've been born again. I know where I'm going when I die. I'm going to heaven.'

Pastor Divine stood, put the newspaper on the chair. 'There, see? Simple. If they're worthy, they'll ask Jesus into their lives. If they're not ready, let your peace come back to you, but either way, finish things up with a prayer. All right. Any questions?'

Penny put a hand up. 'What if they don't want to receive the Lord? Should we keep on talking to them, to convince them?'

'Keep in mind there's lots of reasons why they may not be ready to receive. Maybe they don't like you. Maybe they had a

196

stressful day. Like Job said, you don't teach a Hereford calf how to drink from a bucket. There are some people you just can't bring to the Lord. Don't even try to talk to busy people. If someone starts arguing back, planting the seed of doubt in your mind, don't say another word. You'll waste your time, you'll waste your energy and sometimes they can slime you with their ideas. The devil's already got them. All you're doing is arguing with the devil. Just smile and walk away.'

'But should we, like, focus on hell?' said Penny. 'Like what's waiting for them if they don't accept the Lord?'

'Sure, mention hell,' said Divine. 'But you don't have to scare them to death. It's more important to listen carefully to people. See where they're hurting. Make them feel you care about them, that you're their friend. Let them know God loves them. That's leading their head down to the bucket. Let the Holy Spirit lead you to the despondent, the depressed, those with the ruffled look of the unemployed, the people he's broken and prepared for you. When they're desperate, they'll do anything to stop feeling that way. They're empty vessels, just waiting for God to fill them. That's what we need to be ourselves – desperate. Because when we're desperate, God can work through us. Do I hear an amen?'

'Amen!'

Rod pulled into the parking lot of Bonnie Doon Mall, and his passengers gathered in front of the van. Job stood close to Penny and tried touching her hand to see if he'd been forgiven for failing in front of the group that morning. But Penny pulled away, crossed her arms and shifted her weight to the other hip, away from him. 'I think we should pair up as boy-girl teams,' she said. 'That way we can minister to either gender. I'll go with Rod and you go with Jocelyn. Seeing as how you and me are mature Christians, and Rod and Jocelyn are new to this. You all right with that, Job?'

'I guess,' he said, seeing that he had no choice in the matter.

'Let's bow our heads in prayer,' said Penny. 'Lord, please arrange a divine appointment with the people you want us to witness to. Break our hearts for the people we encounter today, Lord.' When she was done, Penny clapped her hands. 'All right. See you guys back at the van at five o'clock. We'll see who gets the most converts. It's like a scavenger hunt!'

Job watched Penny take Rod's arm as they walked off. She was all but bouncing, pumped up on the excitement of the Lord. She seemed so far beyond doubt, a trait Job suddenly found annoying.

Jocelyn and Job headed up Eighty-second Avenue, walking past a Salvation Army thrift shop, over a bridge and past restaurants, a hydroponics shop and a rental place for gala parties and weddings. They found a corner grocery and picked up a package of Oreos. Job was handing money to the cashier when he saw Liv through the window, bending over the white buckets of flowers outside, with her henna-red hair draped over her face. Her East Indian-print skirt was see-through in the sun, revealing her shorts and thighs. The bracelets on her wrist caught light. She gathered a bunch of red sunflowers from a bucket as Job grabbed his change and cookies and scrambled outside. He called her name before he saw she was a stranger. A chubby face and broad nose. Shining drops of water dripping from the stems of the flowers she held.

Jocelyn caught up with him. 'What?' she said.

'I thought I saw someone I knew.'

'Who?'

'Nobody.'

They ate the cookies sitting together on a bench advertising the Full Gospel Businessman's Association. Graffiti scrawled across the seat in bold black paint read *Please Post Propaganda Here*. Cars roared past, the thump of their stereos. But the city noise didn't overwhelm Job as it once had. The colours the noise generated were faded, all but gone.

A man on crutches stepped in front of them. He was chubby, dressed in a blue shirt and brown vest, a cap that read *Ducks Unlimited*. He offered them a tract, a comic book of sorts, with a frightened-looking devil on the front, and the title 'A Demon's Nightmare.' Jocelyn waved a hand, said, 'No thanks.'

The man shifted his weight on his crutches, and handed Job the tract. 'Have you heard the good news of Jesus Christ?'

'Yes,' said Job.

'Have you been saved?'

'Yes.'

'Are you sure you've been saved? Are you absolutely sure?'

Job didn't answer. He picked up the bag of Oreos and he and Jocelyn walked on. The man hobbled after them a few feet. 'But if you'll just give me a moment of your time!'

Job flipped through the tract as they walked. A grinning evangelist in a suit and tie saved the soul of a tough-looking kid on a bench. But, urged on by the demons, the boy was tempted by friends back into his old way of life. Then, choosing a Wednesday-night prayer meeting over a movie on television, the boy was once again saved from a life of sin. He went on to save countless souls himself, much to the disgruntlement of the demons. The tract ended with the helpful reminder: 'And whosoever was not found written in the book of life was cast into the lake of fire. Revelation 20:15.'

Job cast the tract into a garbage can.

They passed kids selling jewellery from blankets on the street and a ragged man standing on a street corner with his hand out to everyone who passed.

'Aren't you going to talk to anyone?' asked Jocelyn.

'I was waiting for you.'

'You're the mature Christian here.'

'I guess I haven't seen anyone desperate enough.'

'You're not going to talk to anybody, are you?'

Job scratched his cheek. 'Probably not.'

'Want to grab some lunch? Those cookies just left me hungry.'

She led him to the pub of the Strathcona Hotel. A mime stood by the door, his white face painted over with red and blue stripes, acting as though he were a robot or a marionette on strings. Job wasn't sure. An oversized black cowboy hat containing a few coins sat at his feet. 'This is a bar,' said Job.

'They have these great double-wiener hot dogs. Two wieners wrapped in this huge bun. They're famous for them.' She pulled him in by the sleeve. 'It's okay. Nobody fights here. They do, the regulars kick them out.'

The pub had a shuffleboard at one end and a dartboard at the other. A haze of cigarette smoke. The smell of beer. A dark room, without windows, filled with old-timers, the regulars, and university kids from the U of A. The hum of voices, which produced little in the way of colour for Job. Once he would have found the din overwhelming.

They got themselves a couple of hot dogs at the kiosk by the bar and sat at a small round table covered in red towelling. 'To sop up the beer,' said Jocelyn when he pinched it.

A waitress came by wearing jeans and a white shirt. She had

a cigarette hanging out of her mouth with orange lipstick around the filter, and she made Job think of Crystal. 'You want something to wash that down with?' she asked.

'Yes, please,' said Job.

'Got a particular pleasure?'

'No.' Thinking of water. But the waitress set down two sweating glasses of draft. 'Enjoy,' she said, and was off. Job pushed the beer off to the side and ate his hot dog as he waited for the waitress to come back, so he could ask for water. But she was busy with other customers and didn't return. The lunch-hour rush.

Jocelyn drank her beer. 'What are we supposed to do after we bring somebody to the Lord?' she asked.

'I guess that's the whole point of the construction we've been doing. To give the converts a place to go.'

'No, I mean, are we supposed to be friends to these people? Pastor Divine said to make these people feel like we care about them, that we're their friends. But are we supposed to just pretend to be their friends?'

'I don't know.'

'Huh.' Jocelyn finished off her hot dog and wiped the ketchup from her lip with a napkin. She slurped her beer. 'After I started going to church, my neighbour Linda stopped coming over to visit me. I thought we were friends, you know? When I did that whole song and dance with her in the pew, accepting the Lord and all that, Linda gave me a Bible that she signed, "In Christian Love," and for some reason that hurt, made me angry. I couldn't think why until this morning when Pastor Divine said that stuff about making people think you care about them, that you're their friend. That's just it. No one really cares, no one really is your friend. What was important

201

to Linda was that she make me a part of Christ's body. Who I was, was irrelevant.'

'We're supposed to die to ourselves,' said Job. He'd been taught the acronym JOY in Sunday school: Jesus, Others, You. In that order. You were always supposed to come last. A notion Job's father and mother encouraged. At family suppers when he was a child, his mother had convinced him to take the dark meat over the white. 'You like dark meat, don't you?' she asked as she was cutting up a young fryer, a bird she'd raised herself, into segments. Job was setting the table. Jacob and Abe sat on lawn chairs outside the kitchen window. Though Emma had driven the grain truck all day, and Job had driven the tractor.

'It's okay,' Job said. But he preferred white meat. Before Abe said grace, both Job and Jacob scanned the plate of chicken for the breast meat with the wishbone attached, and grabbed their forks with their eyes still closed during grace. 'Come, Lord Jesus, Be our guest, May this food, To us be blest.' At *amen* they both stabbed for the breast, hoping to land the wish-bone. If Job got the wishbone, he could choose his mother to break it with and count on getting his wish. If Jacob got the wishbone, he invariably chose Job to break it with, and Job, so much weaker than Jacob, never won.

'It would make things so much easier at dinner if you just took the dark meat,' said Emma. Dark was what Emma chose. It occurred to Job at that moment that likely Emma also preferred the breast meat but ate the thigh so the men would get the white. It was understood that Abe would always get one of the two chicken breasts Emma served. The boys fought over the other. If Job succeeded in getting the breast to his plate first, Jacob would sulk through dinner and refuse to eat the dark meat that Abe put on his plate. And the evening would be rife with argument because Abe refused to let his boys leave the table until they had eaten every last scrap on their plates. Come bedtime, Jacob was still at the table, sobbing over the dark meat on his plate as Abe shouted at him. All because Job wanted the breast with the wishbone. So Job took the dark meat, as his mother did, as she requested. Not at first. But over time, because each dinner at which chicken was served and Job stuck his fork into white meat, his mother said, 'Can't you leave that for someone who doesn't like dark meat?' He continued eating dark meat to this day, out of habit. It hadn't occurred to him that he could choose to eat white.

Job finally gave in to his thirst and downed the glass of beer. It was good. Refreshing. He licked his upper lip.

'I don't think I'm cut out for this whole church scene,' said Jocelyn. 'At first it was great, everyone was so nice to me. But now.' She shrugged. 'I don't know. I missed the last couple of church services. I just didn't feel like going. I think the only reason I went to the workshop this morning was because I thought you'd be there.'

Job stared at his glass, not really listening. He suspected something terrible would happen, now that he'd drank the beer, though he couldn't think what. But instead he felt mellow, and the colours of the sounds around him were heightened. He watched one of the waitresses prop open the door. On the city streets outside, a ruckus: horns blared, throwing up pale flashes in front of Job's face, like the reflections from the slough on the pumphouse wall. The roar of vehicles tickled his hands. Layers and layers of sound that grew louder on the occasional breezes that blew in, a cacophony that threw rings of translucent colour splashing one into another against the dark of the pub, and trailed ghost fingers across the skin of Job's arms and face, startling him again and again.

He thought of the time in Denver when he drank beer and watched naked women skate. The colours were brighter then too. Maybe the colours and shapes of sounds had nothing to do with God, despite the certainty that accompanied them, the feeling that God was imparting to him some knowledge, though he could never put that knowledge into words. Maybe it was just a trick of perception.

'You're a nurse, right?' he asked.

'Yup,' said Jocelyn.

'Does alcohol ever make you see things?'

'Not unless you're an alcoholic detoxing. Why? You seeing something?'

He hesitated, but the beer was making him bold. 'I always see colours when I hear sound. But it's been fading.'

'Wild. I've read about this.'

'This happens to other people?'

'It's called synesthesia. You really see colours when you hear a sound?'

'I can feel some sounds in my hands. Like the vacuum cleaner is an egg in my hands, a glass egg.'

'How do you know it's glass? You see it?'

'No, it's invisible, but it's smooth, and cool. So it feels like glass.'

'Huh.'

'But then when I see colours, or feel shapes, I get this feeling that's hard to describe. It's like I *know*.'

'Know what?'

'Everything. But not like *I* know everything. It's like God's in me. I feel *certain*.'

'My nephew's an epileptic. He gets a feeling something like that when he has a seizure. He describes a feeling of profound awe, a knowing, that he can't put into words.'

'Yes!'

'But for him the feelings pass. You feel that all the time?'

'The sensations sort of faded recently. But today, after I had the beer, the colours were more vivid. And I feel that certainty again.'

'I remember reading about one guy with synesthesia whose colours got brighter when he drank. He died of liver disease.'

'But why would the colours be fading?'

'You got me. There was something about how more children than adults experience it, so it must fade with time. A fever, or some drugs or a trauma, like a blow to the head, sometimes make it go away.' She waved at a waitress.

'Are we leaving?' said Job.

'No. I'm going to get you another beer.'

They spent the afternoon in the pub, sampling different brands of beer. Pilsner, Corona, Guinness. Job described for Jocelyn the colours of sounds, how the voices and music blended into a fantasia around him, and how his watch, a Bulova Accutron that had once belonged to his father, produced a raised metallic dot that pulsed with each passing second as it hadn't since he'd seen Will kiss Ed, since the duck landed on his head. Jocelyn leaned over the table and laughed in fascination at everything he said. Job was pleased, and saw himself differently, not as bumbling, but as capable. The shift wore well on him, made him randy. That and the beer. With each beer he drank, the colours of voices in the bar, the cityscape around them, became brighter and brighter, and that feeling of certainty, of excitement mixed with calm, grew. Jocelyn brushed her hand against his arm as she reached for a napkin. Held his glance longer as the afternoon wore on. Slipped off a shoe and ran a toe down the calf of his leg. He reached across the table and took her hand. She lifted his hand and put his ring finger in her mouth and suckled on it. A jolt to his groin. He pulled his hand away when the waitress brought them their next round.

'What did you think the colours were?' asked Jocelyn.

'I don't know. At first I just thought they were how everyone heard things. Then, when I figured out other people didn't experience the world that way, I thought maybe it was the Shechinah the Bible talks about.'

'The what?'

'The glory of God, like a shining light or something, evidence of God's presence, made visible, here in this world. When I started to lose the colours I thought maybe it was a test.'

'A test?'

'From God. Pastor Henschell always said if you feel God's love slipping away and you can't pin it down to any sin, and your worship life is good, then it might be God testing you.'

'To see if you're faithful,' said Jocelyn. 'Yeah, Pastor Divine says something like that. It's the old story of Job all over, isn't it? God makes a wager with the devil and says, okay, take away all his goodies, his health, but I'm betting he'll still love me. But think about it, Job. Would you put up with a spouse who treated you like that? A wife who said, "*Prove* you love me. If I piss off, will you still love me?" Why put up with a God like that?'

'He's *God*.'

'It's just someone's idea of God. Who knows what God is like? Or if there is a God? I mean, if there was no God, do you really think the world would be any different than it is now?'

They window-shopped along Whyte Avenue before heading back to the mall, where they sat on the van's bumper waiting for Rod and Penny. A crow landed near by and pecked at an upturned McDonald's french-fry carton. When another crow landed close by, it cawed a navy blue, far deeper than the transparent tongue of sky blue he'd heard in the months since the duck hit him.

'My feet are killing me,' said Jocelyn. She took off her runners and pulled a bottle of suntan oil from her handbag. Her fingers glistened as she worked coconut oil between her toes. Her toenails were painted a sparkling bronze. 'I had a really good time today,' she said.

'Me too.'

'I was thinking maybe we could get together again soon. But I doubt it's going to be at another church function.' She crossed her legs, ran a slippery toe down Job's bare shin. The shine of oil on his leg.

'I'd like that.' At that moment, with the glow of the beer on him, he couldn't think of anyone he'd rather be with.

Across the parking lot, Penny slapped towards them in her flip-flops in the tight, rapid steps of a geisha. Some yards behind, Rod trotted after her. She didn't stop when she reached them, but went on flip-flopping towards the mall. 'I feel led to try the mall,' she called back to them.

Rod slowed when he reached Job and Jocelyn. 'She is so on fire for the Lord!' he said. 'She's, like, full of the Holy Spirit!' He jogged to catch up with Penny.

'She's full of something, all right,' said Jocelyn, standing.

Job and Jocelyn followed a few yards behind Rod and Penny. On entering the mall they lost them, as they were way-laid by a busload of Japanese tourists crushing their way across the corridor to the Kmart. When they found them again, Penny and Rod had parked themselves across from a haggard couple sitting side by side in the orange plastic chairs of the food court. They were in their late fifties and had, as Pastor Divine had referred to it, the ruffled look of the unemployed. Penny already had them both in her grip. She leaned over the table, tugging at the woman's sleeve with her left hand, and with her right she had hold of the man's thumb. Oddly, Job thought, neither the man or woman pulled away or even sat back. They both looked dazed, glassy-eyed. Were they drunk? But they watched Penny steadily, nodding occasionally. The woman went on chewing her beef jerky, replenishing the mouthful with her free hand as Job and Jocelyn walked up to them. 'Do you know what's keeping you from God?' Penny asked them.

'Yep. Bingo and masturbation,' said the man. The woman, still chewing, nodded.

Rod took a scenic drive home, pointing out an ostrich farm, the exotic birds lying on prairie grass, then a pasture of buf-faloes confined within fences like cows. Penny sat with Rod in the front seat. She drummed the van console like a restless child and twirled her hair. Slapped Rod's arm and his thigh playfully. Giggled.

Jocelyn and Job jostled in the back seat of the van, bumping arms. Job wished he'd worn longer shorts, and more support-ive underwear. His privates jiggled and shook loose of his

Stanfields. Limp penis down his sweaty thigh. He tugged the legs of his shorts down farther and tried to think of some tactful way to rearrange things.

They passed a man standing by his truck, peeing. A puddle in front of him. A pair of ducks flew low over the road. Patches of black, scorched earth dotted the fields where farmers had set fire to straw or slough grass. They passed a field where children ran screeching inside a hay devil that made mischief with the brome grass drying in neat rows. A warm spiralling column of air whipped clumps of hay into blue sky, tumbling the neat rows like a father messing his child's hair. The wind plucked caps from the children's heads, kept them floating in circles before dropping them back to the ground. The kids shrieked in delight, leapt into the hay-strewn air, tossed hay up themselves for the joy of watching it sweep circles above them.

Up ahead, a black horse stood by a fence, its huge penis dangling. Job found his own leaping to the sight, thinking of its own accord. Again. Jocelyn nudged Job's knee and grinned. She put a hand to his thigh and found the bulge in his shorts and massaged it through the fabric as they passed the horse by.

'That horse makes me think of a story I heard,' Rod said, raising his voice so he could be heard in the back. Jocelyn cleared her throat, removed her hand from Job's thigh to pick her handbag up from the floor. Job with his arms over his lap, withering.

'There was this guy, goes into emergency with a knife wound to the belly, from a bar fight. They strip him down and find the guy's got a salami duct-taped to his thigh.'

'Trying to impress the ladies?' said Jocelyn.

'More likely trying to impress the men,' said Rod.

'A gay bar?' said Penny.

'No. The guy was a cocky little bastard, trying to show he was packing the goods, you know. Faking it with that sausage. He was looking for a fight. Trying to prove himself.'

Job thought of something Jerry had once told him, about a man he'd seen in the bathroom, who'd stood two feet away from the urinal, showing off. 'He had more to piss with than I can fuck with,' Jerry had said. Job shifted in his seat, tugged at the hem of his shorts, wondered how much was enough.

Jocelyn rummaged in her handbag and brought out the coconut suntan oil. She rubbed her arms and her face, and smoothed it over her collarbone, the upper rounds of her breasts and into her cleavage. She squirted a dollop of oil on her right hand, worked it into her palm as she put the bottle back into the bag with her left. She pulled the leg of Job's shorts up and rubbed the oil into the head of his penis, bringing him to the point of coming within seconds. But he stopped her. He gripped her wrist and pulled her hand back. Blinked and gulped. Caught her eye and tried to smile. She took his hand and placed it at her crotch, widening her thighs to accommodate. When he didn't move his hand, she placed her left hand over his and moved it up and down, while together they watched the backs of Rod and Penny's heads. Her right hand was again at his penis, working him up. A feeling he wanted to hang on to forever.

Rod turned onto an oiled road, a soothing quiet after the rumble of gravel. But Job feared the quiet, wanted the rattle that had cloaked his backseat tryst. Then, behind them, the lights of a police car. Job yanked his hand from Jocelyn's lap and pulled his shorts down, his excitement withered, the guilt of it already on him. Rod pulled the van to a stop and went to sit in the police car to try to explain why he had been speeding.

The flames of gas-well flares licked up into the sky, giving the landscape an apocalyptic feel. Something was off, strange. It was as if someone had flicked a switch, turned off a light. The world looked that different. Job still heard the rumble of the van's engine as it sat idling in park. But sound brought no colour at all, no shape, no sensation to his hands or arms, no certainty, no knowing. The effects of the beer had worn off, and with it what faded colour and sensation he had still heard.

Job kept his hands in his own lap for the rest of the drive, and Jocelyn kept her hands in hers. They each looked out the window on their own side of the van. He avoided grazing Jocelyn's arm with his own and shifted away so that one buttock was nearly off the seat. A Skyhawk in front of them hit a robin. The bird rolled and fluttered in the air currents behind the car, clearly wounded but still trying to fly. It fell to the side of the road.

He had once parked his car behind the Value Drug Mart in Wetaskiwin late on a winter afternoon when the light was failing. When he came out again, darkness had fallen and the sodium lamp bolted to the side of the shop had come on. His truck was the only vehicle left in the parking lot, yet he didn't recognize it. The eerie light from the sodium lamp turned the red of his truck a metallic greenish grey. He had felt momentarily anxious, wondering what had become of his truck, sensing that this one, sitting where he'd parked his own, could not possibly be his. He felt a shift, as if reality were coming unstuck and falling away. The uncertainty stayed with him until he put the key in the truck door and it turned. He felt

211

that same shifting now, reality slipping from his grasp. Without the colours and shapes of sound, the certainty, the knowing, it was a world only half heard, muffled. It was the half-world seen under solar eclipse, the light turned tinny, a landscape of ash.

FIFTEEN

 Job sat by himself in the hired hand's cabin, listening to the vacuum cleaner. After chores he'd made a nightly habit of trying out different sounds and drinking different brands of beer, hunting for his colours, but the fantasia of shapes and light had disappeared altogether. This day, a snowy Saturday, he'd once again brought the vacuum cleaner over from the house, under the pretence of cleaning up, and had left it running for half an hour in the centre of the room. But as usual, the glass egg failed to appear in his hands.

With the vacuum still humming, Job watched the chickadees and pine grosbeaks peck at the bird feeder he'd built and placed outside the window. One of the chickadees was missing a leg. He moved closer to the window to get a better look. The birds, seeing only the reflection of the world outside, didn't rush away. He pressed his forehead, nose, cheeks and lips to the glass, then sat back to look at the imprint his face had left there. A clown's face.

The room lit up. Ruth was at the door, her neck bent to avoid hitting the top of her head on the door frame. 'I knocked but—'

Job clicked off the vacuum.

She closed the door and took off her coat, dripping melted snow on his freshly vacuumed floor. She held out her hands. 'Good to see you!'

Job felt himself wrapped in her long arms, his cheek cradled in her bosom. He held on too long. Ruth pulled away and patted his shoulder as she took a seat. She glanced at the cases of beer bottles stacked in the corner. 'We miss you at church,' she said. When he said nothing, she picked at her nails. She had once told Job that she'd never been comfortable evangelizing. She couldn't sell Tupperware to save her soul. 'Liv was at church a couple of weeks ago.'

'Liv?'

Ruth nodded. 'Jacob said you'd been feeling kind of down.'

'He ask you to talk to me?'

'I guess I should have stopped by before. But so much has been happening. So, what have you been up to?'

Job shrugged. He searched his mind for something to say. 'I'm sorry,' he said finally. 'I just don't feel much like talking these days.'

'Sure. I understand.' But she made no move to leave. 'Interesting news about Penny, eh?'

'What about Penny?'

'Jacob didn't tell you?' She laughed. 'I hear she's gotten pretty serious with that fellow that was here at the revival with Pastor Divine. Bob? Tod?'

'Rod?'

'I heard they were talking marriage.'

Job felt no surprise. No feeling at all. He watched through the window as the one-legged chickadee hopped and fed, expertly compensating for its handicap. It flew off and was replaced by another chickadee.

'Then there's Wade and me.'

'Wade?'

Ruth grinned. 'We're getting married. August 1. Got the church booked. Reception in the basement. That's why I stopped in. I wanted to let you know. And Wade wants to know if you'll be his best man. He doesn't see anything of Jerry any more. Debbie didn't like Wade coming over. Said he made her nervous, just sitting, watching, never talking. Personally I think that's his best attribute.'

'You and *Wade*?'

'It's thanks to you, really. Wade said he always thought you and I would get together. Once you were out of the picture, he asked me out. The rest is history. Anyway, you okay about being best man?'

'Sure. Happy to.' They sat in silence. Too long. 'You see anything of Will?' Job asked finally.

'At church. But I'm ashamed to say I avoid him. He's got so preachy. I understand Jacob's been counselling him. A good thing, I guess. But he's just so self-righteous. He keeps saying, "God's leading me here, God's leading me there."'

Job watched a blue jay fly up to the bird feeder, scattering the grosbeaks and chickadees. The jay hunkered down into the feeder made for much smaller birds, and pecked awkwardly for sunflower seeds. Job's father had hated jays. He called them thieves and shot them. Job had no feeling for them either way, though from habit he banged a fist against the glass, scaring the jay off. 'Have you ever thought what if there were no God?' he said. 'Do you think the world would be any different than it is now?'

Ruth said nothing for a minute. 'I can't talk to you about this kind of thing,' she said. 'My faith is just too precious to me.' She stood and put her coat back on. 'There's a karaoke dance at the hall tonight. Wade and I are going. Why don't you come with us?'

'To a dance? You don't dance.'

'Sure I dance. Just no one ever asked me.'

Job found himself standing on the stage of the Godsfinger community hall, wondering how he had got there. Mike in hand. The recipe box of song lyrics sat beside the tape machine on the table in front of him. A light from above blinded him. He could only see black below. Someone called out, 'Sing something, Job!', jarring him, sending a thump of blood through him. He couldn't think what to sing.

'Amazing Grace.' He knew the words by heart. But as soon as he'd had this thought he realized he couldn't remember anything past the first line. He picked up the recipe box of lyrics and ruffled through the A's. Called out into the darkened dance floor. '"Amazing Grace" is missing.' Someone called, 'Sing, Job!' Others joined in, sounded a chant: 'Sing, sing, sing, sing!' Their voices rang through the hall.

'I've forgotten,' cried Job. 'I don't know the words.' Then the thump of the audience beating their feet against the floor.

Job woke to a knock at the cabin door. It was Jacob, smiling. Job suspected Ruth had had a chat with him and that Jacob was worried for his soul. 'Wondered if you wanted to come along to church with us this morning. Will's coming. He said he wanted to give Bountiful Harvest a try.'

'I don't think so.'

Jacob turned and looked over the silos. The silos leaned so hard Job was sure they'd simply crash down one of these days. He'd warned Ben not to go near them. 'Listen, Job, did I do something to make you stop going to church? I mean, did this whole halfway-house thing turn you off? Or Jack Divine's church? I couldn't live with myself if I was responsible for you losing your faith.'

Job said nothing, thinking of the dream he'd woken to, of trying to sing 'Amazing Grace.' 'Actually, I was thinking it was about time I went back to church,' he said. 'I planned on going this morning. To Godsfinger.'

'Really. Well. That is good news.' But he didn't invite Job over for breakfast.

Job slid into the back pew where the late people sat, and waved when Ruth and Wade turned to smile at him from their pew near the front. Barbara Stubblefield rolled a skinny, crippled man in a wheelchair to the pew in front of Job, and parked the chair, pressing a foot to the brake. The man had almost no control over his limbs and couldn't talk, though he made his feelings known well enough. He grunted, low guttural sounds that sent sprays of saliva out in all directions. He tried to shake his head no, his head wobbling and bobbing on his weakened neck as if it were on wires, the head of a marionette.

Barbara patted his arm. 'Shush,' she hissed. 'Just give it a couple of minutes. If you don't like it, we'll go.'

When the man slapped his armrest, Barbara forced his hand to his lap. 'Enough!' Then, her voice softening, 'It'll be nice, you'll see. We have some fine singers. And Pastor Henschell's messages are always stimulating. And there's coffee and cake afterwards. Mrs. Schultz makes the best almond squares in the county.' A distinction that had once been Job's.

The man swung his head back and forth as best he could, and cried out. When this got no response from Barbara, he let his head lull to his chest, sighed a few wet sighs and sat quietly, his head shaking slightly, apparently capitulating to Barbara's will. Locked in place, it seemed there was little else he could do.

Barbara kept turning in her seat, watching the door of the sanctuary. Finally she waved in a woman in her mid-thirties holding the hand of a ten-year-old girl. The girl was over-dressed for church. Her hair was tied up in a red bow at the back. The woman had the pucker lines of a smoker and was wearing a navy dress, wrinkled and a decade out of date. A run in her nylons. They sat next to Barbara. 'Maybe you'd like to go to junior church with the rest of the children, Sherry,' Barbara said to the girl.

'No.'

'Have you ever been to junior church before?'

'Yes.'

'Did you like it?'

'No.'

Pastor Henschell greeted them. 'Our Bible reading today is from Romans 7. Verses 18 through 25. "I know that nothing good lives in me, that is, in my sinful nature. For I have the desire to do what is good, but I cannot carry it out. What a wretched man I am! Who will rescue me from this body of death?" Thanks be to God – through Jesus Christ our Lord!'

They sang 'Come, Humble Sinner.' 'Come, with your guilt

and fear oppressed, And make this last resolve.' Job mumbled along and looked around the sanctuary, saw it as if for the first time. Without the colours that had once accompanied the singing, there was nothing to stir the awe in him. Plain white walls. Simple crossed windows. The unpainted wood cross was the only decoration. A humble sanctuary, filled with farmers, uncomfortable in their Sunday best.

Barbara in her blue dress, studded with flowers. As she sang she held one hand to her heart and looked heavenward, her face flushed, eyes glistening. Job had seen her put on this performance a hundred times, and he'd always felt a cast of falseness to her. But this morning he saw she really believed the emotion she created in herself. She was also aware of the people watching her and was attempting to create the emotion of awe and love not only for herself but for the rest of the congregation. She was like a Victorian lady swooning over a surprise or indecent remark because she felt swooning was expected of her. Or like a teenaged girl, working herself up into a screaming fit on an amusement-park ride, even though she wasn't particularly frightened, but because the other girls would expect it of her and join in her screams. It was a performance, and though the emotions were manufactured, they were nevertheless real. He was moved despite himself, as if he'd sat through a formula Hollywood movie that he didn't much enjoy, but cried nevertheless at the ending. He felt manipulated.

The song ended and Barbara clutched her hands together across her chest, shaking them gently for emphasis, and, still staring upwards, murmured, 'Thank you, Jesus.'

Pastor Henschell stepped up to the mike. His wide shoulders in a new blue suit. His hair neatly trimmed. 'Today I'm going to talk to you about fence-breakers. We're all fence-breakers. Each of us has looked into that other field, stuck our heads through the wire, worked the wire up and down a little. Even if we didn't step right through the fence, we've all thought about it. Not one of us is without sin.'

Every beef farmer in that congregation had had a fence-breaker in their pasture at one time or another, a cow they'd had to yoke with two-by-fours nailed in a triangle around its neck, so it couldn't possibly get through the wire.

'Just like a farmer puts a yoke around a fence-breaker, God puts a yoke around us. The yoke is our conscience. That sick feeling when we've thought or done something we know we shouldn't have. That's the yoke that should stop us from stepping through the fence. But it doesn't always, does it? A little sin leads to bigger sin. We wiggle that wire a little more, a little more, and before we know it, we're through the fence!'

His voice rose in volume. Annie Carlson, seated across the aisle from Job, rummaged through her purse and pulled out a package of yellow foam earplugs. She rolled them between her fingers, and made a point of holding her arms up as she put them in so Pastor Henschell would take note. He didn't. 'So God uses another kind of yoke! He uses the consequences of our actions to teach us not to break through the fence of his laws. If you break through the fence, if you break God's laws, you will suffer the consequences! If you are an adulterer, you will get pregnant or suffer from venereal disease! Your marriage will suffer! Your spouse will leave you! Your sins will catch up with you. Maybe not right away, but years from now, the truth will come out. God will put that yoke on you!'

That did it. Job felt the familiar stab of guilt in his gut. It was just like Pastor Divine said: *Make use of guilt. It's the best tool in the evangelical toolbox. Everybody feels guilty about something. Make them feel the guilt in their bellies; fire it up! Promise them salvation, the final solution for guilt. Then you've got them.*

The man in the wheelchair cried 'Ma!' in a strangled voice. He rolled his head towards Barbara and, as he couldn't turn completely towards her, he let his head lull heavily on his left shoulder so he could get a good look at her. A bubble of saliva burst on his lips and for a moment Job thought he might spit at her.

They stood, sang 'Almost Persuaded.' 'Almost persuaded now to believe, Almost persuaded Christ to receive.' The man in the wheelchair cried out 'Ma!' again and again, flinging his head from side to side, slapping the armrests weakly. A fledgling pigeon, with undeveloped wings flapping and mouth open. Barbara shushed him, dabbed the saliva from his mouth and pulled his hands down into his lap. 'Quit it!' she hissed. 'Behave!' When he only shook his head harder and grunted so loudly that he competed with Mrs. Henschell's organ playing, Barbara said, 'All right, all right, we'll go!' She turned to the woman and girl sitting with her and said, 'I'm sorry, Carol, Sherry,' as she pressed a foot to the brake on the chair. Red-faced, and without looking at anyone in the congregation, she marched the chair down the aisle and out through the sanctuary doors.

'You can't hide sin from God!' Pastor Henschell called out.

Startled, Job looked around and realized the singing had come to an end and that he had sat with the rest of the congregation. Sherry pulled at the bow that held her hair back. Her mother slapped her hand down.

'He knows every single thing you've done! And he knows you're helpless. Sinning is in your nature! That's why you must

221

confess and ask the Lord's forgiveness, ask for the Lord's help in changing. A leopard can't change his spots, and under our own power we can't change either.'

Sherry piped up, 'Yes I can!'

'Shush!' said Carol.

'But I *can* change. I just decide to and then I do it.'

Pastor Henschell chuckled. 'Out of the mouths of babes,' he said. 'But we know better, don't we? Well, don't we?'

Harry shouted out, 'Yes!'

Carol grabbed her daughter by the shoulder, pulled her close and whispered in her ear. Then she withdrew her arm and sat up straight. Sherry slumped in her seat and kicked the underside of the pew ahead of her until Mrs. Schultz turned, and the girl's mother slapped Sherry's leg.

'We're not good enough,' said Pastor Henschell. 'We'll never be good enough. We're sinners. You can't help but sin. If there's any message I can get through to you this morning, it's that you aren't worth anything without the Lord. Let's pray.'

The congregation, all but Job and the little girl, bowed their heads as Mrs. Henschell softly played 'Why Do You Wait?' and Pastor Henschell prayed. 'I'm a sinner, Lord. I can't make it on my own. Here are my sins. Take my sins, Lord, and wash them clean.' He wrapped up the prayer with an invitation to those who wished to rededicate their lives to God to come forward, while the congregation kept their heads bowed and eyes closed.

Harry tottered forward as usual and lowered himself gingerly down onto the steps in front of the pulpit. Once kneeling, he placed both hands on his cane, bowed his head and wept. For several long minutes he was the only one who came forward.

Finally, just as Pastor Henschell wound down the prayer of rededication, Carol leapt to her feet and scurried down the aisle. She fell to her knees on the steps and stayed there. It was what Pastor Henschell had been waiting for. He stepped back and let her take her time. She clasped her hands together and, swaying slightly, prayed silently with her eyes open, looking upwards. Mrs. Henschell went on playing as the congregation waited on the Lord to move the woman back to her seat. Finally Carol trotted back down the aisle with her head down. A perplexed, embarrassed grin on her face.

Sherry stared at her feet and hissed, 'That was *so* embarrassing.'

'Amen,' said Pastor Henschell. 'The Spirit has moved in this room today. May he move in all our hearts as we go out into the world.'

Job jostled out of the sanctuary with the rest of the congregation and found himself in the coffee line out of habit. He returned a few smiles.

Then a hand on his shoulder. Pastor Henschell. 'Job, I've been meaning to talk to you. Come into my office, will you?'

Job followed him in and sat. So, Ruth had phoned Pastor Henschell as well. He wished for a cup of coffee to occupy his hands.

'I, ah, kept meaning to stop by the farm,' said Pastor Henschell. 'Sorry I didn't get around to it sooner. Jacob and Ruth have both told me you've been depressed.'

'I'm just tired.'

'Jacob says you've been eating meals out in the hired hand's cabin, rather than in the kitchen with them. He says you wouldn't eat at all if Lilith didn't fix you up plates, take them out to you.'

A lie, or a half lie. Lilith had brought Job out a plate once. No, twice. Job bought a few groceries in Leduc and made peanut-butter sandwiches on dry bread. He ate oranges and made coffee but couldn't summon the energy required to cook on the wood stove. 'I feel like I'm intruding on their family time,' he said.

'I understand from Ruth that you've been drinking. Beer.'

'I thought it might help—' he said, but stopped short.

'Alcohol never helps anything,' said Pastor Henschell. 'Then there's the matter of the vacuum cleaner.'

Job looked off to the side, at a poster of a sheepdog, hair covering its eyes, a passage from 2 Corinthians 5:7 written beneath it: *We live by faith, not by sight.* 'I like to keep things tidy, that's all,' he said.

'Lilith tells me she goes into the cabin to get the vacuum and finds you sitting there, listening to it.'

'I keep hoping—' What was he going to say? *I keep hoping the vacuum cleaner will put a glass egg in my hand?* 'I find it soothing,' he said. 'You know, like when mothers leave the vacuum cleaner running to help babies sleep.'

Pastor Henschell appeared relieved at this, an excuse he could choose to believe. 'Jacob was right,' he said. 'You're clearly depressed. The question is, Why? How's your walk with God? Are you praying daily?'

'No.'

'Reading your Bible?'

'No.'

'I know you haven't been going to church.' Pastor Henschell rubbed the oily patch at the side of his nose. 'Ruth said you were asking some disturbing questions. I understand you've been having some doubts.'

Job said nothing and looked past the pastor's head to the window.

'A Christian's walk with God can be completely sidelined by unconfessed sins. Have you got any outstanding sins you haven't taken to God?'

'I don't think so.'

'Are you masturbating?'

Job nodded.

Pastor Henschell grinned. 'Well, there you go! There's the problem. That sin is standing in the way between you and God. Take it to God and you'll be back on track.'

'I don't think masturbation is the problem.'

'Sure it is. I guarantee it. You feel guilty about it, right?'

'I guess.'

'Anything else I can help you with?' said Pastor Henschell.

Job shook his head.

'Well, I'm just glad I could help.'

Job fled the office and headed for the front door. But Steinke stopped him. Dithy Spitzer was at his side, one hand through his arm. 'Job! Glad to have you back. How about giving Dithy a ride home?' He patted Dithy's hand. 'I would, but I'm going over to the grandkids' for lunch. What say?'

'I'd like to, but I didn't get chores done this morning.'

'Come on, Job. It's on your way home.'

Caught. Job nodded and held out his arm for Dithy, though for what reason he wasn't sure. Her stride was as steady as his. He deposited her on the passenger side, praying that the truck wouldn't start, so he could foist her off onto someone else. But it turned over.

Job drove into Dithy's driveway, past the whirligigs pounded into the tops of fence posts that were cast higgledy-piggledy across the snow-covered lawn: ducks with wings that twirled, oil wells that pumped, men who sawed logs with crosscuts when the wind came up and, Herb's *pièce de résistance*, a model of Leonardo da Vinci's helicopter, made from a stack of tongue depressors mounted on a Lazy Susan.

Dithy insisted he come into the house. Cats slept on the kitchen table, on the counters and huddled in groups on the chairs. One jumped on Job's shoulder.

'Molly,' said Dithy. 'Go off and play. Leave us grown-ups alone.' She shooed another cat off a kitchen chair before offering it to Job. 'You don't drink coffee, do you? A nice boy like you wouldn't drink coffee. Have I told you I haven't had a cup of coffee in fifteen years?' She poured them both a cold cup of tea from a pot left on the table. When there was only enough to fill half her cup, she took the lid off the teapot, fished around for the tea bags and squeezed them into her cup. 'Got to savour every last drop of goodness,' she said.

Job took the cup and dabbed a cat hair off the cold surface before setting it down.

Dithy took a sip and made a face. 'This is cold. Why am I drinking cold tea? Doctor's right. I really am losing it.'

'Doctor?'

'In Ponoka. Psychiatrist. Got me on some pills. Says they should help. Said I should have been on them a long time ago.' She filled a kettle and plugged it in. She tapped her temple. 'Screw loose. I didn't feel crazy. Just a little unsettled, on account of God talking to me. I figure that would make anyone edgy.'

She shooed a cat off the table and picked up the teapot to rinse it out. 'You like that Liv, don't you? You don't have to answer. Anyone can see you like her.'

'I haven't seen her for quite a while.'

'Maybe she's working today. You know the co-op's open Sundays now? Sacrilege. Why not stop in at the café, get yourself a decent cup of coffee, maybe ask her out on a date? This stuff I make tastes like shit.'

'Liv's married. I couldn't ask her out.'

'I'm not so sure about that. I heard Darren's truck's been parked over at Rhonda Cooper's again.' She lifted a cat off a plate on the counter, blew cat hairs off the plate and emptied a package of cookies onto it. 'I bet you didn't know I dated your father. Before either of us were married, of course. I broke things off. Abe always had to be right. You couldn't tell him otherwise. It was almost like he figured he *couldn't* be wrong.'

'You got him pegged there.'

She set the plate of cookies on the table in front of him. 'I remember when he first gave up sheep and went into raising beef. God knows why, but he figured if he was raising beef he needed to look like a cowboy. Too many westerns, I guess. He got himself a cowboy hat and boots, and a western tie. Looked like a damn fool. Moseyed into the co-op café all dressed up like that. We all laughed. Called him a drugstore cowboy. He took it, didn't say a word. Next time I saw him he was dressed in a flannel shirt, work boots and cap like the rest of the beef farmers.'

Those cowboy boots and the hat were packed away in the attic. Job had once caught sight of his father standing in front of the mirror on his bedroom dresser wearing that cowboy hat, striking a pose. Job had quickly stepped away, and sat at the kitchen table as if he hadn't seen. His father had come out, clean-shaven and smelling of Irish Spring, but without the cowboy hat. 'He told me once that when he was a kid he wanted to go on the rodeo circuit, be a bronco star.'

227

'I don't suppose there's one of us here doing what we really want. When I was a girl I wanted to be a ballerina. Even bought myself shoes.' She ate a cookie and pulled a cat hair from her mouth. The kettle whistled.

'I've got to go,' said Job. 'Thanks for the tea.'

'Wait. Got something for you.'

She unplugged the kettle. Then disappeared down the hall-way and came back carrying one of Herb's whirligigs, a whale with a toothy grin that carried Jonah, a mast and sail on top. It was fitted with a foot-long spike jutting from the whale's belly, for mounting. A propeller on its nose cranked Jonah into waving his arms over his head.

'Herb was working on this the afternoon he died. Left it and his paints on the kitchen table. I planned on giving him hell for it. Then the police car drove up. You can see where he didn't get around to finishing the swim trunks.' Jonah's behind was bare wood. 'It's yours.' She pushed the whale into his hands, then followed Job as he carried it to his truck. 'Don't know why I hung on to that thing. I hate it. I hate all of them. Couldn't understand why he took this up as a hobby.' She flung an arm at the whirligigs whirring and clicking in the breeze around them. 'Look at it! I've let this whole place go to hell.' She held up the stained skirt of her dress as if for inspection. 'Why did I let this happen?'

Job parked in the yard in front of the cabin and eyed the poppy Abe had pinned to the visor so he wouldn't have to buy another the next Remembrance Day. Job had been driving the truck all that time and hadn't noticed the poppy. He guessed that was how it was with much of his life; he knew it so well he didn't see it. But was looking now.

He glanced down at Herb Spitzer's whale, grinning at him from the seat of the truck. Jonah's arms were raised and waving, as Job opened the door and the cold air caught the propeller on the whale's nose and fluttered the sail on the whale's tiny mast. The cheesy smile of the whale, the pathetic little man. Job lifted the whale and hurled it onto the snow in front of the cabin. He expected the whale to break apart, and Jonah and the mast to splinter off. But the whirligig landed whole and rocked to one side, the propeller on the whale's nose whirring, Jonah waving. He gave the whale a kick and marched off across the road, past the house and across the snowy fields. His anger dissipated as he reached the top of the coulee.

He dropped to the snow and hugged his knees as he looked down into the valley to the frozen lake below. The bawls of the cows behind Job echoed against the far coulee wall. Below, in the valley, a herd of mule deer. He counted ten, led by a large buck, as one by one they ran down the steep hill, across the ravine and up into the bush of the bank just below him, where they gathered for a moment before running back across the coulee again. The sound of them snorting, their hooves against frozen earth and snow. They were playing, enjoying the warmth of the winter sun. It was instinctive; they ran in response to their hearts quickening their blood. They didn't ask God if they could do it, or who they could do it with; they didn't think of God at all.

The little girl named Sherry at church that morning was right. He didn't need God in order to change. Or live. He'd spent his life trying to fulfill the wishes of others, to cater to Abe and Jacob's needs. But why couldn't he think of himself for a change? He could decide what he wanted, and do it. The thought was a revelation, a thrill running through him. But where to start? What did he want?

He ran back to the yard, excitement carrying him, a feeling as though he could hover over the prairies as he sometimes did in dreams, just by choosing to. He stopped short at the whale he'd tossed to the ground and picked it up, then carried it to a fence post along the driveway and, after hunting down a hammer, knocked the whale on its spike into the top of the fence post. Then he set the propeller spinning. The wide-eyed, bare-assed Jonah flung his arms in panic, hoping to be seen and rescued.

SIXTEEN

When Job knocked, the door flew open. Liv was dressed all in grey: grey sweatpants and sweatshirt with an oversized man's sweater over the top. She wore glasses, and didn't look herself. She'd been crying. 'Job,' she said. 'Thought you were Darren, forgetting his key again.' She turned her back to him and blew her nose into a wad of toilet paper. 'He didn't come home last night.'

A hummingbird made of stained glass hung by fishing line in the window, scattering sunlight on the hardwood floor. Job kept his eyes on the light on the floor, wondering if it had really been wise to stop in on Liv. Crystal had told him Liv was at home alone when he came into the café for breakfast, and had urged him to go over to see her. But now that he was here he was afraid of some embarrassing domestic scene. What if Darren suddenly came home and caught him here at this early hour? It wasn't nine o'clock.

'Come into the kitchen,' said Liv. 'I just made tea.'

A good-sized kitchen. A high ceiling. Walls painted periwinkle blue. Pots hung from the rack above the stove. Open shelves were stocked with gallon pickle jars filled with chickpeas, dried kidney beans, rice, flour and oats. Jars of spices labelled neatly in Liv's hand. The smell of cinnamon. A wooden table big enough to hold eight comfortably. 'Steinke had that sitting in his barn,' she said, rapping her knuckles on it. 'I offered him fifty bucks for it and he took it.' She took down blue teacups and saucers to match from a cupboard.

Job lifted a mayonnaise jar of brightly coloured buttons from the shelf. 'My mother kept a jar of buttons in the kitchen,' he said. 'She did her sewing on the kitchen table.' He put the jar back on the shelf as Liv handed him his tea.

'I just like the look of them,' she said. She unwound a fresh wad of toilet paper from the roll on the table and wiped her nose with it. 'They make me happy.'

Job remembered a jar of buttons from his childhood, in his grade one class. One button covered in rhinestone, shining within a jar of others made from horn, bone, jet and coloured plastic. He dumped the buttons on the floor to get at it, then played with it in the sunlight that came in from the window, sending shards of light across the ceiling, distracting the class. He wouldn't stop or hand over the button when the teacher told him to, and pulled his hand into a fist to protect it. As punishment, he stood outside in the sun, on the steps of the school, sending slivers of light over the wall. He had known what he wanted then, and had dumped the jar of buttons to get it. Made a fist to keep it. 'There's something about a jar of buttons,' he said, as he sat at the table with Liv.

'It's the abundance,' said Liv. 'The choice.'

'Mom put buttons of one kind on a safety pin, to keep them together. Jacob and I played with those safety pins full of buttons, making like they were electric razors. Dad would lift me onto the sink and Jacob would stand on the toilet, and all three of us would look into the mirror and shave. The buttons just rolled over my cheeks. I thought I was shaving. Being a man.'

They sat in silence for a while, sipping tea. Liv put her cup back in its saucer. 'So, you come for anything in particular?'

'Just a visit. Ruth said you came to church. Crystal said you'd been asking after me.'

'I thought at least you'd turn up at church, if not the café.'

She *had* been looking for him. There was a crack from the ceiling, then another and another, as if someone were walking overhead. 'That Jason?' said Job.

'No. He stayed overnight with one of his friends. That's likely the ghost.'

'You really think it is a ghost?'

'I don't know. Sometimes I go into a room and feel like I've just scared something off. When the furnace is on, I think I hear a voice. I've even called out a couple of times, thinking Darren or Jason had come home without me knowing, but no one was in the house with me.' She picked up the teapot and refilled both their cups. 'You ever see a ghost?'

'No.'

'But you believe in a spirit, or a soul, right?'

'Yeah, I guess.' Though, increasingly, he wasn't so sure.

Liv poured milk into her tea. 'I remember this one time I woke up outside myself. I was awake, but I was floating just above my chest. It only lasted a moment, but while it lasted, I had this sensation of expansion, as if I were air escaping a balloon. I would have been happy to stay like that and never go back to my body.'

Job sat forward, excitement pumping through him. 'Really? I've had that happen too,' he said. 'The feeling of expansion.' He thought of telling her about the colours he had heard, how he had lost himself to the singing of the church choir. How he missed the colours, the sensations in his hands, that feeling of losing himself, the certainty that God was real. But what if she didn't understand and thought him crazy, a religious nut? As he was sure he'd appeared when he'd been interviewed about the crop circle. 'It's like when you're driving down the road,' he said. 'And you get lost in the sky; you feel like you're a part of it. And then you come to an intersection and wake up and feel small.'

'Yes,' said Liv. 'Exactly.'

Job reached out and took Liv's hand, a rhinestone button in his grip. The thrill, the relief, of finally finding someone who understood this. He could justify himself. Something of his experience was hers too. He wasn't so different, after all. Not so strange.

She squeezed his hand and let go. 'Listen, you want to go for a walk?' she said. 'I don't want to be home when Darren gets back.'

'Sure.'

'Let me put some clothes on.'

Liv came downstairs dressed in a long black skirt with leggings underneath. A pair of black boots. A thick fisherman-knit sweater under a man's tweed jacket. Looking a little more like herself again. She had put contacts in, but she wasn't wearing makeup. Her face was still mottled red from crying. As they stepped from the house, she put on a black fedora over her sweep of red hair and pulled on black woollen gloves. 'What a glorious day,' she said.

Everything, from the roofs of the town to the trucks and cars and surrounding trees, was covered in hoarfrost, casting the world in a brightness that made Job squint. Hoarfrost iced the branches of the trees and drifted down in large flakes that caught the sunlight and glittered like the coloured Christmas lights on the tree outside the community hall.

They passed the hedge of caragana on Dithy Spitzer's fence-line. The whirligigs on her snowy lawn. A large red bow at her gate, a cheerful nod to the season. Chickadees kept up with their pace, flying from tree to tree just ahead of them. A small flock of blue jays flew up as they approached, not as a group, but individually and in a line, one after the other.

'Can I ask you something?' said Job.

'Sure.'

'Why do you stay with Darren? Why don't you just leave?'

'I don't know. I guess it's the practicality of it, for one thing. I can't just walk out the door. I don't know how I could arrange everything, find a place, move all my stuff out before he gets home from a haul. I'd have to come back for things – it's inevitable – and then I'd have to face him, and he'd get into one of his rages. I'd have to ask him for money. I've got Jason to think about. And he is going to the counsellor with me and Jason. He's making an effort.'

'But then he didn't come home last night.'

'Yeah, then he doesn't come home.'

They reached the Sunstrum farm gate. Job thought he should ask her in, but then where to entertain? The dinginess of the cabin. Instead, they stopped at the gate and turned back, heading for town.

'You get angry at this other person for doing this to you,' said Liv. 'But you get more angry at yourself for letting it happen. I mean, how did I go from that girl who hitchhiked by herself across the country to this woman who's afraid to drive a car to the grocery store? Why did I let that happen?'

Job glanced at her to see if she expected an answer, then tucked his chin back into his chest.

A pickup roared up behind them. 'Oh, shit,' said Liv. 'Speak of the devil.'

Darren stopped the truck and jumped out. The crunch of gravel and snow under his boots. 'What the hell are you doing with that freak!' he yelled, and turned to Job. 'You suddenly got a taste for women?'

When Liv turned from him and started walking away, he grabbed her arm. 'You sleeping with this pansy?' He waved a hand back at the Sunstrum farm. 'You stay at his place last night?'

'What do you care?' said Liv. 'Where were you last night, huh? If I'd gone over to Rhonda Cooper's would I have seen the truck parked there? Would I?'

Darren kicked gravel. 'None of your business where I was.'

'I'm your wife, for God's sake. When you don't come home at night it is my business.'

Job stepped back. Of course Liv was Darren's wife. What was he doing with her?

Darren pulled Liv to the truck. 'Come on. I'm not going to discuss this in front of this fairy.'

Liv yanked her arm out of Darren's grasp. 'I'm not going anywhere.'

'What is it? You got a thing for Princess?' He waved a hand at Job. 'You going to take off with him?'

'Of course not,' said Liv.

'What is it, Pretty Boy? You got a thing for my wife?' He pushed Job in the chest. Job stumbled back into the snow-filled

236

ditch and nearly lost his footing. Spittle was on the side of Darren's mouth as he sucked in air in his rage, as Abe had, as he beat unruly cows with a stick.

'Leave him alone,' said Liv. 'We were just taking a walk. We're just friends.'

'What do you need with friends?'

Liv stared at him a moment with her arms crossed, then started walking down the road. Job trotted to catch up to her.

'Wait!' said Darren. 'I brought you a present.' He rummaged in his truck and scrambled to catch up to Liv. He pulled a gift-wrapped box from a brown paper bag and held it out to her.

'I don't want it,' she said.

'Open it.'

'I said I don't want it.'

'Damn it! I went to all the trouble of buying it for you, you'll damn well open it.' He shoved the box into her arms, but she let it drop to the ground. A tinkle of broken glass.

'Jesus Christ,' Darren yelled. 'What the fuck's the matter with you?'

He picked up the box. Job was surprised to see tears in Darren's eyes, and his face screwed up in anguish. 'I got you that what-do-you-call-it, that chalice you wanted. The one in the antique store, with those Celtic designs all over it. The one you saw up in Edmonton. Remember?'

When Liv turned heel and kept walking, Job following behind, Darren ran back to the truck and threw the gift inside. He smacked the hood of the truck with the flat of his hand, then took a fist to it, pounding its metal. Liv, still walking, sobbed.

Darren jumped in the truck and drove up to them. 'Get in the truck,' he said.

'You should go home,' Job said to him. 'And cool down.'

Darren breathed in sharply and began to sob as he drove slowly along beside them. Again, it was a surprise to Job. He held back a nervous laugh and coughed into his hand.

'I'm trying,' said Darren. 'I'm doing like the counsellor says.'

'You didn't come home last night.'

Darren slapped the side of the truck. 'You don't know where I was. You don't know.' He stopped the truck and cried.

Liv held her hands up. 'Let's just go home,' she said and started around to the passenger side of the truck.

Job followed her. 'Maybe you should go to the café,' he said as she got in the truck. 'Or you could come down to the cabin. He seems so angry.'

'She's not going anywhere with you,' said Darren.

'He's just feeling guilty,' said Liv. 'He gets mad when he knows he's in the wrong. I'll just go with him. He'll settle down in a while. I'll be okay.'

Job watched them drive off, anger sliding away to loneliness as he let the hopefulness he'd felt earlier that morning drop like a button from an open hand.

SEVENTEEN

In the milky light of a late April afternoon, Job drove home from the Ponoka auction, pulling his stock trailer, eyeing the sundogs cupping each side of the sun like shining parentheses, wondering if they meant a change in the weather. For a few days in mid-April he'd breathed in the heady smell of thawing earth, before winter had slammed down again, bringing freezing cold and a skiff of snow. Early that morning he'd bundled up and driven two cows down to the auction and waited around most of the day for them to sell, drinking coffee in the bleachers and eating greasy burgers and mashed turnips at the auction café. Now he was returning home with an empty trailer and a cheque in his pocket, enough to get through another month.

Just before the driveway to the farm, the Chevy heavy-half ahead of him slowed. Its bumper sticker read *Keep honking. I'm reloading.* Jerry. Job could see the back of his head as he leaned across the seat. The passenger side opened and the white Samoyed jumped out. Jerry sat up, then, seeing Job in the mirror, sped off. The dog ran after the truck, barking and wagging its tail, as if this were a game.

Job honked the horn and put his foot to the gas to follow, but he was slowed by the trailer and Jerry was gone, lost in a spit of gravel. He turned the truck around and headed for home. When he stepped from the truck the dog was there, jumping up, leaving muddy paw prints on his jacket and jeans. 'Git!' Job yelled. 'Git! Get lost!'

The dog wagged its tail, leapt in the air, barked, chased itself in circles and went nowhere. Then lifted a leg to the truck tire. Job threw a poplar branch at it but hit the side of his truck instead, pockmarking the door. The dog retrieved the stick and dropped it, drool-soaked, at Job's feet. Its eyes were moist and grateful for the attention. Job kicked the branch and strode to the house, the dog leaping after him.

Lilith had the phone receiver in hand and was banging it against the table when Job entered the house. She wore a pink dressing gown and slippers and had curlers in her hair. She wasn't wearing makeup. Freckles covered her nose and forehead and gave her a vulnerable, girlish look. When she saw Job at the door, she dropped the phone and scurried into the bathroom, closing the door behind her. The phone bounced and dangled from its cord. On the table a greasy plate and cutlery left over from breakfast at Jacob's seat, a steaming cup of black coffee at Lilith's. From the bathroom the sound of water running.

Job picked up the phone and listened. When he heard nothing but the dial tone, he dialled Jerry's number and got him in two rings, the whirr of an air compressor charging up in the background. 'Jerry? Come pick up your dog, will you?'

Jerry shouted over the noise. 'Can't you keep it there for a while? Debbie's threatening to leave if I keep that mutt.'

He'd assumed Job would take the dog in without putting up much of a fuss. It was what everyone assumed. A memory came to mind, of Abe on the day he took Job and Jacob to a game park just east of Edmonton. There, in a large fenced compound, two male lions lounged, their heads on their paws, sleeping like house cats might on the living-room rug. Job raised his arms over his head to get some response from the closest lion, but it didn't stir; it merely opened one eye and watched Job lazily, without much curiosity. 'What's the matter with him?' said Job. 'Is he sick? He doesn't look sick.'

Abe shrugged.

Job threw a stone so that it landed just to the left of the lion's nose. The lion raised its head, but that was all. Job turned his back and was walking away from the cage when he heard the wire behind him shudder with a sudden impact. He jumped and found the lion on its hind legs, its fangs bared and claws extended through the mesh of the fence. His roar wasn't like that of a movie lion. It was more like a deep bark, and left Job weak in the knees. 'See? That's how you've got to act,' said Abe. 'You've got to roar a little, or people will walk all over you.'

His father had been right. People would just walk all over him if he didn't stand up for himself. 'Jerry, pick up your god-damned dog tonight or so help me I'll take a gun to it!' He slammed the phone down and raked a hand through his hair, then laughed a little to himself. He couldn't bring himself to kill a gopher, or even a chicken, much less take a gun to a dog. What had gotten into him? He should be fretting now, wrapped in regret, but he wasn't. He should call Jerry and apologize, but he knew he wouldn't.

Lilith called, her voice muffled through the bathroom door. 'Job?'

'Yes?'

'Jacob phoned. He wanted to know if you'd gotten back yet.' When Job didn't reply, she continued, 'He said the cattle were bellowing like they were out of water or something.'

'He didn't think to check them himself?'

'He had to get up to Edmonton. He was late for work.' After Jacob and the few volunteers who'd come down from Bountiful Harvest hadn't managed to get the halfway-house building to lockup before winter fell, Divine had given Jacob work at the church, as an assistant pastor. But the position was only temporary. Pastor Divine already had an associate pastor, a Pastor Wiley, who Job had seen at Bountiful Harvest but had never been introduced to. Job had helped out on the two weekends when they had hammered up the halfway-house structure, putting up the walls and the roof, and nailing on the shingles. But there were no windows or doors; it would be too cold to do any finishing work until spring thaw. Rod and Penny hadn't shown up for either of those work bees. Neither had Jocelyn. He heard she'd quit the church completely.

'Where's Ben?'

'He's in his room; he just got home from school.'

'I asked him to get the fire going in the tank heater this morning. Likely the cows are bawling because the tank's iced over and they can't drink.'

'You want me to get him?'

He listened a moment to the scuffle in Ben's bedroom, knowing Ben could hear every word they said. 'No. I'll get the fire going myself.' Ben hadn't grown up on a farm, and hadn't learned how to work. If Job hadn't moved fast enough, Abe had counted backwards from ten to zero. If he got to zero and Job hadn't got to work, or hadn't speeded up the work he was doing, Job got the strap. He had learned to work quickly, and through anything, even illness. If he complained, 'I'm not feeling well. I've got a stomach ache,' his father would ask him, 'Do you want an ass burn too?'

Job pushed open the door and tripped over Jerry's dog. He stumbled down the concrete steps and knocked his shin hard against the railing, then limped towards the cows, the dog leaping and pawing at him all the way.

Sure enough, Ben hadn't lit the fire in the tank heater that morning and a layer of ice covered the water in the stock tank, forcing the cows to go thirsty. He went to the barn for the coffee can that he filled with diesel. Into this he added a little gas, as the cold left the diesel thick and difficult to light. Too much gas and the mix would explode. He'd done that a few times and singed the hair on his hands. Once he'd singed his eyebrows and burned the edge of his toque.

He brought the can, an armload of wood and a box of Redbird matches back to the waterer. The heater was set inside the tank. It was watertight and made of cast iron. Job removed the lid, cleaned out the ashes and stacked the wood and kindling inside, then poured a sprinkling of the diesel and gas mix on it. He lit a match and dropped it into the heater. Flames whooshed up and died down to a steady flame. Job took off his mitts and warmed his hands over the flame before putting the lid back on. Then, from behind him, the squeak and crunch of footfalls on dry snow. Job turned. Ben. 'I was just getting to it,' he said.

'I bet.'

'I was.'

Job snorted and grabbed a stick from the ground and jammed it into the water surface to break up the ice.

'Let me do it,' said Ben. He yanked the stick from Job's hand, then, jamming it into the ice, snapped it in two.

'Can't you do anything right?' said Job. A thing Abe had said to him a time or two. He pulled the stick from the ice, tossed away the broken half and used the remainder like a pick. The dog leapt around, trying to get the stick from his hands. It jumped up on Job, nearly knocking him into the water tank. Job whirled around, rage like a gas flame, and smacked the dog across the jowls with the stick. It whimpered off to lick the blood from its snout as Job went back to breaking up the ice.

Ben picked up a handful of gravel from the road and sent it pinging against the steel side of the water tank. 'You're just like Dad,' he yelled, and started walking back up the road to the house. 'I thought you were different.'

Job leaned forward, hanging onto the rim of the water tank, listening to Ben's receding footsteps, spent rage leaving him shaky and ashamed of himself. Jerry's dog dropped a cow patty at his feet and looked up at him expectantly, as if the frozen shit were a frisbee, or a peace offering. When Job didn't pick it up, the dog lay down by the patty to chew and lick it.

Job woke that night to Jerry's dog yelping and howling at his door. Outside the cabin window, over the windrow of cotton-wood and willow, there was a glow in the sky. The halfway house.

Job dressed hurriedly and ran to the house to get Jacob. He had his keys in hand, as Lilith always locked the door, but he found the door unlocked and pushed his way in. He yelled for Jacob until he heard him scramble out of bed and then dialled the fire-hall number. He got Carlson, his sleepy voice. Job explained to Carlson, then after he hung up to Jacob, as his brother staggered into the room, belting his plaid robe over his belly. Then Job was outside, running over icy gravel, stomping through snow. Jerry's dog barked and leapt around him. The sparks from the fire drifted and snapped over the trees.

The walls of the halfway house were still standing, but the roof had caved in. The crackle of fire. Billows of black smoke into the night sky. Behind the building, in the glow from the fire, Ben stood in snow, wearing a navy toque and the Mackinaw he wore to do chores. The coffee can he and Job mixed gas and diesel in, to get the fire in the water heater going, sat at his feet. He bent down, picked up a rock from the moist earth and hurled it at the fire. Job remembered this, the compulsion to throw rocks into the fires he'd set as a boy. The frustration he felt; how it was released, along with the stone, into the fire.

Job took a few steps towards Ben, but when Ben saw him, he stepped back and disappeared into the night.

Jacob and Lilith ran up to the fire just as the pumper truck pulled to a halt on the road next to them. Bob Miller and Leslie Stewart, both grain farmers in the county, jumped from the truck and unravelled their hoses, as Arnie Carlson came over to talk to them. 'Anything in the way of explosives in there?' he said. 'Propane tanks? Anything that might blow up?'

'No,' said Jacob. 'We hadn't got it to lockup.'

'All right,' said Carlson. 'Get yourself back. A good fifty feet.'

Job, Jacob and Lilith stepped back into snow. The three of them watched as the firemen put the hoses to the fire at full blast, filling the air with white clouds of steam. When, in a matter of minutes, the flames had died down, they slowed the water pressure but went on dousing the fire.

Carlson walked over to them. 'Looks like you've got a case of arson,' he said. 'There wasn't the V-pattern burn on the wall you usually get from an electrical fire, no single point where the fire started. There's a big burn area like you get if diesel or gas was thrown on the wall, and it doesn't look like the building had been wired yet, in any case. And we found this.' He handed Jacob the coffee can, with the skim of diesel at the bottom. 'You should know I saw your boy lurking around back there, watching. Can you say for sure he was in bed when the fire started?'

'Do you have to report this?' said Jacob.

Carlson took off his hat and scratched his head. 'Well, in situations like this, where the building is on the parents' property, we usually leave it up to the discretion of the parents. But you've got to know, this likely won't be the last fire he starts. Is it the first?'

'I'll handle it,' said Jacob. He marched into the dark, past the fire, and came back some minutes later, dragging Ben by the elbow. Job watched as he pulled Ben across Correction Line Road and over to the house. Jacob was yanking off his belt as, together, they stumbled up the steps of the house. Lilith walked in after them.

The halfway house had been reduced to a pile of smoking rubble. A few charred boards stuck out of the ashes. The heads of nails melted off. All that was left was the concrete foundation. Job was watching the firemen roll up their hoses and put away their gear when he spotted a glow over the trees around the barnyard. The hired hand's cabin. He called to

246

Carlson and pointed, before heading to the cabin himself as the men drove the pumper truck over. Fire licked up the wall. Smoke drifted up from the roof and from between the shingles. Fire in the tiny attic. Jacob came out and watched with Job as Carlson quickly climbed a ladder and, with the pick on his axe, chopped a hole about two foot square in the roof. The other men manoeuvred the hose up to him, and he sent a spray into the hole. In moments the fire was out.

Light had crept into the sky. Across the yard, leaning against the barn, Ben watched the firemen check over the building to make sure the fire was doused. Likely he'd been there watching all along.

Carlson came over to Jacob and Job, taking off his hat. 'I think we better get the RCMP over here.'

'What would they do?' said Jacob. 'Do they lay charges?'

'It depends on the situation. They usually take the child away for questioning. Later they talk to the parents, to see what's behind the fire setting.'

'Can't you let me handle this?'

'I don't know, Jacob. Looks like you got a real problem on your hands.' He waved a hand at Ben. Ben slid back out of sight around the corner of the barn.

'I can deal with it.' Jacob lowered his voice. 'Please let me deal with it.'

Carlson held his hands up. 'All right. But he sets any more fires, I'm calling the RCMP.'

'It won't happen again.'

Job followed his brother to the barn, fearing he might hurt the boy. The rage on his face. A look Job remembered on his father, before Abe yanked the tail of an unruly cow, breaking it. 'Do you really have to strap him again?' said Job.

'His will has got to be broken. If he stays wilful, prideful, he'll be no use to anyone. He's thumbing his nose at my authority. What are Jack Divine and everyone in his church going to think of me now? Ben's ruined me.'

Ben was squatting against the wall of the barn, hugging himself, when they came on him. He didn't try to run away. Jacob yelled, 'What the hell are you doing?'

'Nothing.'

'Are you punishing me? Is that what you're doing? Just what is it you think I've done?'

A vacant look on Ben's face as if he were stunned. Job remembered this. He had never been sure what he was doing when he lit fires, but had been propelled to act, to light the fires, almost as if he were possessed by some outside force.

Jacob grabbed hold of Ben's arm, pulled him up and dragged him across the road and into the house. Job followed a few yards behind, watching as the pumper truck headed down the road.

Lilith was making coffee when Job walked in the house behind his brother. Sausage sizzled on the grill. On the counter a bowl of pancake batter. A Sunday breakfast. She was trying to make things all right. Emma had done this, thrown together an elaborate breakfast during harvest or calving seasons when Abe worked to exhaustion and his rage was quick to ignite.

Lilith took Job's arm as he started to follow Jacob and Ben into the boy's bedroom. 'What are you doing?' she said.

'I'm afraid he might hurt Ben.'

'God knows he deserves a strapping,' said Lilith. 'We can't let this go unpunished.'

Job pulled his arm away and headed to Ben's bedroom, but stopped in the hallway before the door. Jacob had pulled his

248

own pants down, and had knelt and lain over the edge of Ben's bed. Job was embarrassed to see his brother's bare behind. Ben stood a few steps behind Jacob, his father's belt like a heavy snake in his hands. The scene hardly seemed likely to Job, more like something he'd dreamed and then forgotten and was just now reminded of. But familiar. All those times he'd exposed his own behind at his father's bidding. The strap in his father's hands.

'All right, hit me!' Jacob said.

'I don't want to,' said Ben.

'I said, hit me!'

Ben didn't argue, but he didn't move either. Jacob peered at his son over his shoulder, his face tilted nearly upside down, giving him a peculiar, disorienting appearance, like the drawings that depicted a bald man whether held right side up or upside down. 'Hit me!' he said. 'Or so help me God, I'll whip you like you never been whipped.'

Ben hit his father once with the strap. He coughed, as if he might throw up.

'Again!' Jacob shouted.

Ben slapped the strap weakly against skin.

'Can't you do anything right?'

Job watched as Ben brought the belt up, sliced it through air and whacked his father's skin. And again. And again. Ben's face twisted into an angry mask.

Job's heart skipped a beat and raced along. He felt the mix of embarrassment and fascination at seeing something he shouldn't. He knew he should look away, or act, but he couldn't think what to do. He remembered a winter when he'd gone with his father to pick out and butcher a pig at a farm owned by Earl Chamberlain near Leduc. Job and his father, Earl and his two brothers and a hired hand had walked the pig out into the open and used their bodies as a fence. A circle of men in the snow, a pig in the centre, trying to keep a distance from them. Earl stuck the pig, stepping deftly, stealthily, into the circle and giving a quick jab with his knife to the throat. The pig's squeal was a pink burst of light. The men suddenly went into action as the pig tried to escape, lunging this way and that. Then, in resignation, it stood back in the centre of the circle of men with the blood forming a red pool in the snow at its feet. It was not stunned with a blow or shot in the head, a merciful killing, because his father wanted the brains for head cheese; he didn't want the meat bruised or shot through with lead.

Then, like now, Job felt sick to his stomach, but couldn't take his eyes from the dying beast. The pig, weakening, stumbled to its knees, then finally collapsed, the last of its lifeblood pumping from its neck as the men, seemingly oblivious to the pig's suffering, scuffed the snow with their feet and talked of the planting season to come, their hopes for the weather.

Job had thought his father and the other men were indifferent to the animal's suffering, that they possessed a kind of manly strength that Job couldn't summon. He'd been overtaken by a wave of nausea, stumbled away from the circle of men and leaned against the wall of a wooden granary to cough and spit into snow.

Now Job realized why his father and the men had talked of crops and of the weather as the pig bled at their feet. It was embarrassment. The violence of the pig's death was too intimate a thing to witness, so they had turned away from the horror and distracted themselves with small talk.

Job took a step back and hesitated in the hallway between

the bedroom and the bathroom door. He watched as Jacob struggled to get up. 'That's enough,' Jacob yelled. But Ben went on hitting. 'I said that's enough!' Jacob yanked the belt from Ben's hands and threw it to the floor. He pulled up his pants, his hands shaking. 'You see what I did there?' he said. 'I took on your sins. I took the pain of it, just like Jesus took the suffering of all our sins. He cleansed us with his blood, so we could have a relationship with God. You understand? I can't change you. No amount of whipping is ever going to change you. You can't change yourself, even if you wanted to. Only God can do that. The only way you're ever going to be saved is if you give yourself over to Jesus Christ, who died on the cross for you.'

Jacob knelt again and pulled Ben down beside him. 'Now you pray with me, pray for acceptance from Jesus Christ our Lord. Pray that he comes into your heart and changes you.'

At once it was clear to Job. He had once broken his 4-H steers, taught them to follow along on a rope. He got a steer used to the idea when it was still a calf, by tying it to a post with a short rope, so the calf would figure out it couldn't get away – once the calf was broke to the post, it had to be broke to lead. Job would pull the calf around using his own body weight. The trick was to convince the calf that he was stronger than it was. There was a magical point where submission happened, when the animal gave in. Like Abe before him, Jacob was doing exactly that. He was trying to break Ben's will, to master him, to bring Ben to submission, but not before God as he claimed. Jacob was trying to bring Ben to submission before himself. And it was working. Ben, sobbing, repeated what his father said and asked Jesus Christ into his heart. He asked to be born again. 'I pray in Jesus' name. Amen.'

EIGHTEEN

The Out-to-Lunch Café was empty when Job arrived. The breakfast rush was over and the morning coffee rush hadn't begun. Crystal was sitting at the counter drinking coffee and smoking a cigarette that she stubbed out as Job walked through the door. She wore a pair of green capri pants and a green blouse. Her blonde hair was piled on her head in an elaborate coiffure. Job guessed it was a wig.

'Job!' she said. 'Long time no see!'

He glanced back into the kitchen, hoping to see Liv at work.

'She's not on today. What can I get ya?'

'Breakfast, I guess.'

'Come talk to me while I make it. Want the usual?' The usual was The Big Man's Breakfast: three eggs, hash browns, sausage, bacon and a stack of pancakes. She led him into the kitchen and offered him a stool by the prep table.

The space looked like the kitchen in the community hall. Oversized sinks and a gas stove with eight burners, a walk-in

252

freezer and a fridge wide enough to store big boxes of cauliflower and bags of carrots. A rack of pots hung from the ceiling over a large library table that served as the food-preparation area. With a fork she pulled a couple of boiled sausages from a large covered plastic tray and tossed them on the grill before putting the tray back in the fridge. 'So, what're you up to? Still working on that halfway-house thing?'

'No. The building burned down last night.'

'Lord love a duck, Job. I'm sorry.'

'Yeah, well. It was Jacob's thing. I guess I never really wanted any part of it. The cabin burned too, though.' The sound of his voice, as if he were talking of someone else's fire. Job felt the urge to snuggle into Crystal, to bury his face in her bosom, like a toddler hiding in his mother's chest in a strange crowd.

'How the hell did that happen?' When Job didn't answer, she said, 'Never mind. I can guess. Liv was right when she said that boy was heading for trouble.'

'Don't say anything,' said Job. 'It would kill Jacob.'

'My lips are sealed,' said Crystal. 'Not that it'll make much difference. The news will make the rounds in no time. Who took the call at the firehouse? Carlson?'

'Yeah.'

Crystal pulled a handful of cooked and sliced potatoes from a plastic tub and threw them in a frying pan. 'So where you going to stay? Is there room in the house?'

Job shook his head. He could sleep on the couch, or on the living-room floor, or in the attic with the mice and bats. But he didn't want to witness the family disputes that were sure to follow this day. 'I guess I'll have to fix up the cabin.'

'Is it salvageable?'

'I don't know. There's a hole in the roof. I didn't really give it a good look. I just left.' He'd backed away from Ben's bedroom and his brother kneeling with his son, bringing him to the Lord. Jacob's belt on the floor beside them. Lilith had asked if he wanted breakfast, as if everything were all right, as if Ben hadn't burned two buildings in the night. Job had said no, and got in his truck and drove to town.

'You going to rebuild that halfway house?'

'I doubt Jacob could get the support for it now.' He stared up at a clock made out of an old fry pan that hung on the wall, and listened to his breakfast sizzle.

'Liv's been wondering where you got to,' said Crystal. 'I told her she should just go ahead and give you a call, but I guess she never did.'

'No.'

Crystal broke a couple of eggs onto the grill. 'You know Darren's crazy enough to believe his father's still haunting him?'

'Liv said she's seen the ghost.'

'I've got no doubts his dad is haunting him. But not in the way he thinks. I remember when his dad beat him nearly to death and landed him in the hospital when he was just sixteen. That's when he took off and never visited 'til his old man was dead. He was scared of him, and never got over being scared. When men get haunted like that they'll do anything to make sure nobody's got that kind of power over them again.'

She served up his breakfast and watched him while he ate. 'This hair of yours. It's almost white.' She pulled at a ringlet near his ear. 'Those curls natural?'

'Yeah. I know I should get a haircut. Just haven't got around to it.' A thing he often said when farmers taunted him about his girlish curls.

'No! Don't get it cut!' said Crystal. 'Every time I see you I want to run my fingers through that hair, like I used to do with my boys, you know? No. You want to find yourself a woman, you hang on to that hair. You know what Liv said? She said you make her think of a Christmas-card angel. She thinks you're shy. Not like the other guys who come in here. Nothing like Darren. She likes you, you know. Don't think I don't notice how she gives you the biggest piece of pie. The way she talked, I thought you two were getting together.'

'She went back to Darren.'

Crystal refilled his coffee cup and her own. A smudge of coral lipstick on the rim. 'It took me four tries to leave my husband,' she said. 'I'd get myself all settled into a new place and he'd come begging and pleading and making promises, bringing me flowers, and I'd fall for it, 'cause I loved him. It's like giving up cigarettes. You got to give it a few tries before you kick the weed.'

A bell tinkled as the door to the café opened. Crystal glanced over the high counter that separated the kitchen from the rest of the place. 'Huh,' she said. 'Ed.'

'Ed?'

'Why don't you take your plate out there, sit with him.'

'I don't think so.'

She shooed him with her hands. 'Go on. I'll just nuke myself up a muffin and join you.'

Ed sat in Job's usual window seat wearing a cap that read *Specialized Stud Service*. Job had heard Ed had found himself an apartment and got a job packaging orders in a stud-and-bolt factory on the outskirts of Edmonton. He was reading an article in *Bowhunting Deer* entitled 'Grunts, Bleats & Blats! New Calling Tactics That Make Bucks Hunt You.'

'Haven't seen you for ages,' Job said. He put his plate and coffee cup on the table and sat.

Ed closed the magazine. 'I came down to make sure Liv was all right. She left a call on my answering machine. Sounded really upset. Then I couldn't reach her. You seen her? Nobody answered the door at her place. Darren's truck wasn't there. It's probably nothing. She just takes off with Jason now and again. Still, I thought I better check. I figured Crystal might know where she is.'

'She'll be out in a minute.'

'Great.' He went back to reading his magazine as if Job weren't there.

'You hunt?' said Job, pointing at the magazine.

'Used to. With my dad.'

'Huh.'

'What do you mean "Huh"? You don't think fags hunt? I'll have to stick to making almond squares, then, like yourself. Maybe I'll give out jars of jam at Christmas.'

'I didn't mean that.'

'What did you mean?'

'I didn't mean anything.'

Crystal brought out her mug of coffee and sat with them. She winked at Ed. 'Nice to see you boys getting along,' she said.

'You know where Liv is? I got a call from her yesterday. She sounded upset.'

Crystal squeezed a creamer into her coffee. 'Yeah, she came in yesterday afternoon asking for a few days off. She and Jason took the Greyhound to Salmon Arm last night. I guess she and Darren had another scene. She had to get away for a while.' She spooned sugar into her coffee and stirred. 'Did Job tell you he had a fire at his place last night?'

'No.'

'Burned down the halfway house and part of the cabin.'

'Really? That's crappy. Anybody hurt? Lose any livestock?'

'No.'

'How'd it start?'

'They don't know,' said Crystal. 'Thing is, Job's got no place to stay.'

'Oh?'

'Liv tells me you've got a spare bedroom. I understand she's stayed with you from time to time.'

'When she had to get away from Darren. I'm really not set up for guests.'

'Don't you think you could put Job up for a couple of nights? Until he gets things straightened out for himself?'

'That's okay,' said Job. 'Really.'

'You afraid of what people would think?' said Ed. 'You staying with me?'

Job said nothing. But yes, he was.

'There'd be a hell of a lot more talk if you parked your truck at my place,' said Crystal. 'But if you want to do that, it's fine by me.'

'No, really, I'll be okay.' Job waved a hand to show it was all right but saw that his hand was shaking and grabbed hold of his coffee cup, as though it would anchor him to the table.

'You're looking pretty shaken up,' said Crystal. 'Might do you some good to get away. Get Jacob to look after the farm for a few days.'

Job bit an indentation into his lip to stop the tears, self-pity drifting into his gullet like indigestion. Where else could he go? 'Yeah, maybe,' he said.

Ed was holding an armful of shirts and pants when he opened the door for Job. He bent down to retrieve scattered socks as Job came in. 'I wasn't expecting anyone,' he said. A tabby wound itself around Job's legs as Ed disappeared into the bathroom with the clothes. Ed came out a moment later cupping his hands. 'I don't have much to offer you. Coffee?'

'No. I'm fine.' Job stared down at a cat toy near the door. A string hanging from a hook on a stick. At the end of the string, a bell encased in clear plastic.

'I haven't had a chance to do any shopping this week,' said Ed. 'I've got nothing in the fridge for supper. We could go out and get a bite to eat.'

'Yeah, okay.'

'You got a place in mind?'

'We could go to the Strathcona.' Thinking there might have been something special in the beer in the pub to bring on the colours he hadn't been able to find since.

Ed looked surprised. 'The pub? Sure. They don't have much of a menu.'

'They have those two-wiener hot dogs.'

'Hot dogs it is then.'

They took seats at the back of the dark pub. Job ordered a draft to drink with his hot dog, then ordered another, then another when not even a hint of colour appeared. 'You always drink like that?' asked Ed.

'No.'

'You got to take it easy. You don't drink much, it'll hit you fast.'

'I'm okay.' He finished off his glass and listened to his father's watch, but he saw no metallic dot there.

'Watch stop?' said Ed.

'No.' Neither the hum of voices in the pub nor the noise that tumbled in from outside when anyone opened the door produced flitting colours or shapes in his hand. Nothing at all. He waved a waitress over, ordered another draft for himself and asked Ed if he wanted another too. Ed shook his head. 'So Liv stays at your place sometimes?' Job asked.

'Only occasionally,' said Ed. 'When things get really bad at home.'

'She ever talk about me?'

'Yeah, from time to time.'

'You think she's going to stick it out with Darren?'

'You better ask her that yourself,' said Ed. He sipped his beer. 'You see anything of Will?'

'No.'

'I phoned him,' said Ed. 'But he wouldn't answer my calls. A couple of times I went over to the farm, but Barbara wouldn't let me in the house. I hung out at the café for a while, in case he turned up. Talked to Ruth a few times. She said Barbara and Jacob had Will on a pretty tight leash. Doing like that nutcase preacher said, telling Will what to watch on TV, what to read, where to go, watching him night and day. Crazy.' Ed pulled out a pack of gum and folded a stick before putting it in his mouth. 'Jacob talk at all about him?'

'I don't talk to Jacob much.'

'He's right on the farm with you.'

'We kind of avoid each other.'

'Where do you eat meals?'

'I heat a kettle on the wood stove. Eat a lot of sandwiches.'

'Doesn't sound like much of a life. I don't know why you put up with that situation.'

'My dad pretty much trained me to put up with anything,' he said, and was surprised at himself. He listened to himself talk to hear what he'd say, as if he were listening to someone else. 'All my dad ever cared about was what other people were going to think, what people at church were going to think. Now I don't know how to do anything. I've spent all this time feeling guilty about things I've got no reason to feel guilty about. For God's sake, everyone masturbates.'

Ed, caught off guard, scratched his chin.

Job waved a hand. 'I'm sorry. It's just like what Liv said to me. You get angry at these people for doing these things to you. But really I'm pissed with myself, for believing it all.'

'Yeah, well, it's that whole Santa Claus thing, isn't it?' said Ed. 'You find out Santa was your dad with a fake beard on. You get mad at Dad for lying to you, but then you get over it, and you grow up. Then you bullshit your kids into believing in Santa Claus.'

'I never believed in Santa Claus,' said Job.

'Never?'

'Dad wouldn't let us believe. He said if we could stop believing in Santa Claus, we could stop believing in God. He didn't want to set a precedent.'

Ed laughed, making Job, for the moment, feel capable of easy banter. 'I think the thing that pisses me off most is that I spent all that time scared shitless,' said Job. 'When I could have been living.'

'Yeah, I know what you mean. I was just like that, scared

shitless. Scared of my dad, mostly. What he'd think. We were so close. Then, in my early twenties, I couldn't stand it any more and decided not to hide it. I told my folks I was gay. Mom went to the therapist with me. Now when I talk to her about it she says, "I don't care," so I know she still does. But when I told my granddad he said, "I can still give you a hug like I always did, can't I?" And that was it. With him, nothing's changed. With Mom, it's a federal case.'

'How about your dad?'

'My dad? He won't talk to me. I phone ahead and visit Mom when Dad's down at the Legion.'

'You said you went hunting with him.'

'That was then. I spent all those years trying to prove myself to that old fart. To get his approval. Finally I just gave up trying.'

The waitress brought Job's beer. He sipped from it and licked foam off his lips. 'I could never do anything right for my father either,' he said. 'One time I nearly drowned in grain trying to get his approval.'

When he was eleven he had clammered onto the mound of barley rising in the old wooden granary as his father manned the auger that shot the grain through a hole in the granary roof. His feet sank six inches into barley. His back itched and his chest ached from grain dust, but Job shovelled away the cone of barley, which had dropped from the auger, to all four corners of the granary until he was crouching beneath the roof. He could have escaped through the door at the apex of the granary roof, but he didn't, trying to prove his worth to his father, trying to please him, trying to make him see he was a good worker. That he was farmer material, the highest praise his father would allow.

'I was struggling to keep the pile of grain away from the auger's spout so grain wouldn't jam it,' he said. 'And I found myself trapped in the back of the granary, with my shoulders against the roof. I couldn't reach the door. Dad couldn't hear me shouting because of the noise of the auger.'

'So, you got out, obviously,' said Ed.

'Dad cut the motor finally and dragged me out of there. He slapped my back as I spit black and called Mom out to bring me water, and I didn't have to do chores that night because Mom wouldn't let me. But he never apologized or said anything about it. He just read his newspaper in the living room after supper as I coughed and hacked in the kitchen. Things were different after that, though. He started talking like I'd be the one to take over the farm, and not Jacob.'

The waitress came by to take away the glasses and plates and left the tray with the bill. Job, feeling generous, slapped his credit card onto the tray. As they waited for the waitress to return, Ed said, 'Something I was wondering. Will ever tell you I made that crop circle?'

'*You* made it?'

'Sure. I mean, it was Will and me. My idea. I thought I'd give you that sign you were looking for. To go out with Debbie Biggs. Took us less than an hour. We made it just like that professor guy said, the one in the interview with you. I thought you'd stumble on it when you were checking the cows. I never thought Carlson would spot it, or phone the television station.'

'Will never said anything. He let everybody think I was nuts.'

'Hey, you were the one who went on TV holding a dead duck and said all that stuff about demons.' He slapped Job's arm and laughed. 'Come on,' he said. 'It's funny.'

Job nodded grudgingly.

'Listen, Job. I didn't mean to make you feel unwelcome this morning. You want to stay a couple of days, or even a week if you need to, you're welcome.'

The waitress came back with Job's card and receipt. As Job stood to leave, a whirl of vertigo came over him. He sat. 'I think I drank too much.'

'I'll give you a hand out.'

On the way out of the restaurant, Ed held him up from behind, holding both his hands as if they were dancing the schottische. 'Why'd you park so far away?' said Job. 'Everyone's staring.'

'Nobody's staring.'

But people on the street were staring. A man in a plaid shirt and John Deere cap did a double take as he approached. 'Want to take a picture?' said Ed. The man shook his head and walked on.

'How much farther?'

'Not far.'

'Don't hold on so tight.'

'All right. All right.'

A pickup slowed and drove alongside them. Four farm boys still in their teens, two in the cab and two riding in the back, leaning on a bale of hay. One of the boys in the back banged a yellow plastic shepherd's crook against the truck box. 'Hey, look at this, guys,' he said. 'Lover boys dancing on the street.'

'Ignore them,' said Ed. 'Don't make eye contact.'

'Whoo-hoo, pretty boy!' The driver blasted the horn. 'Hey, I'm talking to you!'

The kid in the back reached out with the shepherd's crook, hooked Job behind the knees and brought him stumbling to the sidewalk. Ed grabbed hold of the crook and yanked it out of the kid's hand. 'You looking for a piece of this?' he yelled. He smacked the side of the truck with it, leaving a dent.

'Jesus,' said the driver. 'This guy's nuts.'

'You don't know the half of it!' Ed took a stride towards the truck. The driver put his foot to the gas and sped away. He yelled, 'Faggots!'

'Shit,' said Ed. He threw the yellow crook after the truck and it landed in the middle of the road. The car behind honked. Ed leaned down and took Job's arm to help him up.

But Job pushed him off, pulled himself erect. 'Leave me alone!' he said.

Ed took his arm and tried to lead him to his truck. 'Come on.'

'Get away from me!'

'This is ridiculous. Blame those assholes, not me.'

Job leaned against a power pole, waiting for the dizziness to pass, and watched a man in a wheelchair whiz by, pulled by two huskies. 'I'm going to be sick,' he said.

'Well, puke here then, not in my truck.'

'I want to use a washroom.'

'Why didn't you use it when we were in the pub?'

'I didn't think I was going to be sick then.'

Ed put his shoulder under Job's arm, staggered with him into a nearby café and past the tables to the men's washroom, a single toilet in a room with a mirror and sink. Ed waited outside.

Job spit into the toilet, but now that he was here, he couldn't vomit. He rinsed his mouth out with a handful of water and washed his face. Then stared at his own reflection, thinking of the boys with the shepherd's crook, the rage in their faces.

What Crystal had said about Darren getting beaten up by his father, how it made him act the way he did. How Jason was acting out now. On it went from one generation to the next. If Job had had a son at the age Jacob had, he likely would have used the strap, or even beaten a boy in rage, just as Abe had beaten him. He thought of how he'd acted with Ben the day before, as he broke up the ice in the water tank. The things he'd said and the rage that had burst out of him wasn't really him. It was Abe. And not Abe. It was Abe's father, and who knew who else's before him, on down the line. But how could he escape it? Job, overcome by another wave of nausea, sat on the covered toilet and stared at the sign above the doorknob that read *This doorknob is a bit sticky. It will open with fiddling.*

NINETEEN

When Job pulled the truck into the farm and got out, Jerry's dog leapt up and left muddy paw prints down the thigh of his jeans. He kicked the dog away and stood a moment, looking over the yard. There were no vehicles there; no one was home. He'd make himself coffee to warm up with, and nuke a beef sandwich in the microwave, and maybe spend a half-hour in the house alone. But he was surprised by a compulsion to knock. He felt like a trespasser, stepping inside. It smelled of Old Spice, the scent of his dad on Sundays. A fry pan sat on the stove, still coated with white grease from bacon cooked that morning. A cup and greasy plate sat on the table and a fork lay on the floor. As if his father had just dressed and gone to church, and left his breakfast dishes for Job to clean up. Job ripped off a sheet of paper towel and wiped the fry pan clean, then set it back on the stove. He washed the few dishes in the sink, running a thumb over them to make them squeak, hoping for a sheen of pastels. None appeared. He wiped the table free of crumbs and swept the floor. Then stopped himself and sat at the kitchen table. This had never been his house; it had never stopped being his father's house. The place seemed shrunken in, stifling. A playhouse for children. He couldn't imagine having lived here with his parents and Jacob. Where was the room?

Job put the broom back in the hall cupboard and took out the vacuum cleaner to suck up the crumbs from beneath the table, then left it running in the middle of the kitchen. He leaned back into one of his mother's metal-legged chairs with his hands in his lap, fingers locked, and listened. But felt no glass egg in his hands.

The dog barked and scratched at the front door, and Job felt a blast of cold air at his neck. Lilith was at the door with her back to him, a finger pointing at the dog. 'Sit!' she ordered. 'Stay!' The dog sat and stayed. When Lilith turned, she looked from the vacuum to Job. 'What are you doing?' she said. She closed the door as Job yanked the plug from the vacuum and tugged the cord to let it snake back into the housing. Lilith covered her mouth with her hand when he looked up.

'Just a little tidy-up,' he said. He walked the vacuum into the hall closet.

'I would have done it. I keep a good house.'

'I never said you didn't.'

Lilith, still in her coat, picked up a washcloth and turned her back to Job to scrub the kitchen counter, though it was wiped clean. Job scratched his scalp and felt the confusion of dealing with this woman: a pressure at the back of his skull, two hands pressing a melon.

'Well, don't just sit there!' she said finally, with her hand over her mouth. 'You're as bad as that Wade friend of yours,

267

just sitting, staring, like you know better. Like you're one up on everyone else in the room. So superior.'

A surprise, to be thought of this way. He liked it. Wade must like it as well. What was Wade without his silence? If he spoke he was only a poorly dressed parts salesman.

Job stood and put a hand on Lilith's shoulder, and she started to cry. Job remembered this. Will's hand on his shoulder, the smallest kindness bringing on tears. 'What's the matter, Lilith?' he said.

She ran an index finger under her nose and wiped the finger on her coat. 'Somebody at Bountiful Harvest found out Ben started the fire. Pastor Divine came down yesterday to say they were cutting support for the project. Volunteers didn't want to give their time if Ben was just going to burn everything down. He said if Jacob couldn't control his own son, then he couldn't possibly have the leadership qualities it would take to run the halfway house. Jack fired him. What are we going to do?'

Job watched a drowsy fly land in the condensation that fogged the kitchen window. As it struggled to escape the dampness, it ended up with both wings stuck to the water, sliding down the glass.

'I was always afraid Ben was going to do something like that while Jacob had a church. He nearly burned our house down once, and set the yard on fire. Jacob had to tell the board he'd had an accident with the barbecue. Then I go and duct-tape that awful kid's head to his desk.' She tapped her chest. 'I'm the reason we had to leave.'

Lilith cried, blew her nose, cried some more. 'I think sometimes I did it to get Jacob's attention. Isn't that childish? I was just so tired I couldn't think straight. Any time I tried to talk about how much I hated never having time to ourselves or a day off, he just said the same thing, over and over. "We've all got to make sacrifices for God's work." And he was right. We do. I was wrong to complain. It's just I feel like I can't ever do enough. God is never going to be happy, is he?'

The fly slid farther down the windowpane until it dropped to the sill. Job watched as it struggled to right itself. When it did, he pressed it flat with his thumb.

Lilith yanked a sheet of paper towel from the roll and blew loudly. 'Then this morning I had an appointment to get my dentures fitted and they kept them, to do some work on them.' She let her hand drop from her mouth. She wasn't wearing her dentures. She sobbed, her voice rising to a squeak. 'And then this policeman stopped me for speeding and I didn't have any teeth in, so I didn't say anything, I just handed him my driver's licence. Then I panicked and drove off.'

'You drove off?' Job laughed.

'With him standing there, holding my driver's licence.'

Lilith laughed and cried, a combination that came out like hiccups. A relief, to see her laugh. It made everything seem manageable. For a moment. The dog barked and scraped a paw on the door. 'Where's Jacob?'

'I don't know.'

'Are the cows fed?'

'They were bawling this morning when I left.'

'I guess I should get out there, feed them. Make sure they've got water.' He went to the hallway and sat on the bench to put on his boots.

She tossed the paper towel into the white, square garbage can in the hall. 'Where are you going to sleep tonight? You want to have supper with us?'

'I'm not hungry. I'll sleep in the cabin.'

'It's got a hole in the roof.'

'I'll make do.'

As Job dropped a round bale into the feeder, Jacob drove the station wagon into the yard. He was walking across the road as Job parked the tractor. 'Schultz phoned yesterday,' he said. 'He said he thought the bull was out, down by the lake.'

'You didn't go check?'

When Jacob shrugged and looked away, Job headed to the pumphouse for the hip waders. He'd take the tractor down. Likely the bull was in the lake. Jacob shouted after him. 'Want help?'

'No.'

The bull was dead, its body floating between the ice and the lake's shore, its head below water and only its massive back protruding. Job hooked one end of a chain to the draw-bar of the tractor and dragged the other end with him into the icy water. Hip waders kept the water out, but the cold was sharp enough to take his breath away. He grasped the bull by the tail and pulled it closer to shore, then plunged a hand down into the cold water to slide the chain around the animal's leg. As he was walking back to the tractor, he remembered the terror in the beast's eyes when he got into the water with it the fall before, and the feel of its monstrous head leaning into Job's calming scratch. He wondered at its final moments.

Job cranked up the heat in the tractor to warm himself, sped up the engine and pulled the body of the bull up the muddy bank and then up the road. He'd call the rendering truck and have the body taken away.

The drab yellow prairie stretched out to meet a grey sky. There wasn't yet a hint of green in that landscape. The only colour was the orange of the snow fences in the fields along the roads. Trees were still leafless and wouldn't green out until the beginning of the next month, and even then it could freeze or snow right into June. Just the year before, Godsfinger had had a dump of snow in May that was so heavy it broke the Sunstrums' mayflower tree – already in bloom – in two. He'd taken a chainsaw to it, and it was now a stack of firewood by the cabin.

Job had dragged the body of the bull to the yard before he noticed he was shaking. Cold perhaps. Or nerves humming with fatigue. He wanted a hot shower, and a bed and a place that was familiar, his own.

He opened the door to the hired hand's cabin and startled a pigeon. It flew up through the hole in the roof; under the gap Carlson had opened in the attic, the gyproc had become soaked and caved in, leaving an open patch of sky above Job's head. There were pigeon droppings on the floor, but other than the hole and the smell of smoke, there was little evidence of the fire inside the cabin. He brought in wood and kindling and newspaper from the piles stacked in the barn and got a fire roaring in the stove. Then he crossed the road to the house.

Jacob was in the living room, sitting in Abe's green easy chair with his feet up, reading a paper. 'The bull's dead,' said Job. When Jacob didn't turn to look at him and kept reading as if he hadn't heard, Job said, 'You might have saved him, if you'd checked.' Jacob snapped the newspaper and turned a page.

Job found extra sleeping bags and his mother's blow-dryer in the attic of the house and hauled them out to the cabin. He swept away bits of charcoal and pigeon droppings and arranged the sleeping bags on his bed. Then he plugged in his mother's blow-dryer, tucked himself into layers of flannel and

271

switched the blow-dryer on. It ran for a moment, but it didn't produce a cylinder in his hands. Then it sparked, sent up a plume of smoke and died.

He unplugged the blow-dryer and lay shivering, looking up at a star-studded evening sky through the hole in the roof. It seemed foolish, now, to sleep in the cabin. But he didn't want to face Jacob, to ask him if he could sleep on the living-room floor as they watched the late-evening news. He felt profoundly sorry for himself and gave in to the urge that had followed him for much of the day, and cried.

He woke deep in the night to a chorus of coyotes howling. Above him, through the hole in the roof, northern lights pulsed in hues that were at once saturated and iced, like lime and raspberry sherbet. Startling colours to find in a night sky. He wrapped himself in a sleeping bag and stepped outside to watch as brilliant red bands of aurora pulsed inward from each side towards the corona directly overhead. A heart beating in the sky. He couldn't take his eyes from the sight. He felt rapture in his chest, a tingling thrill up his back. How had he watched this display all those nights and missed this awe? And this terror. As the corona moved across the sky, the pulsing heart shifted to ghostly strands of coloured light, spectres that seemed to rush down on him with such speed that he felt the pumped-blood fright of the chased.

TWENTY

It was already nearly the end of July, and Job was on the tractor, wondering where the days had gone. He was turning over an old hayfield of brome grass and alfalfa that was thin from winterkill; plants had died off in the harsh winters and no longer produced enough forage to make the harvest worthwhile. He planned to work over the field several times that summer, with the disk and later with the cultivator, to break up the sod, and to replant with barley the next spring.

At the headlands, the space at the end of the field where he turned the tractor around, a thought came to mind as he glanced over to the fenceline. It was a fence his grandfather had built, one that Abe, and later Job, had repaired, replacing wire and fence posts as needed. But the fenceline itself had remained there for more than sixty years. When Job was a boy, lightning had travelled along this fenceline, electrocuting the unfortunate cow that had been pushing through the wires to munch on grain in the next field. As a consequence, Job never mended fences under a stormy sky. Abe had told him how that length of fence had been part of the telephone line in his youth; the barbed wire had carried crackling voices up to the house. Now, turning the tractor at the headlands, the notion occurred to Job that the wire might still carry those voices, that if he hooked a telephone up to the barbed wire, he might overhear conversations from decades past. Then it dawned on him that he'd had this exact thought at this very point at the headlands six years before when he last disked the field. Would he have the same thought again in his forties? In his sixties? His father had often complained that with farm work, one year was so like the next that the years seemed to nest in one another and collapse into one, like the plastic cup he owned that was made up of rings and folded down into a pillbox. An effect that made the years at once stand still and speed by, without much change. A thought Job found suffocating.

He straightened the tractor out and headed back down the field, vibrating with the bounce of the tractor wheels over upturned sod. Behind him, red-billed Franklin's gulls lifted and fell as they followed the tractor, feasting on a banquet of newly churned worms and insects. A crow hopped along in front of the tractor, playing a dangerous game of chicken, for no good reason that Job could see. The bird didn't appear to be after bugs. A hawk swooped down and plucked a scurrying mouse from the field as a magician might pluck a rabbit from a hat. Job hadn't seen the mouse until the moment the hawk, still in flight, reached with its claws for it. Maybe it was the mice the crow waited for, though, like Job, the crow was not as adept as the hawk in spotting them. The crow watched with Job as the hawk flew off with his prize.

Jerry's dog sniffed along the edge of the field near the fence, then ran off barking at someone walking down the road. Liv. Job lifted a hand to her and she scaled the fence, the dog leaping and barking around her. She marched across the field, lifting her feet high to navigate the turned sod, holding her long skirt up to keep it from the dirt. She wore a wide straw hat on her head. From a distance she could have walked out of the turn of the century. The wife traversing the field to bring lunch to her husband, who was busy with horse and plow. Job swung the tractor around to meet her, before pulling to a halt and turning off the engine. He jumped down into broken sod, and still feeling the vibrations of the tractor running through his body, he steadied himself like a sailor stepping from a ship onto land. The smell of hot earth. Grit the tractor threw up stuck to his sweaty face. He pulled his handkerchief from his pocket and wiped his brow.

'Isn't this Jerry's dog?' Liv said, patting the dog down.

'Yeah.' Job didn't explain. The effort seemed beyond him. He'd phoned Jerry several times, begging him to pick up the dog. Jerry said, 'Take him to the SPCA, shoot him, I don't care.' But Job couldn't bring himself to shoot it, and the effort of hauling it all the way to Leduc to the SPCA seemed just too much. The dog was everywhere Job was, running after the tractor as he worked the soil and seeded, and later as he brought in his first hay crop. The dog scratched at the door at night, and streaked Job's work jeans with muddied paws. Job had tied the animal up but found it running alongside the tractor later in the day with the gnawed rope dangling from its collar. The yard was littered with scraps of white hair that fell from the dog once the weather warmed up. The limp bodies of the gophers it caught and carried around all day as trophies rotted on the lawn.

'Jerry hardly ever comes into the café any more,' said Liv. 'I guess Debbie's got him going elsewhere.' The dog brought a stick and dropped it at Liv's feet. She threw it and watched the dog run. 'Never see you at the café any more either.'

'I do most of my shopping in Edmonton these days.'

'Ed says he sees quite a lot of you.'

'We catch a movie now and again. I make a lot of meals at his place.' Without access to his own kitchen, Job had craved the opportunity to cook, and Ed seemed happy enough to have a meal waiting for him when he came home from work. He'd given Job a spare key and hadn't taken offence when Job refitted his kitchen with a few pots and pans and kitchen utensils. Job had even catered a couple of dinner parties Ed had had in his apartment, with friends he invited over from work and a guy he'd met at one of the neighbourhood pubs and cultivated an interest in, a dark, barrel-chested soccer player named Claude who had a fascination with tropical fish. After Ed and Claude had started dating, Job had made himself much more scarce. He was busy with field work in any case.

Job waved a hand at the grass of the coulee bank beyond the field. 'Why don't we go have a sit,' he said. 'I could use a break.'

They walked to the bank with the dog loping after them, and sat looking over the valley and lake below. Jerry's dog lay beside Liv, and she stroked his hair as they talked. 'I saw Jacob on the street the other day,' she said. 'He's lost a lot of weight.'

'He's working at Hanke Bullick's feedlot, feeding silage and doing pen checks, looking for sick animals.'

'Jesus, really? Never thought he'd do that kind of thing.'

'Not so different than what we grew up doing. But it's pretty miserable work for not much pay. All those animals crowded together in the muck.'

'And the stink,' said Liv.

'He pretty much hates it.'

'Why is he doing it then?'

'He couldn't find work. He wanted to sell the farm, but Lilith said if he made her move again she'd leave him.'

Liv laughed. 'Good for her!' She brushed white dog hair from her hands. 'I know Ben wanted to stay. He's often said how sick he was of leaving his friends behind every time they had to move. Which was quite often, as I understand it. He still comes over to my place and visits with Jason. He never told me about his dad working at the feedlot, though.'

'I think he's embarrassed by it.' But Job was only guessing. Other than waving hello from across the road, or nodding at them as he passed by the house on his way out to the fields, he saw little of his brother's family. The last dinner he'd eaten with them was at Easter.

'I guess if Jacob did sell, you'd have to give up farming,' said Liv. 'Or would you start again?'

'No.'

'So what would you do?'

'I don't know. Cook, maybe. Own a restaurant.' Now that he'd said it, the notion of having a restaurant of his own sent a thrill running through him. It occurred to him he'd never truly owned a thing in his life. Even the truck he drove was his father's castoff. But he owned this new idea of himself, a cook, owning a restaurant. It was a rhinestone button, tight in his first. A new thing, to know what he wanted. He looked off to the side, at the fence posts crowned with rocks as if the weight anchored the posts from floating off. 'Crystal told me you and Darren split,' he said.

'Yeah, again, eh?' She laughed. 'It's for good this time. We had this big blowout after he came home saying we were going to a party at Hanke Bullick's one night. I never liked Hanke and I was all set for a relaxing evening. I said I wasn't going to go but he was welcome to go by himself. Darren just sort of freaked out. He said I had to go. When I said, "Oh, no I don't," he pushed me down on the couch. He said, "What would it look like if I went to the party alone?" He went into this rant, yelling and yelling, and threw one of my vases against the wall. I didn't say anything. When I saw my chance I ran to the bathroom and locked myself in. He kicked the door for a while. Eventually I heard him leave the house.

'In the morning he came in and sat at the kitchen table and asked me if I still loved him. I said no. He asked me why, what he had done wrong? After all those counselling sessions he still didn't have a clue. I told him he was killing me, that he'd been trying to kill me off for years, and he had this moment of lucidity, where I think he understood. Then he was at it again, hollering. Finally he said, "Don't you love me?" I said, "No, I don't." He went quiet for a while, and then he left. He filed for divorce that week. And that was it. I thought he'd go crazy or something and wouldn't let me go. Like those stories you hear of women all the time, stalked by their exes. But he's been pretty good. I think it helped that he'd never stopped seeing Rhonda Cooper. Isn't that crazy? I'm grateful to Rhonda. I even feel sorry for her.'

Below them, a coyote trotted across the valley floor, its nose to the ground. Jerry's dog watched it with its tongue lolling and ears up but didn't chase after it.

'I'm sorry I didn't phone or come by earlier,' said Liv. 'I just had to let things settle, you know?' She plucked a piece of dry grass and twirled it between her fingers. 'Jason's away, on a haul with his dad. You could stop by this week, if you want.'

Orange-winged grasshoppers flitted, clicking, in the buffalo bean. It was here, right below him, that the deer had run up and down the coulee walls for the joy of it. The thump and crunch of their hooves on snow and earth, their hot breath creating puffs of steam behind them. Job felt like one of those deer now, his heart beating against his chest as though he'd run up that coulee wall himself. A thrill of joy running through him. But he kept his voice calm. 'Okay,' he said. 'I'll try to make it over.'

That night Job got on the phone and asked Jerry if he could stop by the next day and have him look at the truck starter, to fix it finally. He couldn't take Liv out on a date if he was afraid the truck wouldn't start. But he had a second motive. On the way to Jerry's, the dog rode in the back of the truck, blinking into the wind. It leapt from the box, recognizing home, as Job slowed to turn into Jerry's driveway. The smell of spilled diesel, rusting iron. The yard strewn with the skeletons of vehicles and spare parts. Stacks of tires, and hubcaps nailed to the barn wall. Jerry's metal shop was a huge, dark mouth. On hearing Job's truck, he walked from the shop wearing blue welder's coveralls, wiping his hands on a rag. The dog raced for him, leapt up to his chest and licked Jerry's face. A reunion. 'Goddamn it, Job. You have to bring the dog?'

'Your dog.' The look on Jerry's face. Surprise. Appraising. 'Your responsibility,' said Job. 'You take care of it.'

Jerry stuffed the rag into his pocket and scratched the dog's head. 'All right. Let's take a look at your truck.'

As Jerry worked, Job drank a Styrofoam cupful of coffee that tasted of oil. 'Something I've been wondering for ages,' he said. 'How come your dad went up front every altar call? What's he feeling so bad about? Is it your mom being institutionalized? Does he blame himself?'

Jerry straightened up and scratched the side of his nose, leaving a black streak there. 'What? Hell no. He knew Mom was nuts when he married her. Just wasn't much to choose from.'

'What then?'

'Masturbation. He just can't seem to get a handle on it.'

A day later, Job was at Liv's door, wearing Ed's leather jacket and the sunglasses he normally only wore in his truck. Ed had offered to dress him up, to make him look the part of a lover. He had him pose in his apartment kitchen, leaning against the doorway with one hip strutted out. Job wasn't sure if Ed was helping or trying to make him look like a fool. Likely both, though Job had decided to believe the former. He needed friends. He settled himself in position against Liv's door frame, attempting the nonchalant look Ed had demonstrated. The look that said, 'I want you, but not that badly.' 'So as not to scare her off,' said Ed, a phrase he'd repeated as if he were afraid of the possibility. Job balanced a large box on that jutted hip. He didn't like the effect, too much like a woman carrying a child, so he shifted his weight and dropped the box to his side.

It was nearly nine o'clock but still light. The air was muggy, close. Drops of perspiration slid down his sides. He knocked and glanced down at the windowsill beside the door as he waited. A lit match there. A spark. He looked closer. A firefly, blinking on and off. He let it walk on his finger and lifted it up just as Liv opened the door.

'Hey, aren't you that crop-circle guy?' she said. The jangle of bracelets, the rustle of skirts. Her fingers were cluttered with rings, except for the ring finger on her left hand. She grinned.

Job felt his face flush. 'Hello!' he said.

'Wondered when you were going to get around to knocking,' she said. 'Whatever are you wearing? What's with the sunglasses?'

'Oh,' he said, but didn't take off the glasses. Both hands were occupied.

'What's that?'

'Firefly. Lightning bug.' He held it up for her to see.

'You know I've never seen one?'

It flew up just then, past her head, flitting and sparking into the house.

'I'm sorry,' said Job.

'It's all right. Can't be that hard to find a bug with a light stuck to its butt.'

He took off the sunglasses and remembered the box he was carrying. A case of Medjool dates. He had phoned half the grocers in Edmonton to find them, then panicked when he discovered the cost but emptied his wallet anyway. 'These are for you,' he said, and handed her the box, realizing at that moment that the gift was too much. He thought of Jerry's dog, wagging his tail even as he crouched in fear. *Please love me.*

'I don't know what to say.'

'They were on sale,' he said, thinking this might make the gift seem less expensive. But regretted this too. Would she think he was cheap?

'Thank you. Have a seat on the couch. I'll bring us some tea.'

He held his cup by the handle but didn't drink. The weather was too hot. He wanted water instead, or cool lemonade, but couldn't bring himself to ask for it. He wanted to take the jacket off but was afraid of underarm stains. The mud in his mind churned for something to say as he looked around the living room. A cluttered house now. Not with mess, but with furniture. The room had the appearance of a tea house, with tables and chairs placed carefully around the space, dressed up for a conservative clientele. All things cozy. An ancient and ragged framed embroidery hung to the side of the front entrance. *Home Sweet Home.* Below it an overstuffed armchair with a doily over the headrest.

'Darren says I can have the house,' said Liv. 'He doesn't want Jason living in some rented place. And he never liked it here. Too many memories, I guess. And the ghost scared him, though I haven't heard much from it lately.' She waved a hand at the furniture around the room. 'I'm collecting for a bed and breakfast, or a tea house. People around here don't know the value of an antique. They want the new. Their barns are full of this stuff. I just went around asking if anyone had old furniture they wanted to get rid of and I picked it up for a song. This,' she said, patting a side table, 'cost me five bucks. Five bucks! I saw one like it in Vernon when I was down visiting Mom. They were asking five hundred.'

A knock on the door. Job stayed on the couch as Liv answered the door and talked to the boys on her step. Job heard Ben's voice. 'Jason's on the road with his dad,' she told them. 'You'll have to find someplace else to hang out tonight.'

'Why?' said Ben. 'You got a date?'

'Yes, I've got a date. Now go on.'

She closed the door on their singsong 'Liv's got a boyfriend, Liv's got a boyfriend.'

Job tugged at the sleeve of Ed's jacket as Liv sat back down on the couch beside him. *Boyfriend.* 'I was wondering if you wanted to go to Ruth's wedding with me on Saturday,' he asked her.

'As your date?'

'The ceremony is at two. There's a reception to follow. In the church basement.'

'Sure. Sounds like fun.'

Job fiddled with his cup. With the task of this visit now accomplished, he was unsure how to proceed. Should he stand to go? 'I'll be going to the wedding rehearsal tomorrow at three,' he said.

'You wouldn't think there'd be much to rehearse. I assume you'll just be standing there.'

'And handing Wade the ring.'

'Yes, the ring.'

'And I'll be helping to decorate.'

'The church?'

'The basement. For the reception. Ruth's picking up a helium tank, to fill balloons.'

'That's nice.'

'You working tomorrow?'

'No.'

'You're not working Saturday?'

'No.'

'That's good.'

They sat in silence. Too long.

Job pushed himself up from the couch. 'I should be going.'

Liv pulled him back down. 'You can stay. Awhile.' She leaned forward and kissed him. Her tongue like a date in his mouth. Then she leaned back and put his index finger in her mouth. The feel of her tongue and teeth on the pad of his finger. Tingling. She kissed him again. Warm hands on the damp skin of his face, his neck, his shoulders, pulling at the shirt tucked into his pants. They fumbled on the couch, his hands on her breasts, her rump and sliding past the elastic of her skirt. He opened his eyes for a moment and saw a flash in the air above him, and wondered if this, of all things, had brought the colours reeling back, then realized his mistake. The firefly flashed and darted, and flashed again. Job pulled back a little and said, 'Look.' The firefly streaked an arc across the ceiling, blinked out, and streaked another.

'That's the first time that's happened,' said Liv. 'Fireworks.'

The lightning bug flew at them and caught in Liv's hair. She batted at it. Job searched through her hair, trying to find it, but it had stopped blinking, or had fled under one of the many tables or chairs. 'I think it's gone,' he said.

'Let's go upstairs, where it's more comfortable.'

She left the lights off and led Job by the hand up the stairs. She undressed him and then herself as they kissed. Once on the bed, she sat on top of him and guided him into herself. He held her hips as he came and then held her hips to stop her from moving. The sharp pain of her riding his sensitive penis. She pulled herself from him, the pain like a bandage pulled from hair, and lay beside him. Some time later she put his hand on her thigh, as if expecting something, but Job didn't know what. Had he missed something? He rolled to his side and held her and breathed at her neck. The smell of her. Sandalwood. Oranges.

Above their heads the firefly flashed and streaked. He felt a sudden flush of wonder at it. This private display of fireworks. 'Must have come up on our clothing,' he said.

'Yes.' She shifted away from him.

Job lay on his back beside her, feeling the ease of being in accepting company for the first time in his life. 'I'd like to stay the night,' he said. He was already drifting into sleep.

'Fine.'

He spent the morning staring down at her, watching her sleep, waiting for her eyes to open. When she did finally wake, opening her eyes to find him there, she started.

'Hi,' he said.

'Hi.'

'You slept in.'

'What time is it?'

'Ten-thirty.'

'I usually sleep in to about ten when I'm not working. Anyway, I didn't sleep much last night.'

'It's okay. I didn't mean anything. It's nice that you slept in.'

She held the blanket over her and yanked her robe down from its hook beside the bed before pulling it around herself. With her back still towards him she said, 'I guess you must be hungry.'

'A little.'

'I'll make us some breakfast. Brunch.'

He sat up. 'Can I? Can I make you breakfast?' He all but felt his tail wagging, and lay back against the pillow. He put an arm behind his head. 'I mean, I like to cook.'

'All right. Sure.'

Liv watched as he cracked eggs into a double boiler and stirred in lemon for a hollandaise sauce, as he fussed over the poached eggs and worried that he didn't have English muffins and would have to make do with toast. He chose her best china, with a rose pattern, to serve breakfast on. 'I hope that's all right. If you like your eggs done harder, I can redo them.'

'No, no, this is fine. I don't usually eat breakfast, just have a glass of orange juice.'

'You want orange juice? I was going to squeeze some but you're out of oranges. I can run over to the co-op and pick some up.'

'No, no, this is fine. Really. It's great. It's remarkable. I've never known a man who cooks like this.'

She ate and gave Job a forced smile. 'Good!' she said, her mouth full.

'If you want another I'd be happy to make it.' He stood and started for the fridge.

'No. Job. Sit.'

He sat.

'Listen. I appreciate all the trouble you've gone to here this morning. And the dates and everything, but I really don't think this is going to work out.'

Job looked at his hand rubbing the tablecloth.

'I guess it's just too soon for me,' she said.

'Was it last night? Did I do something wrong? I thought you might want something, but I wasn't sure what.'

'No.' She pushed her plate away. 'Yes. It wasn't that you were doing anything wrong. It was just like being a teenager again. All fumbling and then – over.'

Job remembered Jocelyn in the van, placing his hand between her legs, then, when he didn't get it, moving his hand up and down. He felt the tears well up. He wasn't good enough. Not even at this, a thing bulls did without thinking. A knowledge they carried in their blood. He left the kitchen and headed for the front door.

'It wasn't that bad,' Liv called out after him. And a moment later, 'We could try again.' But he couldn't face her. He left the house and shut the front door behind him.

TWENTY-ONE

Outside Liv's house, Job leaned against the wall, feeling he might melt, dribble to the ground in an oily puddle. He was shamed by his inexperience. The small trails he'd travelled. Overhead, navy clouds boiled in a green sky and shot down fingers of lightning. He should get home and take a stab at bringing in the hay before the rain hit. But he heard his name called from across the street just as he settled into the truck. A familiar voice, from a stranger. 'Will?'

Will had lost too much weight and shaved his beard. His jeans and flannel shirt hung off him. His eyes, staring out from blue-rimmed hollows, were at once yellowed and shining. Mad eyes, or stoned. Job had seen this yellowed look before, but couldn't think where. Then he remembered his sister-in-law, Lilith, as she explained why she had put the cat in the dishwasher. The look of someone with one foot in another world and the other on something slippery.

'I thought this was your truck,' said Will. 'Saw it here at dawn, when I went over to do chores.'

Job stayed put. He didn't want conversation, but felt obliged to try. His voice was slow, slurred with the effort. 'You staying at your mom's?'

Will picked a chicken feather off his sleeve. 'We rented out the farmhouse to a couple who work in Edmonton, until they find a house of their own. They've got kids and wanted a bit of country to raise them on. I'm still running the poultry.'

'Staying with Barbara makes getting to chores harder, doesn't it?'

'Easier for Mom to keep an eye on me this way.' He jammed his hands into his jean pockets and looked over to Liv's house. 'Thought maybe your truck had broke down or something. But then I saw you coming out.'

'Uh huh.'

'Haven't seen you in Godsfinger Baptist for ages. You still going to Bountiful Harvest? Or are you going to a different fellowship?'

Fellowship? Job didn't answer. Will spent much of his time under Jacob's counsel and would know he wasn't going to either church any more.

Will gripped the truck's window ledge with both hands. 'Don't you feel the Holy Spirit moving you to go? Don't you feel *convicted* to go?'

Job's hand on the keys in the ignition. He felt the Spirit move him to start the truck, but paused.

'I'm very dependent on the Holy Spirit. Without him I'm afraid of what I might become. Jacob's helped me see that in God's eyes, sin is sin. Homosexuality is just that, sin, no worse than adultery or sex out of wedlock.' He glanced at Liv's door. 'I know now why I had the homosexual impulses. It was pride. I used to think God helped those who helped themselves. But

289

I'm nothing unless I humble myself completely to the Lord. Now that I let the Holy Spirit work through me, everything's changed, everything's easier. I don't feel the temptation any more. I'm healed!'

Over Steinke's canola, a flying saucer floated into view. Purple with green aliens waving out the windows. A hot-air balloon.

Job started the truck, but Will hung on. 'I want to thank you, for saving me from myself. If you hadn't told Jacob about seeing me and Ed, I don't know if I ever would have found the Holy Spirit.'

'I should have kept my nose out of it.'

'Don't say that! You can't begin to understand the kind of favour you did for me. And I want to return the favour. It causes me great grief to see you so separated from the Lord, *backsliding* in this way.' He waved a hand at Liv's house. 'But it's no wonder if you've fallen away from your spiritual practices. When was the last time you picked up your Bible?'

The sky above Will's head rolled like smoke from a chimney. 'I've got to go.' Job eased down Liv's driveway and stopped for the Bullick kid on his bike. The boy with a blanket tied around his neck and dragging in the gravel behind him. Trying to fly again.

'I wish you could experience communion with the Holy Spirit,' Will called after him. 'I'll pray for you!' It struck Job as a threat. He kept his eyes to the road and spit gravel as he sped off.

As Job drove into the farmyard, Jacob was just getting out of his car, pulling his briefcase from the passenger seat. 'Some storm brewing, eh?' he said. 'Knew we were in for something yesterday when I saw a flock of sparrows in the lilac bushes. Swallows were flying low.'

Job slammed the truck door. 'What did you do to Will?'

'Why? What's the matter with him?'

'It's like he's drugged or something.'

'*Drunk,*' said Jacob. 'Drunk on the Holy Spirit.'

'I didn't recognize him.'

'I suggested he get rid of the beard.'

'He's so skinny.'

'He's been having a little trouble with his appetite and sleeping. Probably the effects of the Holy Spirit working on him. I'm sure he'll bounce back soon.'

'But he's so changed.'

'Of course he is,' said Jacob. 'He's totally dependent on the Lord now, the Holy Spirit. That changes a man's appearance.'

Job heard a deep whine. He thought at first it was machinery in the distance, or an electrical line. But he found the source: over the roof of the house there was a mass of mosquitoes, a great ball of moving bodies, thick enough to darken the storm cloud behind. Job kept an eye on the mosquitoes, ready to hightail it should they decide to descend. 'You know Will's living with his mother?' he asked.

'I suggested it. If he were a drug addict in need of treatment, you'd see the need for watching that he didn't get into the drugs again, wouldn't you?'

'I guess.'

'That's exactly the situation we have here. He's got an addiction. And he needs help getting over it. So Barbara and I are watching that he stays away from people and places and ideas that would lead him astray. Where were you last night, anyway? I didn't hear your truck come in. You did come home, didn't you?'

Job didn't answer. He watched the great swarm of mosquitoes and braced himself for a lecture. Jacob sniffed the air. 'You got a fire going in the burn can?' he said.

'No. Why?'

Jacob looked around the yard and caught sight of a thin plume of smoke rising from the back of the house. They both took long strides, Job taking the lead. They turned the corner and there was Ben, watching the flames from a wood fire he'd built lick up the siding on the house. He didn't run or explain. Just crossed his arms and watched as Jacob and Job stomped the fire out.

His town shoes blackened, his face red from exertion, Jacob swirled around and grabbed Ben's shoulders. 'What the hell's the matter with you?'

Ben made a sound like a laugh and went limp in Jacob's hands.

'You think this is funny? You think all this damage you cause is funny? You think ruining my position in this community is funny? Do you *want* to go to hell? Do you? Do you?' Shaking him.

Ben pulled himself free, a surprise to Job, and to Ben, by the look of it, that he was able. 'I hate this house. I hate this farm.'

'It's not yours to hate. You've got no right.'

'I hate you!'

'How dare you talk to me like that!' Jacob's voice was shrill and spittle flew from his mouth. He tugged off his belt with his right hand and held his waistband with his left. 'Pull down your pants,' he said.

'No.'

292

Jacob lifted the belt over his shoulder like a whip, but Job yanked it from his hand and threw it to the ground several feet away. The two brothers stared at it, a brown snake, as though it had leapt from Jacob's hand by itself.

Ben ran to the front of the house. The screen door squeaked open, and the door of Job's old bedroom banged shut. The yard light flickered on. Above them a sky like boiling rags. The drone of mosquitoes from the roof.

Lilith came out in a yellow dress and shoes with heels that punched holes in the lawn. 'What are you two doing out here?' she said. 'You'll get yourself hit by lightning, then what will I do? It's time to head over to the church.'

'Church?' said Jacob.

'To help Ruth and Wade set up for the wedding, remember? We said we'd be there by now. Job, Ruth phoned. She wants you to come in whatever you're going to wear tomorrow. She said she wants to make sure the best man doesn't look prettier than the bride.'

Job stepped from his truck to the gravel of the church parking lot wearing the new dress shoes and blue double-breasted suit Ed had helped him pick out. He stood a moment outside the church, hoping Liv might catch sight of him dressed up, though he sweated in his new suit and wished for shorts. The flying saucer, the hot-air balloon, was nowhere in sight; Job imagined that the pilot, seeing the storm, had landed it in one of the fields. Beyond the community hall, a single sunflower, head and shoulders above the surrounding crop, bloomed in the midst of Steinke's field of flowering canola. Above, a storm blackened sky, so dark that the town lights flickered on. Ants, their blood hot, sped across the gravel under his feet. The air was thick with electricity: the smell of ozone, a metallic taste on Job's tongue.

Ruth called when she heard the church door open. 'We're downstairs!'

Job rattled down the concrete steps to the basement, sounding to himself like a woman in heels; he wasn't used to the clack of dress shoes. Wade was on a chair, and Ruth stood with her arms up, the two of them on either end of a streamer they were taping over the head table. Ruth turned when they were done. 'Thank heavens,' she said. 'I thought Wade and I were going to have to decorate this place by ourselves.'

'So?' Job held out his arms.

'You look fine. I had nightmares that you would turn up in that frilly shirt you wore to grad and upstage me.' It should have hurt. But it didn't.

From outside he heard tires on gravel, and car doors slamming. Jacob, Lilith and Ben shuffled down the stairs, Jacob carrying a box of small white vases of roses Lilith had hastily picked from the bushes in front of the house. 'Sorry we're late,' said Lilith.

'Well, I'm just glad you're here,' said Ruth, taping another streamer in place. 'I've got to get these up before rehearsal. Pastor Henschell will be here in about an hour. You and Ben can put the roses out, centred on the tables. Jacob, blow up the balloons, will you? The helium canister is by the door and there's a box of balloons on that last table. Job, you want to get going on those pompoms?'

Jacob dragged the helium tank over to a table, put the lips of a balloon to the nozzle and tied a full balloon to a chair so it wouldn't float to the ceiling. The balloon was pink with purple writing: *Congratulations! May all your dreams come true!*

294

Job slipped off his suit jacket and sat on the concrete floor beside the box of plastic pompoms. They were packaged flat and had to be ruffled into shape. He looked up at Jacob now and again, assessing his anger, the damage done. Jacob locked gazes with him once as he fixed a string to a white balloon that read *Life is sweet with you by my side.* The balloon slipped from the chair he tied it to, bounced against the ceiling and was drawn into the overhead fan, where it popped.

Job felt the rumble in the concrete floor against his behind before he heard it. The low vibrations of an approaching freight train carried through the concrete of the floor, though no train should have been running at that hour. Then he heard it, a distant, deep roar that created spots of molten orange just in front of his face, like fire in the sky as the sun dipped below the prairie horizon. 'What is that?'

'What?' said Jacob.

Job brushed off his dress pants and trotted up the basement stairs to the front door. Wind licked up dust and bits of paper, pushed and pulled Steinke's canola crop and bowed the sunflower. Lightning flashed and thunder banged hot on its heels. The first few pellets of hail initiated a deluge. Lights throughout town blinked out. Suddenly it was there, illuminated by the blue-white flashes of downed electrical transformers. A looming finger dropped from a fist of cloud, twirling towards them. Job cried down the stairs, 'Tornado!'

'What?' said Jacob, heaving himself up the stairs.

Job pointed as Ben, Lilith, Wade and Ruth joined them on the front steps under the awning to stare at the thing. A roar like jet engines that produced, for Job, licks of harvest moon, streaks of shining yellow and puddles of orange like liquid metal. With the colours came the first blushes of certainty Job had felt in months, a light thrill of knowing.

'It's coming right for us,' said Jacob.

Lilith headed back down the dark stairs, her hand clutching Ben's shirt sleeve, dragging him down with her. 'We've got to get into the cold room,' she yelled. 'It's solid concrete.'

They all disappeared down the stairs, leaving Job alone on the front steps of the church. He leaned into the door frame in order to stand, as the force of the wind nearly knocked him over. It was exhilarating, and deafening: a roar the exact colour of a harvest moon, when thousands of prairie combines kicked dust into the atmosphere, colouring the moon a shining deep red-orange. He coughed dust, and his ears popped as the tornado careened into Steinke's canola field. Canola blossoms spiralled upwards, clockwise, turning the tornado momentarily yellow. Job felt the air pull from his lungs and felt himself lifting, losing his footing, even as he clung to the door frame. Lightning banged overhead and reached out like the legs of a spider across the sky.

Then a black spiral snaked its way up the tornado as Bullick's house and yard were sucked upwards. Debris, like a swarm of bees, rolled together as if orchestrated by one mind. Shattered two-by-fours. The branches of trees. Sheets of siding. A truck. A hot-water tank. The roof of a barn flapped like the wing of a bird before disintegrating. A duck floundered through the whirling air; its flapping slowed, and it lost momentum, clicking through its movements like an image projected in slow motion. Around it, debris hung suspended in place, as if the tornado were about to reverse itself and send Bullick's house snaking back down. But the tornado didn't unwind. It simply stopped.

Quiet. The colours of the tornado hang still in the air in front of Job. Puddles of molten orange, streaked with shining yellow. He touches the colour and his hand sinks into orange. Colour bleeds up his arm and runs into him. He becomes orange, becomes yellow, becomes light. He becomes air, and churning wind. He feels himself balloon outward in all directions until he doesn't feel himself any more. He is all there is. It is all himself.

Bliss.

A shift. A disconnection. A lack, a loneliness. A movement from light to form. A hand, a foot. Stomach. Gender. Self. He laughs and finds voice. Remembers the taste of orange. All at once, everything falls into place.

A hand on his shoulder. Jacob. 'Job!' Job saw him shout, but didn't hear. All around them the thud of falling objects: chunks of wood, slabs of concrete, sheets of siding. A canoe bounced off Job's truck and landed whole on the parking lot that was now a lake of mud. Power poles along the road fell one after the other.

Jacob grabbed Job's arm, pulled him back into the church and down the basement stairs. They stumbled through the dark, pushing tables aside and tripping over the legs of chairs. Above them the crash and tinkle of glass, the snap of two-by-fours and all around a roaring. Job's molten orange was brilliant in the dark. But even brighter inside him was a profound excitement, a presence he had only one word for: God. He fell. Jacob dragged him across the concrete floor and pushed the metal door of the cold room shut behind him. Job's ears popped. A freight train chugged towards them. The snap and thunder of disintegrating boards. Then, nothing.

A crack of light under the door. Behind him in the dark, Jacob, Lilith, Ben, Wade and Ruth murmured to one another that they were all right. Job yanked the door open and stepped into sky. He stumbled over layers of debris at his feet, the wreckage of the church. The organ sat on a pile of studs, insulation and plywood. The church roof sat almost whole out in the mud of Steinke's field. Pews were on end in the graveyard. Children's chairs from the nursery were flung into surrounding fields. The canoe that had fallen from the sky was now cradled in a poplar, but Job's truck was gone. Everything was cast in a green-yellow light.

Job picked his way through mud and debris, careful not to get his new shoes dirty, and headed down Main Street, the yellow blossoms of Steinke's canola crop showering down on him like confetti. Shingles were torn from the roof of the community hall, and paint was lifted from the sides of Barbara's house as if it had been sandblasted. Trees were knocked over, their roots clutching air like tortured hands. On the trees still standing, wads of pink insulation hung like Christmas-tree ornaments. The strings of Ruth's wedding balloons were caught in a rosebush, wrapped around the mirror of a truck and snagged in a crabapple tree. Many of the balloons were still full of helium. Job found a torn garbage bag on the road and collected them, thinking Ruth would want them.

Bullick stumbled through the alley between the community hall and the co-op coated in dirt, carrying a piece of siding in one hand, a chunk of two-by-four sticking out of his shoulder. The brilliant red of blood oozing over mud. Job waved a hand to get his attention. 'Got something on your shoulder there, Hanke.'

Bullick looked back at his shoulder, at the wood sticking out. 'Oh, thanks.' But tucked the siding under his useless arm and bent to collect another piece.

A few windows were knocked out of Liv's place, and the bird feeders were gone. Job pulled a balloon from her caragana hedge and added it to his collection. Liv picked her way out of the basement door and joined Job on the lawn, in the shower of yellow petals. She held her hands out to them, as if to a welcome rain after a dry spell. Yellow in her hair. 'You okay?' she said.

'Fine.'

'What you up to?'

'Ruth's balloons.' He tied a knot in the top of the garbage bag, put it down, and it took flight, sailing into the air above them. It struck Job as funny. He went to all that effort collecting the balloons, only to have them fly off. Wasn't that just the way of things? He laughed.

Liv laughed a little and said, 'What?'

But Job was off, stumbling past the co-op, where a small crowd had gathered outside. Steinke was among them, still drinking his coffee. Crystal came out, refilled his cup and went back inside. Job waved a hand at them and they all waved back, as though they were watching a parade. Liv caught up to Job and walked with him down Correction Line Road, the gravel strewn with yellow flowers. 'You sure you're all right?' she said. 'Weren't hit by something?'

'No. I feel fine.' He did feel fine. Euphoric.

'You going to check on the damage at the farm?'

'Damage?' He couldn't think what she'd be talking about. He wasn't sure why he was heading to the farm. It just seemed important to get there.

299

They passed what was left of Dithy's yard, her house nothing but rubble, her husband's whirligigs scattered for a half mile. Dithy herself sat on an orange couch on her lawn, petting a cat laid across her lap. She called, 'Yoo-hoo!'

Liv waved. 'You okay?'

'Fine, fine.'

'Sorry about the house.'

'It was insured.'

'That cat okay?'

'Don't think so. It's dead.'

'You need anything?'

'No, no. You two young people run along. Enjoy yourselves.'

Along the road a dozen eggs in a carton, all of them whole. A picture of Jesus from a junior-church classroom, ripped nearly in half. Half a nursery chair. A toddler's white boot. A crazy quilt wrapped in the arms of a tree. Will's renters on what had been their lawn. A petite woman in a business suit, and her children, a boy and a girl, sat on chairs, watching their father try to start a lawn mower. The man waved. Behind them the garage still stood, but the house was gone. One of Will's poultry barns was flattened, but the other was whole. Machinery around the yard was left untouched by the storm. There were dead chickens on the road and feathers everywhere. Chickens wandered the yard and pecked at gravel, and a few of them strutted around naked, like strippers in high heels, their only feathers at the tops of their heads. The hot stink of chicken manure.

At the Sunstrum farm, there was mud everywhere. The whale was still on the fence post and Jonah waved and waved. The vacuum cleaner hung in a spruce, and a kid's chair from the church rested in the middle of the yard. The house was

300

nothing but foundation and debris, and the barn had collapsed from the middle inward, as if a giant had sat on it and the barn couldn't take the weight. The metal of the new granaries had unfurled and twisted around trees near by. The hired hand's cabin was simply gone. Only the two silos were left standing. *Jesus is Lord! Hallelujah!*

A creature covered in mud ran across the yard towards Job, mewing. Grace. She was shivering, skinny, pregnant. Job picked her up, sat in the child's chair, and cradled and petted her. He found himself crying over the cat, at having found her again. Then he caught sight of his feet. 'My new shoes!' They were wet through, covered in mud, ruined. He looked up at Liv. 'I wanted to look nice for you.' He saw that his suit was also covered in mud. It had been all along and he hadn't noticed. At that moment he registered the devastation around him, as if the world had suddenly come into creation. The yard and fields around him were strewn with splintered boards, twisted metal, bits of tortured machinery, insulation and the bodies of cows. The cows still alive grazed among the bodies as if nothing had happened. But even this seemed achingly beautiful. Job waved a hand at it all and laughed at the absurdity. 'And I'm worried about my shoes.'

Liv knelt beside him, hugged him, rocked him, smoothed his muddy hair as he rubbed Grace dry with the inside of his suit jacket and put the cat to the ground. The cat mewed and mewed. 'I know this really isn't the time for this,' said Liv, 'but I wanted to apologize, for the way I acted this morning. Ed called, and as we were talking he said he thought you'd never been with a woman before. Not all the way, in any case.' She took his muddy face in both her hands. 'I just wanted to say I'm sorry.'

They sorted through rubble for a time, waiting for Jacob or help to arrive, piling salvaged items on the concrete steps. One of Lilith's dresses. The copy of *Nervous Christians* jammed with bits of pink insulation. A suit jacket. Ben's guitar, with its strings plucked and curled. An iron. Graduation photos of Jacob and Job. A torn family portrait taken when they were still boys: Abe, grim, wearing the suit he'd be buried in. Emma putting on a smile, one hand clenched in a fist. Both Jacob and Job in their tight, nervous grins.

He found his mother's clear glass rolling pin cradled in the kitchen drawer in which he'd kept it. Miraculously intact. He smoothed his hand over it, wrapped it in a mud-stained blanket and placed it carefully on the steps. He picked up Abe's cowboy hat from the rubble and put it on. Liv wriggled her nose. 'It doesn't suit you.'

'No.' He took it off and fiddled with the red feather tucked into the band. He thought of his father wearing the hat and playing cowboy in the mirror. He'd wanted to ride the rodeo circuit and got stuck raising sheep on his own father's farm. 'You know, I don't think I've ever done a thing I wanted,' said Job. 'Not a single, goddamned thing.' He tossed the hat back into the rubble. 'What am I going to do?'

'You could stay at my house, until you get back on your feet.'

'Your place?'

'You can sleep in the spare bedroom tonight. And after that, we'll see.'

Job waved a hand. 'No, I mean, what am I going to *do*?' He didn't know *what* he wanted; he had never considered what *he* wanted. He didn't know where to start. And already he was forgetting the tornado, not that it happened, but the order of things, the details. He knew he'd felt awe and carried a profound light within himself, but he couldn't capture the feel of it. He was surprised at how quickly the moment had drained away. He was already on to the next, wondering at his future.

TWENTY-TWO

The end of April, and fields thawed into gumbo. Above, what Liv called a Monty Python sky: perfect white and fluffy clouds receding in size into an infinite blue horizon. Liv lifted a beer and said that from such a sky she expected an immense foot to descend and stomp them all flat with the squishy, rude noise of a boot stepping into a cow patty. 'God's foot?' asked Will.

'Don't start,' said Liv.

It was under this sky that Job, Liv, Jason, Ben, Will and Jerry had gathered in the stubble of Will's barley field for a Godsfinger tradition: the junk party. They sat on a row of folding lawn chairs on a low hill that afforded the best view of Correction Line Road. The best view of Job's place as well, for this was the day the silos would be taken down.

The Stubblefield farm auction was over; the auctioneer's trailer was gone. Members of the ladies' auxiliary had folded and carted their tables from Will's garage and enlisted their husbands to haul away the coolers of pop and the barbecues on which they'd broiled burgers and wieners. In the back of Will's pickup was a mess the local auctioneer called Nellie's Room, a pile of junk that wouldn't fetch a dollar: a bicycle without pedals or a chain, rolls of tarpaper, the broken handles of garden tools, a rusted submarine tank heater, stovepipes and bits of scrap metal, half bags of moulding seed, a seized slough pump, useless bits of leftover fencing wire, and household odds and ends. Below the junk party, sitting on the side of Correction Line Road, was a toaster that hadn't worked for years. Will had polished it up with his shirt before placing it there, then ran back up through the caragana that hid the lawn chairs on the hill from view. The toaster caught the sun and winked.

Will wore his Mackinaw, his chin covered in a stubble of new growth. He'd gained back most of the weight he'd shed and lost the haunted look, though from time to time he still tried to talk Job into finding a fellowship to attend. Will had found himself an apartment in Edmonton and was attending a church in the city that he said little about, only that it was more comfortable than Jacob's new church or Godsfinger Baptist had been. Jacob called Will a backslider, a black sheep, an ink blot. Job assumed he and Will had had a falling out but had never heard the details, and he didn't ask for them. Job had seen Barbara Stubblefield cross Main Street rather than meet her own son on the sidewalk. Job crossed the street himself if he saw Jacob walking down it. He was tired of his brother's sermons and demands that Job attend service on Sundays. 'How do you think it looks having my own brother refuse to come to my church?' Jacob asked him.

Jacob had put a down payment on Hosegood's sausage factory, and was in the process of renovating the second floor into a large apartment and the first floor into a church, all with the weekend volunteer labour of the church's membership. He'd been holding Sunday services in the midst of sawdust and construction for months, ever since Pastor Henschell, too close to retirement to start over, had handed his resignation to the board. A few members of the old Godsfinger Baptist congregation attended Jacob's church, as the closest Baptist church was in Leduc. But most of Jacob's flock were newcomers, acreage people, or families moving into new subdivisions.

Ben and Jason sat on the ground at Liv and Job's feet. Ben scratched the belly of Jerry's dog with his foot as Liv unwound her long hennaed hair from the bun she kept it in during her day serving at the tea house. Her orange broomstick skirt was fanned out over her legs, her orange silk tank top shining in the sun. Goosebumps on her arms. The vulnerability of her stubby, exposed toes in her leather sandals made Job want to pull her close and never let go.

From across the road, on the Sunstrum farm, came the roar of machines: Caterpillars and scrapers, buggies and a track hoe digging out a slough. The clack of tracks and grind of metal scraping on rock. Dump trucks and gravel trucks came and went, cleaning up the rubble, smoothing out ground, now that the earth had thawed. A couple of Johnny-on-the-spots. A survey team of two men. And a foreman watching it all, with his hands on his hips, from the rubble that had once been the house.

'So how's it feel?' Liv asked Job. She pointed at the machines with her beer bottle. 'Seeing the farm turned into a golf course.'

Job shrugged, felt his eyes sting. It made him weepy to think of it, the land his grandfather had homesteaded sold to strangers. But there it was, progress. And the sale had let him do what he wanted. He'd sunk a little of his part of the insurance settlement and the sale of the land into a half share of Liv's tea house and set up the kitchen the way he wanted. He had a tidy sum in the bank, even after taxes. He felt like a rich man. All that money, tied up in land.

The Sunstrums' had been the first of the Godsfinger farms hit by the Black Friday tornado to sell. It was the coulee that wrapped up the deal, the view of the lake. They'd sold to an Edmonton developer named Schlitt, who was turning the property into a golf course with a subdivision all around, for those hungry for a game of golf after a hard day's work in Edmonton. A sign where the mailbox had been said so: *Future Home of Schlitt Estates. Golf Lover's Paradise!* A man swinging a golf club. Rolling greens beyond. The future clubhouse at the top of the coulee, where Job had watched deer run for the joy of it, to feel blood thumping through their veins. Locals had already taken to calling the place 'Shit Estates.'

Bullick's feedlot was the second to go, sold to a developer who risked October snows to bang up a tidy street of roofed boxes and was at it again now. Rumour had it he'd already sold all the houses planned for the development. Dithy Spitzer had bought one. Families living in ten others already. Liv and Job's tea house was booming, filled with visitors from Edmonton who came to check out real estate and stopped for lunch. A few Out-to-Lunch Café old-timers came to the tea house too, mostly the younger married couples, out on dates. Liv and Job had hired Ben to bus on weekends along with Jason, and to wash dishes after school.

A red Mustang roared down the road but slowed when it came upon the toaster. They all sat forward in their lawn chairs and watched. When the car sped on, they booed and hooted. Jerry's dog, excited by the shouts, leapt up and barked, put its front paws on Jerry's lap and licked his face.

Liv leaned forward to get a look at Jerry. 'Where's Debbie?' she asked him. 'Figured she'd want to see the silos coming down. Or is she too good for us?'

Jerry clapped his hands, yelled, 'Git!' and wiped muddy paws from his jeans. 'She left me last weekend,' he said. He pulled a beer from the cooler and avoided looking anyone in the eye. 'She said I couldn't bring her all God had in mind for her and that she'd found her true soulmate in a welder from Stony Plain.'

Liv caught Job's eye, grinned, and raised her beer in a toast.

From across the road the buzz of an angle grinder droned as a workman cut the last of the anchor bolts of the first silo. Then a minivan drove down Correction Line Road, with a kid in a car seat in the back. The van slowed and stopped. A woman in a wide-shouldered business suit and blue pumps got out, looked around, picked up the toaster and trotted back to the driver's side, holding it like a football. She sped off.

Will jumped and raised his arms. 'Touchdown!' he said, and did a little dance. They all hollered. Will clinked Job's beer with his plastic Thermos cup and took a swig before choosing his next item from the back of his pickup: a transistor radio that hadn't produced a tune for a decade. He ran it down the hill and left it by the side of the road.

A catskinner on a D4 Cat ran the loader into the first silo. *Jesus is Lord!* Job pulled a Coke and a Bud from the cooler. He handed the Coke to Jason and popped the beer open, then took Liv's hand in his. A flock of ducks flew low overhead,

their wings whistling. Northern shovellers with bills like spat-
ulas, shiny olive heads and splotches of reddish brown on
their bellies. Job paid close attention now and noted details.
Since the Black Friday tornado, he'd been searching out and
collecting moments like this one as if they were photos,
mementos, knick-knacks found in the tornado debris. Junk to
anyone else. Precious to him. He replayed these moments
daily, while lying in the bath or just before sleep, to keep the
images fresh in his mind.

There was the moment the month before when he soaked in
the claw-foot bath, up to his chin in the orange-scented bubbles Liv had filled the tub with. Liv was in the bathroom with
him, dancing to the Mozart that played on the boom box she
had carried into the room, her bracelets and earrings jangling.
She grabbed handfuls of bubbles from the bath and blew them
into the air. The clouds of bubbles hung suspended, as if time
had stopped, as if they were held aloft by nothing.

There was the moment last November when Job and Liv
and Jason took a walk down what had been Bullick's long
driveway, to take a gander at the unfinished houses of the new
subdivision. A day sparkling in hoarfrost. Every tree and bush
was frosted white and glittering like coloured Christmas-tree
lights under a clear blue sky. Job turned to look behind him, at
their footprints on the snowy road, at the line of frost-coated
poplar the Black Friday tornado had miraculously left standing. The hoarfrost, just starting to melt in the morning sun,
drifted across the road and floated down on them. Grace and
her four teenaged tabbies followed in a row behind them. The
snow was so dry their tiny feet squeaked when they walked in
it, a sound that had once produced for Job a cloud of transparent blue.

There was that moment just the day before when he was in the kitchen, near closing time, wiping down his prep table. The smells of the day were still in the air: hot cheese from the tuna melts, the lunch special; sauerkraut from the grilled Reubens; the tang of homemade tomato soup; the sticky sweetness of cinnamon buns. From the tea room the clatter of Ben collecting dishes in a tub and Liv moving chairs and wiping down tables. The snap of fresh tablecloths. Sounds that had once produced, for Job, splashes the corrugated beige of fossilized wood that was churned up in the fields; a rain the metallic blue found on a tree swallow's back; honeycombs the red-bronze of a salt lick. But he heard no colours now. No invisible glass egg from the hum of the vacuum cleaner as Liv cleaned up under the tea-house tables. No tumble of sparkling blue spheres from the gravel that hit the undercarriage of the truck. He no longer lost himself to the voices in a church choir, and never would again.

But he would have these moments. Job had tugged his apron off, and tossed it into the basket of whites by the washer, then pulled his blue T-shirt over his head and wiped his face with it before tossing it into the basket of colours. He spooned a cinnamon bun from the pan, cut it in half and bit into it. The kitchen window reflected his image, caught in the afternoon light. His mass of damp curls. The smooth, nearly hairless skin of his arms. And in his face an ease, a happiness, had crept in. If he saw that man on the street, he'd want to know him. Count him as a friend. A tingle of recognition ran through him. This was where he wanted to be, in this moment.

Job collected moments like these, noting the colours in the ducks' wings, the smell of thawing earth, the cool of the beer in one hand and the warmth of Liv's hand in the other. Because if Liv could love him, just as he was, knowing all his foibles and fears, if he could catch his reflection in a kitchen window and like the man he saw, then who knew what else this world might offer him if he was attentive to its details. He might find eternity in the spin of a tractor's wheel. He might lose himself, expand into an arching prairie sky as he drove the paved roads. He might feel the blood thumping through his veins as he watched northern lights pulse across a night's sky. And it might be that God was found, not in a church or some hazy hereafter, but in the tart taste of a beer, in the warm hand of a lover, on the whistling wings of ducks flying low over-head.

The catskinner brought the loader up and lifted the base of the silo. There was a great *woomph* as the silo toppled like falling blocks, heaving up a great cloud of dust and a flurry of escaping pigeons. Jerry's dog barked and leapt into the air. The junk party hollered and clapped, and Job clapped with them. The ease with which the structure fell, as if it had been made of cardboard. As if it hadn't stood for thirty years. Then the Cat ate into the second silo. Another *woomph*. A cloud of dust. More startled pigeons. And Liv shouted, 'Hallelujah!'

ACKNOWLEDGMENTS

As they say, it takes a village to raise a child, and it certainly took one to bring this baby into the world. While I don't have the space here to acknowledge the great many people who contributed to the creation of this novel, I would like to thank my husband and research assistant, Floyd Anderson-Dargatz; my Canadian editor, Diane Martin, and my British editor, Lennie Goodings; my agent, Denise Bukowski; and my mentor, Jack Hodgins.

A number of books inspired me as I wrote this novel. The most influential were *Leaving the Fold* by Marlene Winell; *Bright Colours Falsely Seen: Synaesthesia and the Search for Transcendental Knowledge* by Kevin T. Dann; *The Man Who Tasted Shapes* by Richard E. Cytowic; and *Synaesthesia, Classic and Contemporary Readings* by Simon Baron-Cohen and John E. Harrison. The quote from the Book of Job that opens this novel was taken from a translation by Stephen Mitchell. Other Bible quotes were taken from the *Thompson Chain-Reference Bible*.